A
WEEK
OF
MONDAYS

ALSO BY JESSICA BRODY

The Unremembered Trilogy

Unremembered

Unforgotten

Unchanged

52 Reasons to Hate My Father

My Life Undecided

The Karma Club

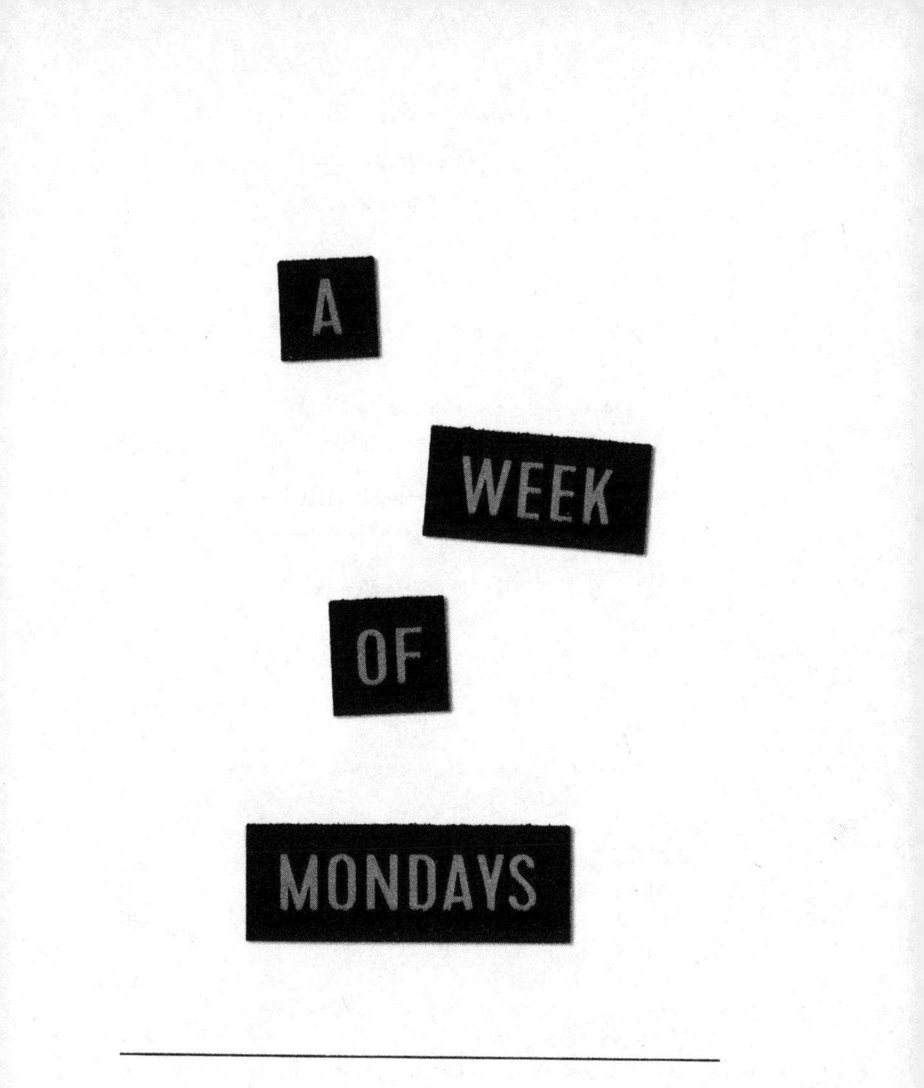

JESSICA BRODY

FARRAR STRAUS GIROUX
NEW YORK

For Jim McCarthy,
who asked to read more

Based on a concept by Jessica Brody and Mitchell Kriegman

Farrar Straus Giroux Books for Young Readers
175 Fifth Avenue, New York 10010

Printed in the United States of America
Designed by Elizabeth H. Clark
First edition, 2016
1 3 5 7 9 10 8 6 4 2

fiercereads.com

Library of Congress Cataloging-in-Publication Data

Names: Brody, Jessica.
Title: A week of Mondays / Jessica Brody.
Description: First edition. | New York : Farrar Straus Giroux, 2016. | Summary: Sixteen-year-old Ellison Sparks keeps reliving the terrible Monday on which her boyfriend, Tristan, breaks up with her and no matter how hard she tries, she cannot seem to set things right.
Identifiers: LCCN 2015022212 | ISBN 9780374382704 (hardback) | ISBN 9780374382728 (e-book)
Subjects: | CYAC: Dating (Social customs)—Fiction. | Friendship—Fiction. | Supernatural—Fiction. | High schools—Fiction. | Schools—Fiction. | BISAC: JUVENILE FICTION / Love & Romance. | JUVENILE FICTION / Social Issues / Emotions & Feelings. | JUVENILE FICTION / Social Issues / Self-Esteem & Self-Reliance.
Classification: LCC PZ7.B786157 Wee 2016 | DDC [Fic]—dc23
LC record available at http://lccn.loc.gov/2015022212

Yesterday I was clever, so I wanted to change the world.
Today I am wise, so I am changing myself.
—Rumi

Monday, Monday. Can't trust that day.
—The Mamas & the Papas

CONTENTS

THE FIRST MONDAY

THE SECOND MONDAY

THE THIRD MONDAY

THE FOURTH MONDAY

THE FIFTH MONDAY

THE SIXTH MONDAY

THE SEVENTH MONDAY

THE FIRST MONDAY

Mountain High, Valley Low

7:04 a.m.

Bloop-dee-dee-bloop-bloop-bing!

When my phone chimes with a text message on Monday morning, I'm still in that dreamy state between sleep and awake where you can pretty much convince yourself of anything. Like that a teen Mick Jagger is waiting in your driveway to take you to school. Or that your favorite book series ended with an actual satisfying conclusion, instead of what the author tried to pass off as a satisfying conclusion.

Or that last night, you and your boyfriend *didn't* have the worst fight of your relationship—correction: the *only* fight of your relationship.

Or that it wasn't completely your fault.

Bloop-dee-dee-bloop-bloop-bing!

But it *was* my fault.

I blink out of my trance and scramble for the phone, knocking over the cup of water on my nightstand. It splashes onto the stack of textbooks and papers next to my bed, soaking the extra-credit AP English paper on *King Lear* that I spent the entire weekend working on. This was my only hope of turning my borderline A to a solid A before first quarter grades are finalized.

I hastily swipe at the lock screen of my phone.

Please be from him. PLEASE be from him.

We didn't talk at all after I stormed off from his house last night. Some hopeful part of me thought he might call, not wanting to leave things the way we did. While some slightly delusional part of me thought he might have taken some unknown back roads and alleyways, driven twice the speed limit to beat me to my house, and would be standing in the front yard with his guitar, ready to play me an apologetic "I'm a jerk, please forgive me" love ballad that he just happened to write on the way over.

(Okay, a *really* delusional part of me.)

Regardless, neither had happened.

My fingers fumble to open the text message app and I nearly collapse in relief when I see Tristan's name. *Twice.*

He sent me *two* text messages.

The first says:

Tristan: I can't stop thinking about last night.

Oh, thank God. He's a mess, too.

This makes me so happy I want to cry.

Wait, that didn't come out right. It's not like Tristan's misery makes me happy. But you know what I mean.

I want to grab Hippo (the stuffed hippopotamus on my

bed that I've had since I was six) and waltz around the room with him while "At Last" by Etta James plays soulfully on my life soundtrack. (The sixties really were the best decade for music.)

But then I see the second text message and Etta screeches to a halt in my head.

Tristan: Let's talk today.

Okay, deep breaths.

Don't jump to conclusions. This could be a good thing. This could be like "Let's talk today so I can apologize profusely for everything I said last night and confess my undying love for you while I run my fingers through your hair and a four-piece band serenades us. Or maybe a six-piece band. You know how much I love the sound of the trombone."

Ugh. That sounded crazy even to *me*.

Honestly, since when does "let's talk" ever foreshadow good things? It's like the universal sign for impending doom.

This is it. He's going to break up with me. I said all the wrong things last night. I overreacted. I've turned into the very thing that Tristan hates.

A drama queen.

And really what happened last night wasn't that big of a deal. I don't know what got into me. I just, kinda . . . flipped. I chalk it up to stress. Severe stress. And hunger. It was a moment of stressful hangry weakness. And now the whole relationship is probably over. The best thing to ever happen to me (okay, pretty much the *only* thing to ever happen to me) and I screwed it all up.

I suppose it was only a matter of time, really. I mean, Tristan is Tristan. Gorgeous. Funny. Charming. And I'm . . . me.

No. Stop. Self pity party *over.*

I can still turn this around. He hasn't broken up with me yet. I can still save this. I *have* to save this. Tristan is everything to me. I love him. I've loved him since our second date, when he took me to his band's show and I saw him singing up on that stage. He just oozed sexytime and poetry.

Can one ooze poetry?

Or sexytime, for that matter?

Whatever. One fight does not a breakup make.

We will persevere. Our hearts will go on!

I send Tristan a quick text back. I infuse it with nonchalance and free-spiritedness. I am Ellison Sparks, Drama Free since 2003!

(Okay, so technically I was born before that, but the first few years of anyone's life are, by nature, dramatic.)

Me: Morning! Can't wait to see you today!

I press Send with a flourish. Then I find "Ain't No Mountain High Enough" in my "Psych Me Up Buttercup" playlist and set the volume to Blast!

It's almost impossible to feel down when Marvin Gaye and Tammi Terrell are cheering you on from the sidelines. It's like this song was written specifically for impeding a breakup. It's the Relationship Saver's Anthem.

I prance into the bathroom, place the phone down on the counter, and sing along at the top of my lungs while I shower.

"Ain't no mountain high enough . . . To keep me from getting to you, babe."

On second thought, this song might also be the Stalker's Anthem.

But it doesn't matter. It works. As I step out of the shower and grab a towel, I actually have the nerve to think:

Today is going to be a good day. I can feel it.

Talking 'bout My Generation

7:35 a.m.

Why do we have to pick out clothes every day? Why can't we just live in one of those cheesy futuristic sci-fi movies where everyone wears the same neon space suit and no one really seems to care that they all look like clones?

Argh.

I stare hopelessly into my closet. It's school picture day and I also have to give a speech to the entire student body for class elections. Rhiannon, my running mate, texted me last night, reminding me to "Look vice presidential!"

Now I have to find an outfit that not only reminds Tristan that he's madly in love with me, but *also* makes every member of the junior class—or at least a deciding majority—want to vote for me, *and* it has to be something that won't totally embarrass me in front of my grandchildren in fifty years when I show them my junior class picture.

So basically, no pressure.

I pull my pair of lucky skinny jeans from a hanger in the

denim section of my closet and move over to the pinks. My wardrobe is coordinated by fabric, color, and season. It's supposed to make clothing selection more efficient, according to an article I read in *Getting Organized* magazine two years ago. (I've been a subscriber since I was ten.) But today, I don't think even a personal stylist could help me pick out the right thing to wear.

I settle on a conservative-but-not-totally-puritan baby pink button-down shirt with a navy cardigan from the autumn section. Then I brave the mirror.

Huh. Not bad.

Maybe I don't need the neon space suit after all.

I blow-dry and flat-iron my hair until it's (relatively) tamed, reprint my extra-credit English paper, and pack up my schoolbag.

7:45 a.m.

Downstairs, the Sparks Family Circus is in full swing. My father is trying to eat oatmeal while playing Words With Friends on his iPad, which usually just ends up with him *wearing* most of the oatmeal.

My mother, the hotshot real estate agent, is her own sideshow this morning. She bangs cabinets and drawers closed as she searches for God knows what.

And in the center ring is my thirteen-year-old sister, Hadley, noisily shoveling spoonfuls of cereal into her mouth between page turns of whatever contemporary young adult novel is at the top of the bestseller list. She has this obsession with reading about people in high school. I've tried to tell her that four years of high school is bad enough. Why on earth would she want to submerge herself early?

She eagerly looks up from her book when I walk into the kitchen and asks, "Did he call?"

I roll my eyes. Why oh why did I tell her about the fight? It was a momentary lapse of judgment. I was a weepy sack of emotions and she was . . . well, she was there. Popping her head out of her bedroom as I climbed the stairs. She asked me what was wrong and I told her the whole story. Even the part where I threw a garden gnome at Tristan's head.

In my defense, it was the only thing within reach.

Then she proceeded to summarize the entire plot of *10 Things I Hate About You* in an effort to make me feel better, which, incidentally, only made me feel like she was comparing me to a shrew.

"No," I say dismissively, reaching into the fridge for the bread. "He texted this morning."

My dad looks up from his iPad and I cringe, waiting for him to ask me what happened. I really don't want to hash out my domestic issues with my parents. But instead he says, "I need a word that starts with T and has an X, an A, and preferably an N in it."

No one responds. No one ever does.

My mom bangs another cabinet closed. This time, miraculously, my dad takes notice. "What are you looking for?" he asks.

"Nothing!" she snaps. "I'm not looking for anything at all. Why would I possibly be looking for something I have no hope of ever finding? At least not under this roof!"

I wince.

Talk about a drama queen.

Oh God. Is this where I get it from? Are meltdowns genetic?

I pop two pieces of bread into the toaster and return the package to the fridge.

"What did the text say?" Hadley asks.

"Nothing," I mumble. "It was just a misunderstanding."

Hadley nods knowingly. "Lost in textation."

I lean against the counter and glare at her. "What?"

"Lost in textation. It's that awkward part of texting where the context of a conversation is lost without being able to see the person's face or hear their inflection."

I sigh. "Will you stop looking at Urban Dictionary? Mom, tell her to get off Urban Dictionary. It's completely inappropriate. Do you know what kind of things are on there? Words you and Dad don't even know."

My mom doesn't respond. She pulls a frying pan from the cupboard and sets it down on the stove top with a boisterous *clank*.

"Textation!" my dad shouts excitedly, tapping at his screen. "Good one, Hads!" But a moment later his face falls. "Not a real word? WTF?"

I groan. How is this my life?

My toast is only half done, but I push up on the lever and force the bread to eject. I smother it with peanut butter, wrap it in a paper towel, and grab my schoolbag. I'm not exactly running late, but staying around here another second will make me want to stick my own head in the toaster.

"Ellie," my dad says.

I stop just short of the door. I almost got out alive. *So close.*

"Yeah?"

At first I think he's going to ask me for another word for his game, but instead he says, "Are you ready?"

I pat my bag. "Yup. Got my speech notes right here."

He looks genuinely confused. "No, I mean, about softball tryouts."

Oh, and I have softball tryouts today. On top of everything else.

"Making varsity your junior year would be huge. The state schools would definitely take notice of that."

I'm itching to get out of this house. And my dad reminding me of yet *another* thing that's looming over this day is not helping. "Yeah," I agree.

He sets his iPad down and stares wistfully into space. "I remember when my varsity baseball team made it to the state championships."

Aaaand he's off.

"Standing on that pitching mound, I'd never been so nervous in my life. Your mom was in the stands. I just didn't know it yet. It probably would have made me even more nervous. Remember that, Libby?"

My mom takes the butter tray from the fridge and slams it down on the counter so hard I think she might have cracked the plastic.

"Is something wrong?" my dad asks.

Quite the observer, he is.

"No," my mom answers sharply, not even looking at him, as she cuts a piece of butter and drops it into the frying pan. "Why would anything be wrong?" It's one of her snakebite questions. I call them that because she coils up, lunges at you, and before you can even answer, you're dead from the venom.

"Are you sure?" my dad asks.

"She's gone mom-zerk," Hadley remarks.

My dad glances down at his iPad. "Ooh. I wish I had a Z!"

That appears to be the last straw. My mom storms out of the kitchen, leaving the burner on and the butter melting in the pan.

I am *so* not getting into the middle of this. I don't need to add "mediate parental dispute" to my to-do list today.

I shove my shoulder against the garage door. "Great story, Dad. Okay, bye!"

Dropping my bag into the backseat of the car, I get behind the wheel and start the engine. It isn't until the garage door opens and I back out onto the driveway that I notice it's raining and I don't have an umbrella.

But there's no way I'm going back inside that house.

The Magic's in the Music

7:55 a.m.

I sing along at the top of my lungs to "Good Vibrations" by the Beach Boys as I take a left at the end of my street, then the first right, and pull into Owen's driveway, putting the car into park. I'm about to lean on the horn when I notice the front door of his house is open, and he strolls casually to the car, not even caring that he's getting totally soaked by the rain.

"Wow. It's really chucking it down out here," he says, opening the door. He stops when he hears the song playing. "Uh-oh. What happened?"

I give him a questioning look.

He plops his backpack on the floor and climbs into the passenger seat. "You only put the Beach Boys on after something bad happens."

I scoff at this. "My life doesn't have to be in shambles to listen to the Beach Boys."

He closes the door. "Yes it does."

"What if I just felt like listening to something beachy?"

But Owen knows me too well. We've been best friends since the summer between third and fourth grade when he talked me into jumping off the ropes course telephone pole at Camp Awahili. "The Beach Boys are in your 'Psych Me Up Buttercup' playlist. And I happen to know that playlist is reserved for emergencies only."

He gives his head a doglike shake, flinging drops of rain from his dark, shaggy hair onto my dashboard. I grab the small cleaning cloth I keep in my glove box and wipe it off. Then I slump in my seat. "Fine. Tristan and I had a fight."

His green eyes open wide and he turns down the music. "You and him?"

"Uh-huh."

"A fight?"

"Uh-huh."

"As in, the two of you actually disagreed about something?"

"Do you not understand what a fight is?"

Owen lets out a low belly laugh.

"Owen," I whine. "What's so funny?"

He stops laughing. "It's just that it's about bloody time."

"You're not British," I remind him. "You can't keep using the word 'bloody.'"

"The Brits don't *own* the word 'bloody.'"

"Yeah, they kinda do. In America—where *we* live—it means 'covered in blood.'"

"It's a good word. It's like the loophole of swearwords."

I scowl. "What did you mean when you said it's about time?"

"I said it's about *bloody* time," he reminds me.

"Owen!"

He sighs. "Fine. I just meant you two never disagree. About anything." He holds up a finger. "No, wait. I wish to strike that from the record."

"So stricken," I say automatically.

Talking like we live in a television legal drama is kind of our thing.

"*You* never disagree with anything," he says, amending his statement.

"I do, too."

"Well, yeah, with *me*. But not with *him*."

"Objection."

"On what grounds?"

"I—" I begin to argue but then realize I can't come up with a single example to prove him wrong. "Well, but that's just because I don't want to be like all the other girls he's dated."

"Superficial and obnoxious?"

I slug his arm. *"Dramatic."*

"Having a differing opinion is not being dramatic. It's being, you know, a person. What was your fight about?"

I groan. I don't really want to rehash it, but I know Owen won't leave me alone until I spill. "His phone."

"You had a fight about his *phone*?" Comprehension flashes on his face. "Oh. Let me guess. He has an Android operating system and you have Apple. It's a compatibility issue. You'll never get along. You may as well just end it now."

I give him another slug. "No. It was what was *on* his phone."

He cocks a scandalized eyebrow. "Now I'm really interested."

"Not that, you perv. Snapchats. From girls. While we were trying to watch a movie."

He shrugs. "So?"

"So?!"

"He's a musician. In a semipopular local band."

I exhale loudly. "Yeah, that's what he said. Well, you know, minus the 'semipopular' part. And I know. I *know.* It was something I told myself I'd have to deal with when we started going out. And normally, I'm able to suppress it. But last night, I kind of just snapped."

"You Snapchat Snapped?"

Owen finds this incredibly amusing. I do not. He wipes the smile from his face. "Sorry. Good joke. Bad timing. Withdrawn."

"Anyway," I go on, "we got into a huge fight. I told him I didn't like the attention he gets from girls. He accused me of overreacting. It went on and on and then I threw a garden gnome at his head."

Owen's jaw drops. "You did what?"

"It wasn't a heavy one," I say, defending myself. "It was mostly full of air. It didn't even hit him. I missed. It hit the paved walkway and broke."

"That doesn't bode well for your softball tryouts today."

I feel myself deflate. "Now he wants to *talk.*"

Owen sucks in air through his teeth. The sound puts me on edge.

"I'm doomed, aren't I?" I ask. "He's going to break up with me, isn't he?"

He takes a beat too long to answer. "No." Then after seeing my doubtful face, he repeats the word with more conviction. "No! It'll be fine. He probably just wants to talk about . . . you know . . . replacing his garden gnome. His mother is undoubtedly pissed that you broke it."

This makes me laugh. It feels good. I'm suddenly glad I confided in Owen.

"Good Vibrations" by the Beach Boys fades away and "Do You Believe in Magic" by the Lovin' Spoonful comes on. Owen turns up the volume.

"Do you really think it'll be okay?" I ask. Despite how much I love this song, my voice still breaks with uncertainty.

"Do you believe in magic?" Owen asks me in return, half speaking, half singing the question.

"Thanks, that's reassuring."

His eyes light up. "Oh! Speaking of!" He digs into his backpack by his feet and produces two plastic-wrapped fortune cookies. "I was so distracted by your shambled life I almost forgot about our Monday morning ritual."

Owen buses tables at the Tasty House Chinese restaurant on Sundays for extra cash. And he makes a lot of it. I think it's his irresistible baby face and the boyish charm he turns on when he refills water glasses. Customers set aside additional tips just for him. He's been bringing us fortune cookies on Monday mornings ever since he started working there.

"Choose your tasty fortune," he trills.

I admit, the familiarity of the gesture does wonders for my frayed nerves. I hover my hand over the two cookies, wiggling my fingers majestically, before finally opting for the one on the left. Owen unwraps the remaining one and cracks open the crisp shell.

"If your desires are not extravagant," he reads aloud from the tiny piece of paper tucked inside, "they will be granted."

He snorts and crumples up the fortune, tossing it into my backseat. "My desires are always extravagant." He pops the pieces of cookie in his mouth and chomps down. "Your turn."

I unwrap mine and bust it open. The small strip of paper reads:

Today you will get everything your true heart desires.

Owen leans in to read over my shoulder. "That sounds promising."

I fold up the paper and slip it into the side pocket of my door. Then I throw the car into drive and pull onto the street. "I sure hope so," I mumble.

But Owen is barely listening. He's too busy singing along—completely off-key—to the song. *"I'll tell you about the magic. It'll free your soul."*

You Better Slow Your Mustang Down

8:10 a.m.

As I pull to a stop at the corner of Owen's street and Providence Boulevard, I lean forward and scowl up at the gray sky. "I really hope it stops raining before the carnival tonight. Tristan and I are supposed to have this big romantic date and the rain will totally ruin it."

Owen ignores my lamenting. He usually does when Tristan is the subject line. "Did you ever get around to watching the season premiere of *Assumed Guilty*?" he asks.

I avert my eyes in shame. "I have it DVR'd," I offer as if this redeems me, even though I know it doesn't.

Assumed Guilty is our favorite legal drama. We usually watch it live and text each other during the commercials, but last night I missed our weekly screening party because I was busy throwing fairy-tale creatures at my boyfriend's head.

Owen bangs his fist on the dashboard. "Bollocks! You need to get on that."

"And you need to stop saying things like 'bollocks'!"

"You missed the *best* episode."

"I'm sorry, I'll watch it tonight," I promise.

"You just said you're going to the carnival tonight."

"I'll watch it after."

Owen looks out the rain-splattered window. "No you won't," he mumbles.

I don't think he meant for me to hear but I do. And the guilt punches me in the stomach. Just another thing on my overly crowded plate that I can't keep up with. The truth is, ever since I started dating Tristan at the end of last year, I haven't had a ton of extra time to do much of anything, including keep up with Owen's and my busy television schedule. Tristan's band had almost nonstop gigs this summer and I volunteered to help with promotion. It only made sense. I'm more organized than any of the band members. When I found out they didn't even have a mailing list, and Jackson, the drummer, asked me how to "tweet the Instagram," well, it was just easier to do it myself than try to explain the art of Internet marketing to a group of musicians who call themselves Whack-a-Mole.

But hanging out with Tristan and his band meant I had to pass up my usual summer job as a counselor at Camp Awahili with Owen.

"Sorry," I tell him again because I don't know what else to say. And I really do mean it. I hate letting Owen down. "Wanna give me a hint about what happened?" I ask, trying to appeal to one of his biggest weaknesses: dishing out spoilers. Owen loves being the one who spoils surprises. I think it makes him feel omniscient or something. But don't ever try to do it back to him. He'll rugby-style tackle you to the ground before you can even utter a single syllable. I made this mistake a while back when his copy of *Harry Potter and the Deathly Hallows* got lost in the mail and I was able to read it first.

"Did Olivia finally get it on with that death row inmate?"

Owen crosses his arms. "Nope. You're not getting any spoilers from me."

"C'mon. Just a little sneak peek. How about I say something and you blink twice if it's—"

"Yellow light," Owen interrupts, nodding to the stoplight ahead of us.

I look up, quickly gauging the distance to the intersection of Providence Boulevard and Avenue de Liberation. My foot hesitates between the gas and the brake pedal. "I can make it."

Owen shakes his head. "You'll never make it."

In a split decision, my foot plunges down on the accelerator. "Totally going to make it."

We sail through the intersection just as the signal turns red and I'm momentarily blinded by the flashes of light that surround the car like paparazzi stalking a celebrity.

"Told you," Owen says smugly.

"What was that?"

"Red light cameras."

My chest hiccups. "You mean I'm going to get a ticket in the mail now?"

"Yup."

"But I was already more than halfway through the intersection!"

"Apparently not." His voice is light. Almost singsongy.

"Great," I mumble. "Just what I need today."

He nods toward the door where I stashed my fortune. "Maybe that's what your true heart desires."

"Yeah, my true heart desires to be grounded."

He cringes. "Your true heart is kind of a masochist."

They Call Me Mellow Yellow (Quite Rightly)

8:24 a.m.

Five minutes later, we pull into the school parking lot. I must have spent too long idling in Owen's driveway griping about my fight with Tristan, because the only spots left are in the farthest row. It's not until I open the car door and see a splotch of rain hit my cardigan that I remember I don't have an umbrella.

"You don't happen to have an umbrella, do you?" I call to Owen. He's already out of the car, tilting his head back to catch rainwater in his mouth.

"I thought you'd bring one," he says without looking at me.

I groan. "I didn't."

"Ouch. And with school pictures today?"

Dang it. I'd already forgotten about that. To be honest, I'm more worried about seeing Tristan than I am about my picture. Drowned Rat is not exactly the look I was going for when I give my big apology speech.

Speech.

Crap! I have to give my election speech today, too. This day is *so* not turning out the way I'd hoped. So much for good vibrations.

I grab my schoolbag from the backseat and hold it up as a shield above my head. "You don't seem too worried about *your* school picture."

He shrugs. "I'm a dude. My hair always looks good."

I hate to admit it, but it's true. Owen could go through a car wash in a convertible and still come out the other end looking like he spent an hour in front of the mirror. Guys have it so much easier.

I lock the car and walk around to his side. Owen laughs at my makeshift umbrella. "Run for it?" he suggests.

I nod, and we take off into the rain.

8:42 a.m.

"Say 'Two more years!'" the overly cheerful photographer chirps.

I give a weak smile and she takes the picture.

Why do people tell you to say stupid things when they're taking your photo? I mean, beyond the age of three when you're required to say "cheese" to ensure you're not scowling or sticking out your tongue.

Does this woman seriously think I'm going to say "two more years" for my school photo? Does she not realize what the word "years" would do to my lips? It would make me look like I was sucking face with an octopus.

"Lovely," she lies, and then calls, "Next!"

I scoot off the stool and walk to the other end of the cafeteria where the rest of Mr. Briggs's chemistry class is waiting.

Of course we would be the first group called in for photos. I didn't have a single spare moment to go to the bathroom to fix my hair. By the time Owen and I made it in from the rain, the first-period warning bell was already ringing and I had to head straight to class.

I manage to catch a peek at the photographer's viewfinder as I pass, and oh my God, it's more horrifying than I thought. My eyes are totally bloodshot from the rain. My makeup has smeared. My hair looks stringy and limp, like a kindergartner attached it to my head with Elmer's glue.

Fortunately I won't see Tristan until next period, and I should have time to duck into the bathroom and touch up before then. I need to look perfect when I see him. Or, at the very least, presentable.

9:50 a.m.

As soon as the bell rings, I jam my earbuds into my ears and scroll through my playlists until I find the one I want. "Mood Altering Substances."

The soothing sound of Donovan crooning "Mellow Yellow" floods into my ears and I feel myself relax somewhat. I keep my head down as I navigate through the crowd toward the girls' bathroom, but a tap on my shoulder makes me jump. I spin around to find—

Oh, please no.

This is not happening. It was not supposed to go down like this. I was supposed to look breezy and happy-go-lucky and, above all else, *nonfrightening* when I first saw him today. Not like I just walked out of the House of Horrors.

I rip my earbuds out and do my best to sound cheerful. "Tristan!"

God, he looks gorgeous today. His dark blond hair is all tousled and oh-so-touchable. He's wearing the faded loose-fit jeans and black leather jacket combo that I love. Although to be fair, he pretty much wears that every day.

He's staring at my face like he's trying to decipher an ancient Egyptian scroll. "Are you trying out for the play?"

Ouch.

I dab uselessly at the skin under my eyes. "No. I was just . . . it was the rain. I didn't bring an umbrella. I was on my way to the bathroom to clean up."

Remember. You are drama free. You are the embodiment of chill.

"I mean, not that I *care*," I add quickly. "What's a little rain, right?"

"Right," he agrees, hitching the strap of his guitar case up his shoulder.

"I just hope it clears up before tonight."

Confusion is back on his face. "What's tonight?"

I wince inwardly. Did he forget?

"The town carnival?" I remind him. "Tonight's the last night."

I've only been looking forward to it since I was ten years old. Okay, so I didn't actually *know* Tristan when I was ten. He moved to our town freshman year. The carnival comes to town every year for two weeks. I've been going to it since I was a kid, and when I was ten I saw this couple there who looked so head-over-heels in love with each other, I kind of became obsessed with them. I followed them around all night, tracking their date like a private investigator.

I looked on whimsically as they held hands in line for the

rides. I smiled a goofy smile as he won her the biggest stuffed animal at the ring toss game. I swooned when they sat down to share a milk shake and he reached across the table to cup her face in his hands, like he was trying to hold her together. I got a crick in my neck following their progress on the Ferris wheel (a ride I've still never gone on due to my paralyzing fear of heights). Then, when their car paused at the top and they shared a moonlight kiss, all I could think was *I want that.*

I want to be in love like that.

To this day, it's the most romantic thing I've ever witnessed.

But until five months ago, I'd never actually had a boyfriend to go to the carnival with.

"We're still going, right?" I ask, cringing at how whiny my voice sounds. Maybe I really *am* turning into a drama queen.

He nods, but I can tell his mind is elsewhere. "Sure. Sounds fun." He clears his throat. "So, that thing. Last night. I thought we could talk about it."

Oh God, he wants to do this now? *Here? While I'm looking like* this?

I take a deep breath. Time to defuse a bomb. "Yeah, I wanted to talk about it, too. Look, I'm so sorry about that. I completely overreacted. It's all my fault. And I'll totally buy your mom a new garden gnome."

This makes him smile and I feel my throat loosening.

Am I doing it? Am I smoothing things over?

I charge on, talking so fast I barely even know what I'm saying anymore.

"I was hungry. And tired. And stressed about the election today. I really think that's what it was. You know, I'm not usually like that. I'm usually totally fine with all the girls. I mean, I *am* fine with all the girls. I mean, not like for you to *make out* with them or anything. But you know, talking to them and doing your . . . rock star thing." I raise my hands in the air and wiggle my fingers to illustrate my point.

Wait. Did I just do jazz hands?

Moving on.

"I wish we could forget the whole thing and pretend like it didn't happen. And—"

"Oh, yeah," he interrupts, his expression shifting to something unreadable. "I forgot about that."

"What?"

"The election. That's today, isn't it?"

Is he still hung up on that part? How fast was I talking?

"Yes. There's a school assembly during homeroom. I have to give my speech."

He taps his fingers against the strap of his case. "Huh."

Huh?

What does "huh" mean?

"So do you think we can do that?" I ask, pressing on. "Forget this whole thing ever happened and start fresh? I'm really, really sorry."

The bell rings.

"We better get to class," Tristan says.

Was that a yes?

He grabs my hand and interlaces his fingers with mine. The warmth of his flesh does more to calm me than any song in any of my stupid playlists. I want to live inside those beautiful strong hands of his. Sometimes when I watch him strum his guitar on stage, or when he's practicing with the band, I get lost in the movement of his fingers. Like I'm in a trance.

And don't get me started on his wrists.

As we walk hand in hand toward Spanish class, I almost

manage to forget the atrocity that is my face. That is, until we step inside the classroom and Señora Mendoza does a double take in my direction. Then she shakes her head, as if to say, "Kids these days! Who can understand them?"

We take our usual seats in the back row as Señora Mendoza starts conjugating the future tense of the verb *ver* on the white-board. I pull a piece of notebook paper from my binder, scribble "Are we good?" and slide it onto Tristan's desk.

He glances down, then winks at me, causing my heart to puddle on the floor. "Yeah," he whispers.

But there's something about the way he turns his attention back to the front of the class—the speed at which he breaks eye contact—that makes me doubt the sincerity of the word. Am I being paranoid or has he suddenly taken a very unusual interest in Spanish verb conjugations?

Then just as Señora Mendoza is in the middle of saying *"Nosotros veremos"*—we will see—a loud *thunk* startles me out of my thoughts.

The entire class turns toward the window as a giant black bird slides down the glass and drops to the ground outside.

"¡Dios mío!" Señora Mendoza cries, holding her hand to her chest.

"Is it dead?" someone asks, racing to the window along with a handful of other students.

"It's totally dead," Sadie Haskins replies.

And that's all it takes for me to burst into tears.

It's Easy to Trace the Tracks of My Tears

10:02 a.m.

The bird is dead. And now I'm a blubbery mess. Which, when you think about it, doesn't make a whole lot of sense. I didn't even *know* the bird. He could have been a total douche bag. He could have been the kind of bird that steals hot dogs right off your plate. Or poops on people's windshields and doesn't leave a note.

But it's not every day you see something die right in front of you. And at the hands of a dirty classroom window. Really, the crow should have known better. There's no way the windows of this prison are clean enough for a bird to mistake them for air.

So, in other words, the bird was a moron.

At least I don't have to worry about the tears smearing my eye makeup. That ship has long since sailed.

The good news is, Tristan seems really concerned about me. He wraps his arms tightly around my back and lets me cry into his chest. He doesn't even seem to mind that I'm totally smudging up his white T-shirt.

"Shhh," he coos, in that sultry soft voice he usually reserves for the stage. "It's okay. He didn't feel anything. He died instantly."

He squeezes me closer and I can smell the piney scent of his aftershave. I can feel the contours of his chest muscles through his shirt. Tristan has what I like to call a sucker punch body. It's the ultimate proof that looks can be deceiving. From the outside, he seems slightly on the scrawny side. His jeans and shirts always fit a little loose. His Adam's apple protrudes from his neck and does this cute contraction when he swallows. But then he takes off his shirt and it's like, *BAM!* Sucker punch! Right to the gut. His muscles aren't huge but they're defined. Like wowza defined. And his chest is completely smooth.

"Viking DNA," he likes to joke. "We Scandinavians are freakishly hairless."

At first it feels nice to be comforted by Tristan. I'm reminded of why I love him so much. He has such a gentle soul. A poet's soul. And I'm certainly not gonna complain about being pressed up against his chest muscles. But then the sound of my own sniffling starts to echo in my ears and I'm reminded of our fight last night. And how I basically went from normal chill girlfriend to strung-out monster in thirty seconds flat.

Tristan hates drama. This has never been a secret. He told me as much the day we met. It was actually one of the first conversations we had. We were at a party at Daphne Gray's house. Tristan had just broken up with Colby, his girlfriend for all of six weeks, and everyone knew about it. Tristan had a long history of short relationships. Maybe that's because he always dated the same type of girl over and over and then broke up with them for the same exact reason. It's like someone who complains about never losing weight but eats an entire box of Oreos every night.

I push away from Tristan's warm, inviting chest and wipe away my tears. "I'm okay," I say. "Thanks."

I have to remedy this. I can't allow myself to become another melodramatic ex-girlfriend in Tristan's life. Five months we've been dating. Five whole months. That's longer than any of his past relationships. We even lasted through the summer, which, let's face it, is like the kiss of death for high school romances. I have to prove once and for all that I'm still the same girl he fell in love with.

"Señora Mendoza. Can I use the pass?"

"En español," she reminds me.

"¿Puedo usar el pase?"

She smiles. *"Sí."*

I grab the straw sombrero from the hook on the wall and bolt out the door. It's time to clean up this mess. Starting with my face.

Everybody's Talkin' at Me

11:20 a.m.

You would think a dead bird outside your Spanish class window would be the low point of your day, but it's not. Things only go more downhill from there. Monday is an odd day, meaning we only have periods one, three, five, and seven. In fifth-period U.S. history, we have a quiz. A quiz I knew about. A quiz I totally forgot to study for due to my attention being elsewhere. Namely on my fight with Tristan.

And it's not one of those essay-style quizzes you can just wing by being vague and witty. It's ten multiple choice questions about the American Revolution, a chapter in our textbook that I did *not* read. I pretty much guess on every single question. I figure I have a twenty-percent chance of getting them right.

After we're finished, Mr. Weylan—hands down the oldest man alive (I think he actually lived *through* the American Revolution)—has us swap quizzes with our neighbors so we can grade each other's.

Needless to say, I bombed it. So much for my twenty-percent odds.

I didn't even get one question right.

Now, the odds of *that* have to be pretty impressive.

Daphne Gray—yes, the same Daphne Gray who threw the party where Tristan and I first met—scribbles a big fat zero on the top of my quiz, beside which she draws a smiley face.

She tilts her head. "Better luck next time, Sparks."

You know that voice people use when they want you to know for certain that they're being insincere? That's Daphne's voice as she slides the quiz onto my desk. Like it brings her immense pleasure to watch me fail.

Here's the thing. Before I started dating Tristan, girls like Daphne Gray didn't even know my name. She never would have given me a second thought. Before that party at her house, Owen and I just kind of existed in our little universe, and that was fine with me. I've never been one of those girls who aspired to higher social status. Being popular wasn't on my bucket list. But the moment word got out that Tristan and I were a couple, it was like someone dressed me up in a silly costume and shone a giant spotlight on my face. Suddenly people knew my name. They knew where I lived. They knew my class schedule.

Girls like Daphne Gray suddenly took notice. And not in a good way. They noticed me the way a supermodel notices a pimple that's just appeared on her face hours before a photo shoot.

Now I constantly feel like I'm locked in a display case. Like one of those caveman exhibits at the museum that curious groups of kids walk by, laughing at the skimpy rabbit-fur clothing that hides practically nothing.

I feel like I'm permanently trapped in the naked-at-school dream.

As Mr. Weylan writes our homework assignment on the board—read chapters 3 and 4 in our textbooks—I carefully stow the quiz away in my binder under the divider tab marked "History" and the sub-divider tab marked "Tests and Quizzes."

I'll have to figure out how to fix this later. Maybe I can convince Mr. Weylan to give me some extra-credit work. If I can speak loudly enough for his hearing aid to pick up.

12:40 p.m.

By lunch, I'm absolutely starving, but I'm way too nervous about the upcoming election speeches to keep anything down. I completely forgot to eat my peanut butter toast this morning and I find it crumpled at the bottom of my schoolbag, the peanut butter now creating an adhesive between my chemistry textbook and my extra-credit paper for English.

Perfect.

At least I had the foresight to store the note cards for my election speech in the interior Velcro-sealed pocket. The speeches are after lunch during homeroom, and I haven't even so much as glanced at the notes all day. Remind me again why I agreed to be Rhiannon Marshall's running mate. Because she asked? No, there had to be a better reason than that. I'd like to think that I was even halfway rational when I decided to say yes. Maybe something about college applications? It's all a blur now.

I pull the cards Rhiannon wrote for me out of my bag and slip them into the back pocket of my skinny jeans. I'll review them a few times during lunch and everything will be fine.

I'm a quick study.

It's the standing-up-in-front-of-fifteen-hundred-people part that's making my internal organs do cartwheels.

Ever since school started last month, I've been eating my lunches in the band room while Tristan and the guys rehearse. I try to practice my speech in there, but I'm way too distracted by Tristan's sexy voice as he croons the lyrics to their most popular song, "Mind of the Girl," and I eventually leave to find somewhere quiet.

The library is my best bet. When I enter, Owen is leading the book club in a passionate debate about the major differences between the movie and book versions of *The Book Thief.* I steal up the stairs to the second floor and lock myself into one of the tiny soundproof booths where language arts students record the oral portions of their exams.

Even in the dead silence of this little cell, I still can't seem to concentrate. I stare numbly at my index cards, but the more I try to focus on Rhiannon's neat handwriting, the more the letters blur and swim in my vision. I'm able to make out words like "vision" and "commitment" and "campaign," but I can't, for the life of me, make them fit together into any coherent thoughts.

What am I going to do? I can't even read the stupid speech! How am I ever supposed to *give* the stupid speech?

Eventually, I give up and proceed back downstairs. I sit atop one of the tables and wait for Owen. When book club wraps up, he comes over and slides onto the table across from me, swinging his legs like a little kid sitting on a too-high stool.

"You should join book club," he says, holding up his tattered, dog-eared copy of *The Book Thief.* "And by the way, I totally stole this book."

I stifle a laugh. "No, you didn't."

"How do you know?"

"Because you only pretend to be a rebel. Deep down inside, you're just like me." I bat my eyes. "Sugar and spice and all things nice."

Owen pulls a half-eaten sandwich from his bag, unwraps it, and holds it out to me. The smell of the tuna makes my stomach turn and I breathe through my mouth. "No, thank you."

"You haven't eaten anything all day."

"How do you know?"

"I know things."

I cross my arms, demanding a better explanation.

"You never eat when you're nervous."

"Who says I'm nervous?"

He doesn't answer. Instead he tries to shove the sandwich into my face again. I turn away and gag.

"You have to eat *something*," he says. "You can't get up in front of the entire school on an empty stomach. What if you faint?"

"At least then I won't have to give this speech." I flash a smile and fan myself coyly with the index cards still clutched in my hands.

Owen reaches out and snatches them. "Let me see those." He flips through a few cards and makes a horrified face. "Did you write this? It's horrible!"

I pretend to be insulted. "What if I did?"

He hands the cards back to me. "You didn't. You would never write anything this bland."

I flip through the cards. "Is it really bland?"

"This speech makes vanilla look like the flavor of the month."

"Rhiannon Marshall wrote it."

"Ah, see, now that explains everything. Why didn't you write your own speech?"

I shrug. "I dunno. She offered to write it and I agreed. Besides, she's the one running for president. I'm only her VP. It's kind of *her* platform."

"Yeah, but it's *your* face everyone has to look at while you give this awful speech. I mean, it reads like she copied it from the *Most Overused School Election Speeches* book."

"That book doesn't exist."

He taps the cards in my hand. "It does now."

I glance at the clock on the wall. Two minutes and counting. My heart races. "Did you know that the number-one fear in America is public speaking?"

"What's number two?"

"Death."

He bursts out laughing, eliciting a few glares from students trying to study. "Are you saying that the average American would rather drive off a cliff than give a speech?"

"That's what I'm saying."

The bell rings and I glance up at the speaker, like a convicted witch looking at the stake that's about to burn her.

"Well, you're not dying today," Owen says, sliding off the table and standing in front of me. "Not on my watch. Let's go."

I slump forward, resting my head against his chest. His body tenses for a moment, as though I took him by surprise, but then he relaxes and pats me on the back. "You'll be fine. You'll give the world's most clichéd speech, everyone will fall asleep, and then it'll be over."

I lift my head and look up at him. "Owen?"

He smiles. It's not his usual goofy smile. It almost looks forced. "Yeah?"

"You're absolutely horrible at pep talks."

And then it's back. The boyish grin I've come to love. He bows like a gentleman in a Jane Austen novel. "Glad I could be of service."

Yummy Yummy Yummy

1:12 p.m.

Gurgloomph.

Owen stops walking halfway to the gym. "What was that?"

I play it off. "Nothing."

"Was that your stomach?"

I walk past him. "Gross. No."

Gurgloooeeeooomph.

"It was!" He says this like he's freaking Sherlock Holmes solving the murder of the century.

"I'll eat after the speech," I promise him.

He grabs my elbow and steers me into the cafeteria. "No, you'll eat now."

"There's no time!"

He points to a table in the corner where a group of scantily clad cheerleaders are counting money in a cashbox under a giant handmade banner that reads BAKE'N'CHEER!

"Grab something quick," Owen commands. "Something with a lot of sugar in it. It'll give you enough energy to get through the speech."

"I don't have any money," I remind him. I had dropped my bag off at my locker after we left the library, opting to bring just my phone and my index cards with me.

"My treat."

I eye the sign skeptically. "Bake'n'Cheer? Is that like Shake'n Bake? Or Bacon Bits?"

But Owen is not yielding. He practically drags me over to the table. "Hold up," he says to one of the girls with her back turned to us. She's packing up individually wrapped Rice Krispies Treats and putting them into a box. "You have one more customer." He turns to me. "Pick something."

The girl spins around, looking extremely inconvenienced, and I see now that it's Daphne Gray. I didn't recognize her from the back because, in their uniforms, all cheerleaders pretty much look alike.

She gives me a once-over, jabbing the inside of her cheek with her tongue. "We're closed."

Here we go again.

I really don't have time for this right now. I tug at Owen's sleeve. "See, they're closed. Let's go."

"C'mon," Owen pleads to Daphne. "One more sale. It'll help you earn enough money to"—he squints at the small printed sign on the table—"buy new pom-poms."

I fight back a groan.

Owen is completely oblivious to the battle waging between Daphne and me. Why are boys so clueless when it comes to girl drama?

Daphne sighs. "Fine. What do you want?"

"What looks good, Ellie?"

I scan the table. "Does the banana bread have almonds in it? I'm allergic."

"Not like deathly allergic," Owen adds. "Her lips just get all swollen and apelike. It's pretty funny actually."

Daphne doesn't look amused. "No."

Owen snatches up a piece of banana bread. "Great. We'll take it." He hands her a dollar and unwraps the bread, stuffing a piece into my mouth.

"Oweh," I complain as I chew and swallow. "I can feed myself, thank you very much."

He hands me the bread and I take another small bite. I admit I do feel better with something in my stomach. As we walk across the hallway to the gym, I peer hesitantly through the open doors. The bleachers are almost full. I can feel the banana bread rising back up in my throat.

"I can't do this," I tell Owen, shoving the bread back into his hand. "I'm gonna throw up."

A moment later, I feel a hand on my arm. "There you are!" Rhiannon says in her usual clipped, imperious voice. "I've been looking *everywhere* for you." She drags me into the center of the gym, and I turn back to see Owen taking a seat in the front row of the bleachers.

"Did you practice your speech?" she asks.

I falter and then ultimately decide that with Rhiannon, it's easier if I just lie. "Yup."

We position ourselves next to the other candidates and I scan the crowd for a friendly face.

Why does everyone look like they're scowling at me?

My gaze lands on Tristan. He gives me an encouraging smile and I feel my stomach settle.

Talk to him, I tell myself. *Give the speech to* him. *Forget about every other face in this room.*

"Calm down, everyone!" Principal Yates, a plump woman with an unfortunate unibrow, booms over the speaker system. "Calm down."

A hush falls over the room. It's punctuated by sporadic coughs and the sound of students fidgeting on the uncomfortable wooden bleachers.

"We're excited for this year's class election speeches!" Principal Yates says, with such fervor it's clear she's expecting a burst of raucous applause to follow, but it's like crickets chirping out there.

She clears her throat. "We'll hear a short speech from each vice presidential and presidential candidate, starting with the freshmen and ending with the seniors."

I find Tristan in the audience again, but he's not looking at me. He's staring down at his phone. So I glance at Owen in the front row. When I catch his gaze, I notice he looks panicked. His eyes are open much wider than usual and he's staring slack-jawed back at me.

I make a "What?" gesture with my hands. He responds by slowly pointing at his mouth.

Oh crap, do I have something stuck in my teeth?

Trying to be stealthy, I reach up and touch my lips, hoping to subtly rub my finger against my gums. But as soon as my hand makes contact with my mouth, I understand what Owen is trying to tell me.

I don't know how I didn't feel it coming on. The numbness. The tingles. The pressure of the skin filling with excess blood.

My lips. They're swelling.

Horrified, I look to Owen, who peers down at the half-eaten banana bread sitting in his lap, then back at me. He mouths one word. I don't need to read lips to understand. It's the same word that's flashing in my mind like a NORAD alarm.

ALMONDS.

I Fall to Pieces

There are really only two possible explanations here:

1) Daphne lied to my face about the almonds in order to see me humiliated in front of the entire school.
2) Daphne didn't *know* about the almonds.

As I stand in front of an entire gym of restless teenagers and try to block out the sounds of the final sophomore candidate's speech, I scan the crowd for Daphne. Maybe I can deduce her motives (or lack thereof) by the smug (or clueless) expression on her face, but I can't seem to find her. Instead, my eyes fall back on Owen, who's pantomiming dramatically to get my attention. I squint, trying to decipher his movements. But, to be honest, they have more resemblance to some interpretive modern dance than actual sign language.

He's either miming that his head is on fire or he's asking me what on earth I'm going to do.

I reach up to touch my lips, hoping to gauge the severity of the reaction. Maybe there was only a trace of almonds. Maybe

I can get my speech over with before my lips turn into full-blown whoopie pies.

But as soon as my fingers brush against the taut, swollen skin, I know I'm in trouble. I can definitely feel my lips on my fingers but I can't feel my *fingers* on my lips.

There's a jab at my arm and Rhiannon is looking at me with bug eyes, as if to say "What's the matter with you?"

"You're up," she hisses.

What?

I incline my head toward hers. "I can't do this," I try to whisper, but the words are garbled and clumsy.

Does she not see my lips? Does she not get how disastrous this is going to be?

She gives me a little shove. "Go."

As I slowly approach the microphone stand, I lock eyes with Owen once more. From the look on his face, I realize he can't believe I'm going through with this.

That makes two of us.

A snicker breaks out among the students. No doubt someone has noticed my inflated lips and is spreading the word swiftly.

I clasp my index cards in my hand and step up to the microphone.

Just keep it brief. Introduce yourself. Read some of the buzz words from the cards and then take cover.

I glance down at Rhiannon's perfect girly handwriting. The ink seems to be running, like someone spilled water on it.

Are my eyes swelling, too?

"Hello," I say into the microphone. I can hear the amplification through the gym's speaker system. The word comes ricocheting back at me a split second later like a distorted boomerang. But it doesn't sound like "hello," it sounds like "he-wo."

The snickers instantly turn to giggles.

I take a deep breath. "My name is Ellison Sparks and I'm running for junior class vice president."

I cringe, waiting to hear what I really sound like. I only catch the tail end of the sentence. *Vife pwesheden.*

This is it. This is the end. I always wondered how I was going to die. And silly me, I thought it would be something epic and tragically romantic. Like sharing a vial of poison with my star-crossed lover. I never thought it would end like this.

Metaphorically stoned by my peers.

Murdered by my own kin.

I rush through the rest of the speech as fast as I can, trying to focus on moving my thick, dragging lips while at the same time attempting to block out the echo of my voice reverberating back at me.

The giggles have escalated to full-blown laughter now. I can feel Principal Yates's muscular arms flapping somewhere behind me, trying to silence the growing unrest with wide sweeps of her hands, but it isn't working.

I peer up at Tristan, hoping he'll pass on some of that confidence he seems to possess so easily. He catches my eye and then looks away. That's when it hits me.

I'm not just embarrassing myself. I'm embarrassing *him.*

All those girls who doubted his sanity when he started dating me—who still doubt it—were right. What is he doing with me? I can't even read a few words off an index card without making a fool of myself.

At least he's not laughing like everyone else.

At least there's that.

“Thank you for your attention and please vote for Marshall/ Sparks for your junior class president and vice president.”

I stuff the index cards back in my pocket and run from the gym. I don’t wait for applause. I know there won’t be any. But the laughter follows me down the hall.

Who's Bending Down to Give Me a Rainbow?

1:39 p.m.

I don't see any reason why I can't stay in this bathroom for the rest of the day. It's got everything I need, really. A toilet. A sink. Plenty of light from the window above the last stall. It's like my own little apartment inside the school. There *is* the issue of food, but after what happened back there with the banana bread, I'm fairly certain I'm off food for a while.

I won't be able to vote. That's one downside to hiding out in here. Students will be casting their ballots when they get back to their homeroom classes. But I don't think it really matters. After that debacle, there's no way Rhiannon and I are winning this thing.

I pull a paper towel from the dispenser and wipe the remnant tears from my eyes and then blow my stuffed-up nose.

I've now cried twice in one day.

I'm on a roll.

I toss the towel in the trash and stare at my reflection in the mirror for a long hard minute. My lips are still absurdly enormous. I contort them this way and that, puckering them like a fish and flapping them like a horse. Anything I can do to try to encourage the blood to flow back out. I guess I should be grateful. I could have been born with a *deadly* nut allergy. I could be in an ambulance right now on my way to the hospital.

I really do look like a cartoon character. And here I thought guys *liked* girls with big lips. Maybe just not *this* big.

I purse my lips in the mirror, giving my best sultry bedroom eyes. "Well, hello there," I say breathily to my reflection. "Come here often? What's that? You think I'm sexy?" I make a kissing sound and then quickly wipe the drool that dribbles out as a result.

I lean forward, pretending to give the stranger in the mirror a big, slobbery, swollen kiss. But my romantic moment is cut short when I hear footsteps outside the bathroom door.

Is the assembly over already?

Panicked, I glance into one of the stalls, searching desperately for help. The porcelain toilet stares unsupportively back at me, as if to say "So what's your brilliant plan now, genius?"

Since I don't live in a *Harry Potter* movie, I suppose *in* is out of the question. And that means there's really no place left to go but up. Cringing, I climb onto the questionably clean seat, perching on my tiptoes along the rim and bending myself awkwardly into a crouch.

Classy, Ellie. Really, really classy.

I silence my thoughts with a grit of my teeth. Right now I just have to concentrate on not falling in. This isn't as easy as they make it look in the movies.

The door opens and someone walks in. I hold my breath. The footsteps pause for a moment, then shuffle hesitantly before pausing again.

What is this girl doing? Is she checking each individual stall for the cleanest one? Get on with it already! This is a public high school. There *are* no clean stalls!

I bite my tongue against the slight quiver in my upper legs. How much longer can I realistically keep this up? But it's not like I can come down now, because then whoever's in here will know that I've been squatting atop a toilet seat.

"Ellie? Are you in here?"

I blink in surprise at the sound of the distinctly *male* voice. "Owen?"

"What are you doing?"

I hop down from the toilet seat, my thighs screaming with relief, and open the stall. There's Owen, all gangly six-foot-one of him, standing in the middle of the girls' bathroom. I remember the summer that he sprouted. It was when we were counselors in training at Camp Awahili. I didn't notice the growth spurt because I was with him every day, but when his parents came to pick him up at the end of the summer his mother nearly fainted when she saw him.

"What are you doing in here?" I ask.

"Looking for you," he says, as though it's obvious.

I awkwardly massage my thighs as I hobble out of the stall.

"Hiding out in the bathroom?" He raises an eyebrow. "A little cliché, isn't it?"

I run the faucet and scrub my hands. "It's only cliché because there's nowhere else to hide in a high school."

"Janitor's closet, theater dressing rooms, that weird little patch of trees behind the track."

I pull a paper towel from the dispenser. "You've spent way too much time thinking about this."

"So," he begins, changing the subject. "I looked up the most popular recipe for banana bread on my phone."

"And?"

He cringes. "And it has almond *extract* in it."

I slump. "Do you think she did it on purpose?"

"Put almond extract in her banana bread on the off chance that Ellison Sparks comes to buy something from the cheerleader bake sale right before her election speech? Now you're sounding like a paranoid politician."

I slap his arm. "No, I mean, do you think she deliberately *lied* to me about there being almonds in the bread?"

"Honestly? No. I think she probably didn't know."

I sigh. He might be right.

"Anyway"—he pulls a small pill from his back pocket—"I got this in the nurse's office. Benadryl. It'll help with the swelling."

Gratefully I lunge for the capsule, popping it in my mouth and swallowing it dry. "Thank you!" I croak.

"I know what you need," he says, pulling my phone from the back pocket of my jeans. A few seconds and several swipes later, the catchy opening bass solo of "Windy" by The Association funnels out of the speaker.

He's accessed my "Bubble Yum" playlist, consisting of all the bounciest pop songs of the sixties.

The gesture is sweet, and honestly, watching Owen jump around the girls' bathroom singing *"Who's peeking out from under a stairway" is* rather comical, but I'm far too depressed to even crack a smile.

I take the phone back from him, turn off the song mid-chorus, and return it to my pocket. "Thanks, Owen, but I'm not in the mood."

"That's the whole point of the 'Bubble Yum' playlist," Owen argues. "To *change* your mood! You said so yourself."

"Yeah. I did. Back when my biggest problem was a B minus on a calculus test and my sister's Urban Dictionary obsession. My life is over now. *Over.* I can never show my face out there ever again."

Now the tears are falling for a third time. Gosh, who opened the floodgates today?

I don't understand. Yesterday my life was amazing. And just like that, it's turned into total cow plop.

I grab for another paper towel and dab at my nose.

"Let me see," Owen says.

"What?" I turn, and before I can react, Owen's hands are on my cheeks, holding me still. His face lingers close to mine. Closer than I think we've ever been before. I glance down. His eyes are determinedly focused on my swollen lips, his brows knitted in concern. I'm actually surprised by how warm his hands are. Did he stick them in his armpits before he came in here, or are they always that warm? I've known him for seven years. How come I've never noticed the temperature of his hands before?

"I think the swelling's going down," he assesses, sounding remarkably like a doctor.

His eyes drift up and, for a brief moment, land on mine. I can see the tiny flecks of brown in the green. I never noticed *that* before either.

It's weird, yet oddly not weird, to be this close to Owen.

And then it feels weird that it's *not* weird.

Owen suddenly seems to become aware of our proximity and steps back, his warm fingers sliding from my face.

"Thanks," I mumble lamely, and look away.

He takes an exaggerated deep breath and glances around the bathroom. "So *this* is what it looks like in here?"

"Does it live up to your fantasies?"

He scowls. "Only pervs fantasize about the girls' bathroom."

"So you're calling yourself a perv?"

He flashes me a mischievous grin.

And just like that, we're back to being us.

"I don't get it," I complain. "What is it about the girls' bathroom that's so enticing? It's not like we come in here, strip off all our clothes, and dance naked together."

"Shhh," Owen whispers desperately. "You're ruining it."

"People *pee* in here. Among *other* things."

"La la la!" Owen sings, covering his ears. "I'm not listening!" He waits to make sure I've finished talking and then slowly lowers his hands.

"Sometimes I come in here and it smells *so* bad it's like a rhinoceros took a huuuuge—"

"LA LA LA LA!" His hands fly to his ears again.

I laugh. Owen watches me, his face breaking into a beatific grin as his hands lower once more.

"What?" I ask, tilting my head.

"You're laughing."

I scoff. "Yeah, because you're acting like an idiot."

"Mission accomplished."

I Can't Help Myself

1:50 p.m.

The bell rings and Owen ducks out of the bathroom before anyone wanders in. I take a few minutes to collect myself. The swelling hasn't completely gone down but it's definitely chilled out a bit, thanks to the Benadryl. Now it just looks like I'm addicted to lip-plumping gloss, as opposed to looking like I just got out of the ring of a heavyweight boxing championship.

If you think this is bad, you should see the other guy.

I comb my fingers through my hair, trying to give it a bit of lift. It's still limp and yarnlike from my jaunt in the rain this morning. But really, the only thing that needs help right now is my attitude.

Owen is right. I need to snap out of it. Change my mood.

I remove the index cards from my back pocket, rip them in half, and toss the pieces ceremoniously into the trash can, watching them scatter like giant snowflakes against the black liner, landing among the other discarded items.

Rhiannon's speech. In the trash where it belongs.

I swipe on my phone and press Play on the song that I so rudely dismissed.

The Association continues cheerfully crooning about Windy and her stormy eyes, and I try to let the music lift me. Eyeing the door to make sure it doesn't burst open, I even bounce a few times along with the bubbly tune. I once watched a documentary about how dancing actually has the ability to alter people's emotional states. For a minute there, it seems to be working. I can feel my heart lightening.

Then I hear the school secretary's voice come over the loudspeaker. "Ellison Sparks, please report to the counseling office."

I stare up at the ceiling and throw my hands in the air. "Really?"

How on earth did I end up on the universe's hit list today?

Just like that, my mood slumps again. I turn off the music and slip my phone back into my pocket. Then I wait for the seventh-period bell to ring. If I have to go back out there, it's not going to be during rush hour.

1:56 p.m.

"Hello! You must be Ellison!" The guidance counselor jumps from his chair as I walk in and sit down across from him. He's a ruddy-faced middle-aged man who is wearing an actual bow tie. He offers me a seat before noticing that I've already taken one. He attempts to slyly turn his outstretched hand into a hair check. "Great to see ya. Really swell. I'm Mr. Goodman. But you can call me Mr. *Great*man, if you want." He guffaws at his own joke and then swats it away with his hand. "Just joshin' ya! So how ya doing? Ya holding up okay?"

"I'm fine," I mumble.

"Well, that's good. Just swell. Really swell. Now, let's get down to business. Junior year. It's a toughie, am I right? Or am I *riiight*?"

Did he just wink? I think he just winked.

Now he's staring at me, expecting me to answer. I worry he might actually hold that disturbing clownlike grin until I reply.

"Yep," I say, forcing a smile. "A toughie."

He chuckles heartily, his trimmed mustache actually oscillating.

"And don't forget about those colleges! It's time to start thinking about your future." He says "your future" in an obnoxious chewed-up baby voice. Then he makes two pistols with his fingers and shoots them in my direction. "Pow! Pow!"

Am I supposed to play dead?

"That's actually why I called you in here," he continues, growing serious. "Us trusty guidance counselors have been assigned to meet with every student in the junior class to talk about the next two years. Have you given any thought to where you want to apply?"

"Uh," I stammer. "Not really."

"Well, ticktock, ticktock! Time's a runnin' out."

He opens a file on his desk and skims it with his finger. "Let's see here. Well, well, you've been a busy bee—4.0 GPA, three AP classes this year, junior varsity softball, running for vice president, honor society." He closes the folder with a pat. "I don't know how you do it. When do you ever find time for yourself?"

I scowl, not understanding the question. "What do you mean? I do all of that for myself."

He purses his lips thoughtfully. "Do ya?"

What is that supposed to mean?

"Look," he says with a sigh. "I saw your election speech, and to be honest, I think you might be a *tad* overloaded." He puts a funny accent on *loaded* making it sound like *looded.*

"I'm fine," I say, somewhat snappishly. "Today has just been a little rough."

He shrugs and turns toward a massive display of pamphlets that covers the entire back wall of his office. He plucks a green one from somewhere in the middle and sends it sliding across the desk to me, like an air hockey puck. "Why don't you take a gander at this when you get a chance?"

I reach out and hesitantly take it. On the front it reads:

You 101: A Guide to Acing the Hardest Subject of All

and it features a picture of a preppy-looking girl walking through a field with her arms outstretched, like she's welcoming an alien spacecraft.

Okaaaay.

"Great," I say, feigning enthusiasm. "This is *super* helpful. Thank you, Mr. Goodman. Uh . . . *Great*man."

He guffaws and does the lame swat move again. "Go on and get out of here, ya little scamp."

He doesn't have to tell me twice.

2:14 p.m.

The receptionist in the counseling office gives me a pass to seventh period. I pop into the library to print yet another copy of my extra-credit paper as the first two were destroyed by water and peanut butter. Then I suffer through the last hour of English class.

After the final bell of the school day rings, I swing by my locker to drop off my stuff before heading to the locker rooms to change for softball tryouts. I keep an eye out for Tristan but he's nowhere to be seen.

Is he avoiding me? Or just busy?

I haven't spoken to him since lunch, and after that horribly embarrassing speech I gave (if you can even call it a speech) I'm worried he'll want nothing to do with me.

The school secretary comes over the speaker system while I'm stuffing my schoolbag into my locker. "Attention, students. I have a couple of announcements before I reveal the results from today's election."

I drum my fingers anxiously on the edge of the locker. Not that I'm expecting anything. Not that I even have the right to expect anything after that humiliating experience.

"First off," the secretary continues, "the cheerleaders would like to thank you for supporting their bake sale today. They raised over one thousand dollars!"

Well, I'm glad my poisoning wasn't for nothing.

"Also, a reminder that the auditions for the fall musical will start tomorrow afternoon. The deadline for signing up to audition is four o'clock today. This fall the drama department will be bringing us the hit musical *Rent*!"

Rent! Oh, I love that musical! I've sung "Take Me or Leave Me" in the shower so many times, my shampoo bottle probably knows all the words by now.

"And finally, here are the results from today's election."

I stand up a little straighter and tilt my ear toward the ceiling. She announces the results of the freshman and sophomore classes before finally getting to the juniors.

"In a landslide victory, claiming a whopping 89 percent of the vote, the junior class president and vice president are Kevin Hartland and Melissa O'Neil!"

I slam my locker door closed.

Everyone knows that Mondays are the armpit of the week, but I'm telling you, this one really takes the cake.

3:35 p.m.

Coach slaps a batting helmet onto my head and gives me a friendly pat on the back. "Look, I know you field like an all-star," he says, "but your batting average last year was not up to varsity standards."

"I know," I say, grabbing a bat. "But I've been practicing all summer. I'm better this year."

Okay, this isn't *technically* true. My dad and I did go to the batting cage a few times in June, but I spent most of my time with Tristan and his band. Coach doesn't need to know the specifics though. I just need to wow him right here, right now.

I need a win today. Any win.

"I'll have Rainier pitch you a few. Show me what you can do."

I step up to the plate and take a few practice swings.

Focus, Ellie, I tell myself. *You don't get another chance. This is it.*

Jordan Rainier, the starting varsity pitcher, winds up and delivers me a fastball. I smash it easily. It goes sailing above the third baseman's head and drops to the ground. I let out a sigh of relief.

"Good," Coach calls from the sidelines. "Again."

Another fastball. *BAM!* Another solid hit.

Coach signals to Jordan, tapping the inside of his elbow twice and then tugging at his ear. "One more fastball," he tells her.

Jordan winds up and the ball comes hurtling toward me, slowing just as it flies over the plate. I swing a second too soon, nearly stumbling from my missed swing.

That wasn't a fastball. That was a changeup. He tricked me.

I hear Coach clucking his tongue. "Listen to the ball, Sparks! Not my voice!"

I nod. "No problem."

He signals to the pitcher again. I try to tune it out.

Listen to the ball.

Jordan coils up again. I watch her body language, noticing the shift in her stance as she unwinds. It's different from the last three pitches. A curveball. But curving which way?

The ball comes at me, blindingly fast. I blink, missing the trajectory. I swing at air as the softball whizzes by my left ear. I bash the ground with my bat.

That's okay. I hear my dad's voice in my head. *You've got the next one.*

But Coach claps his hands twice. "Good work, Rainier."

"Can I have one more try?" I beg. "Please?"

He shakes his head regretfully and I can tell the news is not good. "The JV team still needs a good fielder like you." Then he slaps me on the back and turns away. "There's always next year."

The First Cut Is the Deepest

7:02 p.m.

As I make my way to the fairgrounds, I blast "Ticket to Ride" by the Beatles over my car stereo. It's not on any of my playlists but it seems appropriate.

The house was quiet when I left. Both my parents were still at work and my sister had been locked in her room since I got home from school. I was grateful for the calm. I didn't want to have to explain to anyone—least of all my dad—that I had bombed my softball tryouts . . . and pretty much every other aspect of this day.

I park my car and check my hair and makeup in the mirror. I decided to start from scratch. I showered and picked out an entirely new outfit. I'm ready to save my relationship. If a romantic night at a carnival can't convince Tristan he's still in love with me, then I don't know what will.

From the parking lot, I follow the sounds of laughter and screams and the smell of cooking meat. I can see the Ferris wheel in the distance, all lit up and spinning, and my stomach turns.

I once watched a documentary about traveling carnivals. Some poor girl in Nebraska apparently lost both of her arms riding the bumper cars. The bumper cars! And they stay on the *ground.*

No, stop.

No one is getting murdered or dismembered. Tonight will be perfect.

If there ever was a time to get over my fear of heights, this is it.

I think back to that couple I stalked when I was ten years old. This carnival transformed them. The lights, the music, the sugar, it turned them into Romeo and Juliet, Cleopatra and Mark Antony, Elizabeth Bennett and Mr. Darcy, Taylor Swift and . . . well, whoever she's with now.

Obviously I didn't know the couple's names or anything about them, so I made up my own names and gave them backstories.

He was the strong, silent type. A gentleman who liked to listen to her speak. He needed a simple yet dashing name. I chose Dr. Jason Halloway. I decided they'd met at an urgent care animal hospital in the middle of the night. He was the veterinarian on call at two a.m. when she—Annabelle Stevenson, avid animal lover and owner of six dogs—brought her eight-month-old golden retriever in after he accidentally swallowed a golf ball. Dr. Halloway, looking irresistibly cute in his white coat and rumpled hair, performed one emergency procedure on the dog, and another on Annabelle's heart.

They'd been inseparable ever since.

I've been imagining myself in Annabelle's shoes for six years now. I just never had the guy. Now I do.

Jason and Annabelle's night ended with a kiss atop the Ferris wheel. And I'm determined that mine will, too.

I take a deep breath and start walking. Tristan and I are supposed to meet in front of the ticket booth at 7:15. I check my phone and notice that he's texted me, saying he's going to be late. My shoulders droop slightly in disappointment. I text him back and tell him I'll be at the carnival games.

I find an empty seat at the horse race game and slide in, feeding a dollar bill into the slot.

A buzzer rings and a recorded voice calls out, "And they're off!" as a red ball rolls down the ramp in front of me. I watch my neighbor, trying to figure out how this game works. It appears all you have to do is roll the little ball up the ramp and try to get it into one of the holes marked with the numbers one, two, and three. If you sink the ball into the three hole, your horse moves three paces ahead.

Easy enough.

I chuck the ball up the ramp and watch in dismay as it bounces around the edges of each hole and then rolls back to me. I glance up at my horse—the green one with the number eight on his back. He doesn't budge.

I try a few more times, but I'm still unable to sink the ball into any of the holes. The other horses are soaring past me now, racing toward the finish, while my lame number eight is still at the starting line.

What is wrong with this game?

Does my horse have a broken leg?

I'm a junior varsity softball player for a state champion team. You would think I could roll a stupid ball into a stupid hole.

The ball comes back to me and I give it another try, this

time light and easy, barely a flick of my wrist. The ball glides up the ramp and drops right into the number-one hole. I throw my hands in the air and let out a whoop. I did it!

The buzzer rings, startling me.

"And we have a winner!" the virtual announcer says. "The lucky number two!"

Wait, what?

Someone won already? Didn't we just start? I peer up at the horses. The one with the red number-two jersey is waiting patiently at the finish line, while my slow horse is still way back at the beginning, having moved only one pace thanks to my *one* sunken ball.

Wow. I really suck at this game.

I'm about to try my luck again when a shadow falls over me and I turn to see Tristan standing there. I jump from my stool and throw my arms around him. "Hi! You're here! Isn't this amazing?"

He shrugs and I carefully disentangle myself from him. When I pull back I see he's frowning and his whole body language is off.

"What's wrong?" I ask.

He jerks a thumb over his shoulder. "I just passed the stage."

I glance in the direction he's pointing. There's a giant makeshift theater on the far side of the fairgrounds. It's empty and dark. "So?"

"So?" he repeats, agitated. "There's no one playing on it! I've been trying to get Whack-a-Mole a gig at this carnival for weeks and they kept telling me it was full."

I can feel my perfect fantasy evening slipping away. I have to get Tristan out of his funk. He can't be like this all night.

We have prizes to win and junk food to eat and Ferris wheels to ride.

"Maybe it was a last-minute cancellation," I speculate.

"It was," he grumbles.

Tristan is rarely in a bad mood. He's just not the type.

"So, there you go!" I say brightly.

But this only seems to have the opposite effect on him. His head drops and he stares at the ground. "I wish we knew about the cancellation. We could have performed tonight. We could have rocked this place. All these people would have heard our music. It's such a waste."

Panic flares in my chest. He's getting more and more upset about this. I need to shut it down.

I rub his arm. "I have something that might cheer you up."

He peers at me through his lashes and I nearly swoon. "What's that?"

I go through my mental list of the activities that made up Jason and Annabelle's enchanted evening. "How about the bumper cars?"

Jason and Annabelle waited in line for ten minutes for those bumper cars. Then they hopped in the same car and he drove while she called out directions and pointed out targets, squealing in delight and grasping his leg every time they collided with someone. By the end, they were both laughing so hard, they couldn't even get out of the car. A carnival attendant had to walk over and tell them to leave.

The bumper cars are sure to cheer up Tristan. It's rear-ending people on purpose. What better way to work out your aggression?

"I'll let you drive," I add, sweetening the offer.

He presses his lips together, like he's contemplating the

idea, but then he shakes his head. "Actually, I don't think I'm going to stay."

My heart fills with lead and sinks into the pit of my stomach.

"What? But you just got here." I don't mean to sound so whiny, but I do.

"I know," he says and, for the first time, I notice that he won't meet my eye. "I think I should meet up with the band and strategize. We haven't had a gig in a few weeks and we need to do something about that."

I nod sympathetically. "Of course. I'll come with you. I have some great ideas about—"

Tristan puts his hands on both of my shoulders, like he's trying to keep me from blowing away. Yet he still won't look at me. "No. You should stay here. I actually just came by to talk to you about something. I didn't want to do it over the phone."

I try to swallow but my mouth is suddenly dry. "Okay."

"Ellie," he begins, his voice cracked and uncertain. He clears his throat. "I can't do this anymore."

"What? The carnival?"

"No." He bites his lip. "I mean, *us*."

My breath instantly grows shallow. Someone has locked my lungs in a too-small cage and thrown away the key. I watch, stunned and transfixed, as Tristan presses his thumb against each of his fingernails, like he's checking to make sure they're all there. It's one of his little nervous tics. Something he does before he goes on stage. It used to be so endearing. Now it feels like a sign of the apocalypse.

He closes his eyes. "I'm confused, Ellie. I'm so confused. I don't know what to tell you. I wish I had all the answers, but

I don't. I just know that it's not working. You and me. We're not working. Something is broken and I don't know how to fix it. I don't know if it *can* be fixed."

I open my mouth to speak, to say all the things my heart wants to say.

What's broken?

We can *fix it. I know we can.*

I love you.

But my tongue is useless. Only air escapes.

And then tears.

Tears I try to hold back. Tears I don't want this entire carnival to see.

Tears that fall anyway.

"Oh, Ellie," Tristan says. His voice is so soft. So full of compassion. It makes me cry harder.

I can feel his hand encircle mine. I can see the scenery around us changing as he leads me to a nearby bench and makes me sit. I can't seem to feel the ground beneath my feet. I can't seem to feel my feet *period.* Are they still attached to my ankles?

Tristan plops down next to me, keeping my hand tightly clasped in his. "I'm sorry. I'm so sorry. It breaks my heart to do this, because I really did care for you. I still do. I mean, I always will. We had something good. Really good. Something I've never had before. It just . . . I don't know . . . fell apart somehow. I wish it could have been different. I wish I didn't feel this way, but I do. And I have to stay true to how I feel."

"B-b-but," I stutter between quiet sobs. That's all I manage to get out, though. The rest of the words—whatever they are—remain trapped inside me.

Tristan lets go of my hand and it feels so final. Like I'll never touch him again. Like I'll never feel his warmth. Shiver at his touch. Fall powerless to his gaze. "It'll be okay," he says to me. "You'll be okay."

I want to scream at him that I won't. That I'll never be okay. That I'll never stop loving him. But the only thing that comes out is another sob.

And now people are taking notice. Passersby are stopping. Nosy eavesdroppers are whispering.

I can't be here. I can't have this breakdown here. In front of everyone.

I leap to my feet and take off into the crowd. I swear I hear Tristan's voice calling after me but I don't turn around. Why would I? What could he possibly want to tell me? How sorry he is again? How certain he is that I'll be fine? How broken up he is about this?

What good will any of that do?

There's a crowd of people gathered around the ring toss game, watching someone toss rings at glass bottles like it's a freaking spectator sport. Normally I would politely excuse myself, tap shoulders, and give gentle nudges. But not today. I shove people aside with my shoulders, swatting at my tears with the back of my hand.

I manage to muscle through the throng of onlookers when someone catches me by the arm. I turn around to see Owen, his eyebrows knit together as he takes in my disheveled state.

"Ells?" he asks, his face a giant question mark.

But I can't talk to him either. I shake him loose and continue into the sea of people.

I half expect Tristan to catch up to me, having suddenly

changed his mind and wanting to take back everything he said. But he doesn't.

I push through the crowd alone.

I run for the parking lot alone.

I collapse into my car, press my cheek against the steering wheel, and cry alone.

I Say a Little Prayer

8:22 p.m.

Have you ever noticed how many worlds there are out there? Infinite. An infinite number of worlds. And they all function separately from each other. Like unrelated specks of dirt floating in the air. Sometimes two specks will collide, momentarily affecting each other, but most of the time they just keep on floating, completely unaware that any other specks exist.

You don't really stop to think about this phenomenon until *your* world—your tiny speck of dust that feels more like a planet than a particle—completely falls apart and no one else seems to notice. No one else seems to care. Because their worlds just keep on turning. Keep on zooming obliviously through space, while you're being sucked into a black hole.

That's exactly what's happening to me right now.

My world has disintegrated. My life is over. And yet the cars on the road don't swerve out of the way to let me pass. They go on driving.

Oblivious.

When I get home, the lights are off in the living room and kitchen, and I climb the stairs to hear my parents arguing behind their closed bedroom door.

Oblivious.

When I drag myself down the hallway, I pass Hadley's open door and hear the familiar dialogue from *The Breakfast Club*. Surprise, surprise. Why does she watch the same movies over and over again?

She, too, is oblivious.

Oblivious to my heartache. Oblivious to the end of everything.

Sure, I could tell Hadley. I could stand in the middle of this hallway and shout at the top of my lungs, *My life is over! My heart is crushed! My world will never be the same!*

But what's the point? Of anything, really.

They won't understand. My parents will spout some nonsense about how it's only high school and I have my whole life ahead of me to fall in love again.

Blah blah blah.

And my sister will try to cheer me up by plagiarizing some line from a teen movie. As if every adolescent problem has already been solved by John Hughes.

I take another step toward my room, causing the floorboards to creak. Hadley looks up from the glow of her TV screen. "Hey!" she says brightly. She must not be able to see the smudge of tears and mascara on my face because I'm cast in shadow. "Wanna watch? I can start it over from the beginning."

I shake my head and mumble, "No."

Then I retreat to my bedroom and shut the door softly, before collapsing on my bed in a fit of quiet sobs and deafening grief.

I have every intention of staying in here for the rest of my days. Or until I shrivel up and die. There's no way I can go back to school. There's no way I can show my face in this town ever again. Not after what happened tonight. Not after what everyone witnessed at that carnival.

I'll never survive it. I'll never be able to see Tristan without bursting into tears. And how long will it take before he moves on? How long will it take before one of those hundreds of adoring girls sinks her teeth into him? How long did it take him to move on from Colby to me?

Less than a week.

The idea of seeing Tristan with another girl—*kissing* another girl in the hallway the way he used to kiss me—it's too much. My stomach feels like it's going to eat itself just thinking about it.

How could he do this to us? How could he throw us away so quickly? I don't understand. Nothing he said made any sense. We're broken? We can't be fixed? Those are cop-out lines if I ever heard one. Why didn't I push him for a real reason? Why didn't I speak up and demand an explanation?

Is this because of our fight last night? Because I threw a garden gnome at his head? He can't break up with me for that! It's not fair. He has to give us—give *me*—another shot.

I hear a tapping at my window and nearly let out a startled scream. Then my heart catapults into my throat. It's him. It's Tristan! He's changed his mind. He's driven all the way over here to tell me that he's made a huge mistake. He's climbed up the tree outside my window just like they do in the movies to confess his love for me. It's wildly romantic! And so Tristan!

I brush the tears from my face, leap off the bed, and scurry to the window. I thrust it open and my heart sinks back into my chest.

It's Owen.

Of course it's Owen.

He's been climbing that tree in our front yard since we were nine. He's been entering and exiting through my bedroom window for as long as we've been friends.

"Hi," I mumble, and step away from the window to allow Owen to tumble inside. He never manages to enter gracefully. It's always more of an awkward face-plant than anything. You would think after all this time he'd learn how to squeeze through the window without nearly killing himself.

I plop back down on the bed with my face buried between pillows. I can feel Owen's weight shift the mattress as he sits.

"I suppose I don't have to guess why you left the carnival in tears," he says.

"You mean, you haven't *heard*?" I murmur into the pillows before propping myself onto my elbows. "I thought they'd announce it over the carnival loudspeaker."

He winces. "That bad?"

"I just don't understand! I apologized for the fight last night. I acted normal—"

"Wait, wait," Owen stops me. "Since when is *you* apologizing the equivalent of acting normal?"

I pick up Hippo and throw it at his head. He catches it deftly and brings it up to his ear, as though the stuffed animal is whispering to him. "Hippo says you're better off without him."

I grunt. "Hippo doesn't know anything."

"What's that?" Owen returns the plush toy to his ear. "Oh, right. Hippo also says he wants a real name. He deserves a real name after all the stuff he's been through with you."

"He *has* a real name," I defend.

"Calling something by its literal genus is not a real name."

"I named him when I was six. What did I know?"

Owen places Hippo in his lap. "Well, you're older now. So give him a new name."

"That'd be like you giving yourself a new name after sixteen years."

"Watson," he says without hesitation.

"What?"

"My new name would be Watson."

I crack a smile. "So you could solve crimes alongside Sherlock?"

"What would you pick?"

I sigh. "How about Piggy?"

He scrunches his face in disgust. "You would name yourself *Piggy*?"

I slug him in the arm. "For Hippo! Not me!"

"You can't call him Piggy."

"But he looks like a piggy!"

"Well, now you're just going to give him an identity crisis. Not to mention an eating disorder."

I cross my arms over my chest. "Fine. How about Rick?"

"Why are you asking me? It's your hippo!"

I groan. "You're impossible."

"I disagree. I am completely possible. Like one hundred and ten percent possible." He stops. "What about you? What would you rename yourself if you could?"

I sigh. "Right now, anything but Ellison."

"What's wrong with Ellison?"

"Ellison is the girl who gets dumped by Tristan Wheeler at the town carnival."

"You think he dumped you because of your name?"

"No. I think he dumped me because I'm me."

And just like that, the misery washes back over me and I collapse onto my pillows, staring at the ceiling. The tears well up and run down the sides of my cheeks. I don't even attempt to brush them away. Owen has seen me cry a thousand times. What's one more?

He's fallen silent beside me. I know he's trying to find a way to cheer me up. Like he always does. But it's not that simple this time. I'm beyond cheering up. Beyond fixing.

"I have a secret to tell you," he says after a long while. His voice isn't light and playful like it usually is when he's on one of his "Cheer Up Ellison" missions. It's quiet and serious. Almost hesitant. The shift snags my attention and I sit up.

"What?" There are traces of concern in my voice. Owen and I don't keep secrets from each other. We never have. So what has he been hiding from me?

He sighs and stares down at my comforter. "I wasn't going to tell you because, well, it's kind of humiliating."

I swallow. "Now you *have* to tell me."

"Blimey, okay. You have to swear you won't laugh."

I laugh at this. He shoots me a look. I settle down.

"Seriously," I tell him. "Why would I laugh?"

"Like I said, it's embarrassing."

"I won't laugh," I swear, keeping my voice steady and sincere.

He exhales loudly and hugs Hippo tighter, like he's trying to pull strength from the inanimate object. "Okay, here it goes."

I'm not sure why, but suddenly I feel like the air has been

sucked out of the room. My stomach clenches in anticipation. Am I actually nervous? Why would I be nervous? Maybe because I've never heard Owen's voice quite so grave before. What if it's bad? I'm not sure I can handle any more bad news today.

"Last night I dreamed I went skinny-dipping in the school pool with Principal Yates."

I stare at him openmouthed for a long time and then burst into uncontrollable giggles.

Owen huffs indignantly. "You said you wouldn't laugh."

I laugh harder. "How can I not? Are you kidding?"

He flinches. "No. See? This is why I didn't want to tell you!"

"I'm sorry," I say, trying to regain control. "But why *did* you tell me if you knew I would laugh?"

As soon as the question is out of my mouth, the answer is obvious to me.

He knew I would laugh. That's why he told me. Another mission accomplished. Owen managed to momentarily make me forget about the worst night (correction, *day*) of my life.

"I swear though," Owen warns, "if you tell a living soul, I will murder you in your sleep and make it look like a mafia hit."

"So . . ." I say, nudging his shoulder. "How was she? Was she good? Did she have a rockin' bod?" I crack up again.

Owen shudders. "Eew! Bugger off! I really don't want to talk about this. I shouldn't have told you."

I shake my head. "No, you're right. You shouldn't have. Because I'm going to hold this against you for the rest of your life."

9:12 p.m.

Owen leaves a half hour later. I swallow an ibuprofen to help with the massive headache I'm surely going to have in the morning, turn off the light, and climb under the covers. In the darkness, everything about my day becomes magnified. Like my agony feeds off the shadows and grows darker and more sinister in my head. Then the questions start. The debilitating regret. The "if onlys."

If only I hadn't eaten that stupid banana bread.

If only I hadn't made a fool of myself in front of the whole school.

If only I had been more apologetic to Tristan.

If only I had been *less* apologetic.

If only I had worn a different outfit, styled my hair up instead of down, brought an umbrella.

If only I knew how to fix this.

If only I had another chance.

These are the kinds of thoughts that lead to destruction. That do nothing but harm. Because in the end, there are no second chances. We all know that. There are no do-overs in life. You make mistakes, you live with them, you move on. I know all of this. I do.

And yet, as I drift to sleep, through the blur of tears and heartache, under the heavy weight of remorse that's pressing down on my chest, I find myself thinking the same thing over and over again.

Please just let me do it over.

Please give me another chance.

I swear I'll get it right.

The Way We Were (Part 1)

Five months ago . . .

The very first time I ever spoke to Tristan Wheeler, he accused me of stealing.

Before you go thinking this is another one of those kleptomaniac romances that are all the rage these days, let me set the record straight. I was completely innocent. I didn't steal a thing.

Tristan, on the other hand, stole everything.

My breath, my common sense, my ability to form coherent sentences. He was the ultimate thief. A shoplifter of hearts. A pickpocket of dreams.

He just didn't know it. That was what made him so dang good at it. He had no idea of the things he walked away with in his pocket. The things girls were so willing to simply hand over to him at the flash of one lonely dimple. At the flick of his windswept dark blond hair. At a single chord strummed on his electric blue Fender guitar.

War treaties have been signed for less.

Colonies have been emancipated for *much* less.

Before that fateful night of Daphne Gray's party, Tristan Wheeler was just another high school cliché to me. The cute boy in your yearbook who you show to your future kids and say, "I wonder if he's on Facebook." The seventeen-year-old rock god who exists for the sole purpose of giving teenage girls someone to fight over.

Before that fateful night, Tristan Wheeler was about as viable an option for me as a member of One Direction.

I wasn't even supposed to be at the party. I had gone looking for Owen. He had told me earlier in the day that he was thinking about going. I didn't realize until much later that he was saying this facetiously. Owen likes to attend things facetiously.

Parties had never really been our thing. Owen and I were always perfectly content spending our weekend nights watching reruns of *Law and Order* or trying to beat our high scores at the bowling alley (me: 145, him: 142. Ha!).

As soon as I walked into Daphne's house, I remembered why I didn't go to parties. I felt like a sober zebra in a wild pack of drunk horses.

The noise alone was enough to make me want to walk out. And I almost did. And I almost would have. Had I not bumped into *him*.

I had already done a full lap of the first floor, and having decided that Owen was most definitely not among these people, I opted to exit out the back door because the thought of trudging back through that chaos was about as appetizing as walking across hot coals.

I crept out the glass door to the backyard and slid it shut behind me. The silence was blissful. I stared at the door for a good ten seconds, wondering if it was made from the same glass they use to make the windows of the president's car, because the way it blocked out the noise of all those rowdy teenagers and their rowdy teenage music was nothing short of a miracle.

I didn't expect anyone to be out here. It was a cold night for late April, and judging by the claustrophobia of the living room, every teenager within a hundred-mile radius was packed like sardines inside the house. But there was one person sitting out in the cold.

And he wasn't about to let me slink off unnoticed.

"What did you steal?"

Those were the first words Tristan Wheeler ever said to me.

Later, I would debate whether or not I should needlepoint them onto a decorative throw pillow.

"I really hope you stole something," he went on, "because that would be the perfect crime. Pilfering precious gems in the wake of a high school house party. Way too many suspects to narrow down."

"Huh?"

And that was the first word *I* ever spoke to Tristan Wheeler. Definitely not throw-pillow worthy.

I turned around to see him sitting on the edge of the pool. His shoes and socks were off and his feet were dangling in water that had to be as cold as the stuff that killed fifteen hundred Titanic passengers.

"The way you left that house," he explained. "It was very . . . criminalistic. You are definitely running from something." He stopped to contemplate. "Or some*one*? Let me guess again. You cheated on your boyfriend, you're feeling horribly remorseful, and now you're disappearing into the night before he notices you're gone."

"I've never had a boyfriend."

That was the second thing I ever said to Tristan Wheeler.

Yup, I was on a roll. I wanted to vanish right then and there. I wanted to dive into that pool and never resurface.

His eyebrow cocked. "Never?"

I was still standing there like an idiot, not sure if I should dash to the side gate and make my getaway or continue along with this scenario, which I'd now completely convinced myself was a dream.

"Not even like one of those two-hour relationships in third grade where you exchange valentines and then discover she actually gave the same valentine with the same message to three other guys?"

I barked out a laugh. "That's *really* specific."

He bowed his head in shame. "Yeah, I know."

"What was her name?"

"Wendy Hooker."

I couldn't help but snicker. "That's . . . an unfortunate name."

And then it happened. That was the first time I saw it. The single-dimpled, heart-stopping, cocky grin that would change my life forever.

"I should have known, right?" he joked.

I stared at my feet, hiding the grin that was spreading across my face.

"So," he went on, but I didn't have the courage to look up. I could already feel the world shifting. I was already memorizing this entire conversation to play back over and over again in my head. "You never answered my question."

Why was it suddenly so hard to breathe? Had I entered that party and exited on another planet? One with a significantly thinner atmosphere?

"No," I said to the stone pathway under my feet. "I've never had even a two-hour relationship."

His chuckle made my head whip up and my face flush with heat. Was he laughing at me? At my humiliating lack of experience?

"I meant," he clarified, "what did you steal?"

"Oh." And there went all the blood that once called my head home. "Right. Um, nothing."

He pulled his feet out of the water and hugged his knees to his chest. "A likely story."

I jerked my thumb over my shoulder. "I was just looking for my friend. I wasn't actually invited."

"I don't think this is the kind of party you have to be invited to. Or if it is, then I wasn't invited either."

"I hardly doubt that." All the breath in my chest left with the words, and I couldn't manage to get any of it back. It was like my lungs were suddenly closed for business. Out of order. On strike. Please try again later.

I ducked my head so he couldn't see the blush that was inevitably making my cheeks glow like the alien's finger in that *ET* movie.

Thankfully he chose to ignore my humiliating comment. "So, this friend that you allegedly couldn't find—"

"Allegedly?"

"Yes," he said in all seriousness. "Allegedly. I have no proof that your alibi holds water."

"Are you interrogating me?"

"Do you have a reason to be interrogated?"

I laughed at this. I couldn't help myself. "I'm a minor, so technically you can't interrogate me without a legal guardian present."

"Are you saying I should call your parents?"

Stupid. Stupid. Stupid.

I'm 89.97 percent sure Tristan Wheeler was just flirting with me and I had to go and ruin it by talking about my *parents*?

Seriously, what was wrong with me?

Apparently I watch way too many legal dramas and not nearly enough normal teen dramas.

"I should go," I said, starting toward the gate. I needed to get out of there before I could embarrass myself any further.

"I don't know if that's such a good idea," Tristan said behind me. I froze, too afraid to turn around.

"I'm not sure I should let you out of my sight," he continued. "I'm still highly suspicious. And if the police find something valuable missing, I'd like to claim the reward when I turn you in."

The smile was impossible to stop. I turned around. "You'd turn me in?"

He dipped his feet back in the water. "I might. You definitely have 'shady character' written all over you."

"And what about you?"

He blinked in surprise. "What about me?"

"You're pretty suspicious-looking, too."

He leaned back on his hands, looking highly amused.

"Exhibit A," I began, "you're out here alone. Exhibit B"—I gestured to the ice-cold water that his feet were submerged in—"you're clearly a vampire."

He broke into laughter. "A vampire?"

"That water has got to be close to freezing and you've barely even flinched. What other conclusion am I supposed to come to?"

He tilted his head, considering my question. "Come here."

I balked. "What?"

He patted the cement beside him. "Come over here."

My heart was galloping as I weighed my options. This was one of those moments, wasn't it? When you feel like the rest of your life hinges on one decision, ten lousy footsteps, the lopsided-smiling invitation of a guy so hot he belongs in men's underwear commercials.

The way I saw it, I had two options: I could go over there, take the kind of leap my heart had never dared take before. Or I could run toward that gate, hop in my car, drive back to my house, hide under the covers with Hippo, and pretend for the rest of my life that I wasn't the biggest coward to ever walk the earth.

The decision was easy. My legs were the challenge. I had to bully them into walking. Scold them silently in my head until they finally moved. Until I was finally inching closer to him.

I sat down, keeping at least a foot of space between us. Then I looked at him, like I was waiting for him to tell me what the rest of my life would look like.

"Take off your shoes," he commanded.

I leaned over and stared into the pool. "You're crazy."

"You asked me what other conclusion you were supposed to come to. I'm giving you another option."

I sighed and removed my shoes, holding my hands over the toes of my socks to hide the unsightly hole. Why oh why didn't I pick out cuter ones?

Maybe because I never, in a zillion quatillion years, thought I'd be sitting shoeless next to the cutest guy in our entire school.

"Socks, too," he ordered.

"My feet will freeze. I have warm blood running through my veins. Unlike some people."

There was that smile again. But he didn't say anything. He just stared intently at my socks.

I slipped them off and stuffed them into my sneakers.

Then suddenly Tristan Wheeler's hands were touching me. Well, technically they were touching my jeans as he leaned over and rolled the hems up to my knees. But his fingers brushed my legs more than once and I prayed to God the shivers I felt on the inside didn't show on the outside. I was also extremely grateful I had shaved my legs that morning.

"Now," he said, nudging my knee with the backside of his hand. "Stick your feet in."

I shook my head. "No way."

"Come on. Trust me."

That's when I looked up at him. That's when our gazes crashed together. It would be the first of many explosive collisions complete with fire and smoke and an electric vibration of the air around us.

He didn't look away.

He could have. We both could have.

But he held me tight with his eyes, like he was cushioning me, protecting me from the sheer slicing pain that would accompany the water as I slowly slid my bare legs into the pool.

But the pain never came.

The water was delicious. Warm and tingling and welcoming. I gasped in surprise.

"There," he said, looking mighty proud of himself. "The *other* conclusion."

"The pool is heated," I whispered.

"The pool is heated."

"You're not a vampire."

"I am most definitely *not* a vampire."

THE SECOND MONDAY

Let the Sunshine In

7:04 a.m.

When I was nine years old, I went to Camp Awahili for the first time. My family had just moved to town and I was starting a new school in the fall. They wanted me to get a jump start on making friends so they sent me to a local sleepaway camp. That's where I met Owen.

One night, a girl from my bunk accidentally left our cabin door open and every blood-sucking mosquito within a fifty-mile radius was invited to a free, all-you-can-eat sleeping-children buffet. I woke up the next morning with bites all over my face, including on both eyelids. My eyes were so swollen, I couldn't open them for half of the day.

Bloop-dee-dee-bloop-bloop-bing!

When I hear the text message ding on my phone the next morning, I'm afraid to open my eyes. I'm afraid that it'll be just like that horrific morning at camp. Not because I was attacked by hungry mosquitoes but because I was up half the night crying, and that never bodes well for your face in the morning.

I sigh and drag my eyes open. Surprisingly, they offer little resistance.

Bloop-dee-dee-bloop-bloop-bing!

Who's messaging me this early? It's probably Owen asking how I'm feeling.

Well, I can tell him right now: like someone ran over my heart with a truck.

There's no way I'm going to school today. I can't face everyone. Not after what happened yesterday. It all comes back to me in a tidal wave. The rain, the school picture, the speech, the puffy lips, the election results, and then—a sob hiccups in my chest—Tristan.

Everyone has to know by now that he broke up with me. At our school, that kind of news can never stay buried for long.

So, nope. Definitely not going back there.

I wonder how long I'll have to fake sick before the whole thing blows over and people stop talking about it. A week? A month? I better be ready to fake the plague, if necessary.

I reach for my phone, knocking over a cup of water in the process.

That's strange.

I don't remember getting water last night.

I swipe the screen and the air catches in my throat when I see Tristan's name.

He texted me?

Oh, holy Smurf poop.

My fingers are suddenly useless fat sausages as I try to select the message so I can read it. When I finally get it open, I see that he didn't send me only one text, he sent *two*!

Tristan: I can't stop thinking about last night.

Tristan: Let's talk today.

I bound out of bed like a superhero breaking through a glass ceiling and let out a triumphant *whoop!*

He changed his mind! He wants to get back together! Happy, happy day!

I text him back, choosing my reply carefully.

Don't seem too eager, Ellison. Remember, play it cool. Cool as a cucumber, that's me.

Where does that phrase even come from? Are cucumbers inherently cool? Imagine how much cooler they'd be with sunglasses on.

I giggle at the image as I type my response.

Me: Sure. Meet you at your locker before class?

A minute later, he replies.

Tristan: OK.

Huzzah! This is it! My second chance. The one I begged and pleaded for last night as I drifted off to sleep in a sea of my own tears like Alice, in Wonderland. Thank you, Universe. I will not fail you this time!

I shower quickly and then stand in front of my closet, taking in the rows of color-coordinated clothes. If I thought yesterday's clothing decision was stressful, this is something else entirely.

What do you wear on the day your boyfriend wants to get back together with you?

It has to be something stunning that doesn't look like I'm trying too hard.

I finally opt for a pair of jeans, an off-the-shoulder sweater, and flats.

As I fashion my hair into a loose high bun, I keep looking at my phone, double-checking to make sure those messages are real.

I can't stop thinking about last night.

Let's talk today.

There's nothing else that could mean, right? Why would you want to talk to your ex-girlfriend the day after you dumped her, unless you changed your mind?

The words do feel familiar, though. Didn't he text me the exact same thing yesterday after our fight?

I'm about to scroll back up to check yesterday's messages, when I notice the time.

Yikes!

I gotta go. If Tristan and I are meeting before first period, I can't be late. I need to allow plenty of time for him to confess his undying love for me. How long do reconciliation conversations usually take? Two minutes? Three? I mean, it's not like there'll be a lot of resistance on my part. I'll just stand there quietly, listen to what he has to say, nod in all the right places, and then when he gets to the "Do you want to get back together?" part, obviously I'll pretend to think about it for a few seconds because, you know, cool cucumber and everything, and then I'll say something totally casual and uneager, like "Sure. I guess so."

I place my phone in my schoolbag, pausing when I notice a stack of textbooks next to my bed.

Did I do homework last night? In the middle of my emotional breakdown?

I let out a gasp.

Do I do homework in my sleep?

That would be like the best superpower ever!

I grab the textbooks and the water-soaked pile of paper on top and stuff them into my bag. Then I hurry down the stairs.

So what if he used the same words as yesterday? That's Tristan. There's always some hidden poetic meaning in everything he does. Like song lyrics. You repeat the chorus several times throughout because it has the most significance. I think it's romantic. The same words that drove us apart are now bringing us together again.

7:46 a.m.

When I enter the kitchen, I hear the bang of a cabinet door and see my mom glaring evilly at my father, who's deeply absorbed in another Words With Friends game on his iPad.

They still haven't made up? That must have been some fight.

Hadley looks up from her cereal and the book she's reading the moment I walk in. "Did he call?"

Huh?

I don't remember telling Hadley about the breakup last night. Actually, I distinctly remember *not* telling her. Why would she ask that? Did she hear me and Owen talking from her room? She was probably listening at the wall with a water glass held up to her ear, the little snoop.

"No," I say dismissively, hoping my tone clearly conveys that I do not want to talk about this with her. Especially after she completely eavesdropped on my life.

I walk to the fridge and pull out the bread, popping two pieces into the toaster.

My dad glances at me over the top of his iPad, his face pulled in concentration. "I need a word that starts with T and has an X, an A, and preferably an N in it."

My mom bangs another cabinet closed.

"What are you looking for?" my dad asks.

"Nothing!" she snaps. "I'm not looking for anything at all. Why would I possibly be looking for something I have no hope of ever finding? At least not under this roof!"

Slowly, I turn from the toaster and stare at my circus of a family. There's something weirdly familiar about this conversation.

"Craydar," Hadley says knowingly, interrupting my thoughts.

I glare at her. "What?"

"It's when a guy can tell whether or not a woman is cray cray just by looking at her. Maybe you set off Tristan's craydar and that's why he hasn't called."

"No," my dad says, shaking his head disappointedly at the screen. "I don't have a Y or a C."

I squint at Hadley. "You don't know anything about anything. And stop looking at Urban Dictionary. Mom, I told you—"

CLANK!

My mom has just slammed a frying pan onto one of the burners.

I have to get out of here. This place is even more unbearable than yesterday.

I force my toast out of the toaster, slather it with peanut butter, and wrap it in a paper towel. "I gotta run," I tell no one in particular.

"Ellie," my dad says, stopping me as I'm halfway to the door.

Great. He's going to ask me how softball tryouts went yesterday. I was really hoping to avoid this conversation until later. Much later. Like when I'm fifty.

"Yeah?" I reply unassumingly.

"Are you ready?"

I tilt my head, confused. "For what?"

Now *he* looks confused. "Softball tryouts."

Wait, what?

Has he completely forgotten about the conversation we had right here in this very kitchen? I swear he plays that game way too much. It's starting to affect his brain.

"Okay," I say slowly.

"Making varsity your junior year would be huge. The state schools would definitely take notice of that."

Now I *know* he's lost it. Isn't that exactly what he said to me yesterday? I glance around the kitchen to see if anyone else seems to have noticed that Dad is losing his marbles. I mean, I know forty-four is old, but I didn't think it was *that* old. Hadley has gone back to her book and my mom is rummaging loudly through the fridge for something.

I make a mental note to Google the signs of dementia later today.

My dad sets his iPad down. "I remember when my varsity baseball team made it to the state championships. Standing on that pitching mound, I'd never been so nervous in my life."

What is this? Some kind of joke?

Why is no one else fazed by the fact that my dad has launched into the same boring story he told yesterday?

I can't deal with this. Not right now, anyway. Parental breakdowns will just have to wait until I smooth things over with Tristan. "Great story, Dad," I interrupt before he has a chance to really get going. "But I have to run."

My mom slams the butter tray down on the counter. It makes the same cracking sound.

"Is something wrong?" My dad turns his attention to her.

"No," Mom barks as she cuts a piece of butter and drops it into the frying pan. "Why would anything be wrong?"

"Are you sure?"

"She's gone mom-zerk," Hadley says, glancing up from her book.

My dad excitedly reaches for his iPad again. "Ooh. I wish I had a Z!"

Then my mom storms out of the kitchen, leaving the burner on and the butter melting in the pan.

I stare openmouthed at the scene before me. Talk about déjà vu. It's like my family is rehearsing a scene in a play. They perform the lines and the exits exactly as they did yesterday.

Wait, *are* they rehearsing for a play? Is this some family bonding exercise they're doing without me?

Whatever, this is too weird. I have to get out of here. I practically run to the door, nudging it open and tumbling into the garage. I hop in my car, rev the engine, and squeal out of the driveway. I cannot drive away from that house fast enough.

My family is certifiably crazy. Or as Hadley would say, "certifiably cray cray."

If You Believe In Magic, Don't Bother to Choose

7:54 a.m.

Why is it raining *again*?

And why did I forget to bring an umbrella *again*?

I have a weather app for this very thing. It might help if I, you know, checked it once in a while.

I select my "Psych Me Up Buttercup" playlist from my phone again, hit Shuffle, and turn the volume up.

"Good Vibrations" by the Beach Boys starts to play as I turn left at the end of my street. That's weird. There must be something wrong with the shuffle feature. This is the same song that came on first yesterday. Good thing I happen to really like this song. I sing along at the top of my lungs as I turn onto Owen's street and pull into his driveway.

"Wow. It's really chucking it down out there," he says when he opens the car door. "Uh-oh. What happened?"

"What do you mean?"

He drops his backpack on the floor and settles into the

passenger seat. "You only put the Beach Boys on after something bad happens."

A shiver passes through me. Isn't that what he said yesterday, too?

He shakes his damp hair out and I watch the tiny drops of rain splatter across my dashboard like they're moving in slow motion.

Is it just me being anal or did those drops land in the exact same spots yesterday?

I reach into my glove box and pull out the cleaning cloth.

"So why are you listening to an emergency-only playlist?" Owen asks. "Did you and Tristan have a fight or something?"

I stare at him in disbelief. Is he kidding? Is he trying to make light of my tragic state? Well, it's not very funny and I don't appreciate him turning the worst night of my life into a joke.

I open my mouth to tell him exactly this when I notice he hasn't changed his clothes since yesterday. He's wearing the same loose-fitting black jeans and the same gray T-shirt over a long-sleeve thermal.

"Did you sleep in your clothes?" I ask.

"No, why?"

"Did your mommy forget to do your laundry?"

He looks at me like *I'm* the crazy one.

"Anywaaaay," he says, completely ignoring my insult. "You can't tell me you had a fight. I refuse to believe that. You two agree on bloody everything."

"We do not—" I start to argue, but the overwhelming sense of familiarity in this exchange is freaking me out, so I put the car in Reverse and back out of the driveway. I had planned to show him Tristan's text messages and ask for a guy's opinion on the matter, but if Owen is going to be an insensitive jerk about this, I won't talk to him.

As I reach the stop sign at the end of Owen's street, the Beach Boys song comes to an end and "Do You Believe in Magic" begins. Baffled, I look down at my phone. The shuffle feature is definitely buggy. I knew I shouldn't have installed that new update the other day. Everyone knows you're supposed to wait at least three days for them to fix all the bugs.

I swipe down to access the notifications window, checking to see if they released another update to fix the last one, and that's when I notice that my phone is still displaying yesterday's date.

Monday, September 26.

What the . . . ?

Jeez, that update really screwed everything up. My whole calendar is wonky!

"You know you only have to legally pause for like a second at a stop sign."

I glance up at the empty street in front of us and toss my phone into the compartment under the radio, easing on the accelerator and pulling onto Providence Boulevard.

Owen turns up the volume and starts singing along.

"Owen," I say carefully, turning my windshield wipers up a notch. "Have you ever had déjà vu?"

"Only all the time," he says, reaching down into his bag. "Oh, I almost forgot." When he sits back up, I let out a stifled gasp when I see the two plastic-wrapped fortune cookies in his hand.

"W-w-what are you doing?" I stammer.

"Choose your tasty fortune!" he says, like it's nothing. Like we didn't just do this whole thing twenty-four hours ago.

"Wait," I protest. "I thought you only worked at the Tasty House on Sundays."

"I do."

This is going to be a strange day, I can tell.

I reach for the cookie on the left, but then remember that's the one I picked yesterday, so I grab the one on the right and drop it in my lap.

As I drive, Owen nosily unwraps his cookie and snaps open the shell.

"If your desires are not extravagant," he reads aloud, "they will be granted."

I swerve the car to the side of the road and slam on the brakes.

"Whoa. Drive much?" Owen complains.

"Let me see that!" I swipe the piece of paper from his hand and read it.

If your desires are not extravagant,
they will be granted.

No. It's not possible.

I toss his fortune back and hastily unwrap mine. My hands are trembling as I break open the cookie and pull out the message.

My lips feel heavy and numb as I read.

Today you will get everything your true heart desires.

But . . . it can't. It's . . . what are the odds of this happening? A gazillion to one? I don't know, I've never actually studied fortune cookie statistics. Is that even a thing? Is this fortune cookie factory simply printing the same two fortunes over and over again? But Owen and I have never gotten these fortunes before.

"Did the Tasty House change fortune cookie distributors?"

Now Owen is looking at me like I need to be locked up. "Noooo," he says slowly.

Maybe their printer malfunctioned and printed a billion duplicate cookies.

"Is this a joke?" I ask, waving the fortune at him. "Did you do this?"

"Do what? What are you talking about?"

"This fortune. I already got it. I . . ." My voice trails off and I dive my hand into the pocket of the door. I grapple around, feeling for the tiny piece of paper I crumpled up and stuck in there yesterday. The one with the same exact message on it. It has to be in here.

But all I feel is the smooth, clean interior of the compartment. As if it disappeared into thin air. As if yesterday morning never even happened.

Suspicious Minds

8:11 a.m.

"Did you ever get around to watching the season premiere of *Assumed Guilty*?" Owen asks.

I cringe. With the horrific day I had yesterday, it totally slipped my mind. "Not yet. I will soon, though. I promise!"

After Tristan and I have reunited and I'm back in a state of gorgeous boyfriend bliss.

Owen bangs his fist on the dashboard. "Bollocks! You need to get on that."

I scowl at his reaction. "I know, I know. And *please* stop saying 'bollocks.'"

"You missed the best episode."

"I *know*," I repeat, growing annoyed. He doesn't have to keep telling me it's the best episode. I already feel bad enough.

Owen points to the intersection ahead. "Yellow light."

What?

I glance at the street sign. Avenue de Liberation. It's the same dang intersection.

This time I know I can beat that stupid light. I *have* to beat it. I have to prove that I'm not going crazy. That the world is not stuck on some weird Repeat button. That today is different.

I floor the accelerator. Owen grips the door handle.

"Um . . ." he says.

I sail through the intersection just as I'm attacked by a barrage of flashing bulbs.

Dang it!

I swore I'd make it. That's two red light tickets in two days. My parents are going to kill me.

"Ouch," Owen says, cringing.

"Shut up," I snap.

"Objection. Argumentative."

"Withdrawn," I mumble.

8:25 a.m.

How did I manage to be late again? It must have been the time I spent on the side of the road freaking out over my fortune cookie. I told Tristan I'd meet him at his locker before class and now I'll have to go straight to class. He'll think I stood him up.

On second thought, maybe that's a good thing. A little hard-to-get might actually work in my favor. At least I won't seem eager.

Cool as a cucumber.

Owen forgot his umbrella again, too, so we make another run for it.

Tuesdays are even days so I head straight for my second-period class—calculus with Mr. Henshaw. I burst through the door just as the bell is ringing and slide into my desk.

"Excuse me," a haughty voice says, and I look up to see Daphne Gray standing there in her cheerleader uniform, with her hands on her hips. "You're in my seat."

Wait, Daphne Gray isn't in my calculus class. The girl can barely count.

I glance around the room. Actually, I don't recognize any of these people.

"Ellison," Mr. Henshaw says, staring strangely at me from the front of the classroom. "If I remember correctly, you're in my second-period class."

"This is second period," I say, but there is no confidence in my words.

Isn't it?

Daphne leads the room in a round of laughter.

"Today is an odd day," Mr. Henshaw says.

It most certainly is.

What on earth is going on around here? Tuesdays have always been even days. Since I started going to this school. Did they suddenly change it up this year?

"This is my first-period algebra class," Mr. Henshaw continues.

Daphne clears her throat. "Ahem. My seat."

I slowly stand and pull my bag over my shoulder.

"You should get to your *first-period* class." Mr. Henshaw enunciates "first-period" as if I might actually be hard of hearing.

As I make the walk of shame to the door, I hear Daphne hide the word "drunk" under a cough, causing the whole class to erupt in laughter again.

I race down the hall and up the stairs to chemistry. When I get there, all the students are filing out of the classroom, chattering noisily.

"Okay," Mr. Briggs calls out, clapping his hands. "Can we keep it down? There are classes in session."

"What's going on?" I ask, shoving my way to the teacher.

"School pictures," Mr. Briggs says. I can tell he's trying to decide whether or not to reprimand me for being late. But then Aaron Hutchinson starts playing drums on a nearby row of lockers and Mr. Briggs scowls and darts away, deeming that the more heinous crime.

School pictures?

But we did that yesterday. Are they doing retakes already? I thought they waited at least a few weeks for that. Maybe something happened to the photos. Maybe the photographer lost the memory card and now we have to redo them.

As I stand in line in the cafeteria, waiting to get my picture taken for the second time this week, I'm suddenly reminded of my hair. It's a disaster.

Again.

"Say 'Two more years!'" the photographer trills as I sit down on the stool.

My mouth falls open in shock just as she snaps the photo.

"Lovely! Next!"

As I'm shuffled away, I steal a peek at the camera's viewfinder again. This time I look like a dying fish. Tack on the scariness of the hair and smudged makeup and I'm a dying *zombie* fish.

So there goes that. I don't think I can count on the memory card being lost a second time. I guess I'm destined to be the laughingstock of the yearbook.

9:50 a.m.

As soon as the bell rings, I make a beeline to the girls' restroom. Priority number one is to fix my face before I see Tristan. I can't get back together with my hot boyfriend looking like a zombie fish.

But I'm startled when I see Tristan standing outside my classroom.

He's waiting for me?

Well, well, well, how the tables have turned. I guess my little no-show act worked like a charm.

"Hey," he says, sidling up and falling into step beside me.

"Hey," I say back. *Very* cucumber-like.

I can feel him peering at me out of the corner of my eye, studying my face. "Are you trying out for the school play?"

I slow. Did he really ask me that a second time?

"No, it's raining again. Remember?"

He looks momentarily confused before saying, "You didn't show up this morning. I waited at my locker." He sounds like an injured puppy. My heart does a little quickstep in my chest. He's sad that I stood him up.

Oh, this is so happening right now.

"Sorry." I coat the word with a smooth nonchalance. "I was running late. Had to head straight to second—er, first period."

He nods. "I was hoping we could talk."

"Isn't that what we're doing?" I hoped for that to sound coy and flirtatious, but he clearly doesn't interpret it that way.

Tristan inhales sharply. "You're still mad."

I feign innocence. "About what?"

"About last night."

"Mad? No. A little confused maybe."

"Yeah," he says, running his hand over the back of his neck. "Me, too."

Ah-*ha*! Confusion! Confusion equals second-guessing equals regret equals we are *so* getting back together.

But the third-period bell is about to ring, so let's move it along.

"What are you confused about?" I ask, hoping it will encourage him to spit it out already.

He sighs. "About some of the things you said last night."

"Me?" I blurt out. I can't help it. The idea that *I* had anything to do with the events of last night is preposterous. I was the one standing there speechless while he was the one who destroyed everything we had in a matter of minutes. "*You're* the one who broke up with *me*."

Wow. He really *is* confused. I can see it all over his face. He stops walking. "Broke up?" he sputters. "Ellie, we had a fight."

"Yeah," I say helplessly. "And then you broke up with me?"

"No, I didn't. I was upset, sure. But I never said I wanted to break up." His eyes fixate on a spot above my head, like he's trying to remember the exact conversation.

Meanwhile, *I* remember the conversation perfectly, and he said . . .

Wait a second.

My pulse sputters to a stop. My mind is reeling. Did he ever actually say the words "I want to break up?" Or anything remotely similar?

I replay his words in my head.

I can't do this anymore.

This isn't working.

Something is broken and I don't know how to fix it.

Holy crap on a stick. Did I completely make this up in my head? Did I misinterpret the whole thing? Was it really just another fight?

Did I cry myself to sleep for *nothing*?

"So you *didn't* break up with me?" I ask slowly, unsure if I can trust the words coming out of my mouth.

He takes way too long to answer. "No . . ." It sounds like he wants to add more, but he falls silent.

And then I very eloquently say, "Oh."

Oh?

The worst night of my life has been revealed to be an illusion and all I can say is "Oh"?

"But I still think we should talk about—"

Just then the bell rings. We look at each other and then make a dash to Spanish class. Señora Mendoza gives us a sour look as we slip into our seats, but thankfully she doesn't say anything.

I glance at Tristan out of the corner of my eye and he gives me a conspiratorial half smile. I feel relief fill me up and I expect it to lull me into a state of calm. But for some reason it doesn't. It's like taking a deep breath but never being able to exhale.

It was all a big misunderstanding. Everything is totally completely fine.

Isn't it?

Why do I still feel so uneasy? Like there's something I'm missing?

I tear a piece of notebook paper from my binder and quickly scribble "Are we good?" then slide it onto Tristan's desk.

He gives me an adorable wink and whispers, "Yeah," just as

Señora Mendoza says, "*¡Nosotros veremos!*" in her bright, bubbly tone.

My head whips to the front of the room.

Didn't we conjugate this same verb yester—

But the thought is cut short as a massive black blur crashes against the classroom window.

Oh, I Believe In Yesterday

There's only one rational explanation. The local crows have formed a suicide pact. I saw a documentary about this once. Not with birds, obviously, but with people. A bunch of lonely souls get together and decide to commit suicide around the same time.

I'm no avian expert, but I imagine it works the same with birds.

I mean, how else do you explain *two* birds crashing to their deaths against the window of my Spanish class?

It's either that or they really hate the sound of Señora Mendoza's voice.

Fortunately, this time I don't burst into tears. I got that little problem under control. But I do feel pretty queasy when Sadie Haskins confirms that the bird is dead. Tristan looks to me, almost like he expects me to start crying again, but I hold it together.

See, I'm improving already.

Reining in the drama.

11:20 a.m.

In history, Mr. Weylan actually hands out the exact same quiz as yesterday. When is this poor old man going to retire already? It's kind of embarrassing.

Although I guess what's really embarrassing is the fact that I still don't get all the questions right. I remember some of the correct answers from yesterday's quiz, but I'm ashamed to say I don't get a hundred percent today. And neither does Daphne Gray, whose test I have to grade again. I try to share a conspiratorial eye roll with her when we trade back papers. Something that says, "Can you believe this guy is allowed to keep teaching?" but I must not convey the sentiment properly, because she just stares blankly back at me. Like she can't understand why I even exist.

She hands me my test with a big 76 percent marked on the front. Well, it's an improvement, at least. Let's hope old man Weylan also managed to forget yesterday's results and uses these instead. Or better yet, let's hope he forgets again tomorrow. I'll surely be able to ace it by then.

"Homework for tonight," Mr. Weylan announces in his wobbly voice as the class comes to an end. He turns and writes something on the whiteboard. His handwriting is so shaky it's barely legible.

For Tuesday: Read chapters 3 & 4.

I let out a snort and Daphne turns her dark cat eyes on me. "What?"

"He assigned us the same thing yesterday. And he got the day wrong."

Not that I did the assignment anyway. I was too busy getting ambiguously broken up with.

"Um, are you on drugs?" she asks in response.

First I'm a drunk. Now I've apparently upgraded to drug addict.

No, I want to reply, equally snotty, but then I look around the room and notice that everyone is furiously writing down the assignment. Like the mistake doesn't even faze them.

It's right then that a tingle starts in the pit of my stomach. Like a quiet murmuring of some foreboding truth.

I turn back to Daphne and whisper, "Isn't today Tuesday?"

She shakes her head at me, clearly believing I really am on drugs. "No, it's *Monday.*"

"But," I argue, my voice lacking confidence. "It was Monday yesterday."

Daphne sighs, like she really doesn't have time for this. She digs her phone out of her bag, swipes it on, and shoves it in my face. She points to the time and date stamped at the top.

Monday, September 26.

The tingling in my stomach turns to full-grown schizo butterflies.

How is that possible?

Did the update mess up her phone, too?

I grab the device from her and turn it around in my hand, studying the construction from all angles. It's a completely different model than mine. Then I stare intently at the screen, blinking several times.

The date does not change.

What on earth is going on?

"Excuse me," Daphne says hotly, snatching the phone back. The bell rings, ending fifth period, and even though the entire class leaps out of their seats, I can't bring myself to move.

The screen of Daphne's phone is ingrained in my mind.

Monday.

It's still Monday.

But it *can't* be Monday.

I dive for my bag and rifle around until I find my own phone. I turn it on and stare at the calendar app.

Monday, September 26.

I go to CNN.com, Yahoo.com, even Time.gov, which is run by the United States government. Every single one of them confirms what my brain does not want confirmed.

Today is Monday, September 26.

But things happened yesterday. A lot of things. Awful things. The banana bread and the election speeches and the softball tryouts and Tristan's messages.

My fingers fly across the screen until I find the texts from this morning.

Tristan: I can't stop thinking about last night.

Tristan: Let's talk today.

It was the exact same thing he texted me yesterday.

Yesterday.

Also Monday.

I hastily scroll up, searching for the identical messages, but there's nothing. All I find is the text from Sunday afternoon, when he invited me to his house to hang out. Before we had the big fight and I threw a garden gnome at his head.

Ellie, we had a fight.

Those were Tristan's words to me today. *Monday.* He swore he never broke up with me. He acted like yesterday never happened.

And now that I think about it, *everyone* has been acting like yesterday never happened.

My dad asked me about softball tryouts.

Owen offered me fortune cookies.

Mr. Henshaw said it was an "odd day" even though everyone knows Tuesdays are even days.

That bird hit the window.

Mr. Weylan gave us the same quiz.

But I was there. I lived through that dreadful day. It was *real.* I didn't just make it all up. I don't think I could have made up a day that awful if I tried. Stephen effing King couldn't have dreamed up that horror.

But if today is Monday, then what happened to yesterday?

Where did it all go?

Lucy in the Sky with Diamonds

12:40 p.m.

What if Daphne was right? What if it *is* drugs? What if I've been drugged and I don't even know it? I shouldn't have taken that ibuprofen last night. It was probably laced with hallucinogenics or something. I once saw a documentary about a batch of ibuprofen that had to be recalled because they found traces of meth in it. Meth!

Come to think of it, how long have I had that bottle in my medicine cabinet? Does ibuprofen ever go bad?

My head is suddenly swimming. When I look up at the clock I notice that lunch is already half over. I leap out of my seat and shuffle to the door.

Mr. Weylan seems to notice my lingering presence for the first time and startles when I approach. "Oh, oh," he fumbles, collecting himself. "Ellison. Did you have a question?"

I smile politely. "No, Mr. Weylan. Thank you."

He blinks back at me through those massive bottle-glasses of his.

I head straight for the library and burst through the doors just as Owen is making an impassioned case about the narrator of *The Book Thief.* He sees me and smiles. "Are you finally joining book club?"

I don't answer. I grab his arm and yank him out of his chair, pulling him up the stairs and barricading us in one of the tiny recording booths.

"Um . . ." Owen says warily.

"Something is happening to me."

"Okaaaay." He elongates the word like he's afraid if he ends it too soon, I might snap.

"I think I might have brain damage."

He cracks a smile. "Well, I could have told you *that.*"

"I'm serious, Owen," I say, and he schools his face. "I'm losing it. I'm going crazy. Today, I woke up and it was yesterday. I mean, yesterday is actually today. It's the same stupid day. It's happening all over again. Everything. The fortune cookies. The history test. The school pictures."

He can't hold his serious face any longer. He breaks into a knowing grin. "Did you finally watch *Groundhog Day* like I've been telling you to do for *years*?"

"What?" I shake my head. "No. Listen to me. I. Am. Losing. My. Mind."

He's so much taller than me, he has to bend down to get eye-level. "Your pupils *are* a bit dilated."

"Because I'm freaking out!"

Gurgloomph.

Owen gives me a strange look. "What was that?"

"Nothing."

"Was that your stomach?"

"No."

Gurgloooeeeooomph.

"Have you eaten today?"

I think back to the pieces of bread I toasted this morning. The peanut butter is probably smeared all over the bottom of my bag again.

I look away. "Not technically."

"Well, there's your problem." He grabs me by the wrist, opens the door, and leads me back into the library. The entire book club has stopped their discussion and is now staring at us.

I break free from Owen's grasp but he doesn't stop walking. "C'mon, Looney Toons, we're taking you to get something to eat."

I follow Owen obediently out of the library and down the hall. We get to the cafeteria just as the lunch lady shuts the metal grate, closing all access to the food line. Not that it's a huge loss. The culinary selection in this place leaves much to be desired.

A voice comes over a speaker. I immediately recognize the grating, shrill squeaks of Daphne Gray. "This is your last chance to support the cheer team and buy some delicious homemade goodies!"

Owen turns his attention to the table set up in the corner where Daphne is speaking into a microphone under a sign that says BAKE'N'CHEER.

"Bake sale," he says, grabbing my wrist again and pulling me toward it. "Bingo. Come on, my treat. I'll buy you some banana bread."

I pull to a halt. "Oh no. Nuh-uh. I'm not putting anything they make into my mouth."

Owen gives me a disapproving look. "Ellie. You need to let

go of this grudge you have against cheerleaders. They're just normal people."

"Normal people who poison you!"

"What?"

"Yesterday Daphne Gray told me there were no almonds in the banana bread and guess what! Almonds! My lips totally inflated!"

"Yesterday was Sunday."

"No! Yesterday was today!"

"You're losing it."

I sigh. "That's what I've been trying to tell you."

"It's the stress," he diagnoses. "You've been taking on too much lately. Are you nervous about the speech?"

Speech?

What speech?

Oh, flub. The election speech. I have to do it again!

This is officially my worst nightmare. The universe is punishing me. But for what? Not studying for my history test?

Really, Universe? I'm the best you could do? You couldn't find anyone more devious to torture?

The bell rings, signaling the end of lunch.

I think I'm hyperventilating. I've never hyperventilated before, but I suddenly sound like a woman in labor.

"It's going to be okay," Owen assures me, putting his hands on my shoulders. "Where are your speech notes?"

I pat my back pocket but come up empty. "I . . . I threw them away."

He blinks rapidly. "Why would you do that?"

I throw my hands in the air. "Because I already gave the stupid speech yesterday!"

"Okay," he says, "take deep breaths. It's going to be fine."

"How is it going to be fine? I don't know what to say. I'm going to die up there. Again!"

I have to sit down. No. I have to run. I have to get as far away from this death trap as possible. I glance at the cafeteria doors, watching the hundreds upon hundreds of students filing into the gym on the other side of the hallway. Then I glance at the back door, the one that leads to the parking lot.

Yup. I'm so getting out of here.

I turn to leave but a bony, pale hand is suddenly on my arm.

"There you are! I've been looking *everywhere* for you." Rhiannon Marshall's steely blue eyes are trained on me.

I barely have time to hand Owen my bag before Rhiannon is dragging me out the door. Toward my second demise of the week.

I Can't Get No Satisfaction

1:33 p.m.

"Running for vice president of the junior class, here's Ellison Sparks, Sparks, Sparks, Sparks." Principal Yates's voice echoes in my ears as I step up to the microphone. The room is blurring in and out of focus. I look for Owen. He gives me an overly enthusiastic thumbs-up from the front row.

I'm doomed and we both know it.

I stand speechless and motionless, trying to figure out what to do. Maybe this is all a really bad dream. Maybe I'll wake up in my bed and it'll be Tuesday morning.

I squeeze my eyes tight.

Wake up, wake up, wake up!

I hear tiny snickers spread through the crowd. This time, they're not laughing at my blown-up lips, they're laughing at *me.*

I snap my eyes open. I'm still in the gym. The entire student body is still staring at me with expectant eyes. I find Tristan in the crowd. He's looking very concerned. If I fainted, would he run up here? Would he carry me to the nurse's office, knocking people out of his way like some war hero action film star?

I clear my throat. "Hello," I say. My voice sounds high and squeaky. I try a lower register. "Hello."

Whoa. Too low.

"Hello." Third time's a charm.

They're already chuckling. I've barely even said anything. High school is the worst.

"I'm Ellison Sparks and I'm running for junior class vice president." I rack my brain trying to remember the speech Rhiannon wrote, but for the life of me, I can't recall one horrible word.

"Um," I say haltingly. "I'm Ellison Sparks and I'm running for junior class vice president."

Crap. I already said that.

Guffaws from the peanut gallery.

"I'm sorry," I continue shakily, "but this whole day has just been really, really weird."

Silence.

Huh.

They stopped giggling.

I keep going. "Have you ever felt like you're just stuck in the same exact day? Like yesterday never even happened?"

I glance around. Some people actually seem interested. Tristan leans forward. Behind me, Rhiannon is hissing through gritted teeth. "What are you *doing*?"

I look to Owen, who gestures for me to keep going.

"Like we're just running on an invisible hamster wheel and nothing we do makes any difference?"

I catch sight of Mrs. Naper, the psychology teacher. She's smiling and nodding emphatically.

"That's how I feel today. Like I've done this all before and I already know the outcome."

I swallow. I'm still surrounded by rapt silence. I've somehow managed to snag their attention.

"You won't vote for me and Rhiannon." I point behind me to our opponents. "You'll elect them. At least that's how it happened before."

Now I think I've just confused everyone.

Wrap it up, I scold myself.

"But I hope today—*this* version of today—you'll do it differently. Thank you."

I step away from the mic as the crowd breaks into tentative applause, like they're not sure whether to clap or write me off as a wacko.

"Well done, Ellison," Principal Yates says, equally hesitant.

I step back in line with the other candidates. I think all I've managed to do today is baffle everyone. It's a political tactic I don't think I've ever seen before, but at least I wasn't laughed out of the gym this time. At least I'm not hiding in the girls' bathroom right now.

I don't know about you, but I consider that a vast improvement.

1:45 p.m.

After the speeches are concluded, we're sent back to our homeroom classes to cast our votes. I open my bag to pull out a pen and spot the peanut butter toast on the bottom, smashed between a textbook and the paper I spilled water on this morning.

My extra-credit English essay.

I get a sudden niggling suspicion about something.

I open the interior Velcro pocket and hesitantly slip my hand inside. My stomach seizes as I pull out the carefully paper-clipped stack of index cards.

The speech Rhiannon wrote for me.

The one I had ripped up and tossed into the trash in the girls' bathroom.

Yet, here it is. Fully intact in my bag. Exactly where it was yesterday.

A shiver runs down my spine as I stuff the cards back into the pocket. The bell rings. I quickly fill in the "Marshall/Sparks" bubble on my ballot and deliver it to the teacher's desk.

I've barely made it two steps into the hallway when the school secretary comes over the loudspeaker.

"Ellison Sparks, please report to the counseling office. Ellison Sparks to the counseling office, please."

Oh, thank GOD.

Someone to talk to! Someone who is trained in the vastly complicated wasteland that is the teenage mind.

I take off at a run. I barge into Mr. Goodman's office and collapse into the chair.

"Hello! You must be Ellison!" His voice is just as annoyingly chirpy as it was yesterday . . . or today . . . or whatever. "Great to see ya. Just really swell. I'm Mr. Goodman, but you can call me Mr. *Great*man, if you want." He guffaws at his own joke and then swats it away with his hand. "Just joshin' ya! So how ya doing? Ya holding up okay?"

I sigh dramatically and launch into my story. "No. I'm not. Not at all. Look, I really need to talk to someone and you're the closest thing this school has to a shrink. You see, this morning I woke up and it was yesterday. I mean, it was today, but it was the same day as yesterday. I've been reliving the same Monday *twice.* And I don't mean that every day feels like a Monday. I mean it's the exact same day. Down to the stupid red light ticket that I got! And I don't know what's happening to me, but I'm pretty sure it has something to do with the ibuprofen I took last night that may or may not have been ibuprofen because I saw this documentary once about ibuprofen that's not really ibuprofen and I thought, 'What if *my* bottle of ibuprofen is one of those bottles that's not really ibuprofen?' Because who knows how long I've had that bottle in my medicine cabinet. I don't know how long it takes for ibuprofen to turn into meth. And it's not like I take a lot of ibuprofen. I'm not one of those hypochondriacs who thinks she's dying all the time or that every headache is a brain tumor, but I *do* take ibuprofen occasionally, because you know, everyone has headaches. But I think whatever was in that bottle is causing some kind of crazy chemical reaction in my brain. I mean, it's totally possible that today doesn't really exist. That I'm not really here. That I'm sitting in a comatose state in my room, dreaming this whole thing up. But I don't know, do *you* feel real?"

I pause and suck in a huge breath. I think I just used up all the oxygen in the school.

Mr. Goodman blinks hard at me. He takes his glasses off and gives his eyes a rub. I stare at him expectantly, waiting for his words of wisdom. Waiting for him to tell me that what I'm going through is perfectly normal. In fact, in this month alone, he's seen three kids with the same exact problem.

"Well," Mr. Goodman begins, returning his glasses to his face. "This is a very interesting . . . um . . . dilemma you're facing. A real toughie."

He swivels around in his chair and faces the giant display of pamphlets on the back wall. He scans them with his index finger, plucking an orange one from the bottom row and sliding it across the desk at me. "This should do the trick."

"Another pamphlet?" I ask incredulously.

"Have I given you one before?"

I sigh and pick up the brochure. This one reads:

Saying No to Drugs: A Guide for Teens

It shows a blurry photograph of a girl with her hand outstretched against an unseen stranger who's clearly offering her something illicit. The only part of the picture that's in focus is the palm of her hand.

This one is admittedly more artistic than the last.

As I stare at the brochure, I quickly realize what a massive waste of time this has been. This guy's not going to help me. Did he even go to guidance counselor school? *Is* there such a thing?

"Thanks," I mumble, and stand up. "You've been a huge help."

Mr. Goodman cracks a goofy smile and swipes at the air. "Aw, shucks."

Clearly he doesn't have a pamphlet back there about the meaning of sarcasm.

Discouraged, I shuffle out of his office. If this man is helping shape the minds of America's youth, we're all doomed.

Take a Sad Song and Make It Better

2:02 p.m.

I've got it. I've finally figured it out.

I'm on a reality show.

Everyone I know must be in on it. My family, Owen, Tristan, Daphne Gray, even the counseling office receptionist who hands me a pass back to class. They're being paid to pretend this is real. There's probably hidden cameras set up all over the school. Then three months from now, I'm going to be a hit show on a major network.

It'll be called something snazzy like "Sparks Will Fly" or "Ellie's Island."

Although that doesn't really explain the date on all those Web pages I checked. I highly doubt a reality show would hack into a government Web site just to fool me into believing some big, elaborate scheme.

Okay, let's think about this for a minute.

What if I really *am* repeating the same day—even if it's just a dream, or a result of over-the-counter painkillers gone bad, or whatever. Shouldn't I at least make the most of it? Shouldn't I use my knowledge of yesterday to improve today? That's the smart, opportunistic thing to do, right?

I think back to all the horrible things that happened the first time I barely survived this day. Obviously one thing stands out above everything else: the carnival.

Tristan barely even gave it a shot. We didn't get to do any of the things on my romantic fantasy date list. Maybe if we had, he'd realize that we aren't broken. That we *do* still work. He was too bent out of shape about the stage being empty and his band missing the opportunity to perform.

I cover my hand with my mouth to keep the gasp from escaping.

That's it.

That's what I have to fix. That's what set the whole night on the wrong track.

I glance down at the pass in my hand. Too bad it's stamped with a time. Otherwise, I might have been able to pull this off without getting into trouble. I'll just have to try really hard not to get caught.

I've never, *ever* ditched school in my life.

Like I said to Owen, I'm sugar and spice and all things nice.

And look how well that's turned out for me so far.

This is my moment. If I have any hope of winning back Tristan's affections and making him forget about that stupid fight, I have to do this.

If I succeed, it may not just save my relationship, it may save my whole Monday.

Worryin' 'bout the Way Things Might Have Been

3:09 p.m.

Success!

I am victorious. I have triumphed!

Playing tonight on the main stage (okay, the *only* stage) at the final farewell evening of the town carnival is . . .

Whack-a-Mole!

(Cue the applause and confetti!)

I'm actually surprised by how easy it was to convince the carnival manager to let Tristan's band play. Maybe he's in on the reality show, too. I arrived at the fairgrounds ready to desperately plead my case like the losing attorney in a crumbling civil suit, armed with one of the Whack-a-Mole demo CDs that I always keep handy in my bag for just this reason. I marched into the carnival's messy (and smelly) trailer office, introduced myself as the band's manager (which, okay, is technically not true, but you know, trivial), and started to zealously sing their musical praises.

The guy—a grubby planet of a man—stopped me before I

even hit my stride and said, "Look, sweetheart, I don't care if you get up there and start banging on a bunch of pots and pans, as long as that stage isn't empty tonight."

"So the spot is mine? I mean, theirs?" I asked, unable to believe my sudden change in luck.

"Sure, sure. Now get out of my hair, kid. I got a lot of work to do around here."

I strode off, feeling a renewed sense of purpose. On the drive back to school, I put on something from my "World Domination" playlist—songs I usually reserve for a high test grade or when I win an especially brutal game of Sorry! against my dad.

I sing along to "Proud Mary" by Creedence Clearwater Revival at the top of my lungs as I turn into the parking lot of the school and find the same spot I vacated when I left.

I check the clock. Only a few minutes left of seventh period. I can do this. I can totally make this happen. I'll just wait until the bell rings, then I'll blend into the swarm of people exiting their last class.

It's the perfect plan, if I say so myself.

I don't know why I don't ditch school more often. I'm clearly amazing at it.

The song appropriately comes to an end right as the bell rings. This day is totally turning around. All it needed was a little nudge in the right direction. A small shift in perspective and everything falls into place.

Whack-a-Mole will play at the carnival tonight. Then Tristan, having just come off an onstage high, and I will have the romantic night I've dreamed about since I was ten.

I see the swells of students exiting the outer bungalows and heading toward the main building. I ease into the stream like a fish, glancing around to make sure no one gives me suspicious looks.

So far, so good.

I can't wait to find Tristan and tell him the good news. There's no way he can be mad at me after I landed his band this gig.

I will have to eventually figure out a way to explain to Ms. Ferrel, my English teacher, why I never showed up for class, and why I was unable to turn in my extra-credit paper, but that shouldn't be too hard. I'm a rebel now. I'll improvise!

I'm two steps away from the safety of the main building when a large hand clamps down on my shoulder. "Ms. Sparks," a gruff female voice says. With butterflies already stirring in the pit of my stomach, I slowly turn around. Principal Yates is standing behind me, looking like an ogre among all these students. "I hope you have a very good reason for missing seventh period."

I Fought the Law and the Law Won

3:18 p.m.

I take it all back. I'm not a rebel. I'm not even a radical. I'm barely an agitator. I'm not cut out for the criminal life. I buckle too easily under pressure. I would fare miserably in prison. And an interrogation room? Forget it. I'd squeal the moment the police officer straddled his chair.

Case in point, Principal Yates does nothing more than pin me with an accusing gaze before I totally crack.

"I'm sorry," I blubber. "I'll never do it again, I swear. It was a onetime thing."

I pray that Principal Yates will take pity on me as a first-time offender.

"One time or no," she says regretfully, "I have to punish delinquency. As a matter of principle."

I feel the strong desire to crack a joke, *A matter of principle. 'Cause you're the principal? Get it?* But I hold my tongue.

Probably the smartest thing I've done all day.

"Detention after school today," she concludes. "3:30 to 4:30."

My mouth falls open. "What?! No, but you can't. I have softball tryouts. I have to go. My dad will be crushed if I don't make varsity."

She gives me a disapproving look. "I guess you should have thought of that *before* you left school grounds without permission."

3:20 p.m.

I run to Tristan's locker, knowing I'll beat him there since he's coming from the math hallway on the other side of the building. When he appears around the corner, the entire world brightens. It's like Tristan brings warmth and energy and light wherever he goes. I want to start singing *"Here comes the sun!"* at the top of my lungs, but obviously I refrain.

He sees me and a small hesitant smiles works its way onto his lips. Does he look happy to see me? Or is he still angry about our fight?

You know what? It doesn't matter. Because after he hears what I have to tell him, everything will be forgiven *and* forgotten. All will be fixed.

He walks toward me like he's in one of those slow-motion scenes in a high school movie, all hair and swagger. It's hard to miss the stares he gets from other girls as he passes. I certainly notice, even if Tristan doesn't appear to.

See, Ellison. He doesn't care what other girls think. He only cares what you *think. Why can't you just believe that?*

I do. I believe it. I'm done with this insecure jealousy nonsense. It's highly inconvenient.

"Hey," he says when he approaches. "I was hoping I'd see you here."

"Well," I say, giving my hair a playful toss. "Here I am."

He looks uncomfortable, his gaze shifting to just over my shoulder.

"I thought we could continue our conversation. You know the one we started before first period."

Suddenly there's a huge boulder in my throat. The day comes spiraling back to me. The whole, awful, cringeworthy day. Like I'm being sucked back down the space-time continuum and plopped right back where it all began.

"Of course," I say breezily. "But first, I have some good news."

His eyebrow cocks. "You do?"

I can't hold it in any longer. The words bubble out of me. "I got you guys a gig!"

He tilts his head to the side like he didn't hear me correctly. "A gig?"

"Yes!" I squeal. "Tonight!"

He's still not getting this. "You did? Like a real gig?"

"That depends," I reply coyly. "Do you consider the main stage of the town carnival a real gig?"

"WHAT?!" Tristan screeches. "Are you serious?"

I shrug, like it's no big deal. Just fulfilling my basic girlfriend duty. "Yeah. I heard there was a last minute cancellation so I went down to the fairgrounds and talked to the manager. It took some convincing but once I told him how awesome you guys are—"

My words are cut off because my feet are suddenly no longer on the ground. Tristan has wrapped his arms around my waist and lifted me into the air. And now the room is spinning.

"Ellie!" he shrieks, causing at least a dozen people to turn and look.

Good. Let them look. Let *this* be the image they remember me by. Easy-breezy-adored-by-her-boyfriend Ellie. Not bumbling-like-an-idiot-election-speech Ellie.

"This is amazing!" He sets me down and looks right into my eyes. "*You* are amazing."

I feel an intense urge to kiss him. Just tip forward and fall into his beautiful pink lips. It would be the most perfect moment for a kiss. While this sizzling energy of excitement is streaming between us. While he's looking at me like I'm the goddess of awesome sauce. While his hands are still wrapped around my waist.

But I can't. Not after what happened last night. He has to kiss *me*. He has to make the first move. I have to *know* that this has worked.

I keep my eyes locked on his. I keep my lips curled in a loose smile. I keep my body language open and accessible. I even lean forward just the slightest bit.

And then . . .

Sigh.

He closes the space between us. He presses his warm lips against mine. His hands urge my body close, closer, closest. Until we're tangled up in arms and tongues and passion.

If there's one thing that Tristan does better than singing, better than pounding out awesome guitar solos, better than walking down hallways in seeming slow motion, it's kissing. I swear he could teach a workshop or something.

When he pulls away, me and half the hallway are in a state

of post-smooch bliss. It's as if the pheromones are seeping out of my pores and infecting everyone within a half-mile radius.

He rests his forehead against mine and whispers, "You're the best, Ellie. I don't know what I'd do without you."

I close my eyes and bask in his words. The fireworks and celebratory trumpets are blaring in my head so loudly, I barely hear the school secretary's voice as she drones over the intercom system. Something about the results from today's election.

But I don't dare pull out of this cocoon of reunited relationship bliss. I can't even bring myself to care when she announces that Rhiannon and I lost by an even bigger landslide than yesterday.

Because I've already won.

Daydream Believer

3:30 p.m.

Detention is not as bad as I thought it would be. It's *worse.* I imagined it would be more like *The Breakfast Club*, where we get to sit in the library and talk about our feelings. But no. We're forced to work. We actually have to spend the whole hour picking up trash around the school. It's humiliating.

When this reality show is over, I'm going to have a serious talk with the producers.

Because this is unacceptable.

When the clock finally inches its way to four-thirty, I drop the trash bag I'm carrying into the nearest bin and make a mad dash outside to the softball field. I don't even have time to change, which means I'm not only going to have to convince Coach to let me try out, but I'm also going to have to convince him that I can run bases in ballerina flats.

Just as I suspected, the tryouts are winding down when I finally make it out to the field, huffing and puffing from my sprint.

"Coach," I pant, my hands on my knees. "I'm here. I'm ready to try out."

He gives me a once-over, taking in my jeans and sweater. "Sparks," he begins in that you're-not-going-to-like-what-I-have-to-say tone. "I—"

"Please," I beg him before he has a chance to finish. "I have to do this. I have to make varsity this year. My dad . . ." I pause to catch my breath. ". . . is counting on me. I'm ready. I can do it."

I watch pity and compassion cloud his expression as he glances at the girls coming in from the outfield. "I'm sorry, Ellie. But the JV team still needs a good fielder like you." He slaps me on the back and turns away. "There's always next year."

I wouldn't bet on it, I want to say in return as I trudge off the field. *There may not even be a tomorrow.*

It's the Same Old Song

8:12 p.m.

Jackson beats his drumsticks together four times, kicking the next song of the set into gear. The space around the stage is packed with people writhing to the music. I've never seen Tristan look so radiant before. He's practically glowing up there, and his glow makes me glow. It's a contagious glow. Especially when I think about how I'm the reason he's up there. It's because of me that he got the gig. Sure, I got detention as a trade-off and I wasn't able to turn in my extra-credit paper for English, but seeing him up there, crooning into the mic, sweat dripping down his forehead, pounding on his guitar like he's going to blow the strings right off—well, it's worth it.

I stand in the front row of the massive crowd and let my body be moved by the music. Tristan catches my eye for the third time since the set started and I beam back at him, bobbing my head to the beat. When we first started dating and he took me to a gig, I wasn't sure what to do. I'd never been to a live rock show before. Most of the musicians I love are dead or no longer performing. I stood in the back and watched everyone. Like a sociologist observing an indigenous tribe with crazy, archaic rituals. That's how it felt. It was so foreign to me. So intimidating. And yet so fascinating at the same time. I was a stranger in a strange land with even stranger customs.

I lingered in the back and played scientist. I loved watching the people almost as much as I loved watching Tristan. The way they responded to him. The way they all absorbed the beat of the song, like they'd contracted a rhythmic airborne virus. Half of these people had undoubtedly never heard his music before, yet they were pulsing to it like it was their own heartbeat.

That's what Tristan's music does to people.

It moves them.

Literally.

I fell in love with Tristan while he was on that stage. I fell in love with how effortlessly he won them all over.

By the second show, I was right there in front. A convert. A member of the tribe. I wore the sacred uniform, I danced the secret dance, my mouth learned how to form the ritualistic sounds.

I became a true fan.

I admit, Whack-a-Mole's music is still not my favorite in the world. The guitars are a little too rough. The bass lines a little too piercing. The melodies a little too hard to follow. But I've learned to appreciate it. At least it doesn't sound like noise to me anymore. That's probably because I know all the lyrics by heart now and can sing every single song in the shower.

The song finishes with a climactic drum riff leading up to Tristan's solo on the guitar. The crowd goes nuts. I jump up and down, clapping wildly and screaming with the rest of the diehards.

"Okay, we have one more song for you tonight," Tristan pants into the mic, brushing a strand of sweaty hair from his forehead. "This one is dedicated to the girl who got us this gig. Thank you for being so freaking awesome, Ellie Sparks."

The band launches into the song and I immediately recognize the slow opening riff of "Mind of the Girl." It's one of their newer songs—an upbeat punk pop track—and it was an instant fan favorite the first time they played it. Tristan wrote it the week after he met me.

And now he's playing it.

That has to be a good sign, right?

That has to mean that I've successfully changed the outcome of this day. How can he dedicate a song to me—a song written *about* me—and still plan on breaking up with me?

The heavy guitars drop out and Tristan steps up to the mic, softly breathing the first verse into the mic.

"She.
She laughs in riddles I can't understand.
She.
She talks in music I can't live without."

Holy crap, he's hot up there. He's like a rock god. His hands caressing the strings of that guitar, his forehead glistening with sweat (do gods sweat?). Every girl in this crowd is ogling him, wishing she could be the one he comes to when he steps off that stage. And yet it's me—ME!—he's hanging out with tonight. I'm the one who gets the man when the god puts his guitar away.

Or at least I hope I still am.

I hope that yesterday was just a fluke. That today will end differently. With Tristan and me kissing at the top of that Ferris wheel.

Sometimes it's hard for me to believe. It's been five months and I still feel the need to pinch myself to make sure I'm not dreaming. Pretty much every girl in our school has been in love with Tristan since the moment he moved to this town freshman year. Since before he even formed his band. There was just something about him. I don't know if it was his confidence, his laid-back, worry-free attitude about everything, his looks, but people just felt drawn to him. Even the teachers. There's something simply magnetic about Tristan Wheeler.

Most new kids walk into their first day at a new school with fear hunching their shoulders and uncertainty diverting their gazes to the floor. But not Tristan. He walked down that hallway like he already owned it. He stepped into my first-period class like he'd already aced it. With his guitar strapped to his chest and his dark blond hair falling into his eyes. When he pronounced his name to the teacher—Tristan Wheeler—I swear I heard even the walls sigh.

And then two years later, he chose me.

Of all the people in all the world—or, okay, maybe just this school—he chose me. Ellison Sparks.

Don't get me wrong. I'm not one of those pathetic girls who hid in a corner her whole life waiting for the perfect guy to shine his light and bring her out of her shell. I was perfectly content with being an unknown entity. I had no desire to be in the spotlight. People didn't really know who I was, nor did they care. And that suited me fine.

But everything changed the night I was spotted talking to

Tristan at Daphne Gray's party. It was right after he'd broken up with Colby. No one was surprised that they were over. Tristan had broken up with every girl he'd dated at our school. Seven of them, to be exact. Not that I was counting. What did surprise everyone was how long he talked to me that night. Sixty-two minutes, to be exact.

Okay, maybe I was counting.

When you talk to the most sought-after recently eligible bachelor in the school for sixty-two minutes, people notice.

They also notice when you date him for four months longer than any other girl.

Not only do they notice, they disapprove.

That's why the summer was so blissful. For the most part, we were able to steal away from those inquisitive eyes and snickering comments. It was just us. No one else. But now, as I stand in this sea of people all staring up at Tristan, I can't help but feel like they're staring at me, too. Judging me. Deeming me not good enough. Not pretty enough. Not cool enough.

And to be honest, sometimes I wonder if they're right.

"Thank you everyone! We're Whack-a-Mole. I hope you had a great time tonight! Come see us again real soon!" I blink up at the stage. The set is over. The crowd is going crazy. I can feel the energy radiating off Tristan. The post-gig high has already started. It's my absolute favorite time to be around him. When he's floating on the echo of the crowd's cheers and his feet don't touch the ground. Everything you say is groundbreaking, every joke you make is hilarious, every kiss you steal is earthshaking.

Tristan hops down from the stage and is immediately swarmed by people. New fans, old fans, pretty girls, not-so-pretty girls. I squeeze through them, trying to stay close to him, but I keep getting shoved back. Everyone wants to meet Tristan. Or at the very least, stand within ten feet of him.

Finally I grab his hand to keep from getting lost in the storm.

He looks down at my fingers interlaced in his and then up at me, flashing me a warm but hurried smile.

"Give me a minute?" he says. "I'll come find you."

Oh.

I keep my game face on. "Sure! Of course. I'll be by the carnival games."

"Awesome. I'll meet you there." Then he brings my hand up to his lips, kisses it, and lets go.

I try to catch his eye again for one last smile, but he's already turned his back to me to take a selfie with someone.

I push through the swarm and wander over to the aisle with all the games. I take a seat at the horse race game again. I pick horse number seven because aren't sevens supposed to be lucky?

I do better this time. I manage to sink two balls instead of just one and my horse moves a whole four paces, but the buzzer goes off announcing the winner before I've even started to get the hang of it. How do these people win so fast? Do they practice at home? Do they have little ball ramps set up in their basements?

I play two more games and still lose miserably. I scowl as I watch the carnival employee hand some tween girl a giant stuffed polar bear and congratulate her on her victory. That girl is barely Hadley's age. She's probably a plant working for the carnival.

Fortunately Tristan finds me before I pump the very last of my dollars into this money pit.

I jump up from the stool, wrap my arms around him, and kiss him.

I wait for the fireworks. The lightning. I wait for my knees to crumple beneath me at the feel of his strong mouth pressing against mine. But none of it comes. That amazing, contagious post-gig high is nowhere to be found. In fact, he barely even kisses me back.

I pull away and untangle my arms from his neck. "You were amazing up there!" I say, trying to reinvigorate him. Trying to get back a smidgen of what I know I saw in him on that stage.

He smiles weakly. "Thanks."

"I'd ask you if you were ready to rock this carnival, but apparently you already have."

Another puny smile that doesn't reach his eyes. "Actually," he begins somberly, "I don't think I'm going to stay."

Dread rips through me.

No. It can't be happening. Not again.

"What?" I protest. "But you just got here."

Wow, I sound even whinier than I did last night.

"Yeah, but—"

"You can't possibly need to meet with the guys again. You got a gig! I fixed it!"

Confusion clouds his eyes. Of course it does. To him, I'm not making any sense.

"Actually I do need to meet with the guys," he says warily. "That gig was off the hook and I'm so grateful you got it for us. I think it's brought us to a whole new level. We got like five people interested in booking us tonight alone. So we really need to meet and strategize our next move."

I feel a scream of frustration boiling up inside me.

I remind myself to stay calm. This doesn't mean he's going

to break up with me again. It only means he has to meet with the band. There's absolutely nothing to worry—

"But I wanted to talk to you about something before I left, and I didn't want to do it over the phone."

The ground beneath my feet drops out and I'm suddenly plummeting into the bubbling hot, liquid lava center of the earth.

I close my eyes. Maybe if I squeeze them tight enough, I'll wake up. Maybe if I can't see him, he can't go through with this.

"Ellie," he begins, and I hear the same pain in his voice. He clears his throat. "I don't think I can do this anymore."

I keep my eyes shut and shake my head. "This isn't happening," I murmur quietly to myself. "This isn't happening."

"I'm confused, Ellie," he whispers back, and I don't need to open my eyes to know that he's doing that same fidgety thing with his fingernails again. "I'm so confused. I don't know what to tell you. I wish I had all the answers, but I don't. I just know that it's not working. You and me. We're not working. Something is broken and I don't know how to fix it. I don't know if it *can* be fixed."

My eyes snap open. *"No!"* I shout.

Tristan is completely taken aback. "What?"

"No," I repeat. "You can't do this to me again."

"Again? I don't under—"

"What is broken?" I demand. "What can't be fixed?"

He runs his fingers through his hair. "That's the thing. I don't know."

"That's not an answer," I fire back.

He blinks in surprise. "I'm sorry, Ellie. I don't know what else to tell you."

"Is this about the fight last night?"

He shakes his head. "No." But I'm not sure I believe him. He doesn't meet my gaze when he says it.

"Then what?" That's when my voice cracks. Tears are welling up in my eyes. I thought I might be able to keep them at bay this time, but no such luck. "Then what, Tristan?" I repeat, much softer this time. Much more broken.

"Oh, Ellie." He grabs my hand and leads me over to a bench. I immediately notice that it's the exact same bench. This makes me cry harder. He sits next to me, clutching my hand. "I'm sorry. I'm so sorry. It breaks my heart to do this because I really did care for you. I still do. I mean, I always will. We had something good. Really good. Something I've never had before. It just . . . I don't know . . . fell apart somehow. I wish it could have been different. I wish I didn't feel this way. But I do. And I have to stay true to how I feel."

Then something snaps. I don't know if it's the repetitiveness of his words, the familiarity of this scene, the same people passing by and staring at me like I'm a leper, but I can't take it. I rip my hand from his and launch to my feet.

"No. You don't get to do this again. You don't get to say the same stupid things that mean nothing. I want an explanation."

"Ellie," Tristan falters. "I—"

"A *real* one."

"I . . . I don't know."

"Yes, you do," I press.

"Well, I mean, you're a little clingy sometimes. But that's not—"

"Clingy?!" I shout the word and then quickly lower my voice to an urgent whisper. "I'm not clingy. When have I ever been clingy?"

"Look, I'm not saying that's the only reason, I'm just . . ." But he doesn't finish. He breathes out like he's surrendering in a war before he stands up, steps toward me, and kisses me gently on the forehead. "I'm sorry, Ellie. I really am."

Then, with a pitying look on his face, he walks away, leaving me alone all over again.

Come See About Me

9:20 p.m.

I don't expect to see anyone when I get home, which is why I don't bother to clean up my mascara-smeared face before skulking through the door. I tiptoe toward the stairs, nearly jumping out of my skin when my dad calls my name from the pitch-black guest room.

Was he just sitting alone in there? In the dark?

I flip on the light switch and that's when I see that he's lying in bed. The covers are pulled up around him and he's propped up against two pillows.

He's sleeping here.

I'm suddenly reminded of what I heard last night when I returned from the carnival. I came upstairs and my parents were fighting. But that was earlier in the evening. Did they fight again tonight? Did my mom kick him out of their room?

"Are you okay?" he asks me, probably noticing the tear tracks on my face.

"Are *you*?" I throw the question back at him, nodding toward his bed for the night.

He sighs. "Yeah. Just a little misunderstanding between your mother and me."

"Little?"

He chuckles. "Your mom has a tendency to overreact."

"I think it might be genetic."

"What happened?"

I feel more tears stinging my eyes and I almost tell him. I almost spill it all. How I tried to save my relationship . . . *twice.* How I failed . . . *twice.* I almost tell him about my day, the suspicious ibuprofen, the dreamlike déjà vu, but then I see the crease between his eyes. The worry marks of a father who cares too much, and I realize I can't burden him with this. Not when he's clearly dealing with his own mess.

"Nothing," I say quietly. "It's nothing."

He nods, like he believes me, or at the very least he's respecting my decision to keep it to myself. "How did softball tryouts go, by the way?"

A pang of guilt strikes me in the chest. "Fine. I got in."

I don't have the heart to tell him the truth. That I missed them altogether because I got detention. Or that I probably wouldn't have gotten in anyway. I'll save that bad news for tomorrow.

His tired, weary eyes brighten. "That's great! I knew you could do it!"

I change the subject before he has a chance to make too big a deal about it. "What about you?" I ask, nodding to the guest bed. "What happened here tonight?"

He turns his head and looks out the window. "Oh, nothing

you need to concern yourself with. Some days I just wish I had a do-over, you know?"

I crack a smile. "Yeah."

"Go get some sleep."

I bend down and kiss his forehead. "Do you want me to shut off the light?"

He nods. "Thanks, sweetie."

I flip the switch and climb the stairs. When I pass my sister's room, I hear *The Breakfast Club* playing on her TV again. It's a little more than half over. Like last night, she invites me to come and watch with her, but like last night, I turn her down.

I collapse onto my bed and stare at the ceiling, thinking about what my dad said.

Some days I just wish I had a do-over, you know?

I do know. It's exactly what I wished for last night. I may get my dramatic side from my mother, but I definitely get my idealism from my dad.

I think about the words my mind whispered into the darkness as I was falling asleep.

Please just let me do it over.

Please give me another chance.

I swear I'll get it right.

What if today *wasn't* a curse? What if today was actually some kind of wish fulfillment? A prayer being answered? Was I given a second chance only to fail miserably again?

Will I be given another chance tomorrow? Or was that it?

A onetime thing. A fluke.

I hear a tapping at my window and I sit up.

"Owen?" I call out.

"Yeah. Let me in."

The window is already unlocked. I hoist it open and he

tumbles ungracefully inside, ducking and rolling before jumping unsteadily to his feet.

"I suppose I don't have to guess why you left the carnival in tears," he says, after the same long pause he took last night.

I had passed Owen again on my way to the parking lot. This time he was wandering around one of the concession stands, but I still couldn't bring myself to talk to him.

I let out a soft whimper. "Yes, it's true. He broke up with me . . . again."

Owen looks confused. "Again?"

I sit down on the bed. "Owen, if I tell you something will you promise to believe everything I say?"

He looks skeptical. "Is this a trick question? Are you going to tell me you formed your own cult and now I'm going to be stuck joining it because of this promise?"

I roll my eyes. "No, it's not a trick question."

He sits, pulls Hippo onto his lap, faces him toward me, and raises Hippo's left leg in the air, like he's being sworn in. "Okay, fine. We promise to believe you."

I look down at Hippo's beady black eyes, then up at Owen's inquisitive green ones.

"Something weird happened to me today. I think I might be stuck in the same day."

He lets out a groan and turns Hippo around so they can share a look of disbelief. "This again?"

"You promised to believe me. You both did."

He and Hippo exchange another glance. "That's before we knew you were, you know"—he spins his finger next to his ear and whispers—"craaaazy."

"I can prove it to you," I offer.

"Ah, yes, the moment of proof. This is where you tell me

some deep, dark secret that I just happened to have divulged to you on a different version of this same day."

"Last night you had a dream that you went skinny-dipping with Principal Yates in the school pool."

Owen's mouth literally falls open. I think this is the first time he's ever been stunned into silence.

"You mean like that?" I ask, struggling to hide a triumphant smile. The shock on his face is too priceless. I would take a picture but I can't be certain it would be on my phone in the morning.

"H-h-how did you . . ."

"You told me about it. Last night."

"I most certainly did not. Besides, I just had the dream last night."

"Yup," I say. "That's the problem. Last night for you was Sunday night. Last night for me was tonight. I mean, Monday night. This whole day and night has been a complete duplicate."

"You mean Tristan broke up with you twice?"

The reminder is like a knife into my heart. I swallow. "Yes."

"And we've had this conversation before?"

"Well, not this same conversation, but similar. Some details have been changed."

He crosses his arms and rests them on Hippo's head. "Like what?"

"Like last night, you tried to cheer me up by insisting I rename Hippo."

"He *does* deserve a real name."

"That's exactly what you said last night."

"Alternate me is one smart guy."

"Then I said that he does have a real name, and you said—"

"Hold up. Calling something by its literal genus is not a real name."

I laugh. "Exactly. That's exactly what you said."

"Holy crap, Ells."

"I know."

"I mean like *bloody hell.*"

I nod in agreement. "Bloody hell, indeed."

"How does it work?"

"That's the thing. I have no idea! I just woke up and it was . . . today."

"What are you going to do? Like tomorrow?"

I shrug. "I don't know. I don't know if this will even happen again tomorrow. Maybe it was a onetime thing and I botched it up."

"But what if it's not? What if you *do* get another chance? What would you do differently?"

I stop and think about that. "Everything."

"Everything?"

"If I do get another chance, there's only one logical explanation for it. I have to fix what I messed up, right?"

"I guess."

"And the biggest thing I messed up was Tristan. I have to get him back. Or, you know, stop him from leaving."

For a flash of a moment, Owen looks disappointed in my answer. What was he hoping I would say? That I'd join book club? I don't think the universe is rearranging itself just to convince me to discuss *The Book Thief* at lunch.

"So that's your big plan, then?" he asks.

"Do you have a better idea?"

"No. I guess not." He sets Hippo aside and stands up. "Well, I better get home. I don't want to poof into thin air at midnight or anything. That can't be good for me."

He steps onto the window ledge and grabs the overhanging tree branch for balance.

"Svnoyi Ostu." I tell him good night in Cherokee. It was one of the phrases used at Camp Awahili.

He cracks a smile. *"Svnoyi Ostu."*

I'm about to shut the window when I notice Owen pause and look back at me. "Ells?"

I stick my head out. "Yeah?"

"Did you rename Hippo? I mean, the last time we had this conversation?"

I smile at the memory of how effortlessly Owen cheered me up and how he made me temporarily forget my heartbreak. "Yeah, you wouldn't stop badgering me so I named him Rick."

"But you're still calling him Hippo."

"Because yesterday never happened, remember?"

"Ah, right." He gives me a small salute. "See you tomorrow."

I close the window and lean my forehead against it. "Or today," I whisper, my words turning into fog against the glass.

10:42 p.m.

I lie in bed for a long time, thinking about the events of the day and my conversation with Owen.

What if you do *get another chance?*

I glance at my nightstand. The cup of water I spilled this

morning is still sitting there empty. My phone is plugged into its charger. I grab the phone, tap on the Instagram app, and aim the tiny camera at my face.

I smile weakly, snap the selfie, and type out a caption.

I was here.

The Way We Were (Part 2)

Five months ago . . .

"So what *are* you doing out here?" I asked as I splashed my legs through the warm, heated water of Daphne Gray's pool. It felt so good on my skin. A shiver-inducing contrast to the freezing-cold air that swirled around us. The party still blared inside, a million miles away from here.

He stared at our feet, which were warped and distorted under the water. "I had to get out of there. It was too . . . too . . ."

"Much?"

He chuckled. "Yeah. Way too much."

I sighed. "Me, too. I just came to look for my friend and—"

"So you claim."

"I just came to look for my friend," I repeated pointedly, shooting him a sideways glare. "And it was way too much. And oh my God, what is that noise they're playing in there? It's horrendous!"

He tipped his head back and laughed. A loud belly laugh.

"What?"

"That's my band. We're called Whack-a-Mole. Daphne's playing our demo."

Suddenly all the heat got sucked right out of the pool. I turned a hundred shades of white. I wanted to disappear under the surface of the water. I remembered he played in a band, I'd just never actually heard his music before. But now it made total sense. Tristan was a rock star at our school. It went along with his popularity.

"Well," I said, pulling my legs out of the water and readying myself to stand up. "That's my cue to leave."

But he pulled me back down. "Don't."

"I just insulted your art. You can't possibly want to spend any more time with me."

"*Au contraire.* It makes me want to spend even more time with you."

I gave him a dubious look. "Because you're . . . demented?"

"Because you're honest," he corrected.

"I wouldn't give me too much credit for honesty. If I had known that was your band, I would have lied to your face."

Smile.

Heart.

Puddle.

"Well, I'm glad you didn't know then."

"You're not making all that much sense, you know?"

He gazed up at the night sky. "I know. I'm just kind of tired of it."

I wasn't following. "Of people liking your music?"

"Of people *saying* they like something that they don't. Of the fakeness." He nudged his chin toward the NASA-manufactured sliding glass door that was so soundproof I almost forgot half of our school was on the other side. "The girls in there. They're all the same. They say the right things. They wear the right clothes. They post the perfect pouting duck-face selfies on Instagram."

I was starting to think this wasn't about every girl in there. I was starting to think this was about one girl in particular.

Colby Osbourne.

Tristan Wheeler's girlfriend until two days ago.

He pulled his eyes away from the stars and looked at me. "I guess I'm tired of all the drama."

I nodded. "Yeah."

"So you get it?" I wasn't sure why he sounded so surprised.

"Sure. I get it."

Of course I got it. I dealt with those kinds of girls every day. I knew exactly what he meant.

"You seem so different, though."

I laughed. "From the girls in there? I hope so."

This wasn't a lie. I never felt like I fit into that crowd, that scene, that exclusive, members-only club.

"I know so," he said, with such confidence it startled me. I tore my eyes away from the water and looked at him as he went on. "You seem so much more chill, you know? Laid back. Not a drama queen at all."

The truth was, I didn't know who I was. Particularly not when it came to relationships. Was I the dramatic type? The pouting type? The jealous type? He didn't seem to think so. Was it possible he'd gleaned more about me in the ten minutes we'd been talking than I'd learned in my entire life?

I was so ready to be the person he thought I was. The person I thought he needed me to be at that moment.

"Oh, totally. I *hate* drama. It's such a waste of energy."

That dimple again. "That's a relief."

I nodded earnestly, like I understood his frustrations. "Drama is the worst. If drama was an ice cream flavor, it would be Rum Raisin."

I felt guilty as soon as I said it. I actually liked Rum Raisin. Owen and I were probably two of the only people in the universe who did. But my comparison made Tristan laugh again, so I didn't take it back.

"My last girlfriend, Colby, was queen of the drama. She lived off it, thrived off it. If she saw the chance to make a scene, or start a fight, or rock the boat, she took it. I think maybe it was some sick way of making sure I was paying attention to her."

There was a long drawn-out silence, and I could tell he was waiting for me to speak, waiting for me to comment on this revelation he'd just dumped into my lap.

So I chose something eloquent. "Ugh." *And* I made an equally elegant face to go with it. "That's super annoying."

He stared at me like I was the most fascinating thing he had ever seen. Like he was an extraterrestrial researcher no one took seriously and I was alien life.

"I like you . . ." He faltered, realizing for the first time that he didn't know my name.

I tried to ignore the dagger in my chest.

"Ellie." I helped him out.

"Ellie," he repeated, and my heart, liver, kidneys, spleen, and frontal lobe joined the strike. "I like you, Ellie."

I bit my lip to keep the grin from leaping off my face.

"Although," he added a moment later, "you do have dreadful taste in music."

THE THIRD MONDAY

The Girl with Kaleidoscope Eyes

7:03 a.m.

I wake with a start and dive for my phone, knocking over a cup of water on my nightstand. It spills all over the pile of textbooks and paper next to my bed.

Full cup of water.

Textbooks and English paper next to my bed.

Did it happen? Did the day start over again?

I open Instagram and check for my picture. The selfie I posted just before I went to sleep last night.

It's not there.

I check the clock. One minute until 7:04 a.m. That's when the text messages come. That's when Tristan tells me he can't stop thinking about last night and wants to talk today. That's when I know for sure that I've been given a third chance to fix this.

I count the seconds, feeling my grasp around the phone tighten with each passing moment. There's a swarm of agitated butterflies flitting around in my stomach. There's a thousand-pound gorilla sitting on my chest. There's—

Bloop-dee-dee-bloop-bloop-bing!

YESSSSSSSSSSSSSSSSSSSSS!

I spring out of bed, holding the phone high over my head as I do a victory lap around my bedroom.

I click on the message and everything around me gets a hundred shades brighter.

Tristan: I can't stop thinking about last night.

Wait for it. Wait for . . . *it.*

Bloop-dee-dee-bloop-bloop-bing!

Tristan: Let's talk today.

There it is! It's real. This is actually really truly definitely happening. For once, me, Ellison Sparks, and the epic, ever-expanding universe are officially on the same side. Our agendas are aligned. Our visions are one and the same.

Today is victory day. Today is where it all turns around. If I succeed today—which I fully intend on doing—tomorrow will be Tuesday. I'm sure of it. I made the wish. I asked for another chance to set things right. So once I succeed in doing that, life will go on and Tristan and I will be together forever.

Whoa, what a story to tell our grandchildren.

Well, I almost messed it all up and Grandpa almost left me. If I hadn't been given a magical opportunity to set things right, you guys never would have been born!

Now, I just need a plan. A solid, bulletproof plan.

And when all else fails, there's only one place to turn.

I sit down at my laptop and type "How to stop a boy from breaking up with you" into a Google search.

The first result is a YouTube video of an interview with someone named Dr. Louise Levine. I click the link. It's a segment from some morning show a few months ago.

"Welcome back!" the interviewer trills to the camera. "Today on the show, we have author and male behavior psychologist Dr. Louise Levine."

I lean forward in my chair.

Male behavior psychologist?

I didn't even know they had those! This is exactly what I need.

"Dr. Levine has written a very popular book called *The Girl Commandments,* which teaches women how to hold on to a man. Dr. Levine, won't you tell us a little bit about your new book?"

The camera pans to the author in the adjacent chair. She's a polished woman in her early forties, dressed in a red skirt suit with matching lipstick and high heels. Her hair is so big, it looks like it's been glued on.

"Of course," Dr. Levine says, "and thanks for having me on the show. The idea behind *The Girl Commandments* is very simple. Women, as a gender, have lost sight of our femininity, our special womanly flower. The very thing that makes us desirable to men. Women in the fifties and sixties—our grandmothers and great-aunts—they knew what it took to keep a man. They knew it wasn't easy and that it required effort every single day."

I nod emphatically, drinking in this woman's words like I haven't had a drop of water in weeks.

"*The Girl Commandments* teaches young women through basic, easy-to-follow, step-by-step rules—or *commandments*—that utilize the very same tactics women have been relying on successfully for centuries. You know, in our grandmothers' generation, divorce wasn't an option. You fell in love with a man and you lived happily ever after. There was none of this back-and-forth, push-and-pull, on-again, off-again, power-struggle relationship drama. Women knew where their true power lay and they used it to their advantage."

This is sheer brilliance. Why am I just learning about this *now*?

"So tell us," the interviewer says, "what makes you qualified to write a book like this?"

"Well, Anne," Dr. Levine says, "I have a Ph.D. in male behavioral patterns and I've spent the better half of my life studying the male species."

The interviewer lets out a hearty laugh. "Species! I love it. It's like they're primates in the wild."

Dr. Levine smiles politely. "In a way, they actually are. Everyone likes to think men are these complicated, difficult-to-comprehend creatures, but they're actually not. They're very easy. Biologically they haven't changed much since the caveman years, and neither have we. It's our society that has convoluted our gender roles. I study men the same way a zoologist might study apes in the jungle."

Wow. I didn't even know you could get an actual degree in deciphering the male brain. This woman really *is* an expert on the opposite sex!

It immediately makes me realize how little I know. I mean, Tristan is the first guy I've ever dated. My first real relationship. (And no, I don't count the seven minutes I spent kissing Alex Patterson in the closet in eighth grade.)

Here I was thinking I could solve this Tristan dilemma on my own, but the truth is, I am completely clueless about boys.

I stop the interview—I've seen enough to convince me—

and pop over to my favorite online bookstore, where I still have leftover funds from my last birthday gift card. I search for *The Girl Commandments* by Dr. Louise Levine.

This book *is* popular. It's ranked #4 in all self-help books. At least I know I'm not alone out there.

I purchase the eBook and download it to my phone. A minute later, I'm looking at the table of contents. There's an introduction and then ten chapters, one for each of the commandments. I don't have time to read it all now so I simply skim the chapter titles, feeling like I'm being bulldozed by a new revelation with each one.

Girl Commandment #4: Thou shall NOT text or call him back right away.

Well, there's my first mistake right there. I always text Tristan back right away. I've been doing it the past two Mondays.

I glance at my phone, rereading the messages from Tristan. He wants to talk about last night? Well, he'll just have to wait. Ha!

Moving on.

Girl Commandment #5: Thou shall always be a Creature of Mystery.

I slap my forehead. Of course! Be mysterious! I'm never mysterious. I'm always so . . . well . . . whatever the opposite of mysterious is.

I select the chapter and scan the text. It has additional hints on exactly how to be a Creature of Mystery. Things like:

- **Answer his questions with a question.**
- **Don't say exactly what you mean.**
- **Avoid the drama! Don't let him know when you're upset.**
- **Don't laugh too hard at his jokes.**
- **Never eat in front of him.**

Crap. I eat in front of Tristan like every day! They should really teach this stuff in school. It's so much more valuable than chemistry. This is like *life* chemistry.

Now that I have the rules to live by, this day is going to be a piece of cake.

I drop the phone in my schoolbag and prance into the shower.

Ten minutes later, I'm back in front of my closet, staring down my wardrobe choices.

Girl Commandment #2: Thou shall always look feminine and refined on a date.

The book says that boys like when girls *look* like girls. It reminds them of their own masculinity and their place in the relationship.

I search the Web for some inspiration and finally decide on a pink lace knee-length dress that my mom bought me two years ago but I've never worn because I always thought it was too girly, and pair it with a belt. Then I style my hair into soft, feminine waves. For my makeup, I choose a palette of pinks and warm earth tones.

I finish off the outfit with a gold heart-shaped pendant around my neck.

When I look at myself in the mirror, I have to admit I look pretty dang good. I don't think Tristan has ever seen me like this before. Come to think of it, *I've* never seen me like this before.

7:47 a.m.

"Good morning, beautiful family!" I say a few minutes later as I float into the kitchen like a summer breeze.

My brand-new self comes as such a surprise to everyone, I actually manage to halt the circus mid-act. My dad looks up from his iPad, my mom looks up from her cabinet door banging, and my sister puts her book down on the counter.

"Wow," Hadley says. "I guess that means he called."

I just smile in response and swing the fridge door open with a flourish.

"You're in a good mood for a Monday," my dad points out.

I remove the bread and shut the door, nodding emphatically. "I think it's gonna be a good day."

"It's raining," Hadley points out.

"Is it?" I ask wistfully as I push my bread into the toaster. "Well, that just makes it all the more romantic."

"What the fuh?" Hadley asks, referencing what I can only guess is another offering from Urban Dictionary.

I pat her head. "You're adorable."

"Mom," Hadley whines, "Ellie's on drugs. When was the last time you checked her room for narcotics?"

I glance over my dad's shoulder at his screen. "Narcotic," I suggest, pointing to a triple word score space.

He taps it in. "Ninety-six points! Yes!" He holds his hand up for a high five and I deliver.

My mom bangs a cabinet door closed.

My dad looks up from his iPad. "What are you looking for?"

"Nothing!" she snaps. "I'm not looking for anything at all. Why would I possibly be looking for something I have no hope of ever finding? At least not under this roof!"

When my toast pops up, I slather it with peanut butter and take a bite. This time, I'm determined for it *not* to end up squished at the bottom of my bag.

"Ellie," my dad says.

"Don't worry," I tell him, walking over to plant a kiss on his cheek. "I'll make the team. There's no doubt in my mind."

I swing my schoolbag over my shoulder and head for the garage door. I pause, looking back long enough to say, "I hope you all have a beautiful, fulfilling day. I'm off to change the world."

Now I'm a Believer

8:02 a.m.

"Wow, it's really chucking it down out there," Owen says, getting into the car and giving his wet hair a shake. I watch the tiny droplets of rainwater land on the dash but today I fight the urge to wipe them away.

When I don't respond, Owen turns and stares at me, his eyes lingering on my clothes a beat longer than normal, like he can sense something's different but can't figure out what it is.

"You like?" I say, flipping a lock of hair over my shoulder.

"Uh," he stammers, but never quite finishes. Instead he chooses to comment on my music choice.

"New playlist?"

I put the car in gear and back out his driveway. "Yup, I made it this morning. It's called 'Brand-New World Order.'"

He grabs my phone and scrolls through the songs. "It's very . . . bouncy."

I bob my head to the beat of "I'm a Believer" by the Monkees. "What can I say? I feel bouncy."

Admittedly, I'm a little disappointed that Owen didn't comment on my outfit. It would have been nice for him to confirm that my new look is working, but whatever. I didn't dress up to impress my best friend. I dressed up to impress my boyfriend.

"Oh, I almost forgot!" Owen reaches into his bag and removes two fortune cookies. "Choose your tasty fortune!"

I look at the wrapped cookies in his hand and select the one on the left. Owen opens the other and reads aloud. I almost mouth the words along with him.

"If your desires are not extravagant, they will be granted." He crumples it up and tosses it into the backseat. "My desires are always extravagant."

I toss my cookie into the cup holder.

"You're not even going to open it?" Owen asks.

"Nah," I tell him. "I already know what it's going to say."

He snorts. "That's impossible."

I hear a rustling beside me and I glance over to see Owen reading my fortune.

"Be the best version of yourself."

I nearly swerve off the road. "What?"

"Whoa. Drive much?"

I grab the message from his hand and read it for myself.

Be the best version of yourself.

But that's different. How can it be different?

"I thought you said you already knew what it was going to say," Owen points out, and I don't miss the smugness.

"I . . ." I stammer. "I thought I did, but I guess it changed."

Then suddenly I understand.

Of course it changed! It's my fortune! I've already set a new series of events in motion today. I've already started changing my fate.

"Uh, yellow light," Owen says, interrupting my revelation.

I blink back to reality, dropping the fortune into my lap. Instinctively, I slam on the brakes, screeching to a halt right before the light turns red. The car next to me decides to make a run for it. I watch in awe as the intersection explodes in a series of bright flashes.

"That guy is totally getting a ticket," Owen says.

Goose bumps crawl up my arms.

It's working.

I'm changing it. I'm fixing this day.

I glance down at the tiny piece of paper in my lap.

Be the best version of yourself.

Touché, Universe.

That's exactly what I intend to do.

Raindrops Keep Fallin' on My Head

8:05 a.m.

Before we get to school, I decide it might be a good idea to try out some of the advice from *The Girl Commandments* on Owen. You know, take it for a little test run before the real thing. I mean, Owen *is* a guy and Dr. Levine says all men are biologically hardwired to respond to the commandments. And let's be honest, when it comes to being a Creature of Mystery (Commandment #5), I need all the practice I can get.

"Have you watched the season premiere of *Assumed Guilty* yet?" Owen asks as we wait for the light to turn green.

Answer his questions with a question.

"Have *you* watched the season premiere of *Assumed Guilty* yet?"

Owen gives me a blank stare. "Um, yeah. I texted you last night to tell you I was watching it."

I sigh. Okay, so that didn't really go anywhere. "No, I haven't watched it."

He bangs his fist on the dashboard. "Bollocks! You need to get on that. You missed the *best* episode." He waits for me to reply, and when I don't he adds, "Do you not even care about the show anymore?"

The guilt returns, punching me in the gut for the third time. I want to tell Owen I'm sorry but . . .

Don't say exactly what you mean.

"Well," I begin, clearing my throat. "I'm . . . regretful that you feel slighted by . . . my lack of enthusiasm for . . . this particular episodic television entertainment, but you should know that . . . I have good intentions to . . . observe the episode in question this . . . nightfall."

Okay, now I just sound like a walking thesaurus.

Owen gives me another weird look. "What's gotten into you?"

"What's gotten into *you*?"

"I mean, why are you acting strange?"

"Why are *you* acting strange?" I retort.

"I'm not acting strange!"

"Neither am I."

He guffaws. "Objection. Misleading."

"Overruled."

"You can't overrule my objection."

I shrug. "Sure I can."

"On what grounds?"

"On what grounds yourself?"

He throws his hands in the air. "Gah! Why are you being so infuriating?"

"Why are *you*?"

"Didn't we play this game when we were ten?"

I bite my lip. I think I'm doing this wrong. Owen looks really annoyed. I don't think that's the goal of the book. Are you supposed to exasperate your boyfriend into staying with you?

That doesn't sound right.

I turn in to the school parking lot. "Never mind," I mumble. "You wouldn't understand."

I park and kill the engine. I can almost feel the confusion radiating off him. I grab my umbrella from the backseat as Owen gets out of the car and closes the door.

I reach for the handle but pause when I remember:

Girl Commandment #8: Thou deserve to be treated with chivalry.

Dr. Levine says that you should never open your own doors or pay for your own food. Men like doing that stuff because it makes them feel important.

Owen taps on the glass but I still don't move.

He'll get the point eventually.

He doesn't.

After a few more seconds, he finally opens *his* door again. "Ells, what on earth are you doing in there? Did you forget how to use a door? I'm getting soaked."

I let out a sigh and kick open my door. Whatever. So maybe the commandments don't work on every guy, maybe just the guy you're in a relationship with. Which makes perfect sense. Why would Owen care about opening doors for me?

I pop my umbrella and step out. Ahhhh . . . so this is what it feels like to be dry.

Once I've locked the car, I expect Owen to make a run for it again because he still doesn't have an umbrella, but he walks beside me, keeping the same pace as me and getting completely drenched in the process. I offer to share, but he simply shrugs and says, "A little rain never hurt anyone."

He only says that because he didn't see my last two school pictures.

When we make it to the front entrance of the school, I close my umbrella and reach for the heavy metal door. But Owen stops me, gently tugging on my elbow. "Wait."

"What?"

He looks at his feet, fidgeting with the strap of his backpack.

"Owen," I whine, "It's freezing out here and the rain is—"

"I like it." He spits out the sentence, like he's afraid he might swallow and choke on it if he doesn't get it out fast enough.

I tilt my head. "The rain?"

"No. The . . . um . . . the outfit."

I admit I'm a bit surprised by his admission, but before I can say thank you, Owen has yanked the door open and disappeared into the building, like he's desperate to get away from me.

Oh Happy Day

8:47 a.m.

It's official!

I heart this day.

Everything is going exactly according to the Plan of Awesome. (I just coined that term, by the way.)

Umbrella? Remembered.

Red light ticket? Avoided.

School picture? Rocked.

When I slide off the stool and peer at the viewfinder, I am pleased to see that I am the embodiment of poise and togetherness. Not a hair out of place. Not a single smear of makeup. Which, if you think about it, is exactly how a school picture *should* be. You know, if you're not me.

Even the photographer's assistant compliments my picture. She certainly hasn't done that before.

On the way back to chemistry, I steal a peek at my phone and see that Tristan has messaged me again.

Tristan: Did you get my texts? Wanna meet before Spanish?

Well, well. Do I sense a little bit of desperation in his voice? Interesting.

I don't text him back, because Commandment #4, and when the bell rings, I go straight to Spanish. I do not pass Go (or Tristan's locker). I do not collect two hundred dollars. I am a Creature of Mystery, and Creatures of Mystery don't go tracking down their boyfriends. They let their boyfriends track *them* down.

I am not clingy or desperate. I am confident and deserving of chivalry.

As I approach our Spanish classroom, I hear hurried footsteps approaching and suddenly Tristan is in front of me, looking, might I add, a little winded.

Did he just run to catch up to me?

Very, *very* interesting.

"Hey," he says, breathless. "Did you get my texts?"

Girl Commandment #3: Thou shall always appear busy and important.

I feign confusion and take my phone out of my pocket to look at the screen. "Oops! There they are. I just saw them. Sorry. This morning has been a little crazy." I flash him a winning smile.

He looks deflated. I keep on smiling.

"Oh. You've been busy?"

I sigh like the weight of the world is on my shoulders but it doesn't faze me in the slightest. "Yeah, the election speech is today and I have this history quiz next period I forgot to study for and softball tryouts are this afternoon. So much is going on, you know?"

"Right," he says, but I swear he sounds conflicted. "Well, do you think maybe you'll have some time to talk today? I thought we could chat about what happened last night."

I pretend to check the calendar on my phone and pull my face into a grimace, sucking air between my teeth. "Eeek. Today is tough, but I'm sure we'll figure something out."

I turn on my heel and head into the classroom, taking my usual seat in the back row. Once again, Tristan runs to catch up and falls into the desk next to me. I stare straight ahead but I can feel him watching me, studying me. Like he's trying to figure out where he knows me from.

"Are you . . . mad?" he asks, his voice still tinged with confusion.

I give my hair a flip as I turn to flash him another beatific smile. "About last night? Of course not. It was a silly misunderstanding."

"It was?"

"Of course. I don't blame you at all."

There's a long, stunned silence. "You don't?"

"Nope."

I face forward and pretend to be completely rapt in the conjugations Señora Mendoza is writing on the whiteboard, but silently, on the inside, I'm squealing with delight.

It's working. It's actually working!

Unfortunately, however, I'm so busy trying to *look* busy, I completely forget about the bird that flies into the window until the giant *smack* makes me jump.

"¡Dios mío!" Señora Mendoza cries, hand to chest.

"Is it dead?" someone asks, racing to the window along with a handful of other students.

"It's totally dead," Sadie Haskins confirms.

I'm completely overcome with guilt. I should have remembered the dang bird! I could have saved him. But my grief is short-lived when I notice that Tristan is barely paying attention to the commotion the bird has caused. His gaze is trained on me. Once again, he looks like he's trying to decipher the unbreakable Code Ellison.

Señora Mendoza redirects the class's attention and continues on with her lesson plan. When she turns her back, I see Tristan scribbling something on a piece of notebook paper out of the corner of my eye. He checks to make sure Señora's attention is still diverted and then slips it onto my desk.

I count ten full seconds before looking at it, because, you know, Creature of Mystery! Totally busy and important. But in all honesty, it's the most excruciatingly long ten seconds of my life.

I casually glance down, pretending to notice it for the first time.

Are we good?

I can't help but shiver. Those are the exact words I used when I was the one passing the note.

I shift toward him long enough to smile and give a quick thumbs-up.

For the rest of class, I only have one thought drifting through my head.

Oh, how the tables have turned.

Do-Wah-Diddy

12:40 p.m.

After acing my history test—third time's the charm!—I head to my locker to stash my books. As expected, I find my speech notes in the interior Velcro pocket of my bag, just as I did yesterday, and stuff them into the pocket of my dress.

When I turn around, Tristan is approaching from down the hall. I quickly turn and stare into my locker, trying to busy myself with rearranging something. Anything! But par for the course, my locker is already immaculate. Not even a single pencil out of place. So I grab a notebook, flip it open, and pretend to be engrossed in whatever I've written on that page.

I feel warm lips press into my neck. I stifle a giddy squeal.

"Hi there," I say, keeping my gaze locked on my notebook.

Tristan gently turns my shoulder so that I'm facing him and then his mouth is on mine. His kiss is deep and urgent. Like he hasn't kissed me in weeks. One hand snakes around my waist, pulling me into him, the other roams through my hair, his fingers tangling in the soft waves I spent so long perfecting this morning.

The notebook I was pretending to be absorbed in slips from my quickly numbing fingers as my whole body wilts into him. Thankfully, he's got one arm around me, or I'd probably sink to the floor right along with my notebook.

I'm so completely wrapped up in his lips moving against mine, I almost forget about the seventh commandment.

Commandment #7: Thou shall always end the date and the kiss first. Leave him wanting more!

It takes every ounce of mental strength that I have, but I finally manage to pull away. I try not to act completely swooned by what just happened, but in reality I think my kneecaps have entirely melted. I brace my wobbly body against the locker behind me.

"That was nice," I say lamely, bending down to pick up my fallen notebook.

Tristan lets out a laugh. "*Nice?* That was like the world series of kissing."

I teeter my head from side to side. "Perhaps."

Perhaps?

Am I a Creature of Mystery or a character from *Downton Abbey*?

Tristan leans in and rests his forehead against mine. "What's going on in that pretty head of yours?"

"What's going on in that pretty head of *yours*?"

He guffaws. "After that kiss? I'm not sure you want to know."

A deep blush creeps up my neck. Do Creatures of Mystery blush?

I lower my head, averting my gaze.

"I mean," he says, lifting my chin to meet his eye, "are you sure you're okay?"

"Are you sure *you're* okay?"

His face contorts in confusion. "Yeeaaah." He draws out the word, like he's buying time until this conversation makes sense. "Are you coming to the practice room during lunch with us?"

"Are *you* coming to the practice room during lunch with us?"

Okay, I'm not sure Commandment #5 applies to *every* conversation.

"Huh?"

I bite my lip. "Never mind."

"So, are you coming?"

My heart is practically doing somersaults in my chest, screaming "Yes! Yes! Yes!" but my brain is bringing down the gavel, reminding me of Operation Boyfriend Recovery (okay, I just coined that phrase, too).

Girl Commandment #10: Thou shall never accept a date request less than forty-eight hours in advance.

Although, technically, he's not asking me on a date. And technically, given my current, highly unusual predicament, he's not really physically (cosmically?) capable of asking me out more than forty-eight hours in advance. So, *technically*, I could say yes right now.

But I won't.

Everything is turning out so well, I don't want to screw it up by messing with the formula.

"I would love to but . . ." I have to force my lips to form the words. They are still tingling from that kiss and on the verge of waging a full-scale rebellion. "I really should go somewhere quiet to practice my speech." I pull the index cards from my pocket and wave them in the air, offering proof. "I don't want to totally make a fool of myself in front of the entire school."

Again, I add silently in my head.

Tristan hooks his finger into my belt and pulls me toward him. "But I'll miss you. I feel like I haven't seen you all day."

Now who's the whiny, clingy one?

"You'll see me tonight," I remind him. "At the carnival. After your gig, I'll be all yours."

His fingers slip from my belt. "Wait, what gig?"

Uh-oh.

I forgot. That part doesn't come until later, and I'm the one who has to actually *get* him the gig. But going out of my way and getting myself thrown in detention just to snag my boyfriend's band a gig probably breaks at least three commandments at once.

I should tell him now. Tell him I got him the gig, then sneak out during lunch and secure it. But then I won't be able to practice my speech, which I actually really need to do. I'm not bombing that thing a third time.

"Uh," I stammer. "Did I say gig? I meant *jig.* You know, after your jig?"

His eyebrows knit together. "My jig?"

"Yeah," I say, my mind reeling for something to say that doesn't make me sound as ridiculous as I do right now. "You know, your jig." I bounce up and down and wave my index finger in the air like I'm dancing in a bad western movie.

This conversation certainly went downhill fast.

"I . . ." Tristan stammers. "I'm not sure I follow."

I flash him a mischievous smile, like this is all some big fancy surprise I've been cooking up for months. "I guess you'll find out soon enough! Gotta run!" I give him a peck on the cheek. "Have fun at practice."

Then I book it down the hall, feeling Tristan's eyes follow me the whole way.

At least I'm holding his attention. That's gotta count for something, right?

Light My Fire

12:42 p.m.

I swing by the cafeteria to grab some food. No more giving important speeches on an empty stomach. I've learned that lesson twice.

The cafeteria is a madhouse. This is why I never eat in here. Even before Tristan and I started dating and I began eating my lunches in the band room while he practiced, I always ate in the library.

This place is like an introvert's worst nightmare. If the sheer number of people stuffed into one place is not enough to make you cry inside, the roving, judging eyes should do the trick.

I pay for my prewrapped sandwich and bottle of juice (hands down the safest options), and make a beeline for the exit. The less time I spend in here, the better for my complexion.

I'm halfway to the door when a loud clatter echoes across the unforgiving tile. I turn to see a slender girl with creamy skin and raven-colored hair sprawled out on the floor, the contents of an overturned lunch tray scattered around her.

The entire lunchroom stops to stare and I hate myself for doing the same thing. When the girl pushes herself up, I'm able to see her face but I don't recognize her. I bet she's new.

I cringe inwardly. Falling flat on your face on your first day of school? Ouch.

Has that happened the past two days as well? It must have. I just didn't know about it because I wasn't here to see it.

I notice Cole Simpson—a guy with a permanent spot in detention—high-fiving some of his idiot friends. He was probably the one who tripped the poor girl.

I take a step toward her, vowing to help her up and introduce myself, but I notice she's already getting assistance from some guy who was sitting at a nearby table. As he bends down to help her scoop up her food, I see that the front of his shirt is covered in the chocolate pudding that was previously on her tray.

Well, he seems to have everything under control. I tuck my juice under my arm and set off for the library.

When I arrive, Owen is giving his same impassioned argument about Death as a narrator in *The Book Thief*, and I head up the stairs to the recording booths again.

This time, I'm determined to get this speech right.

I flip through the cards, reading each one carefully, and, for the first time, really absorbing what they say. Owen was right. This speech is pretty awful. But it's not like I'm about to sit down and rewrite it twenty minutes before I'm scheduled to give it.

The speech could use some punching up, though. It's terribly vague. It really needs to include more specific ideas about *how* we're going to improve the school, instead of just a lackluster promise to do it.

I take a bite from my sandwich and keep reading. I have to admit, I'm slightly less sick at the thought of standing up in front of the entire school today. Having already done this twice *and* having failed both times, I find it considerably less intimidating. Maybe public speaking really does get easier with practice.

I've just finished reading the entire stack of cards twice when the door to the tiny cubicle swings open and Owen ducks inside.

"Whatcha doin'?" he asks, sidling up to me and glancing over my shoulder.

"Practicing the most boring speech of all time."

He takes the cards from my hand and flips through them. "Whoa, this speech makes vanilla look like the flavor of the month."

I smile. That's exactly what he said the last time he read these cards.

"Rhiannon Marshall wrote it. I'm just doing her bidding like the good little puppet that I am." I jerk my thumb over my shoulder. "Did you win?"

He glances questioningly behind me. "Huh?"

"Your epic debate about the movie versus the book? Did those pinheads see the error of their ways?"

He grins impishly. "Always." But then the smile slides from his face. "Wait, how did you know that's what we were debating? Was I that loud? I thought these rooms were supposed to be soundproof."

For a moment I consider telling him again. I was able to convince him to believe me last night, I'd certainly be able to convince him now. But I'm not sure what difference it would make. Operation Boyfriend Recovery is headed for success.

I've already managed to completely turn this day around. Owen doesn't need to be dragged into my inexplicable cosmic drama.

I shrug. "I just know you. That's totally something you would debate. And you would be wrong. The real reason Death isn't as powerful a narrator in the movie is because in the book, his voice was our own. Every reader was able to hear it as they believed it should be heard. The movie spoils that by literally giving Death a voice."

He cocks his head and looks at me, a lopsided half smile making its way onto his face. I suddenly become aware of how small this room is and how incredibly crowded it is with both of us in it. It's not really meant for two people. It's only meant for one person and a recording device.

His eyes flash with sudden comprehension. "You cheeky monkey, you."

"What?" I ask.

"You read it."

"Read what?"

"The Book Thief."

"No, I didn't," I tell him. "Why would I read that?"

"Because you secretly want to join the book club but it would get in the way of your little lunch dates with Mr. Rock Star."

I make an awkward, overly drawn-out noise with my tongue that sounds something like *puh-sush-uh-shush.* "Uh. Objection. Relevance."

"Objection. Totally relevant."

"Objection. Badgering the witness."

"Objection. Failure to answer the question."

"You never asked a question!"

He leans back against the wall and crosses his arms. "Fine. Have you or have you not read *The Book Thief*?"

I punctuate my one-syllable answer with a distinct head shake. "No."

"Objection. Lying."

"That's not a real objection."

"We're not in a real courtroom."

I huff. "Okay, whatever. I read it over the summer."

His eyes narrow at me. It's his pressure-cooker look. It makes you feel like you're locked in a vacuum-sealed container with no air and no escape, and if you don't give him the answer he wants you'll eventually explode.

"Fine!" I say, exasperated. "I read it last week."

"What other book club books have you read and not told me?"

I stuff my index cards into my pocket, crumple up my sandwich wrapper, and squeeze past Owen toward the door. I shove it open with my shoulder. "I don't have time for this. I have a speech to give in, like, seven minutes."

He follows close behind. "Why don't you just join the book club? I don't understand."

"Because I don't have time. And if Rhiannon and I win today"—I pause, correcting myself—"*when*. When Rhiannon and I win today, I'll have even less time."

He tries to give me the pressure-cooker look again but I refuse to meet his gaze.

"That's total codswallop and you know it. Now tell me the *real* reason you won't join book club. It's because of him, isn't it?"

"What?" I squawk as we exit the library and take a left toward the gym. "No. Don't be ridiculous. Tristan wouldn't care if I joined book club."

"No, he wouldn't," Owen says. "But *you* do."

"Objection . . ." I start to say, but I can't finish the sentence.

"What?" Owen prompts. "See, you can't even think of anything, because it's true."

I let out a deep sigh. I don't have time for this right now, but apparently Owen has all the time in the world because he doesn't let up.

"You don't want to commit to something that interferes with his band schedule. You want to be available for him at all times."

I scoff. "That's so not true."

"It's totally true. It's why you dropped out of being a camp counselor with me this summer. It's why you didn't watch *Assumed Guilty* with me last night. Sometimes it seems like everything you do, you do for him."

"Owen," I say, exasperated, holding my hand up and turning around. He smacks right into my palm. I'm actually surprised when I feel lines of definition under his shirt.

Owen has pecs?

Where did *those* come from?

He certainly didn't have those at the beginning of the summer when I last saw him in swim trunks.

The unexpected discovery makes me lose my train of thought for a moment. I look down to see my hand is still on his chest. He looks down, too, then back up at me as if to say, "Now what do we do?"

I quickly remove my hand.

"What?" he asks.

"I'll have you know," I chide him, "that I passed up an opportunity to do something for him just today because it would interfere with *my* schedule."

"Oh yeah? What's that?" Owen crosses his arms over his chest and I find my gaze drifting down to his biceps, which are also bulkier than I remember.

What did he do all day at camp? Lift weights?

"Um," I say, regaining my focus. "I found out the band that was supposed to play at the carnival tonight canceled and I *could* ditch school to go and get Whack-a-Mole the gig, but I'm not going to because I have other things to do."

And because I follow the Girl Commandments, I add silently in my head, worried that if I say it aloud, I'll just sound like a brainwashed cult member.

Owen rolls his eyes. "Oh, big deal."

I let out a loud huff and open my mouth to argue with him, but then quickly change my mind. "You know what? I can't deal with this right now. I'm really worried about my speech. I need to concentrate and you're stressing me out."

He drops his gaze to the floor. "Okay, sorry." But he doesn't sound sorry. It's just a lifeless word on his lips.

"I'm sorry"—I try—"but this election is really important to me and—"

"Is it?" he interrupts. "Is it important to you?"

"Yes! Why would I do it if it wasn't?"

Owen shrugs. "I don't know. I guess I'd just like to see you live one day for yourself."

I'm so taken aback by his comment, I actually stumble backward. "What does that even mean?"

"It means—" But he never finishes the thought. "You know what? Never mind. Good luck on your speech."

He steps around me and I watch in stunned disbelief as he takes off down the hall without me.

There! I've Said It Again

1:15 p.m.

Well, perfect. Now I'm in a bad mood. Thanks a lot, Owen. He had to do that right before my speech? He couldn't wait to bring up my life's choices until, I don't know, maybe *after* I had to stand in front of the entire student body and read the most boring election speech in the history of high school elections?

I dig my earbuds out of my bag and jam them into my ears. I flip through the playlists on my phone until I find the new one I created this morning—"Brand-New World Order"—tap Shuffle and crank up the volume. Then I continue my march down the hall to the sound of "Sugar, Sugar" by the Archies blasting in my ears. I need to get back to my confident Creature of Mystery state.

The state that Owen so rudely crapped on with his sudden need to play psychiatrist.

"There you are!" Rhiannon grabs my arm. "I've been looking everywhere for you." She drags me into the center of the gym. I pull my earbuds out and stick them back into my bag.

"Did you practice your speech?"

I pull the note cards out of my pocket. "Yeah, about that. I was thinking—"

I can see the disapproving look on Rhiannon's face as we position ourselves next to the other candidates.

"I really like it," I'm quick to start with. "The whole 'we're going to make this school a better place' is great! I'm just wondering if maybe I should add some specific ideas of what we're going to do to accomplish that. You know, like maybe—"

"Stop. Just stop." Rhiannon looks like she swallowed a habanero pepper. "This is not going to be one of *those* campaigns."

"The kind that win?" I venture, and immediately regret saying it when I see the monster flash in Rhiannon's eyes.

"The kind," she admonishes testily, "that uses fake promises and impossible changes that are only designed to win votes and that have no hope of ever getting done. This is an honest campaign. Not a popularity contest. We aren't going to throw around words like 'pizza' and 'karaoke' just to get a cheer from the crowd."

I take a moment to glance around the gym. The bleachers are nearly full now as the kids continue to file in. The sea of faces is starting to look familiar. I don't have to scan the entire gym for Tristan, I know exactly where he's sitting. He gives me an encouraging smile.

"Just stick to the script, okay?" Rhiannon finishes and I turn my attention back to her.

I shrug. "Okay."

Principal Yates steps up to the mic and settles everyone

down. Instinctively, I look to the front row where Owen sat the last two times, ready to share a conspiratorial smirk with him, but he's not there. I do a quick scan of the crowd but don't see him.

Is he even here?

Is he so mad that he decided not to come?

I feel a pang in my chest. Maybe I was too snappy in the hallway. He was probably just trying to help, like he always does. But if that's the case, why did he attack me like that? We didn't have a fight yesterday or the day before. Why this time?

Was it because I slipped up and revealed that I had read the book? Did the whole argument escalate because of one stupid comment? Or was that just the key that unlocked the door to something he's been holding in for a while?

"And now, running for junior class vice president, please welcome Ellison Sparks, Sparks, Sparks."

Like yesterday, the applause is forced at best. I step up to the mic, gripping the index cards in my hands and continuing to search the crowd for Owen. For some reason, I don't think I can start this until I know where he is. Until I can apologize with just a look the way only he and I can do.

This is certainly not the first fight we've ever had. When you're friends with someone for as long as we have been, you get into a few skirmishes from time to time. But for some reason, this feels bigger than that. Deeper, somehow.

Is it because of Tristan?

I sweep my gaze across the bleachers one last time but I see no sign of my best friend. My stomach feels like it's full of lead. He's not here. He didn't even come. How could he abandon me like that?

My eyes land on Tristan instead and he gives me a nod and another smile.

That's all I need.

I take a deep breath, glance down at my cards, and begin speaking as clearly as I can into the mic.

"Fellow students and members of the faculty. My name is Ellison Sparks and I'm running for junior class vice president. It is my great honor to stand up here today as a candidate and a fellow student and I . . ."

Swap card.

". . . am excited about the things that my running mate, Rhiannon Marshall, and I have planned for the upcoming year. This is a great school."

The room erupts in groans and quiet complaints of dissension. Principal Yates silences them all with a single look.

"A great school," I start again. "But if you elect Rhiannon Marshall and me, we can make it even better. Rhiannon is the kind of girl who gets things done. She has a vision for what this place can be and she's not afraid of the hard work and commitment it will take to achieve that vision. When Rhiannon asked me to . . ."

Swap card.

". . . join her campaign, I was overjoyed. The thought of working alongside such a visionary was both inspiring and invigorating."

I glance toward Rhiannon, standing off to the side. She's smiling proudly at my words. Or rather *her* words.

This speech really *is* awful. It sounds even worse over the speaker system.

And who says "invigorating"? Apart from someone trying to sell you protein powder on an infomercial.

"Together Rhiannon and I will do amazing things." I look up at Rhiannon again, tempted to add in a few of those things I suggested to her, but she gives me a stern shake of the head.

Whatever.

As my eyes drift back down to the card, I catch sight of a figure leaning against the doorway of the gym.

It's Owen.

Our eyes lock, and with just the subtlest tilt of his head, and the faintest curve of my lips, the message is conveyed.

All is forgiven.

By both of us.

I stand up straighter, slide the cards back into my pocket, and speak clearly into the microphone. "Thank you for your attention and please vote Marshall/Sparks for your junior class president and vice president."

Lackluster applause breaks out in the crowd. I find Tristan again and he gives me a thumbs-up.

I did it!

I finally got through that dreaded speech, with my dignity—and my normal lip size—intact.

As I step away from the mic, I glance back to the doorway, ready to flash Owen a triumphant grin, but he's gone.

Stand By Your Man

3:15 p.m.

When the final bell of the day rings, I leap out of my chair like an Olympic sprinter off the starting block.

Victory is mine!

I survived the school day!

No, not only survived . . . *rocked*. Killed. Pulverized.

In my mind, I'm running down the hallway in slow motion, high-fiving all the people on the sidelines as they clap and cheer me on and *Chariots of Fire* plays in the background.

Obviously, in reality, I don't do that.

But I do notice there's much more of a strut in my step than usual. After the election speeches, the day only got better. I didn't ditch school to get Tristan's band the gig. I went straight from my counseling appointment (where Mr. Goodman gave me yet another pamphlet) to English class. I turned in my extra-credit English paper, solidifying my A for the quarter.

I don't need to score Tristan a gig to convince him not to break up with me. I just have to be my beautiful, calm, and mysterious self. Which is also why I don't seek Tristan out at his locker after class. I hang out at mine waiting for *him* to come to *me.* He's bound to come eventually, right?

And then right on cue, almost like I summoned him from the heavens, he's there. He taps me on the shoulder while I'm stowing my books and bag in my locker.

I spin around and Tristan plants a delicate kiss on my lips. "Nice speech today. You were great up there."

"Thanks," I say.

"Are you heading to the locker room for softball tryouts?"

"Yeah."

"Cool. I'll walk you there."

Wow. These commandments really do work. I'm going to have to write a very passionate fan letter to Dr. Louise Levine expressing my undying gratitude to her and her book.

I'm about to close my locker door when I hear a high-pitched, grating voice behind us.

"Hey, Tristan."

I flinch at the sound, knowing full well who will be standing there when I turn around.

"Hey, Daphne," Tristan says, stiffening slightly as he glances between the two of us. At first I don't know why he's acting so strange, and then suddenly it hits me. He thinks I'm going to flip out again. Like I did Sunday night, which for him was *last* night. That fight is still totally fresh in his mind.

Well, that just goes to show how much he knows me. This is my moment to prove to him that Sunday night was a fluke. An alternate, hangry version of Ellison Sparks. I am the real version. The cool, collected, my-boyfriend-can-talk-to-cheerleaders-as-much-as-he-wants-and-it-won't-affect-me-in-the-slightest version.

I paint on a breezy smile. "Hey, Daphne! How was the bake sale today? Did you guys make a lot of money?"

See. Easy, breezy, Creature-of-Mystery Ellie.

Daphne gives me a look that says, "Consider yourself lucky I even tolerate you."

I fight an urge to roll my eyes.

"So, Tristan," she says, turning back to my boyfriend. "I have some excellent news."

Tristan once again casts a glance at me and I smile and turn back to my locker, pretending to be totally absorbed in my magnetic pen holder.

Magnets are pretty amazing, aren't they? I mean, they just stick to metal naturally! It's mind-blowing!

I pull the pen holder from the door and stick it back. Then do it again.

Fascinating!

"I found out that the band playing at the carnival tonight dropped out and they have an open slot. So I pulled some strings and I got Whack-a-Mole the gig!"

The pen holder slips from my grasp and crashes to the floor, pens, pencils, and highlighters scattering around my feet.

She got him the gig? But *I* was supposed to get him that gig.

Except I didn't. Because I chose to go straight to English class instead and turn in my extra-credit paper.

Because I chose to play by the rules and follow those stupid commandments.

But how did she know about it? There's no way she could have known. The only reason *I* knew was because I've lived through this day before, but I certainly didn't tell anyone.

As soon as the thought is out, my whole body freezes.

I did tell someone. I told Owen. On the way to the gym for

the speeches. I was trying to prove to him that my life did not revolve around Tristan.

The words come rushing back to me like a bucket of ice water dumped on my head.

I found out the band that was supposed to play at the carnival tonight canceled and I could *ditch school to go and get Whack-a-Mole the gig, but I'm not going to because I have other things to do.*

Daphne must have overheard me. Or someone must have overheard me and reported it back to Daphne, and then *she* went and got Tristan's band the gig.

I watch in horror as Tristan freaks the freak out in almost the exact same way he did with me.

"Are you serious?!" he screeches. "Daphne! That's amazing!" He leaps forward to hug her and then swings her around. Thankfully he leaves the kissing part out. Daphne catches my eye just as he's setting her back on her feet.

I close my mouth and force it into a smile.

Girl Commandment #6: Thou shall never act or appear jealous.

"That's amazing!" I echo. I turn to Tristan and hug him. "I'm so happy for you!"

I never really considered myself an actress before but this is an award-winning performance if I ever saw one.

"How did you do that?" Tristan asks.

Daphne shrugs. "Oh, it was nothing. You just have to know the right people."

I snort and both Daphne and Tristan look at me. I pretend to have something in my nose and reach for a tissue from my locker.

You just have to know the right people? What a bunch of codswallop, as Owen would say. I know for certain that she just drove down to the fairgrounds and asked the sweaty bald guy like I did. But did she get detention because of it? Or is she better at the whole school evasion thing than I am?

"So, I guess I'll see you tonight, then?" Daphne asks, running her hand down Tristan's arm.

"You bet!" Tristan says, and I swear he sounds like a ten-year-old boy who's just been invited to meet the real Spider-Man.

Daphne disappears down the hallway and Tristan turns to me with a grin so wide, I'm afraid he might break some important jaw muscle. "Amazing," he breathes. "I wasn't even that excited about the carnival, but now . . ." He does a little leap. "I can't wait to tell the guys!"

Wasn't even that excited about the carnival?

What is that supposed to mean? That being at the carnival with just me is nothing to get excited about?

I can feel the red-hot frustration bubbling up inside me—the green-eyed monster rearing its ugly head—and I almost open my mouth to demand an explanation, but I manage to rein it in just in time.

"Amazing!" I repeat, feeling like this word has lost all meaning for the rest of eternity.

"She really didn't have to go out of her way to do that," Tristan remarks.

"No. She really didn't," I agree, hiding my gritted teeth behind a smile as I contemplate the leniency of another commandment: Thou shall not kill.

My Little Runaway

3:22 p.m.

So, an overly bouncy, malnourished, almond-poisoning cheerleader is after my boyfriend? So what? This is not a game changer. This is absolutely nothing new. Every girl in this school would date Tristan if they had the chance. Some are just more . . . proactive about it than others.

I will not let this derail me. I will continue the course! If I had one of those motivational posters on my wall it would be the one with the mountain climber that says PERSEVERANCE!

Tristan is my mountain. And I will get to the top!

Daphne and her way-too-short-to-qualify-as-dress-code-appropriate cheerleading skirt is just an obstacle in my way. Like a boulder or a tree.

I tell Tristan again how happy I am about the gig and promise to meet him at the carnival later tonight.

First, I have a varsity softball team to get on.

As I head into the locker room to change, the school receptionist comes on over the loudspeaker to remind people to sign up for the school musical auditions by the end of today. Then she announces the election results.

Oh yeah, I forgot about those.

"And in a landslide victory, claiming 72 percent of the vote, the junior class president and vice president are Kevin Hartland and Melissa O'Neil!"

Really? We lost again? Even after my improved election speech? I'm beginning to think that vice presidency is simply not in the cards for me.

Truth be told, though, I'm not that bummed about it. Did I really want to spend the rest of the year catering to Rhiannon's every whim? Probably not. Plus, being on student council sounds like a really big time-suck. This way, I'll have more time to spend with Tristan and the band.

I change into my training clothes and jog out to the field. When it's my turn at bat, I recognize the signals Coach gives to the pitcher—thank you, previous two Mondays!—and knock each one out of the park.

"Wow," Coach says as he watches the last curveball sail into the stands. "You've really improved your swing, Sparks. The varsity team could use a hitter like you."

I drop the bat like a rapper dropping the mic and step off the field. I have to restrain myself from saying "Sparks OUT!" because that might be a tad overkill.

4:25 p.m.

The drive home is always a little lonelier without Owen. He doesn't do any after-school sports or activities, so he usually takes the bus. But today, the car feels emptier than most days after our weird fight in the library. What was that all about, anyway? Was he really angry at me because I'd read *The Book Thief* and didn't tell him? That seems like a totally inane thing to be mad about.

Or was it about something else?

I slow to a stop at the red light on the corner of Providence Boulevard and Avenue de Liberation. The scene of the crime. I glare up at the cameras hidden stealthily around the intersection. I've already scored two tickets here, although thankfully this morning I was smart enough to avoid one. Actually, I've managed to avoid a lot of things today: public humiliation, detention, a severe allergic reaction, a failed history test, and hopefully, if all goes to plan, a devastating breakup later tonight.

And yet Owen hasn't talked to me since lunch.

Why do I feel like I've managed to improve upon every aspect of this day, but when it comes to my best friend, things are actually getting worse?

The light turns green, but I'm too lost in my own thoughts to notice. A loud *honk* comes from behind, jolting me back to reality. I blink and move my foot to the gas pedal. But it's right then that I notice someone in the crosswalk to my right. A girl. She's small and frail and, from the looks of it, sopping wet. Her hair is matted to her forehead. Her clothes are clinging to her body. It takes me a beat to recognize her.

Hadley?

Another impatient *honk* echoes from behind me, causing the girl to look over. Our eyes meet and a flash of panic registers on her face. She bows her head and picks up her pace, as if she's hoping I won't notice her.

Oh, but I noticed her.

I slam on the accelerator and veer the car over to the curb, screeching to a halt a few yards in front of her. She pretends not to see me, keeping her gaze on the sidewalk and walking briskly past me. I hop out of the car, leaving the engine running.

"Hadley!" I call. But she doesn't look up.

I have to full-on sprint to catch up and intercept her.

"Hadley, what are you doing?" I stand in front of her. She tries to get around me, but I'm too quick. I duck left and then right, forcing her to finally stop, but she still won't make eye contact. "Why are you walking home? Why didn't you take the bus?"

"I missed the bus, okay?" Her tone is sharp and snappish. Not anything like the Hadley I spoke to this morning.

She missed the bus?

Did she miss the bus yesterday? And the day before that? No, I'm pretty sure she was locked in her room by the time I got home. But on those two days, I spent at least ten minutes moping around after softball tryouts, lamenting my failure. Today, I left as soon as I made the team.

Maybe she's been walking home on every version of this day, and I just never knew.

"Why did you miss the bus?" I take in her drenched clothes and soggy hair. "And why are you all wet?"

"I don't want to talk about it." Another whip of a response.

"Okay." I glance at my running car, the door still ajar. "Well, do you want a ride?"

She considers this for a moment, silently debating her options: continue to walk home soaking wet, which can't be very comfortable . . . or warm. Or ride home with me and be potentially forced to endure more questioning.

"I'll walk," she decides.

I shake my head. "Hadley, don't be ridiculous. Get in the car."

She sidesteps me and keeps walking.

What is her deal? Do I seriously need to grab her and stuff her into the car like a kidnapper? Too bad I don't have a potato sack in my trunk.

"Hadley!" I call after her, but she doesn't stop.

"Leave me alone, Ellie!"

I sigh and return to my car. Frustrated, I yank the gearshift into Drive and creep alongside the curb, keeping pace with my sister, which is currently four miles per hour. I stay right behind her, watching her the whole time. She has to know I'm there, even if she refuses to acknowledge me. At this rate, it takes us ten minutes to get home. She scurries up the driveway and into the garage door that I just opened with my clicker.

I park the car and jump out, following her into the house. She's got a decent lead on me as she storms up the stairs. She makes it to her room a few seconds before me and slams the door in my face.

I rap gently on the door three times. "Hadley? Can I come in?"

"No!" she shouts, and I can hear her voice crack. I'd recognize the sound of a girl crying anywhere. After all, I've had a lot of practice the last few days. "Go away!"

"I just want to talk."

"No, you don't! You want to ask me what happened and I'm not telling you. So just leave. Go to your stupid carnival with your stupid boyfriend!"

Stupid carnival?

Stupid boyfriend?

Since when did she think Tristan was stupid? She's always

liked him, and she's always been interested in our relationship. Like *overly* interested. To the point where it got annoying.

I think back to the past two variations of this day and try to find any additional clues as to what might be going on. When I spoke to Hadley this morning, she seemed fine. She was chipper and spouting Urban Dictionary phrases as per usual. But at night? What happened at night?

I feel a stab of guilt as I realize that for the past two days, I barely said two words to my sister after leaving the house in the morning. That first night, I stopped by her room and she asked me if I wanted to watch *The Breakfast Club* with her, but I said no. I was too wrapped up in my heartbreak, too distracted by my own problems to spend any time with her. Was she upset? Is that why she was rewatching her favorite movie for the ten millionth time?

I bite my lip and stare at Hadley's closed door. It's clear I'm not going to get through to her now. If she's anything like me, she needs some time to cool down.

"Okay," I call. "But I'm here if you want to talk."

"I don't." She says it so harshly it feels like she's slammed the door in my face for the second time today.

I Saw Her Standing There

8:11 p.m.

"Thanks so much for coming out tonight! We're Whack-a-Mole and if you like what you hear, please follow us on Instagram!"

I stand in the back of the crowd, keeping one eye on Tristan and one eye on my phone. I'm trying not to appear *too* interested in what's happening on the stage because I don't want to break Commandment #3: Thou shall always appear busy and important. So far the commandments seem to be working like a charm. Tristan texted me twice to make sure I was going to the show.

I didn't text him back, per Commandment #4, and I made a point of getting here late, arriving right as the band was taking the stage. But I made sure to make eye contact with him and flash him a coy smile (Creature of Mystery!), so he'd know I'm here.

The band launches into their second-to-last song of the set, "Fall Down," and I feel my body automatically start to pulsate to the beat. It's like an instinct now. I stop myself and glance down at my phone, scrolling through my Instagram feed to keep myself distracted.

Too clingy, huh, Tristan?

Well, look at me now. I'm barely even listening!

About halfway through the song, I click over to Whack-a-Mole's feed and check their follower count. After spending the summer as their unofficial publicist, I just can't help myself. They've already gained fifty-three new followers tonight. That's pretty solid.

I thumb through their feed and freeze when I see a picture of Tristan and Daphne posing together like a cozy little couple. He has his arm wrapped around her tiny waist and their heads are tilted toward each other. They must have taken this right before Whack-a-Mole went on. If I squint, I can see the Ferris wheel in the background. This is what happens when you're late to your boyfriend's gig. He takes photos with skanky boy-stealing cheerleaders!

I close the app and stuff my phone into my pocket.

"Thou shall never act or appear jealous. Thou shall never act or appear jealous," I whisper to myself, shutting my eyes and trying to ignore the hot fire pokers jabbing at my rib cage.

Tristan belts out the final lyrics of the song's bridge and I melt in relief. Only one more song after this and then it's over. Then he's all mine. Tonight is the night. My fantasy carnival date is finally going to happen. I've set everything in motion. I've played by the rules. I've followed the commandments. And now I can finally reap the rewards.

I glance around the crowd. For some reason it seems even more packed than last night, which I know is impossible. It probably just feels bigger because I'm standing in the back, so I can see everyone. Yesterday I was so focused on the stage right in front of me, I hardly noticed anything else.

There's a couple a little farther ahead of me, watching the show with mild interest. She's slim with black hair and pale skin. He's tall and wearing dark jeans and a gray sweater. I instantly recognize the signs of a first date. The fidgety hands that want to touch. The space between their two bodies that grows smaller, then larger, then smaller again. The game of pivoting heads when you try to steal peeks at the other person without getting caught.

It's not until she steals a glance at him that I recognize her. It's the girl from the cafeteria. The one who was tripped by Cole Simpson at lunch. I can't see the guy's face, but I watch as his hand slips uncertainly into hers and their fingers tangle. It makes me smile. It looks like her first day at school wasn't so bad after all.

Jackson performs the closing drum loop, crashing the cymbals with a flourish. The crowd screams. I almost join in but then limit myself to a polite clap.

"Okay, we have one more song for you tonight," Tristan says breathlessly into the mic, swatting at the sweaty lock of hair that's fallen into his eyes. "This one is dedicated to the girl who got us this gig."

I freeze.

Then I hear the sound. It's not one obnoxious chipmunk squeal, it's a chorus of obnoxious chipmunk squeals. I follow Tristan's gaze down to the front row where the entire varsity cheerleading squad is camped out. Daphne jumps up and down, and for a moment I think she's going to lead the squad in a

Go-Team-Tristan cheer, complete with syncopated claps and herkies.

He flashes her a smile. But it's not just any smile. It's that smile. *My* smile. "Thank you for being so freaking awesome, Daphne Gray."

Oh. My. God.

I can't breathe. The words. They're the same exact words. The only thing that's changed is the name. It's as if the dedication itself doesn't even matter. He can just cut and paste a girl's name in and it's all the same.

He starts the song. *My* song. The one he wrote about *me.*

"She.
She laughs in riddles I can't understand.
She.
She talks in music I can't live without."

Another cold front hits me like a bus.

What if it's not about me?

What if it's just some generic song about some generic girl? If he can plug and play his song dedications, what's to say he can't plug and play his lyrics, too?

The words don't say "Ellie smiles in riddles I can't understand." They just say "She." But apparently *she* can be anyone. Me. Daphne. The redheaded girl with freckles and pigtails on the Wendy's sign.

Tristan should really learn to be more precise with his lyrics. If I turned in an English paper with the word "she" written all over it, I would get a big fat C minus with a note from Ms. Ferrel that said "Be more specific."

Whatever.

Before they even reach the first chorus, I trudge away from the stage, vowing to find something else to do. You know, besides feel sorry for myself.

I sit down at the horse race game again—this time opting for horse number three. Maybe it'll have some kind of cosmic significance. This is, after all, my third time living this same day. My third time at this carnival. My third time playing this game. I feed my dollar into the slot. Before the game starts, I whip out my phone and snap a selfie with the backdrop of the horses all lined up, ready to race.

I quickly type in a caption.

Having a blast at the carnival! Place your bets on me!

I was aiming for fun, flirty, and of course busy and important, but when I post the picture to Instagram all I see is heartbreak in my eyes. Even with the Cupcake filter, which usually makes me look so chipper.

The buzzer rings and I stuff my phone back into my pocket and try to focus on the game. It comes as no surprise to me, however, when horse number three finishes last.

Take Another Little Piece of My Heart

8:43 p.m.

"Woo! That was amazing! Did you see us up there? Did you see the crowd?" Tristan hasn't stopped moving for the past five minutes. If he's not bouncing on his heels, he's punching the air or doing some new skip/spin move I've never seen before.

"I saw it," I reply serenely. "Everyone was really enjoying themselves."

Tristan barely seems to hear what I said. "God, I love it up there! The energy! The screams! The music! We were on fire tonight. I don't think we've ever sounded so good. And by the time we got to 'Mind of the Girl'—BAM! They were all just putty in our hands."

I flash a tight smile. "Yes. Putty."

His high is already rubbing off on me, lifting my spirits, chasing away my sour mood. But I'm careful to keep my responses contained, remembering Commandment #2 about looking feminine and refined on a date. Refined ladies don't jump around and squeal. They sit up straight and cross their legs.

Okay, so we aren't sitting down right now, but I'll be sure to cross my legs when we do.

"At least five people came up to me after the show asking us to play at another venue!" he goes on, punching his fist into his palm.

"That's . . ."

Refined. Controlled. Feminine.

". . . stupendous."

Stupendous?

Tristan gives me and my word choice a strange look before nodding back at the carnival. "So, what do you want to do?"

"What do *you* want to do?" I lob the question back at him almost instinctively. I'm getting pretty good at this Creature of Mystery thing.

Although as soon as the question is out of my mouth, all the items on my fantasy carnival date list stream through my mind. Things like bumper cars and the Ferris wheel and the ring toss game.

"Ooh," Tristan says, pointing to a nearby booth. "What about the ring toss game?"

So much for acting like a lady. The grin that covers my face is anything but refined.

Tristan notices. "I guess that's a yes?"

I nod.

We walk over to the game, where a carnival employee hands us five tiny rings in exchange for a dollar. I glance up at the prizes hanging from the ceiling of the booth, immediately spotting the one I want. It's a giant stuffed white poodle, almost identical to the one that Dr. Jason Halloway won for Annabelle six years ago. Next to it is a sign that says 4 RINGS.

He has to land four of the five rings on the bottle necks in order to win it. I bite my lip and watch as Tristan psychs himself up, adjusting his stance.

He lets the first ring fly.

It's short. It bounces off the table in front of the bottles and falls to the ground. Tristan looks discouraged.

"That's okay!" I pipe in. "That was a practice round."

He readies himself again, shifting his weight around until he's evenly balanced. Then he flings the second ring. It hits one of the bottles and ricochets off to the side.

Disappointment fills me but I try not to let it show. So what if Tristan can't win me a stupid stuffed animal? What counts is that he's here with me. He's playing the games. We're spending time together, just as I wanted. It's more than I can say for the previous two Mondays.

Tristan spends another three dollars on three more games, but he still can't manage to land one ring on one bottle neck.

"It's rigged," he gripes a few minutes later, as he bites into a churro he just bought from a nearby concession stand. "It's gotta be rigged. I bet the bottle necks are wider than the rings."

"Totally," I agree. "That's the only explanation."

I try to ignore the tiny voice inside my head reminding me that Dr. Jason Halloway managed to get four rings on four bottles. I saw it with my own eyes. So obviously the game is *not* rigged.

Stop it, I scold myself. *Dr. Jason Halloway doesn't exist. He's a figment of your imagination. That guy was probably not even a veterinarian.*

Tristan holds the churro up to my mouth. "Want a bite?"

I instantly light up. A shared churro isn't the same thing as a shared milk shake but it's the idea that counts, right?

I lean in to take a bite but stop when I hear Dr. Louise Levine's words in my head.

Never eat in front of him.

It's part of Commandment #5: Thou shall always be a Creature of Mystery.

But that churro looks really freaking good.

Stupid Commandment #5.

I pull back. "No, thanks. I ate a huge dinner."

Tristan shrugs and takes another large bite, wiping cinnamon sugar from the corners of his lips.

"What do you want to do next?" I say, looping my arm through his and cozying up to him.

He pulls his phone out of his jeans pocket and glances at the screen.

Is he checking the time? Does he have somewhere else to be? Is he going to tell me he has to go meet with the band again?

Commandment #7: Thou shall always end the date . . . first.

Right. Time to take action. Time to take back my control of this night. Of this relationship.

I peer at his phone screen. "Oh my God, is that the time? I really need to go. I forgot I have this big history quiz to study for."

He tilts his head. "I thought you had history today?"

"Did I say history?" I fumble. "I meant calculus. I'm always getting those two mixed up."

Another odd expression. I need to shut this thing down before it gets worse. I unhook my arm from his. "So, yeah, I better get going."

I stand on my tiptoes to kiss his cheek. "Thanks for a great night. See you tomorrow."

I turn and disappear into the sea of people. My legs want to run. Sprint. Fly. Get me out of here as fast as possible. Before he can say anything. Before he can ruin this day for the third time.

I compromise with a brisk power walk, feeling sweet relief when I finally get to my car.

I made it.

I did it.

I'm leaving the carnival and Tristan and I are still together!

I fish my keys out of my purse, hit the Unlock button, and swing the door open.

That's when I hear it.

My name.

His voice.

The footsteps.

"Ellie?"

Heart pounding, stomach twisting, I turn. He's there. Jogging to catch up with me. He slows to a stop a few feet away. "Before you go, I was hoping maybe we could talk."

Only the Lonely

9:51 p.m.

The stairs in my house have never seemed so insurmountable. I heave my body up each step, feeling like I weigh a thousand pounds. When I passed the guest room a second ago, I could hear my dad snoring softly inside. Apparently his night didn't get any better either.

I don't understand.

I did everything right this time. I was the perfect commandment-following girl. I was a Creature of Ultimate Mystery. But in the end, Tristan still wasn't mystified. He still broke up with me.

He used the same exact words. The same vague, tormented speech.

I don't think I can do this anymore . . .

I'm confused, Ellie. I'm so confused. I don't know what to tell you . . .

I just know that it's not working . . .

"But I don't understand!" I blubbered through my tears.

More and more tears. Always tears. "I was different today. I wasn't clingy. Yesterday you said it was because I was clingy!"

He seemed genuinely confused by this. I couldn't blame him. It must have sounded like nonsensical babble.

"Is this about our fight? Is this about the garden gnome I threw at your head?"

He cracked a tiny smile at the memory, but it was gone almost instantly. "No. I swear it's not."

"Then what?" I pleaded.

"I don't know, Ellie." He held me against him and rubbed my back in smooth, solid strokes. "I just don't think we're a match."

"Not a match!?" I screamed, breaking away from him. "How can we not be a match?"

He didn't respond. He simply shook his head and stepped forward to kiss me on the forehead. "I'm sorry, Ellie. I really am."

I knew what came next. I knew he was about to walk away from me again, and I couldn't go through that. So I turned my back on him instead. I got into the car, slammed the door, and started the engine.

I refused to glance out the window. I refused to suffer through another pitying look from him.

I reached for the gearshift, ready to squeal out of this parking lot in a cloud of dust. But I couldn't move. Nothing worked. My hands, my feet, my lungs. They all shut down. Only my tear ducts seemed to be in operation. They were pulling overtime. Fat drops rolled down my cheeks. I rested my head on the steering wheel and sobbed.

Now, with much effort, I finally reach the second floor of my house and pause on the landing, rubbing my puffy eyes.

Not a match?

What kind of ridiculous response is that?

Does he not remember our first night together? Does he not remember the things he said to me? How different I was from every other girl he'd dated? How refreshing I was?

Refreshing!

I'm the freaking soft drink of girls!

Why can't he still see that? Why can't he hold on to what we had the way I am so desperately trying to do?

Even though he swore it's not, it has to be about the fight on Sunday night. I never should have reacted that way. I never should have thrown that stupid garden gnome. Why can't I go back and relive *that* day over and over? Instead of this one? Then I'd know exactly how to fix this. Then Tristan and I would still be together.

When I pass my sister's room, I hear the familiar sound of *The Breakfast Club* playing. I almost walk past for a third time until I remember what happened this afternoon.

The heartbreaking look in her eyes as she walked home from school soaking wet is too much to forget. Too much to ignore. I stop and knock on the partially closed door.

"Come in!" she calls.

Hadley is under the covers, propped up on about a thousand pillows. Her knees are hugged up to her chest and her face is clean and devoid of any unsightly mascara streaks. I probably can't say the same for mine, but I'm hoping the darkness will obscure the evidence.

I sit on the edge of the bed and turn toward the TV screen. It's nearing the end of the movie. They're all sitting in a circle, pouring their hearts out.

I want to ask her again about this afternoon, but I also don't want her to get angry and kick me out. She seems so calm right now. I'll just watch the movie. If she wants to talk to me, I guess she will.

As I listen to Emilio Estevez tell his sob story to the group, I hear a soft whisper behind me. I turn to look at my sister. She's quietly reciting the lines, right along with him. She doesn't miss a single word.

Just as I can sing along to every song in my countless mood-altering playlists, apparently my sister can recite every word of this movie, and who knows how many others. I glance at her tall bookshelf. The top three shelves are devoted to all her contemporary teen romances. The bottom three shelves are stocked with DVD cases, every single one of them a movie centered around high school.

"Hads," I say, interrupting Emilio's climactic monologue.

"Hmm?" she says.

"Why do you watch these movies?"

She shrugs. "Why does anyone watch movies?"

"I mean, *this* kind of movie. About high school."

Her eyes never leave the screen. She's so enthralled by this dialogue between the members of *The Breakfast Club*, you'd think it was her first time watching it. But the way her mouth syncs perfectly to every character's line tells another story.

She picks up the remote and pauses the film. "I'm starting high school next year. Did you forget?" She says this like the answer is obvious. Like I should feel stupid for not having come up with it myself.

I glance at the still frame on the screen. Molly Ringwald and Ally Sheedy are sitting on a banister in the library. Side by side, they are the perfect contrast. The prom queen and the weirdo. The popular girl and the outcast. The one who's accepted and the one who hides in plain sight.

"You think these movies are going to help you survive high school?" I say, the realization hitting me like a curveball to the side of the head.

"Duh." Hadley presses a button on the remote and the movie continues.

I stare incredulously at my little sister, then at her bookshelf. Suddenly it all makes sense. This is research. The books, the movies, the obsession with Urban Dictionary. She's trying to prepare for something you can never prepare for.

I eye the remote. I want to grab it, pause the movie, and put an end to this nonsense once and for all. I want to shake her until she understands. There is no shortcut to surviving this world. To succeeding in high school. If there was, everyone would take it. I want to explain to her that she's only setting herself up for disappointment.

But then I turn and watch her watching the movie, her sweet heart-shaped face lit up by the screen, her wavy hair pulled back into a messy bun, her eyes wide with fascination as she watches Molly Ringwald lead Ally Sheedy into the bathroom for the big makeover scene. Some invisible force keeps my mouth sealed shut.

I can't be the one to burst her bubble. I can't be the one to tell her that in the real world, high school doesn't look like it does in the movies. That no matter how many films you watch, no matter how many books you read or how much slang you memorize, you'll never feel like you fit in.

No matter how perfectly you set up your day—your *life*—you'll still fail.

Just as I have.

No. I won't tell her this. At least not today. I'll let her continue to live her life, believing that the world makes sense. Believing that effort equals success.

I'll just sit here next to her until the movie ends.

I lean back against the wall, getting comfortable. Hadley passes me a pillow and I prop it behind my back. Molly Ringwald puts the final touches on her extreme makeover. I can feel Hadley tense beside me, waiting for the big reveal. This must be her favorite scene.

A few moments later Ally Sheedy walks out of the bathroom, looking like a completely different person—her hair swept away from her face, her dark eye makeup cleared away, her whole face bright and uncluttered. Emilio Estevez's reaction to her is priceless. His mouth literally drops open as he suddenly sees her in a whole new light.

My mouth drops open, too, and I let out a quiet gasp.

Hadley shoots me a strange look. "You've never seen *The Breakfast Club*?" Her tone is accusatory and aghast.

I don't answer her. I scoot off the bed, mumbling a hasty good night, and then I'm scurrying down the hall into my bedroom. I tear open my closet door and scan my selection of clothes. I won't have a ton to work with, but I'll have to make do. It's not like I can buy an entirely new wardrobe at ten o'clock at night. I start pulling hangers off the rack and assembling the new look on my bed, trying out different combinations.

Emilio Estevez didn't see Ally Sheedy as his match until she transformed herself. She'd been hiding under that awful bag-lady disguise her whole life.

Maybe I've been doing the same thing.

Maybe I've been afraid to truly be myself.

I hear a creak near my bedroom window and my head whips around. My face breaks into a smile. I can't wait to tell Owen my big plan. He'll love it.

I run to the window and thrust it open, reaching my hand out to help him with his entry, but there's no one outside. Only the wind blowing through the leaves of the tree.

Then I recall the events of the night. I didn't see him at the carnival. I didn't run out crying. There would be no reason for him to come check on me. We're still in that uneasy place where we left things today.

I feel a stab of guilt in my chest, but I quickly push it away. Tomorrow, Owen won't even remember that fight. Tomorrow, I'll fix everything. I'll make it up to him.

I assume I'll get another chance. Another Monday. Why wouldn't I? I haven't successfully fixed this day yet.

After a half hour of costume trial and error, I finally piece together the perfect outfit. An outfit Tristan is practically guaranteed to respond to. He doesn't think we're a match, huh? Well, wait until he gets a load of *this.*

I'm about to take a picture of the ensemble with my phone when I realize it won't be there tomorrow morning. So instead I take a mental snapshot, then scoop up all the clothes and return them to my closet.

I'm hanging up the first item when an idea hits me.

Why am I bothering to put all of this away? Won't everything just magically be put back into place tomorrow morning when the day resets?

A mischievous grin spreads across my face. Ever since I was a little girl, I've never ever had a messy room. Everything has always been put into its proper place. My mom used to brag to her friends about how tidy I was. My favorite game to play as a kid was "housekeeper."

I look down at the clothes in my arms and suck in a huge breath.

Then . . .

I let go.

The clothes and hangers fall into an unsightly heap at my feet. I cringe, fighting the urge to pick them up so they won't wrinkle. I glance around my neat, orderly bedroom. My posters perfectly aligned on my wall. My bookshelf meticulously alphabetized by author. My collection of glass figurines precisely positioned on my dresser. The string of soft fairy lights hung over my bed. The labeled folders stacked on my desk.

After another deep breath, I release a quiet battle cry and lunge into action. I become Hurricane Ellie. A category seven. A force of destruction. I dump books on the floor. I pull clothes off their hangers. I yank posters from the wall. I destroy everything. Until there's nothing left of my old, safe world.

This is the new Ellison Sparks. She is reckless. She is determined. She is not to be messed with.

Panting, I collapse on my bed, my heart racing. I feel like a wild animal who's finally been let out of its cage and has wreaked havoc on the poor neighboring village.

I sit up and survey the damage.

It's impressive. I can barely even see my carpet anymore.

The old Ellie would be totally freaking out right now. I can feel her buried deep down inside me. I can feel her trying to steer my body, manipulate my muscles, will my legs to move, my arms to pick up, my hands to clean. But I repress her. I shove her further and further down.

She had her chance and she failed.

She lost the boy.

She blew it.

It's time to try something completely different. It's time to become someone new.

The Way We Were (Part 3)

Five months ago . . .

"I beg to differ," I argued, pulling my wet legs out of the pool and hugging them to my chest in an effort to thwart the bitter wind that was sweeping through Daphne Gray's backyard. "I have amazing taste in music. If my taste in music were an ice cream flavor, it would be—"

"Rocky Road," we both said at once.

Tristan grinned. "I don't know, Ellie," he said, sounding like an old-timey boxer about to challenge me to a fight. "I'm having serious doubts."

"Just because I thought your music was . . ." I trailed off.

"Noise," he was nice enough to remind me. "You called it noise."

My cheeks turned the color of cherry tomatoes. The super-ripe ones. "Sorry about that."

"So, if you don't like my music, what kind of music *do* you like?"

"Um," I bumbled, "you know, like, old music."

"*Old* music? Are we talking Renaissance? Medieval? Because I could play you a really mean Baroque concerto on the electric guitar."

I giggled. "No, I mean like from the sixties."

"Ah. So you're a hippie?"

"Not all sixties music is hippie music."

He leaned back. "Okay, hippie. What's your favorite song from the sixties?"

I slumped. "That's impossible. You can't make me pick."

"Um, I think I just did."

"Um, I don't have to answer."

He reached around me and grabbed one of my sneakers, clutching it possessively to his chest. "If you want your shoe back, you do."

Of course, as my heart was racing like a hamster on a hamster wheel, all I could think was *I really hope that shoe doesn't smell.*

"Hey!" I made an effort to reach for the shoe.

He pulled it out of reach. "Nuh-uh. Shoe for song."

"I can't choose my favorite! There are too many."

"You don't have to write it in blood. No one's going to know if it's really your favorite or not. I won't wake up Jim Morrison in his grave and tell him you gave him the shaft."

I let out a huff. "Fine. I guess I would say 'You've Really Got a Hold on Me' by Smokey Robinson and the Miracles."

He pursed his lips in deep concentration, and then declared, "Nope. Don't know that one."

My mouth fell open. "How could you not know that song? It's a classic. And you call yourself a musician."

He slammed the sole of my shoe against his chest like it was a dagger burying into his heart. "Ouch!"

I recoiled. "Oops. Sorry. Again. But seriously. You have to know that song."

He shrugged. "I don't. How does it go? Sing it for me."

I instinctively scooted away from him. "Oh no. No, no, no, no, no, *no*."

He threw his hands up. "What?"

"I am *not* singing. Especially not for you."

"Me? I'm only a guy who *calls* himself a musician, but in reality I'm just a bunch of noise."

The words were hostile but his face was one hundred percent flirt.

"Go on," he urged. "Sing. I'm waiting to hear this classic masterpiece of a song that is so not noise."

I shook my head. "Nope. Not doing it."

"Why not?"

"Because I can't sing!"

"Everyone can sing."

"Fine. I can't sing *well*."

He lifted an eyebrow. "Even in the shower? Everyone sounds better in the shower. You do sing in the shower, don't you?"

"Sure I do, but—"

Suddenly there was a tug on my hand and I felt myself being yanked to my feet. He leaned down, grabbed my second shoe and paired it with the other under his arm. "Come on, let's go."

The feeling of his hand wrapped around mine made my tongue too big for my mouth. "Where are we going?"

"To the shower. I need to hear this song."

I tried to pull my hand away but he kept it tightly clutched in his. "Um. Excuse me?" I protested. "I'm not getting in the shower with someone I just met."

He kept walking. "We're not running the water. It's for the acoustics. You can keep your clothes on." He paused and peered down at my shoes tucked under his arm. "Well, except for these, which you'll get back after I hear you sing."

I followed behind him as he led me back through the sliding glass door and into the wild, flapping arms of the party. Jolts of nervous energy were shooting through me with every step. I could feel a thousand pairs of eyes on us. I could hear their screaming thoughts, their silent shouts of disbelief.

What is he doing with her?

Is that where he's been all this time?

Why is he holding her shoes?

Or better yet, why is he holding her hand*?*

Tristan Wheeler was not allowed to walk back into this party with *me*. The planet was not allowed to be knocked that far out of orbit.

But for some miraculous, impossible-to-explain reason, I didn't care what they thought. Maybe it was because Tristan didn't care. Heck, he didn't even seem to notice. He was the wolf in this room and they were his sheep. And wolves don't lose sleep over the opinions of sheep.

He guided me up the stairs and into a bathroom off the main hallway. He didn't let go of my hand the whole time. Not even when he closed the door behind us, which he had to do with the elbow of the arm that was holding my shoes.

"I thought the deal was I got my shoe back when I told you my favorite song," I objected.

He dropped my hand then and reached for the first shoe he stole from me. "You're right. Here you go." He handed it over but still clung tight to the second sneaker. "This one is for the performance."

He pulled back the rubbery shower curtain with a *swish* and stepped into the tub. He sat down cross-legged near the faucet, making himself comfortable, cocooning my shoe in the gap between his legs.

He patted the base of the tub in front of him. "Come on. Plenty of room."

I choked out a laugh. I couldn't believe this was happening. Less than thirty minutes ago I was resigned to driving home and watching a rerun of *Law and Order*, maybe two if I was feeling especially bold, and now I was about to get into an empty bathtub, fully clothed, with Tristan Wheeler.

This doesn't just happen to girls like me. This doesn't just happen to *anyone*.

Reluctantly I placed my sneaker on the sink counter, stepped into the tub, and slid down the back wall until my knees were under my chin.

Tristan slid the shower curtain back into place, sealing us alone in this little fiberglass heaven. Then he looked at me and waited.

"Do I really have to do this?"

He motioned around us. "We're in the shower. No one sounds bad in the shower, remember?"

I took a deep breath. My hands were shaking. My heart was pounding at Mach speed.

I opened my mouth and hesitantly let the lyrics of the first verse tumble out. *"I don't like you, but I love you . . ."*

The melody was so soft, so convolutedly tangled up in my sporadic breathing, I wondered if he could even hear it. I prayed he couldn't.

But his gaze was trained on me. His jaw hanging in a slack smile. His eyes dancing. I closed mine tight. I couldn't bring myself to look at him while this was happening.

I'm singing! To Tristan Wheeler! What is this parallel dimension of my life?

As I neared the chorus, I thought about ending it right there. He didn't say I had to sing the whole song. But then suddenly my voice was lifted. It sounded richer somehow. Fuller. I realized it was because someone with a much deeper register was harmonizing with me.

I opened my eyes and our gazes crashed together for the second time that night. A collision that I was sure I would never survive. Not even with four seat belts and all the airbags in the world.

We sang the chorus together. Me taking the melody, him taking the lower third. *"You really got a hold on me."*

When we reached the end of the stanza I squinted suspiciously at him. "I thought you said you didn't know it."

He tossed my sneaker to me. I caught it.

"About that," he said, grinning. "I may have lied to get you in the shower."

THE FOURTH MONDAY

Papa's Got a Brand New Bag

7:04 a.m.

Bloop-dee-dee-bloop-bloop-bing!

I sit up with a start, rub the sleep from my eyes, and gaze around my room.

Carpet. I can see my carpet.

Bookshelf. Every title is back in its proper, alphabetized place.

Desk. Papers stacked in neat piles.

Wall. Posters pinned up in perfect alignment.

Everything is as it should be. Everything is perfect. It's like last night's Hurricane Ellie never even happened.

THIS IS SO COOL!!!!

Bloop-dee-dee-bloop-bloop-bing!

I shove the covers from my legs, stand up on my mattress, and start dancing. Dancing and singing and jumping and squealing and kicking the air like a mixed martial arts champion.

Hadley bursts into my room a moment later. She stops in the doorway, staring up at me in utter bewilderment. I do a karate chop in her direction, belting out a *"hi-ya!"*

"Um," she begins warily. "What are you doing?"

"Life is amazing, isn't it?" I call out at the top of my lungs. Bounce. Bounce. Bounce. "How come I never knew how bouncy this mattress is?! Hads, you have to try this!"

"Ummmmmmm," she repeats, elongating the word until it's way too many syllables. "I'll pass."

I stop bouncing, drop my head back, and let out a loud, witchlike cackle.

"Are you on drugs?" Hadley asks.

"Nope!" I drop onto my butt and spring to my feet, sticking the landing with my arms up like an Olympic gymnast. "9.6 from the Russian judge!"

"Mom!" Hadley yells into the hallway. "Ellie's on crank! She's a crankenstein!"

I hoot. "Crankenstein! Good one!"

My sister takes off and I close the door and start getting ready.

Forty minutes later, I've been totally transformed.

I took a black lace tube top that I usually wear under lower-cut shirts to make them "school appropriate" and turned it into a miniskirt. I paired that with a formfitting black long-sleeve shirt that I attacked with a pair of scissors, making it a crop top. I caked my eyes with dark shimmery eye shadows, rimmed my lids with heavy black eyeliner, stained my lips a deep, sensual red, and painted my fingernails black.

Yup. Extreme Makeover: Ellie Edition is in full swing.

The only thing I'm missing is the shoes. But I think I know exactly where to get them. I swing my schoolbag over my shoulder and head into my parents' bedroom. My mom keeps all her old Halloween costumes at the back of her closet. I find the vampy lace-up boots from when she went as a Spice Girl four years ago and slide them on over a pair of fishnet stockings I wore for a camp play once. The boots fit perfectly, but it takes me about a year and a half to lace the darn things up. Once I do, my outfit is complete.

I stare at my reflection in Mom's full-length mirror, admiring the brand-new me. The *improved* me. I am no longer Ellie Sparks. I am *Elle*, the confident, sultry, ready-for-anything vixen. There's no way Tristan—or any other guy on this planet—will be able to resist Elle.

Ooh, which reminds me. I dig my phone out of my bag and see the two text messages from Tristan.

Tristan: I can't stop thinking about last night.

Tristan: Let's talk today.

I quickly tap out the response I spent an hour formulating last night as I was trying to fall asleep.

Me: Oh, I'll give you something to talk about, Tristan Wheeler.

I press Send with a giddy squeal and start down the stairs. I saunter into the kitchen like I'm on a fashion week runway in Paris. The Family Circus comes to a screeching halt. Hadley slams her book closed. My dad's iPad nearly falls from his hands. My mom—who is about to slam a kitchen cabinet closed—lets her arms fall limply to her sides.

I grab an apple from the fruit basket and take a big, luscious bite.

Toast is for softies. New girl. New diet.

"What?" I ask, my mouth full of pulpy fruit.

I wait for the protests to begin. This is the part where my dad says, "There's no way you're leaving the house wearing that, young lady!" Or, "Go back upstairs and try again, missy!" Or, "Honey, I think you forgot to put your pants on."

But it never comes.

Every member of my family is way too stunned to say anything. Well, except Hadley, who whispers, "Told you," to my mom.

I grab my umbrella and swagger to the garage door, stopping long enough to turn around and say, "Oh, Mom. I borrowed your shoes. I hope that's okay."

She nods dazedly.

"Aren't they bitchin'?" I ask Hadley, staring down at my feet. I pull my phone out and take a quick picture. "Shoefie!"

Then I disappear into the garage.

What I wouldn't give to have a hidden camera in that kitchen right now.

I settle in behind the wheel of my car, start the engine, and click on my seat belt.

Bloop-dee-dee-bloop-bloop-bing!

I pull out my phone, grinning when I see that Tristan has responded to my last message.

Tristan: Is this Ellie?

I laugh aloud and press Shuffle on my "Wowza! Yowza!" playlist. "Good Golly Miss Molly" comes on and I crank up the volume.

No, Tristan, I think as I back out of the garage. *This is most certainly* not *Ellie.*

Get Back to Where You Once Belonged

8:01 a.m.

"Wow, it's really chucking it down out—" Owen stops midsentence and stares into the car, dumbfounded.

"Yes?" I ask, pouting with my red-stained lips.

He doesn't get in. Instead he closes the door, locking himself outside in the rain.

"Owen!" I call to the closed door. "What are you doing?"

I watch through the sporadic swoosh of the windshield wipers as Owen walks around the front of the car, bending down to examine something on the bumper. Then he gets back in, spraying water onto the dash with a flick of his hair.

"Well, it's definitely her license plate," he murmurs to himself.

"What was that about?"

"But it's certainly not her driving the car."

I roll my eyes. "Owen."

He twists his mouth in concentration as he peers around the interior of my car. "That doesn't leave a lot of credible explanations, apart from the obvious one."

"Owen."

"The aliens have finally made contact. They've taken Ellie to their home planet for a series of very invasive, yet admittedly sexy, experiments and left a robot decoy in her place."

I sigh. "Ha ha. I get it. I don't look like myself."

He continues to ignore me, working out his theory like a detective in a film noir. "It was a very advanced humanlike model, of course, as the alien race was clearly light-years ahead of Earth in the technology race. But the decoy evidently wasn't given any instructions on the proper attire or mannerisms of the human it was replacing. So it simply Googled the word 'teenager' and came up with this"—he gestures to my outfit—"staggeringly unrealistic representation of the modern adolescent."

I groan and back out of the driveway.

"Or maybe—" Owen says with a stroke of inspiration.

"Owen."

"Yes, Ellie impersonator?"

"If I tell you something, do you promise not to think I'm crazy?"

"I would never make a promise so impossible to keep."

I turn left out of the subdivision and onto Providence Boulevard. "Something kind of strange has been happening to me."

"Clearly."

"I didn't tell you about it yesterday but I told you the day before and now I want to tell you again."

"And," Owen says, transitioning back into his detective voice, "it would seem the robot decoy—let's call her Paral-Ellie—is malfunctioning. A faulty wire in its programming, perhaps? A circuit shorted by the rain?"

"Can you be serious for a minute?"

"Can *you*?"

"I am being serious!"

"It's hard to believe that when you look like you just stepped out of a music video."

"I'm just . . . trying something new today." I release a breath.

"Clearly," he says again.

"I want to tell you this time because, I don't know, yesterday it felt kind of lonely without you in it. I mean, in *on* it."

He reaches behind me, fiddling with the back of my top. "There has to be a control panel back here somewhere. If I can just pry it open and—"

"I'm reliving the same day over and over!" I finally yell. "I wake up every day and it's Monday. *This* Monday. Where it's raining and you say 'It's really chucking it down out there' and it's school picture day and I have to give a horrible election speech and the cheerleaders are having a bake sale and lying about the ingredients, and a bird commits suicide outside my Spanish classroom, and Coach tries to psych me out with a curveball, and it's the last night of the town carnival, and Tristan dumps me, and I'm going to get a ticket right"—I glance up to see the light turn yellow at Avenue de Liberation just ahead. I slam down on the accelerator, speeding through the intersection as the cameras start flashing—"now."

I peer over at Owen. He's quiet but not looking at me. He's staring at his hands.

So I keep talking. "And I don't know why. I mean I *think* I know why. And I've been trying to fix it and it hasn't been working, so now I'm trying something extreme, because I don't know what else to do."

He opens his mouth to interject but I cut him off. "And before you say anything, last night you had a dream you went skinny-dipping in the school pool with Principal Yates."

His mouth stays open but no words come out. We drive in silence for what feels like hours. Seasons change outside. The earth makes a complete rotation around the sun. And yet it's still Monday.

I turn in to the school parking lot and park in an empty spot, keeping the motor running. "Say something," I urge him. *"Please."*

"He dumped you?"

I scrunch up my face. "Really? Of all the things I just told you, that's what you're clinging on to?"

He blinks rapidly, like he's trying to wake himself up from a dream. "Sorry. No. I mean, I . . . why did he break up with you?"

I slump against my seat. Elle, the bold, courageous music video star fades into the background as the shy, insecure Ellie makes a cameo. "I don't know. He gives me a different stupid answer every day. But see, that's what I have to do to fix it. To move on. I have to stop the breakup. It's the only explanation."

He tilts his head, confused. "Why is *that* the only explanation?"

"Because I made a deal with the universe!" I say, exasperated.

"Is that like a deal with the devil?"

"No. Yes. I don't know. I told the universe if I could just have another chance, I'd get it right. And so now I'm stuck in this day until I get it right."

He glances dubiously at my outfit. "And this is getting it right? Dressing like a not-so-classy hooker?"

I huff and open the car door, grabbing my umbrella from the backseat. "Never mind. Forget I told you."

His hand is suddenly on my arm. "Ellie, wait. I'm sorry."

His voice has softened. I turn back around and peer into his pleading green eyes.

"*Classy* hooker," he amends. "Very, very classy. I'm talking like a million dollars an hour."

I shake off his arm and get out of the car, popping open the umbrella. It's time to get back into character. It's time to rock this day. Hard.

I slam the car door with the sole of my boot, take a deep breath, and stride purposefully toward the building, trying to ooze confidence and sex appeal with every step.

I don't care what Owen thinks. He's just . . . just . . . a stupid boy who can't handle the fact that the best friend he's known since he was nine is growing up. Maturing. Becoming a stronger, more vitalized woman.

Little Ellie is gone.

Today, and every day after, belongs to Elle.

"Wait!" Owen shouts, jogging to catch up to me. I can hear the crinkle of plastic in his hand. "You forgot to choose your tasty fortune!"

"Don't need it. Don't want it. Don't care!" I call over my shoulder, and strut off into the rain.

Born to Be Wild

8:25 a.m.

Owen finally catches up with me at my locker while I'm checking my hair and makeup for my *fourth* school picture of the week.

"Okay, so let's say you're telling the truth." He leans against the locker next to mine.

I flick a stray hair away from my face. "I *am* telling the truth."

"Right. So that's how you knew about my dream last night?"

"Mmm-hmm."

"Because I told you in another version of this day?"

"Yup."

"So we've had this conversation before?"

I apply a fresh coat of red lipstick and press my lips together with a smack. "Well, not this exact conversation but similar."

"Where?"

"Where what?"

"Where was the conversation?"

"In my room. After Tristan broke up with me. You saw me crying at the carnival and climbed through my window."

"Last night? Or last Monday? Or . . . whatever."

I hesitate. "No. Two nights ago."

"And he breaks up with you every night?"

Not tonight, I think confidently.

"Uh-huh."

He looks over both shoulders, checking for eavesdroppers, and then whispers, "So when did I tell you about the skinny-dipping dream?"

I start walking toward my chemistry class. Owen falls into step beside me. "The first night before this all began. You were trying to cheer me up and it worked." I giggle at the memory.

Owen's face suddenly turns ashen. "I swear, Ellie, if you tell a living soul, I will murder you in your sleep and make it look like a mafia hit."

My giggle turns into full-blown laughter. "That's exactly what you said the first time."

He grins. "What can I say? Alternate me is a smart guy."

I shake my head. "So I've heard."

8:42 a.m.

"Say 'Two more years!'" the photographer's shrill voice calls from behind the camera.

I strike the sultriest pose I can manage, channeling my inner Marilyn Monroe. I don't smile. Smiling is for children. I angle myself on the stool, pull my curled hair over my shoulder, thrust my chest out, and contort my mouth into one of those duck faces people post on Instagram. I always thought those looked so ridiculous, but when I peer at myself in the viewfinder, I'm surprised by how much I like it. I look sophisticated and sassy. Like someone you don't want to mess with.

"Very . . . *nice*," the photographer says unconvincingly.

That woman really needs to learn how to lie better. Especially given the nature of her job.

Not that I care one bit about what she thinks. She wants me to look like America's sweetheart girl next door so she can sell a thousand prints to my relatives.

Well, not today, lady.

9:50 a.m.

When the end of first period rolls around, I head straight for Tristan's locker. He's already there, grabbing his Spanish textbook. He looks up as I approach, blinking rapidly as he tries to figure out who I am. The recognition doesn't register on his face until I'm two paces away from him.

I can see his Adam's apple contract as he swallows. "Ellie?"

I grab him by the elbow, slam his locker closed, and drag him to the room marked Janitor's Closet. As soon as the door shuts behind us I push him against it and dive for his lips. I kiss him harder than I've ever kissed him before, pressing my body into him so he can feel every inch of me.

He grabs my arms and pushes me back. "Ellie?" he asks again. "What are you doing?"

"Isn't it obvious?" I kiss him again, forcing my tongue into his mouth. I reach under his shirt and run my hands all over his smooth, toned chest.

He lets out a deep groan and then his hands are on my

back, running up and down, twisting around my waist, clutching at the fabric of my top.

The bell signaling the beginning of the next period rings but neither of us even flinches. We're way too absorbed in this kiss.

As I pull away, I bite down on his lower lip, raking my teeth against it before letting it snap back into place.

The look on his face at that moment is priceless. A mix of confusion, breathlessness, and arousal. His pupils are the size of quarters. His hair is mussed. His mouth is stained red. I wipe the lipstick from his lips and chin.

"Did you want to talk about something?" I ask, playing with the hem of his shirt.

He looks like I've just asked him to explain Einstein's theory of relativity. "Huh?"

I run a black-polished fingernail down the front of his shirt. "In your text you said you wanted to talk. What about?"

"I . . ." he fumbles, blinking rapidly. "I don't remember." Mesmerized, he loops a finger through one of my curls, watching it snake around his finger. "God, where did you come from?"

I shrug. "Maybe I've been in here all along and you just haven't noticed."

The heart-stopping grin is back, the single dimple lighting up this dark closet. Then he reaches out, grabs my hips, and yanks me to him. I tip my head back, letting him bury his mouth in my neck.

Screw the Girl Commandments. One minute with Elle and my relationship is already back on track.

Keep Me Hanging On

9:59 a.m.

Obviously we're late to Spanish, but no one seems to notice. They're all huddled around the window staring at the dead bird that's lying on the grass outside.

Oh right, I forgot about the douche bag bird.

Again.

Tristan and I are able to slip into our seats at the back of the classroom before Señora Mendoza continues her lesson. A lesson I've heard three times already.

If I can't conjugate this verb by now, there's no hope for me.

In history, I once again ace my test and revel in Daphne's cold, dead eyes when she hands my graded quiz back to me. And I don't miss the pointed, disapproving look she gives my outfit when she does so.

Sorry that I'm just better than you in every way, Daphne.

At lunch, Tristan asks if I want to join him in the band practice room. "Nah," I say, "I think I'll sit in the cafeteria today."

"Then I think I'll join you," he replies.

"You don't have to do that," I murmur, leaning dangerously close to his mouth.

"I know," he says, diving forward to kiss me. "I want to."

Victory has never tasted so sweet.

We get several stares in the cafeteria. Probably because Tristan rarely ever comes in here. I can feel Daphne Gray seething at us from her perch at the bake sale table as Tristan sits sideways on the bench, one knee on either side of me, his arms hanging loosely around my waist.

He brushes my hair over my shoulder so he can kiss the hollow part between my shoulder and collarbone. "I like this new look of yours," he whispers into my skin, sending shivers through my body.

I grin and take a bite of my turkey sandwich. "I thought you might."

He pulls away, running his eyes over my outfit. "Where did you even get those boots? They're so . . ." He searches for a description.

"Punk rock chic?"

Tristan lets out a growl. "That's so freaking hot!" Then his lips are on my shoulder.

Out of the corner of my eye, I glance at the bake sale table. Daphne looks like one of those cartoon characters with steam coming out of her ears and red spirals where her eyes are supposed to be. I flash her a goading grin.

She mumbles something to one of her fellow cheerleaders and huffs out of the cafeteria. I feel pretty darn smug right about now. Everything is going exactly according to plan. Elle was just what the doctor ordered. By tonight, there's no way Tristan will ever break up with me. Plus, his infatuation with me has seemingly made Daphne Gray so ill she had to leave the cafeteria.

I admit it wasn't my end goal, but it's a nice bonus.

"So," I say, taking another bite of my sandwich.

"Hmm?" Tristan murmurs into the bare skin of my shoulder. It's like his lips have been surgically attached to my body. Just wait until I get his band the carnival gig later. He starts kissing down my arm.

"What do you think I should wear to the carnival tonight?"

"This," he says, tightening his arms around me.

I think about the romantic date I had planned for tonight. The one I've been fantasizing about since I was ten.

"I was hoping we could play some of those cheesy carnival games."

His lips return to my neck. "Whatever you want."

"And maybe ride the Ferris wheel."

Tristan moans into my skin. "That sounds hot."

I giggle and pull away from his mouth. "You think everything sounds hot."

He pulls me back to him. "With you, everything *is* hot."

Wow. Who knew all it took was a change of clothes and a little attitude adjustment? I should write to that author of *The Girl Commandments* and tell her not to bother with those stupid rules. Or better yet, I should write my own dating guide book.

Step 1: Be confident and wear sexy clothes.

Step 2: There is no step two. That's it.

Step 3: See Step 1.

I had no idea guys were so easy. If I had only known this earlier, I could have saved myself four days. I think about all those teen girl magazines and self-help books and dating gurus who make men out to be so complicated and hard to decipher.

I mean, I hoped this new sexy, self-assured temptress thing would work, but I had no idea it would work *this* well.

Suddenly, there's a faint alarm going off in my head.

Is it possible this is working too *well?*

I quickly squash the thought down.

Don't be ridiculous, Ellie. This is what you wanted. What you've been trying to accomplish for four days.

It's true. This *is* what I wanted. Exactly what I wanted.

So why do I feel like something's missing?

Before I have a chance to analyze the thought further, there's a towering, burly figure hovering over us.

"All right, lovebirds. Break it up."

I peer up to see Principal Yates glaring down at me. She does a double take at my outfit.

"I would expect more from you, Sparks," she says before stomping away.

Tristan catches my eye and we both stifle a laugh.

"Don't you have a speech to give in, like, ten minutes?" he asks, his foot finding mine under the table.

"I thought I'd wing it."

His eyebrows shoot up.

"What?"

"I've dated you for five months, Ellie. You don't wing things."

"I can wing things."

"You're not a winger."

I take a sip from my juice. "Well, maybe I'll surprise you."

Out of the corner of my eye, I see a girl with a tray walking from the food line to a table at the far end of the cafeteria. I know that girl. I saw her yesterday in this very cafeteria. She's the new girl. The one who gets tripped by Cole Simpson.

Just as the thought enters my mind, I see the scene begin to unfold. Cole, sitting at a table not too far away, nudges one of his buddies, telling him to watch. He positions his foot against his backpack, ready to kick it out in front of her.

My eyes dart to the girl. She's peering around anxiously, looking for a place to sit. She's walking right into his trap.

I launch out of my seat. "Hey!" I call, throwing my arms over my head.

Cole gives his backpack a swift kick, it slides across the linoleum floor, stopping right in front of her.

"Hey, you! New girl! Over here!

She stops just inches from tripping over the bag and glances in my direction, confusion etched into her face. Her dark eyes widen, as if to say "Who me?"

"Yeah, you!" I call, still waving frantically like a crazy person. I beckon her over to the table. She turns, barely avoiding Cole's bag, and heads toward us.

"What are you doing?" Tristan asks, turning to see who I'm waving at.

"Being hospitable." I smile at the girl, who's now appeared behind Tristan. "Sit with us."

She looks delighted and incredibly relieved as she slides onto the bench across from us. My heart swells. Not only did I just save this girl from total social humiliation, but I also provided her with a place to sit—something that is in short supply on your first day of school.

"Hi," I say cordially. "This is Tristan and I'm Ellie . . . but, um, some people call me Elle."

Tristan shoots me a look. "They do?"

I kick him under the table.

"Hi," the girl says quietly. "I'm Sophia."

"That's pretty," Tristan says, as his eyes graze the length of her body, lingering just slightly too long on her chest.

Okay, what is he doing?

Maybe it wasn't such a genius idea to invite her over here.

Tristan realizes that I'm shooting daggers with my eyes and quickly clears his throat, returning his gaze to me and plastering on a smile.

Seriously?

I shoot him a pointed look before asking Sophia, "Is this your first day?"

"Yeah."

"Where'd you move from?"

"Los Angeles."

"No way!" Tristan says. "What was that like?"

She sighs. "Crazytown."

"I need to get out there," he says emphatically. "I'm a musician, and as you know, L.A. is like *the* music scene."

"Yeah, I know. My dad is a studio engineer at Capitol Records."

I think Tristan just had a heart attack. He's grabbing his chest like he's about to keel over. "Your dad? Works for Capitol Records?"

She nods. "He's still out there. My parents just got divorced and my mom moved us here. I guess she grew up around here or something."

Tristan dons his sad face. "I'm sorry about that. My parents got divorced a few years back. It was awful. If you ever need someone to talk to about it . . ."

He doesn't finish the thought. He doesn't have to. Sophia understands loud and clear what he's saying. Which is why she blushes and bows her head a little, murmuring, "Thanks. You're really sweet."

Tristan playfully brushes off the compliment. "Well, I do eat a *lot* of sugar."

Sophia giggles.

Wait. What is happening here?

Is he flirting with her?

I can't believe this. I try to do a good deed and Tristan goes and hits on it. I know, he's probably only sucking up because of the connection to Capitol Records, but still! Does he have to do this right in front of me? It's like that Snapchat conversation from Sunday night all over again. He didn't have to read his *thirty* Snapchat messages from cute girls while we were trying to watch a movie together. And he doesn't *have* to do this whole "I'm here for you, baby" routine while I'm trying to eat.

Who does this Sophia chick think she is? I do her a huge favor, save her from becoming a social pariah for life, and she repays me by giggling at my boyfriend's lame joke?

Well, I do eat a lot *of sugar.*

Har har har. How flipping original.

I'm suddenly wishing I had another garden gnome to throw at his face.

No, I scold myself. *Calm down. It's that same irrational, emotion-driven thinking that got you into this mess in the first place. Take deep breaths. Rein it in. You got this.*

I exhale and snap back into character. I give my hair a sultry toss and slowly begin to move my left boot up the inside of Tristan's leg. He jolts to attention, his gaze whipping back to me. I tilt my head as a flirtatious smile dances across my lips.

"I should probably go practice my speech. You know,

somewhere quiet and maybe a little secluded." I run my tongue over my teeth. Slowly so that Tristan has time to pick up on my innuendo.

Oh, he picks up on it all right. He leaps up from the bench faster than a rocket blasting into space. "You probably need help."

I let out an exaggerated sigh. "I do." I flash Sophia a smile. "It was nice to meet you. I hope your first day goes well."

She looks slightly disappointed at our sudden departure but quickly returns the pleasantry. "Thanks for inviting me to sit here."

"We would stay longer," I add quickly, "but I'm running for junior class VP and I have to give a speech in ten minutes, so . . ."

"Oh, no, that's fine!" she rushes to say. "I totally understand. Maybe I'll see you around?"

"Definitely."

"My band plays around town," Tristan puts in. "You should come to one of our gigs."

"I'd love that," Sophia says quietly, looking completely harmless in that moment. I suddenly feel guilty for thinking badly of her. She really is sweet, and maybe she didn't even realize we were together.

"Okay, see ya," I say, and head for the cafeteria doors. I don't have to look back to check that Tristan is following behind me or that he's watching me walk with all the interest of a scholar.

Some things a girl just knows.

And Then He Kissed Me

There's really only one thing that should be on your mind when a six-foot, blond-haired rock 'n' roll sex god is sticking his tongue down your throat. I'm just not quite sure what that one thing is. Maybe something along the lines of . . .

Great!

Heavenly!

Mind-blowing!

I've been trying out words for the past seven minutes while Tristan and I have been locked in the recording booth on the second floor of the library in a marathon make-out session, but I can't wrap my head around the perfect descriptive phrase. My mind keeps wandering back to the cafeteria. The way Tristan's eyes *lingered on* that poor new girl while I was sitting right there.

What's the matter with him? Does he think she's hotter than me?

No. Those are not the things you're supposed to be thinking about right this minute. How about . . .

Hot?

Reckless?

Scandalous!

Yes, scandalous is definitely a good one. After all, we *are* on school grounds. And right outside this door, people are going about their daily lives—checking out books, researching papers, sending out emails—with absolutely no idea that Tristan and I are rounding second base in this tiny, soundproof room.

It is pretty tiny, too.

My elbow has bumped against the wall like five times already.

But it was during the throes of passion, so it totally didn't hurt.

Except it kind of hurt. I mean, it was right on my funny bone. All five times. I think I'm going to have a bruise there now.

Also, my mouth is like really drying out, but Tristan is still going at it. Kissing me like the world is ending and our liplock is the key to humanity's salvation. Does Tristan have any saliva left? How is that even biologically possible? My saliva glands are running on hyperdrive over here trying to keep up.

And what exactly are you supposed to do with your hands when you're making out with someone for this long?

I already did the hair muss, the shirt grab, the lower back push, the face cup. All the things you see girls do in the movies, but now I've run out of moves. What should I do? Put them in my pockets?

No, that would be really weird. And awkward. I don't even have pockets.

I bet that new girl Sophia would know what to do with her hands. She's from Los Angeles. They probably teach make-out session hand placement in school. It's probably an elective. And she probably aced it.

Stop.

Stop thinking about Sophia.

Tristan is here with you. *Not her.*

But that's really only because I practically dangled this in front of him like a carrot in front of a cart-pulling donkey. Would he have come with me if I hadn't offered a clandestine make-out session? If I hadn't been wearing the shortest skirt I've ever put on in my life? If my legs weren't covered in fishnet stockings?

What would he have done if I'd just *asked* him to come with me?

Would he have chosen to stay in the cafeteria with the new girl and make more lame jokes about his sugar intake?

The bell rings and I feel a glimmer of relief. My chin was starting to get raw from Tristan's face stubble. I pull away and stare at my boyfriend. My beautiful, sexy, rock star boyfriend. His eyes are still closed. His touchable dark blond hair is even messier than it usually is.

"Wow." He breathes the word more than speaks it.

"Yeah," I agree. "Wow."

That's the word I was looking for!

Duh.

"Well," I say, straightening my top. "I should probably get to the gym. You know, big speech and all."

I reach for the door handle, but Tristan's hands are on my waist, pulling me back to him. "Wait. Don't go. Stay a little longer."

A little longer?

How much longer can two people be expected to kiss?

It's not that I don't like it. I do. I really, really do. Tristan is so incredibly sexy, but, you know, I have my speech to think about.

I disentangle his arms from my waist. "No, no," I say, trying to keep my voice light and playful. "I have things to do. People to impress. Elections to win."

I lunge for the door before he has a chance to pull me back again. The blast of fresh air is startling. Did we use up all the oxygen in this tiny cubicle?

I step out and head for the stairs that lead to the main floor of the library. I'm halfway down when I hear my name.

"Ellie!"

My body tenses. Is Tristan seriously trying to lure me back inside the oxygenless make-out lair again? But then I realize the voice is coming from in front of me, not behind me.

I look down and see Owen standing at the foot of the stairs, beaming. I skip down the last few steps to greet him. "How was book club?" I ask.

"I would tell you, but I have a feeling you already know."

"Death. Narrator. Movie. Yadda yadda yadda."

He smirks. "How's the new look working out for you?"

Just then, Tristan appears at the top of the stairs. Owen glances back and forth between us, most likely noticing Tristan's disheveled hair and clothes, and my certain lack of lipstick. "Ah," he says, putting the pieces together. "I guess pretty well, then."

Tristan trots down to us, wrapping his arm around me. "Hey, Reitzman." He nods to Owen.

Why is it that guys always have to call each other by their last names?

"Wheeler," Owen responds in kind, but his voice sounds weird. It's all deep and scratchy, like he's trying to disguise it. He turns to me. "I'll see you in the gym."

"That's where we're heading," I say. "Walk with us."

Something indecipherable flashes across Owen's face. It reminds me of the look he got in the sixth grade when Jacob Hurtzlinger hit him smack in the gut with a dodge ball. "You know, I just remembered I've got that junior counseling appointment thing right now, so I'll have to catch up with you later. Good luck with your speech."

I know right away it's a lie. Not only because Owen does this strange squinty thing with his eyes whenever he lies, but also because I've lived this day four times now and this is the first time he's had a counseling appointment.

But before I have a chance to argue Owen darts off, leaving Tristan and me alone at the foot of the stairs. And leaving me wondering why, for the first time in our seven-year friendship, Owen felt the need to lie to me.

Time Is on My Side

1:34 p.m.

The common misconception about high school election speeches is that you actually have to *give* a speech. It turns out, standing up there and telling dirty jokes for three minutes works just as well, if not even better.

By the time Principal Yates physically rips the microphone from my hand, I have the entire student body in stitches. They're cheering and catcalling and pumping fists in the air.

When I get back to homeroom and fill in the little bubble next to my name on the ballot, I'm feeling pretty good about my chances.

1:57 p.m.

"Hello! You must be . . ." Mr. Goodman's voice trails off when I strut into his office and he gets an eyeful of my outfit.

"Ellison, yes. That's me."

He clears his throat as I sit down, sounding like a wild boar snorting. "Uh . . . right. Pleased to meet you." But he doesn't exactly sound pleased to meet me. Or look it. He looks like he was just thrown into a snake pit. Is that sweat beading on his forehead?

He stands up from his desk and walks over to the door I closed. "I'm just gonna . . ." But he doesn't finish. He cracks the door open. "There we go."

He sits back down and wipes the sweat from his face. Good. That was really going to bug me.

"So, um, where were we?"

"You were about to tell me that junior year is a toughie."

He gives me a blank look. "Right you are. Right you are. A real toughie."

"And then you were going to say, 'And don't forget about those colleges!'" I do my best Mr. Goodman impression, complete with clownlike grin and finger pistols. "'It's time to start thinking about my future! Pow! Pow!'"

He sits speechless in his chair, staring at me.

But I really don't have all day. So if he's not going to get this thing moving along, then I better just finish her up.

"You've been assigned to meet with every student in the junior class to talk about the next two years." I recite the speech I've heard three times now. "Have I given any thought to where I want to apply? No? Well, ticktock, ticktock! Time's a runnin' out."

Mr. Goodman rubs his mouth with his hand, tugging down on the corners of his lips.

"Now this is the part where you tell me I'm living my life wrong and give me one of those pamphlets behind you."

Dazedly, he spins in his chair and practically startles at the sight of the pamphlets. As if he forgot they were there. He plucks a red one from the rack and slides it over to me.

I eye the brochure. It has a picture of a girl sitting on the edge of a bed, holding her head in her hands. A boy is out of focus in the background. Across the top it says:

Making the Right Choices About Sex

I force a smile. "Great!" I scoop up the pamphlet and give it a brusque tap with the back of my hand. "Thanks for this. I can't wait to dive in. Super-duper helpful!"

As I leave Mr. Goodman's office and approach the receptionist for a pass back to class, I eye the digital clock on the wall. It's 2:08 p.m. I'm suddenly struck with an idea.

I turn toward a nearby bulletin board and pretend to be very interested in the colorful display about self-esteem, keeping one eye on the clock. As soon as it clicks over to 2:10, I approach the desk.

"Hi!" I say brightly. "I need a pass back to class."

The receptionist smiles at me. "Of course." She glances up to check the time.

"2:10," I say way too urgently. "It's 2:10."

She gives me a strange look, but writes 2:10 in the time slot and hands me the pink slip.

I thank her and duck out of the office. As soon as I'm in the hallway, I pull a black pen from my bag, hold the pass up against the wall, and with two quick pen strokes, expertly turn the one into a four.

There. Now I have until 2:40 to get my butt down to the fairgrounds, convince that greasy carnival manager to give my boyfriend the stage gig, and get back here before I'm thrown in detention.

That's a little less than thirty minutes. Not ideal, but not impossible either.

I dart out the back door and into the student parking lot, smiling to myself the whole way.

Apparently this outfit is not only making me a better girlfriend, but also a better delinquent.

That's called progress, people.

I Get Around

2:39 p.m.

I make it back just under the wire. After parking the car, I grab my bag and sprint for the building. The conversation with the carnival manager was short and sweet and now the stage belongs to Whack-a-Mole.

I'm only a few paces from my English classroom when the massive shadow of Principal Yates falls over me and I slow to a stop.

"Ms. Sparks." She pronounces my name like she's a warden in a prison movie.

I turn. "Ms. Yates." I try to replicate her tone. She doesn't look amused by that.

"I do hope you have a pass."

I give her a big toothy grin. "But of course. Who do you take me for? Some kind of rabble-rouser?"

Not even so much as a lip twitch.

Tough crowd.

I produce the pink slip from my pocket and hand it over. "I

was just coming from the counseling office. Mr. Goodman is meeting with all the juniors. Gotta start thinking about those colleges. Ticktock ticktock!"

Yates slides her reading glasses onto her nose and glares at me over the rims. She studies the pass for a lot longer than necessary and I start to get antsy. Is she comparing the pen strokes? Will she determine that the four is a fake? I half expect her to hold it up to the light like she's checking a counterfeit hundred-dollar bill.

My heart leaps into my throat. I can't go to detention again. I can't suffer through that pit of despair and risk missing softball tryouts.

Principal Yates pushes her glasses back onto her head and hands the pass back. I breathe out a sigh and start for my classroom.

"Interesting speech today," she says from behind me.

Apparently we're not finished here.

I slowly turn back around. "Thanks!"

"If you could even call it that."

I shrug. "A politician's gotta do what a politician's gotta do."

She makes a grunting sound. "Be careful, Ms. Sparks. Telling people what they want to hear is not the same thing as winning."

Um, okaaay. What's up, random cryptic pep talk from the principal?

"You're a good kid, Ellie. I'd hate to see you go down a bad road."

I force out a smile. "Well, I appreciate that."

She nods and takes off around the corner. I almost want to snort aloud. Bad road? Just shows how much she knows. Right now, my road has never looked better.

My Boyfriend's Back

3:22 p.m.

"And, in a landslide victory, claiming a whopping 82 percent of the vote, the junior class president and vice president are Rhiannon Marshall and Ellison Sparks!"

I stop walking. I'm halfway to my locker after seventh period but my feet just kind of congeal to the spot. People are hurrying past, bumping into me, tripping to get around me.

We won? We actually won?

After three days of losing, I kind of started to think that winning an election with Rhiannon Marshall as your running mate was impossible.

But today we did it!

"Nice going, Sparks!" a voice says, and I turn around to see some jock in a letterman jacket extending his fist toward me. "Awesome speech!"

Random jocks are fist-bumping me?

I tentatively lift my fist and tap it against his. He nods like we do this every day. "Yeah!" he says.

"Yeah," I echo with significantly less enthusiasm.

What is going on here?

"Go, Ellison!" I hear someone else say. I turn around and a girl I've never spoken to in my life draws me in for a hug. "You killed it today. I knew you could do it!"

"Um, who are you?" I say into her shoulder.

She laughs and pulls away, tweaking my nose. "You're hilarious!"

This is too weird.

Is this what it feels like to be popular? Everywhere you go people acting like you're best friends?

My feet finally unfreeze and I stumble down the hall toward my locker. It takes forever to get there. Everyone in the world suddenly feels the need to say hi to me or give me a hug or a high five. Despite how strange it all is, it's admittedly exhilarating. No wonder so many narcissists go into politics.

I mean, after Tristan and I started dating people suddenly knew who I was, but it wasn't like this. They saw me as a threat. A challenge. A victor to overthrow. Now it's like I'm everyone's hero.

Just because I told a few inappropriate jokes?

When I get to my locker, Rhiannon is waiting for me. She looks positively jubilant. When she sees me approach she gives a little bounce. "Oh my God. We did it! I knew we could do it! I'm totally not surprised. Politics basically runs in my veins. Did you know my dad was county commissioner for eight years in a row? I was practically a shoo-in for president. I was a little worried after that horrific rando speech you gave—seriously, Ellie, what were you thinking?—but I could tell I reeled them back in with my speech. Good thing one of us was prepared, right? I worked on that speech for weeks, and it definitely paid off."

I bite my tongue as I dial my combination. "I dunno," I say casually, unzipping my bag and unloading my books. "I think maybe my speech helped."

She leans against the locker next to mine with a sigh. "Don't be ridiculous. It was atrocious. You should consider yourself lucky that you're running with me. I *saved* you today, Ellison."

I taste blood in my mouth. I want to grab her by her dainty little shoulders and shake her. Shake her so hard her pink headband pops right off her head. I want so badly to tell her that her speech actually sucked big-time. That it lost three days in a row, and that the only reason we won today was because of *me.*

But I don't.

Because what does it matter now? We won. The rest is just semantics.

"Anyway, we should get together tomorrow and start coming up with our yearly plan," Rhiannon says, smoothing a lock of her blond bob against her cheek.

"Sure," I tell her. "I have a ton of ideas. Like a Battle of the Bands competition or maybe—"

"Whoa, whoa, whoa. Slow down. Who's the president here?"

"Excuse me?"

She flashes me the fakest of fake smiles and tilts her head like she's talking to a child lost at the mall. "Ellie. I'm so thrilled that you have so many ideas. Like *so* thrilled. But to be perfectly honest, you have no experience in politics. I do."

"Because your dad was county commissioner?"

"For eight years in a row."

"Wasn't he impeached?"

A flash of horror contorts her creamy white features for a flicker of a second. "He was wrongfully accused."

I nod. "Right."

She stands up straighter. "Anyway, I think the best plan of action is for you to shadow me this year."

"Shadow you?"

"Yeah, you know, like an intern. I'll teach you everything you need to know. It'll be great."

I shove my bag into my locker and slam the door. "Rhiannon—" I start to say, but am immediately interrupted by a pair of arms around my waist, yanking me off the ground and spinning me around.

"Congrats, baby!" Tristan exclaims. He kisses me and I wince in pain. My lips are still swollen and chapped from our make-out session in the library earlier. "My little president."

Rhiannon clears her throat behind us. "*Vice* president."

Tristan doesn't seem to hear. Or if he does, he's smart enough to ignore it.

"I'm so proud of you!"

"You are?"

"Hell yeah. Politicians are hot. Making executive decisions. Wearing short suit skirts. Banging gavels. Hot. Hot. Hot."

I laugh. "I don't think we actually wear suits. And gavels are for judges."

"Humor me." He bends down and presses his mouth into my neck.

Rhiannon lets out an impatient sigh. "So, are we good? On my plan?"

I shoo her away. "Yeah. Sure. Whatever."

Tristan moves his lips to my mouth again, his hands pressing into my lower back. I close my eyes, listening to Rhiannon's footsteps retreating down the hall.

I'm not sure how I'm going to be able to put up with her and her delusional power trips for an entire year, but right now I can hardly find the energy to care.

Unchained Melody

3:25 p.m.

When Tristan finally comes up for air, I'm able to tell him about the gig, and that leads to another round of kissing and whooping and spinning me around. Unfortunately, I have to extricate myself in order to make it to softball tryouts on time, although my lips are grateful for the reprieve. I think they feel more swollen now than they did when I ate that stupid banana bread.

As I peel off my sexy vixen costume and don my training clothes, I tell myself this whole attached-at-the-mouth thing is temporary. We're just going through a period of renewed excitement for each other. A second honeymoon period, if you will. Every day in our relationship is not going to be like this. I remember the days after our very first kiss. Those long summer nights when there was nothing else to do but make out, and nowhere else to be but with each other. I couldn't get enough of him. It was like I was gravely ill and Tristan was the cure. I was dying of thirst and Tristan was water. I was surrounded by silence and Tristan was music.

So much music.

All the time.

Streaming in my eardrums 24-7. Serenading me when I was awake. Lulling me to sleep.

Tristan was the soundtrack of my summer. The beat I walked to. The melody I breathed in and out. The lyrics I lived by.

And now suddenly, this day, this *version* of this day, it's like someone has turned him back on. Full volume. Full blast.

Like I've synchronized to his beat again, after falling out of step for too long.

4:09 p.m.

After crushing it in softball tryouts again, I race to the locker room and quickly change back into my miniskirt and boots. I want to try to find my sister before she leaves the middle school. I figure if I can catch her earlier, I might be able to figure out what happened to her. I stuff my training clothes into my gym locker and make a dash for my car.

The middle school is next door to the high school, so fortunately I don't have to go far.

I pull up in the parent drop-off lane and watch the front doors. I did the math. If I saw her at the intersection of Providence Boulevard and Avenue de Liberation at around 4:30 yesterday, that means that she must have left the school right about now.

A moment later, I hear a slam and a group of five giggling girls come running out a side door, around the corner from the front of the school. My sister is not one of them. I watch as they blather on and run to a waiting car, which I assume belongs to one of their mothers.

I can't hear what they're saying with the windows rolled up, but they look just like the girls did when I was in a middle school a few years ago. Thirteen-year-olds trying to be thirty-year-olds. Tanned legs, barely-there shorts, too much eye makeup. I watch both the front and the side doors, waiting for my sister to come out, but there's still no sign of her.

That's strange.

I drive in a loop around the parking lot, my eyes glued to the exits. Finally, as I'm about to give up and head home, I see movement out of the corner of my eye. It's coming from the empty soccer field.

I turn in my seat to get a better view and there's my sister. Sopping wet again, running across the field in the direction of the parking lot. I get out of the car and walk toward her. She sees me and halts in her steps, wiping at her face.

"Ellie? What are you doing here?"

My mind is screaming with questions. I want to lob them at her all at once.

Why are you drenched?

Why were you on the soccer field?

Why are you at school this late?

But I know she'll only shut down again, so I hold my tongue and pretend to not even notice her shambled state. "I dunno. I had a hunch that you'd be here and I came to see if you wanted to go knock off a candy store with me."

She cracks the faintest of smiles.

It makes me feel like I just won the lottery.

"What if we get caught?" she asks, right on cue.

I shrug. "I'm not afraid of juvie. Are you?"

"I'm not afraid of anything."

"Good." I point to my car in the lot. "Let's go then."

Hadley adjusts her backpack straps and walks to the car. I notice a slight bounce in her step.

Candy Stripers is a game we used to play when we were little, mostly around Halloween. We would write our initials on pieces of our candy stash with Sharpies and then hide them around the house. The sister with the most pieces of the other person's candy would win the game.

The name Candy Stripers originated because we'd heard the term in a TV movie once and neither of us knew what it meant. I said it sounded like the workers who painted the witch's house in "Hansel and Gretel." Hadley said it sounded like professional candy burglars. We settled on her interpretation and it eventually morphed into a game. It wasn't until much later that we learned a candy striper is actually someone who volunteers at a hospital. But by then, our definition had already stuck.

When we got a little older we started to joke that we should take Candy Stripers to the next level. We should rob (or "stripe") an actual candy store. We would spend hours planning our heist, choosing our target (this part was easy as there's only one candy store in town), studying maps of the surrounding area, selecting the best candy to stripe (anything gummy because it doesn't melt in your pocket), and drafting our big plan (which usually involved one of us distracting the person at the register with stupid questions about candy while the other lifted a pocketful of goodies from the bin).

"What if we get caught?" Hadley asked me on our first "job" as we waited outside the store for the most opportune moment.

"I'm not afraid of juvie," I told her. "Are you?"

"I'm not afraid of anything," she vowed.

"Good. Let's go then."

We never actually stole anything. We'd always chicken out and pay for the candy, but it didn't stop us from plotting the next job and the one after that and the one after that.

"So," I say as Hadley buckles her seat belt. "Usual plan? Do you want to be the diversion or should I?"

She glances up and down at my outfit. "I'm going to go with you."

I nod knowingly. "Wise choice. Maybe it'll be a boy working the register and I can flash him a little skin."

She giggles and I bite my lip to hide the triumphant smile that threatens to blow my cover. "Ells?" she asks after a long beat.

"Yeah?"

She appears anxious about what she's going to say. Like she's afraid I'll be disappointed to hear it.

"What is it?" I ask, trying to sound as supportive as I can.

"Can we just go and buy the candy? It's what we always end up doing anyway."

I tip back my head and let out a laugh.

"What?" she asks.

"Nothing. I thought you were going to say something else."

Her eyebrows furrow. "What did you think I was going to say?"

I subtly eye her soaking-wet clothes and hair and the streaks of mascara on her face. I lean over to the glove box and pull out a tissue. I hand it to her without uttering a word.

She takes it and begins wiping her face.

Maybe I went about this all wrong yesterday. Maybe nothing has to be said. Maybe no questions have to be asked.

Maybe all I needed to say was "Sure, Hads. Let's go buy some candy."

Because she's right. It's what we always end up doing anyway.

Come Together Right Now

8:16 p.m.

"This one is dedicated to the girl who got us this gig. Thanks for being so freaking awesome—and might I add *hot*—Ellie Sparks!"

I'm back in the front row, screaming my head off along with the rest of the crowd. As Tristan jams the opening guitar riff of "Mind of the Girl," I use all my strength to hoist myself onto the stage. I run over and stand beside him, swaying my hips provocatively with the beat. Tristan looks surprised to see me up here—I've never in our five-month relationship gotten on stage with him—but his surprise quickly turns into a grin and he rubs his back against mine as he strums ferociously on his electric blue guitar.

I haven't changed my clothes, and I have to say, it totally fits. *I* totally fit. Owen was right, I do belong in a music video. I feel amazing up here. Is this what it's like to be a singer? No wonder Tristan loves performing so much. I'm shocked at how comfortable I feel. Normally, I'd be terrified of performing in front of a bunch of people, but as Tristan starts in on the first verse, my body just moves all on its own. I let the music take me over. I let it command me. Tristan's eyes never leave mine. He sings the entire song to me. The crowd is cheering my name.

If I thought Tristan's secondhand post-gig high was blissful, it's nothing compared to this firsthand version. This is sheer ecstasy. I feel like I could do anything. Skydive. Sumo wrestle. I'd even eat Daphne Gray's almond-infested banana bread again.

Where is the little boyfriend-stealer, anyway?

I peer into the crowd, scanning the first row where she was standing yesterday, but she's not there. In fact, her entire posse appears to be MIA.

I scan the sea of faces, all singing along and swaying to the beat and feeding off this energy that Tristan and I are sending out.

I spot the new girl, Sophia, somewhere in the middle. She's dancing, too, but I notice the guy she was with last night is not there. I wonder what happened to him. I hope she's not here to try to make a move on Tristan. Well, if she didn't realize we were a couple in the cafeteria today, then she has to have picked up on it by now.

The song comes to an end. Tristan plays a final, powerful chord on the guitar while Jackson pounds on the cymbals. The noise from the audience is deafening, and yet it's the most beautiful sound I've ever heard.

"Thank you!" Tristan calls, his voice all hoarse and sexy. "We're Whack-a-Mole. I hope you had a great time tonight. Come see us again real soon!"

Heart pounding, ears ringing, I make a split decision. I run to Jackson on the drums and whisper something into his ear. He nods and I ask the same question to Lance on bass and Collin on backup guitar. They both give me a thumbs-up.

I push Tristan away from center stage and pull the mic from the stand. "Actually," I say, flinching at the sound of my own voice reverberating over the speakers. "We have one more song. A surprise song. But it's one of my favorites and it has very special meaning."

Tristan takes a sip from his water bottle, his eyebrows shooting up. "What are you doing?" he yells to me over the screaming crowd.

I flash him a coy grin. "You'll see." I grip the mic and tilt my head to Jackson. "Hit it, boys."

Jackson kicks off the beat and Collin comes in a moment later with a cool, edgy version of the song's original riff. I sway back and forth, my nerves threatening to close my throat.

Am I really going to sing in front of all these people?

I've never sung in front of anyone before. Well, except for Tristan in the shower that night of Daphne's party.

But I can hear the first verse coming like a freight train and I'm tied to the tracks. There's no getting out of this now.

I close my eyes, raise the mic to my lips, and start to sing.

"I don't like you, but I love you."

I can feel someone standing beside me. When I open my eyes, Tristan is there, bending down to share the microphone. Just like we did that night in the shower, he harmonizes the chorus with me, rounding out the sound so perfectly that chills cover my entire body.

"You really got a hold on me."

The audience loves this. They are letting out all sorts of whooping sounds and catcalls. I can feel myself blush but I don't care. Not when Tristan is standing here next to me, our shoulders brushing, our voices tangling together.

After the song is over, Tristan slides his sweaty hand into mine and we take a bow. When we come back up, I see he's watching me, beaming. I lean in to whisper, "Was there something you wanted to talk to me about?"

"What?" he calls back over the noise.

I place my palm on his soft, damp cheek. "This morning, in your text message. You said you wanted to talk."

He laughs and shakes his head. "I can't even remember anymore!"

I smile, victorious. "I figured as much."

I'm so absorbed in the lights, the applause, Tristan, I don't even notice Owen in the audience until I'm about to leave the stage. He's standing in the back, his arms crossed, his expression inscrutable—either because he's too far away for me to read it, or he's purposefully hiding it from me.

Something twists in my stomach. Something I can't identify.

Guilt?

No. That's ridiculous. What reason do I have for feeling guilty? It's not like I broke any promises to him. It's not like we agreed to come to this carnival together. He knew I had plans to be here with Tristan. And yet, when our gazes connect across this giant, pumped-up crowd, I can't help but feel like he's judging me.

I break eye contact and turn to jump off the stage, but Tristan grabs my elbow and yanks me to him. I crash against his chest. Our lips melt together. His hand grips my lower back. His tongue finds mine.

The kiss is hot and sweaty and overflowing with adrenaline.

The crowd loves it.

When he pulls away, I'm left breathless and embarrassed. Talk about a public display of affection! Without thinking, my eyes instantly dart back to where Owen stood only a moment ago.

I'm not sure why I thought he would still be there. And I'm not sure why I feel almost sick to my stomach when I see that he's not.

I Think We're Alone Now

8:32 p.m.

After the show I say goodbye to Tristan, giving him a deep, lingering kiss before making up an excuse about curfew and heading for the parking lot.

I don't really have a curfew. The truth is, I don't want to risk anything going wrong. I want to end the night on a high note. Pun intended.

Sure, we didn't get to do any of the things on my fantasy carnival date list—and technically I'm still a Ferris wheel virgin—but so what? What we did was even better.

Tristan and I sang together. On stage. He kissed me. On stage. In front of everyone. He told me he couldn't even remember what he'd wanted to talk about this morning.

I can't imagine the night getting any better than that.

We created our own fantasy carnival date and it was magical.

Yet, as I make my way to the parking lot, I can't help but feel like the victory is empty.

Yes, I won. I stopped Tristan from breaking up with me. But was it a real win? Or did I somehow cheat at the game?

I flash back to what Principal Yates said to me outside my English classroom.

Telling people what they want to hear is not the same thing as winning.

But that's ridiculous, right? Who cares *how* I won, I still won. I should be happy that Tristan and I are still together. This is what I wanted from the beginning. This is what the day has been all about. I need to stop overanalyzing everything like a crazy person. I need to start appreciating a good thing when I have it.

I press the Unlock button on my keys and watch the headlights flash on my car.

That's it. No more whining.

No more second-guessing.

This isn't a softball match. I don't have to analyze what I did right and what I did wrong so I can replicate the win. There's no need to replicate anything this time. The day is over. I accomplished what I set out to accomplish. Tomorrow will be Tuesday, and that's that.

Life goes on.

"Leaving so soon?" I hear someone say as I open the car door.

I look up to see Owen walking over to me, his hands stuffed into his pockets, his shoulders hunched up near his ears. It's what he does when he's nervous about something. Like the time in fourth grade when he got angry and tipped over all the paints and I made him confess his crime to the teacher. He shuffled to her desk, hunched over like a turtle trying to disappear into his shell.

But what is he so nervous about now?

"Yeah," I say. I'm about to repeat my curfew lie but I stop myself. Owen knows I don't have a curfew. I've never had one. I've never been the kind of girl who needed one. "Nice performance," he says.

I grin. "Thanks. Wait, do you mean on stage?"

He shrugs. "Sure. We'll go with that."

"It was kind of exhilarating. Being up there. I can see why Tristan likes it so much."

"I bet." He stops when he reaches the hood of my car. "I don't see any tears. I assume that means your plan worked."

I beam. "That it does. Mission accomplished."

"Well done."

Well done?

Why is he acting so weird? Why doesn't he just talk normally?

"Thanks?"

He purses his lips, like he's trying to think of something else to say, until he finally comes up with "So, it's all over then?"

My brow furrows in confusion.

"Monday," he clarifies. "The weird déjà vu, history-literally-repeating-itself thing. It's over? Tomorrow will be Tuesday?"

I shrug. "I guess. I mean, yeah."

He jerks his chin at my outfit. "Does that mean you have to dress like that every day?"

I peer down. I have to admit it's pretty silly. I mean, fishnets and crop tops? Two months ago I wouldn't have been caught dead in anything like this, even on Halloween. But I guess that's what life is all about. Changing. Adapting. Moving forward.

"I don't know. I haven't really thought that far ahead."

He nods, still standing awkwardly at the hood of my car, his hands still stuffed into his pockets.

I gesture to the passenger seat. "Do you need a ride home?"

He glances back to the lights of the carnival. The noise of the people and rides and games has faded into a soft din. "Actually, I was thinking maybe we could, you know, like, hang out."

Jeez, why does Owen sound so freaking edgy? Is this "costume" I'm wearing making him uneasy? The way he's ducking his head and averting his eyes, you'd think he was asking some girl he's just met on a date. Not asking his best friend to hang out. And I can't really tell because it's so dark, but it almost looks like Owen is blushing.

"Like here? Or back at my house?" I ask, feeling just as awkward. It's normally so easy between us. There's no fumbling. No asking. We just, I don't know, hang out. But this suddenly feels like we're trying to plan a state dinner or something.

"Here," he says quickly, like he wants to get the word out before it burns a hole in his cheeks. "At the carnival. It *is* the last night. You know, with tomorrow being Tuesday and all."

"Right," I say haltingly. "Tomorrow. Tuesday. That means no more carnival."

"Right," he repeats.

Okay, this is just too much. First he lies to me in the library. Now, we're standing here bumbling like idiot strangers. I had planned on fixing this weirdness with Owen today. I was going to make things right, but apparently I've somehow only managed to make things worse. Owen and I need to return to normalcy, like, stat. I can't take much more of this awkwardness.

I steal a peek at my phone. Tristan's sent me two texts. One that says how amazing tonight was, and the other that says he's heading to Jackson's to strategize next steps with the band. That means there's no chance of me bumping into him at the carnival and screwing everything up.

I close the car door with a decisive *bang*.

"Okay," I say, trying to sound casual. Nonchalant. *Normal*. But it comes out way too bubbly. "Let's go . . . um"—I point vaguely in the direction of the carnival—"hang out."

There's a Moon Out Tonight

8:43 p.m.

The conversation doesn't get any easier. Owen and I walk around the carnival on Mute, like two strangers who have nothing in common. My mind struggles to make sense of it.

This is Owen! The guy who climbs through my window and makes jokes about my stuffed Hippo.

The guy I used to raid the canteen with at summer camp.

The guy who brings me Benadryl when I accidentally eat almonds.

Why is there suddenly a wall between us? Why has this crazy repetitive day turned us into two people who can't even find *one* thing to talk about?

"So do you—"

"Maybe we should—"

We speak at the same time. I chuckle. "You go."

"I was just going to ask if you wanted to play some carnival games."

“Yes!” I say with way too much enthusiasm. Anything that will give us something to do but wander around in silence.

“Great!” His enthusiasm sounds about as manufactured as mine.

We head over to the games and Owen stops at the ring toss booth.

“Oh,” I say, remembering the disappointing experience I had last night. “I’m pretty sure this game is rigged.”

Owen confidently slaps a dollar on the counter. “I’ll take my chances.”

The carnival employee places five rings in front of Owen as he flashes a bogus, gold-toothed smile. I give him a guarded look. I trust these guys about as much as I trust the structural integrity of that Ferris wheel.

I tear my eyes from Gold Tooth and turn to Owen. He appears to be in the middle of some very intense preparation routine. He’s stretching his neck from side to side, swinging his arms forward and back, and hopping from foot to foot like a boxer waiting to go into the ring.

“O?” I say cautiously. “What are you doing?”

“Warming up.”

“For what?”

He punches the air. Left. Right. *Bam! Bam!* “These games are all about muscle memory. I’m warming up my muscles.”

I turn back to the carnival employee. We now share a look of disbelief.

With a clap of his hands, Owen grabs the rings and tosses them one by one toward the bottle necks. His movements are fluid, almost rehearsed. Each fling looks identical to the last, a subtle, yet earnest flick of the wrist. And every single one sails through the air, finding a solid resting place around the neck of a bottle.

"We have a winner!" the employee announces.

I stare at Owen in amazement. I'm not sure what I just witnessed. A miracle? A superhero at work?

"Uh," I stammer, glancing around at the group of spectators that have gathered to watch. "What just happened?"

Owen barely hears the question. He's too busy pumping his fist and jumping around, yelling, "Oh yeah! Who's the man? That's right, it's ME!"

Even the carnival employee looks impressed. "Someone's been practicing."

This brings Owen's victory dance to a halt. He stuffs his hands back in his pockets. "Nah. I think it was beginner's luck."

"Beginner's luck?" I repeat dubiously. "Owen, no one does that their first time."

He shrugs and points to the menagerie of stuffed animals hanging from the ceiling of the booth. "Which one do you want?"

"You won," I argue. "You should pick."

He waves this away. "No. You pick."

"I can't. You really should do it."

He points to the big white poodle—the same one I had my sights on yesterday. The employee lowers it and hands it to Owen, who in turn proffers it to me.

"Are you sure?" I ask.

"Well, *I* certainly can't go home with this. Here. Take it. I won it for you."

My throat prickles and I attempt to swallow as I take the

fluffy stuffed dog from him and hug it to my chest. "Thank you. I love it."

He nods, looking away. "Don't mention it."

We start walking again, and Owen clears his throat loudly. "So, what's next? Bumper cars? Sharing a milk shake? A moonlight kiss at the top of the Ferris wheel?"

I stop walking, my head whipping toward him. I'm relieved when I see the goading grin on his face. "You remember?"

He chuckles. "Of course I remember, Ells. You made me follow that nauseating couple around for hours. I felt like a stalker. What was it you named them? Angie and Dr. Johnson?"

"Annabelle and Dr. Jason Halloway," I murmur, hiding my smile behind the dog's flappy ears.

"Riiight. How could I forget Dr. Jason Halloway? It sounds like some guy on a soap opera who disappears and comes back two seasons later after he's had massive plastic surgery so they could cast a new actor."

I slap him with the dog. "It does not. It's a romantic name."

He snorts. "Sure. To an eleven-year-old."

"I was ten."

"Even worse."

"I can't believe you remember that."

"Ells," he says solemnly, like he's about to deliver bad news. "I remember everything."

She's Got a Ticket to Ride

9:08 p.m.

I stare up at the spinning wheel of death and feel a jolt of fear shoot through me. "I can't do it," I resolve, stepping out of the line.

Owen grabs my arm and pulls me back. "Yes, you can."

I shake my head. "Nope. I can't. I'm not ready to die today."

He laughs. "You won't die. It's just like the ropes course, remember?"

I remember. It was how Owen and I met. It was the summer between third and fourth grade. At Camp Awahili. My bunk and Owen's bunk were signed up to do the ropes course and I refused to participate. I sat on the sidelines and watched as all of my bunk mates climbed a telephone pole that seemed to stretch up to the sky. Then they balanced on the very top of it and leaped to a nearby trapeze swing.

Even though everyone was secured with a harness that the counselor assured me was perfectly safe and tested for quality control every year, I refused to do it.

Why would I purposefully tempt death like that?

The activity period was almost over and I was itching to get to the canteen and drown my sorrows with a large Coke, but then Owen came over and sat with me. He was a stranger then. A skinny, freckle-faced boy with dark hair, crooked teeth, a slightly turned-up nose, and green eyes that squinted when he smiled.

He asked me why I didn't want to join in. I told him I was terrified of falling.

He laughed at this and I tried not to be offended. "Are you kidding? Falling is the best part!"

I looked at him like he was crazy.

"Seriously!" he defended. "It's so much fun, because you've got this harness on"—he jostled the straps around his chest—"and the bouncy net is under you. It's like doing a seat drop on a giant trampoline! Sometimes I fall on purpose, just so I can land on that thing."

"You do?"

He made a *pshh* sound with his lips. "Only all the time. You should get up there and totally fall on your butt. It will be so fun, and then it won't be scary anymore, 'cause you'll have already fallen."

It took a little more coaxing but I finally agreed. I allowed myself to be strapped in. I climbed to the top of that pole, stood on the top, and fell. Right into the net.

That's how Owen got me over my fear of the ropes course.

I glance up at the Ferris wheel again. "This is nothing like that, Owen. There's no harness. There's no net. And I don't think that contraption has been tested for quality control in years."

Owen still hasn't let go of my arm. I glance down at his hand wrapped around me.

"What's the worst that can happen?" he asks me.

"Um, I die."

He makes the same *pshh* sound. It brings me back to that day at the ropes course, when nine-year-old Owen talked me into strapping on that harness. "Don't be daft. You won't die."

"Objection. I could die."

"Objection. Lack of foundation."

"I have plenty of foundation," I counter. "I watched this documentary once about traveling carnivals and—"

"You and your documentaries!"

"Yes, me and my documentaries. They're very informative."

"Whatever. I don't care. You're getting on that Ferris wheel."

"No, I'm not. I'm sorry, Owen. I can't do it. I'm not as brave as you."

I feel his hand slip from my arm, leaving behind a cold spot where his skin used to be. He stares off for a moment, looking conflicted. "I'm not that brave." He says this so softly, I almost don't hear it over the sounds of the carnival around us.

"Yeah, right. You're the bravest person I know."

He drops his gaze to the ground. "Trust me. There are plenty of things I wish I could do, but I can't."

"Like what?" I challenge.

He rubs absentmindedly at his chin and peers over at me. Our eyes meet somewhere in the middle of this small space between us. He takes a deep breath, like he's sucking in invisible courage from the air. "Like—"

"Excuse me!" someone behind us yells. "Are you gonna move up?"

We both blink and turn our heads. The line has progressed several feet and there's now a giant gap in front of us. Owen moves up, and when I hesitate he grabs me again—this time by the hand—and coaxes me forward.

I stand on tiptoes to count the heads in front of us. There are only ten more people until it's our turn. My stomach does a full somersault.

"I really don't think I can do this."

He sighs, losing his patience. "You can."

"My stomach is in knots. I think I'll just sit off to the side and let you go."

"What if *he* asked you?" The question comes out of nowhere. Like a slap to the face. Owen's tone has an unexpected edge to it.

"What?"

"What if he asked you to ride the Ferris wheel with him? You'd do it, wouldn't you? Without a moment's hesitation. You'd suck it up and you'd get on the stupid ride."

"Objection," I complain. "Argumentative."

"Oh, stop it, Ellie. You know I'm right." Now he sounds downright angry. Where did this come from? What happened to the kind, funny, normal Owen I was waiting in line with a few seconds ago? How many faces does he have?

"I don't even know what you're talking about."

"I'm saying with him, you're different. You lose yourself around him. You're not you. You're someone else. Someone you think he wants to hang out with. It's like you play dead around him."

My skin feels itchy. I scratch at my arms. "That's not true."

Owen barks out a sharp, cynical laugh. "Oh no? What are you wearing?" He gestures to my skirt. "What is this? It's certainly not *you*."

"It's the *new* me," I argue, but the rationale feels weak and thin on my lips.

He turns his back to me. I'm so mad now, I'm about to leave. He can ride the stupid ride himself. I'm going home.

But before I can take a single step, Owen spins around again, his face all flushed, his eyes narrowed. "You just don't get it, do you? You don't have to do this. Any of this. You don't have to be someone else. He should like you for who you already are. You are one of the most unique, crazy, quirky, *passionate* people I know. You fight. You argue for things. You speak your mind. You get jealous."

An invisible rock forms in my throat. I try to swallow it down but it lodges itself somewhere in my windpipe.

"But around him," he goes on, "it's like you're on Mute. You shut it all down. You pretend to be this quiet, demure, agreeable, boring person."

"I resent that," I spit back irritably. "I am not boring."

"Exactly!" Owen waves his hands. "That's what I'm trying to tell you! You're the least boring person I know." He bites his lower lip before adding, "As long as you're not around Tristan."

There it is. He said his name. I didn't realize how strange and misshapen it sounds on Owen's lips until now. Maybe that's because in the past five months, I'm not sure I've ever actually heard Owen say it.

How can seven lousy letters suddenly sound so different?

How can a single name—a name that normally makes me feel like I'm flying—suddenly make me feel like I'm falling from a telephone pole and there's no net to catch me?

"Fine," I snarl, pulling up the rope and ducking under it. "If I'm so boring, then I'll save you the burden of having to hang out with me."

I storm off, tears springing to my eyes with every step. Part of me wants Owen to chase after me. Part of me hopes he doesn't. Because then he'd see me crying. Then he'd see what kind of effect his words have on me.

"I still won," I murmur to myself as I stalk to my car and plop down behind the wheel. I wipe at my wet cheeks. "I still won."

But the victory doesn't just feel empty anymore. It feels pointless.

Will You Still Love Me Tomorrow?

10:02 p.m.

"You seem distracted," Hadley says as I sit on the edge of her bed, watching the last ten minutes of *The Breakfast Club.* I missed most of it tonight due to Owen's and my impromptu carnival date.

Date?

Why did I say that? I meant hang-out. Chum session. Friendly jaunt.

Not a date. Obviously not a date.

But it kind of felt like a date, didn't it? Until we got into that huge fight and I stormed off.

Why did it feel like a date? Because we were alone?

But I've hung out alone with Owen a million times. He's been my best friend since forever. I know Owen almost as well as I know myself. Maybe even better. And yet, tonight, I felt like I was hanging out with him for the first time.

"Yo, Ells!" My sister's voice breaks through my reverie and I look over at her. She's paused the movie and is staring at me.

"Sorry. What?"

She laughs. "I said you seem distracted."

I focus back on the screen. "I'm not. I'm totally, one hundred percent, focused."

"Is this about Tristan?"

My head whips back to her. "What? No. Sort of. No."

"No?" she says.

"No," I resolve. "It's not about Tristan."

She nods to the stuffed poodle that I'd set on the floor next to her bed when I came in. "So did he win you that at the carnival?"

My chest squeezes. "No, Owen did."

"Owen?" Hadley asks in disbelief. "Owen has hand-eye coordination?"

This makes me laugh. I think about how ungraceful he always is when he climbs through my window. Will he ever climb through my window again after the things we said to each other tonight?

"Why were you hanging out with Owen?" she asks. "Did you and Tristan get into another fight?"

I shake my head. "No. Actually Owen and I did."

She waves this away. "You and Owen always fight."

She's right. We do. But never about anything serious. Never about anything real. Tonight it felt different. Tonight it felt . . . *final.*

"You're lucky you weren't here," Hadley says. "Mom and Dad had a huge fight. I heard them yelling. It was bad."

I think about the past four mornings, my mom banging pots around the kitchen, my father sleeping in the guest room. "Do you know what it was about?"

"He forgot their anniversary."

I cringe. "Yikes. Mom is big on anniversaries."

"I know. But it gets worse. Not only did he forget, he made plans with his work friends so he didn't get home until late. She thought maybe he was surprising her with some big fancy night out, so she got all dressed up and waited in the living room for him to come home."

"Oh, God. That's bad."

"Yeah." She looks at me and bites her lip. "So did you and Tristan make up or was it just a reconfusiliation?"

"A what?"

"You know, when you try to reconcile with someone but they have no idea why you're even mad."

I shake my head. "Uh. No. It wasn't a reconfus—it wasn't that."

"So everything's good between you two again?"

I glance at the TV. Hadley has it paused right on the part where Ally Sheedy emerges from her makeover and Emilio Estevez is staring at her all openmouthed and googly-eyed. Suddenly it occurs to me that this movie is incomplete.

What happens *after* this?

Do they stay together forever?

Do they break up?

Do they eventually get married and have lots of babies?

The movie never tells us what happens after they all go home as their new and improved selves. Sure, Emilio ends up with Ally and Molly Ringwald ends up with Judd Nelson. But that's like one afternoon. What happens the next day? Or the day after that? Do they fall back into their old ways? Regress to their old personas? Or do they wear those new personalities forever?

The question Owen asked me earlier tonight in the parking lot is screaming in my mind.

Does that mean you have to dress like that every day?

I didn't have an answer then and I still don't have an answer now.

What will tomorrow look like?

"Yeah," I tell her, pushing out a smile. "Everything's great between us."

This seems to satisfy her taste for gossip. She unpauses the movie and hugs the pillow to her chest as the final scenes play out. Molly Ringwald gives Judd Nelson one of her diamond earrings. Emilio Estevez kisses Ally Sheedy goodbye.

I peer over at Hadley. She looks about as giddy and bouncy as Ally does after that kiss.

Of course things are going to work out for them, I tell myself. Otherwise, there'd be no point to the movie. Otherwise, the story wouldn't affect as many people as it does. People like my sister.

That gives me hope.

Tristan and I are fine. More than fine. We're great. Today, I reminded him of what he'd be missing if we were to break up. Today, I reminded him of why we got together in the first place. We have chemistry. I don't have to dress like this every day. I've proven my point and that's all that matters.

The final scene of the movie comes to a close as the voice-over talks about how the Breakfast Club members are a brain, an athlete, a basket case, a princess, and a criminal.

Beside me, Hadley lets out a deep sigh, and I notice her wiping at her eyes.

"You really like this movie, don't you?" I say.

She nods. "It's so true to life. It's so real."

I want to argue that she actually knows nothing about high school so how could she possibly be so sure? But I keep my mouth shut. After the events of today, something tells me that my sister needs this moment to comfort her.

"It's like you, you know?" she adds.

This takes me by surprise. "What's like me?"

Hadley nods at the credits rolling over a frozen image of Judd Nelson punching the air. "You're a brain and an athlete and a basket case, and even a princess, ever since you started dating Tristan." She pauses to think about her analogy. "You're kind of all of those things. Except the criminal."

I choose not to mention my various run-ins with the "law" over the past few Mondays.

"You're all over the place!" she jokes, and I playfully punch her in the arm.

Although I admit she's kind of right. I *have* been all over the place lately, but it's only because I've been trying to figure out how to get myself out of this crazy black hole of a day.

Now everything can finally return to normal.

I say good night to Hadley, scoop up my stuffed poodle, and retreat to my room. I strip off my thigh-high boots and miniskirt and scrub the heavy black makeup from my eyes. As I climb into bed, I send Tristan a quick text. Just to check.

Me: Good night.

A few seconds later, his response comes.

Tristan: Good night, sexy. See you tomorrow.

See, I think to myself as I plug in my phone and set it on my nightstand.

All fixed.

The Way We Were (Part 4)

Five months ago . . .

"I thought we were going to get pizza," I said as Tristan led me up the stairs of his house and into his bedroom.

"We are, but there's something I need to do first."

With his hand firmly clasped around mine, sending tingles up the length of my arm, he sat me down on his bed and closed the bedroom door.

"Uh," I said, glancing around—bedroom? closed door? bed?—"this is our first date."

He laughed that beautiful ballad of a laugh. "Not *that*. Jeez, Ellie, what kind of guy do you think I am?"

The sound of my name on his lips made me grateful I was sitting down.

"The kind that hits on girls at parties and then takes them into the shower."

He walked over to his desk, opening a drawer and riffling around inside. "May I remind you that I did not touch you in that shower." He turned and flashed me a devilish grin. "As much as I wanted to."

My cheeks burst into flames.

It had been four days since the party. Three days and twelve hours since Tristan texted and asked me out, and I still couldn't bring myself to believe it was actually happening. I glanced around the room, taking in the posters on the wall (all bands I'd never heard of before) the navy blue color of the carpet, and the collection of real records in place of books on his shelf. That's when it finally hit me.

I was in Tristan Wheeler's bedroom! The whole thing was so surreal, I might as well have been on Jupiter.

"But I am a man of honor," Tristan went on, pulling a pair of giant black headphones from the desk drawer and detangling the cord from a gnarled knot of other unidentified wires.

I giggled. "A man of honor?"

He feigned offense. "Yes. Honor. A gentleman. And a gentleman always asks first." He approached the bed and gestured toward the empty space next to me. "May I sit?"

I nodded.

"See?" He lowered himself to the bed, pulled his phone out of his pocket, and plugged the end of the headphones into the jack.

"So what is it you absolutely needed to do before we could get pizza? Because I'm starving."

He held up the headphones. "I need you to listen to my music."

I leaned away, like the idea repulsed me. "No way. Not that noise."

He closed his eyes for a brief second, pretending to gather

his patience. "That's the thing. I fear you were introduced to my music in the wrong setting. You were under duress. You had just stolen priceless gems from Daphne Gray's house—"

"Allegedly," I corrected him. "You still haven't proven anything."

"Fine. *Allegedly* stolen priceless gems from Daphne Gray's house. You were desperate to leave. The speaker system there was crap. The party was loud. The circumstances were inadequate to say the least."

"Inadequate?" I repeated, trying and failing to hide my grin.

He nodded. "Yes. Inadequate. Therefore, I feel that you need to give my music a second chance. Under better circumstances."

I gesture around me. "In your bedroom? On your bed?"

He held up the headphones. "With these."

"Those are going to make your music sound better? Are they magic?"

He nudged me with his shoulder. "You said my music was noise. These are noise-*canceling* headphones."

I laughed. "I see."

"But seriously. Songs are meant to be listened to on good-quality speakers. The kind that bring out the mix and the flavor and the nuances of the music."

I sighed. "Okay, fine. Nuance me."

He arched an eyebrow.

I slugged him. "With the music, perv."

He blinked. "Right."

I held my breath as his hands reached toward me, as he pulled the headphones apart and gently placed them on my head.

As his fingers brushed against my hair.

"I'm going to play you one of our newer songs. I wrote it just this week. We recorded it yesterday in Jackson's garage."

My heart fluttered in my chest.

This week?

Meaning, he wrote it after he met me?

"It's called 'Mind of the Girl,'" he went on. "It's about that feeling you get when you meet someone new and you can't stop thinking about them and you desperately want to know everything about them. Everything that's going on in their head. The good and the bad. What makes them smile *and* what makes them fall apart."

There went my lungs again. Back on strike.

"It's not finalized yet." He thumbed through his phone, finding the song. "The mix is still really rough. So don't fault it for that." Then he looked at me, his finger hovering over the Play button. "Ready?"

For this?

No.

Never.

I forced myself to nod.

He pressed Play. A fast and peppy drum line blasted into my ears. It was so loud but I didn't want to insult him by pulling the headphones away or asking him to lower the volume so I just focused on the music and tried to move my head to the beat.

He propped his knee up on the bed so he could turn his body toward me. So that he could watch me. The guitars came in. Eager and electric, followed by the full band. I tried to concentrate, but it was difficult with Tristan sitting there so close to me. All I could see were his hands on the bed, inches from my leg, his eyes intense and anticipating, studying my face for a hint of emotion.

The music cut out and then it was just a simple drumbeat, single keyboard chords, and Tristan's voice.

Oh holy cannoli, it was sexy.

Deep and throaty with just the right amount of angst.

"She.
She laughs in riddles I can't understand.
She.
She talks in music I can't live without."

Only one word flitted through my head.

Wow.

I don't know if it was the lyrics, the edgy guitar riffs that played between stanzas, or the way Tristan bowed his head and looked up at me from under the veil of his lashes as I listened, but it was the most amazing song I'd ever heard.

His lips started to move. I couldn't hear what he was saying because the music was turned up too loud. I reached for the headphones, pulling them off my head, but he stopped me. His hands landed atop mine, the warmth of his soft skin sinking in.

"Don't take them off."

He gingerly guided my hands until the headphones were securely back in place.

He glanced around and then suddenly he was scrambling over to his desk and grabbing a notebook and a pen. He scribbled something on a blank page and then sat down next to me and held it up.

Do you like it?

I nodded vigorously. "It's incredible!" I yelled over the music, before realizing I didn't have to shout. "Sorry," I whispered.

He bent his head over the notebook and began scribbling again.

Keep listening.

I closed my eyes, letting the song pour into me. Tristan was right. It wasn't noise. It was beautiful. Soulful and gritty. Hard and soft at the same time. The music started to ramp up. I felt every instrument in every part of my body. I held my breath in anticipation of Tristan's voice again.

"Tell me where to go.
To know the things you know.
Kiss me in the street.
Where everyone can see."

When I opened my eyes, Tristan had scrawled another message on a blank page of the notebook and was holding it in front of his chest.

You look adorable in my headphones.

"Adorable?" I asked, pretending to be offended. I had to fight off the silly grin that threatened to blow my cover.

Tristan flipped the notebook back over, his hand moving furiously. A moment later, he revealed his amendment to the message.

You look ~~adorable~~ sexy in my headphones.

I broke out in laughter. Tristan held a finger to his lips and pointed to his phone.

I schooled my expression into one of quiet contemplation. A serious record executive listening to a serious song.

No one had ever called me sexy before. No one had ever called me *anything* before.

He flipped to a blank page and scrawled out another question.

Are you a fan yet?

A fan? I was already brainstorming the Instagram handle for my fan *club*.

The chorus started and I attempted to focus back on the lyrics of the song, but Tristan's body next to me was so distracting. It felt like he was inching closer with every drumbeat, even though I knew he hadn't moved.

"Inside the mind of the girl,
Is the reason we lose sleep.
A map through the best dreams.
The secret to everything.

Inside the mind of the girl,
Time passes in light-years
Ships sink in the atmosphere
But someday I'll get there.
Someday I'll get there."

The chorus eased to an end and the second verse started. Tristan lowered his head to write something. I leaned forward to try to read it, but he tilted the notebook toward his chest. So I focused on the lyrics of the second verse instead, my stomach knotting tighter and tighter the closer I got to that mind-numbing chorus again.

Inside my headphones, Tristan sang,

"Tell me where to go,"

Across from me, Tristan turned his notebook around.

Tell me where to go . . .

Inside my headphones, Tristan sang,

"To know the things you know."

Across from me, Tristan turned the page.

To know the things you know.

My heart exploded, fire shooting through my veins and taking me over. Tristan started scribbling again. The music picked up. A big, powerful ramp-up to the second chorus.

A ramp-up I already knew the words to.

Lyrics I already knew by heart.

"Kiss me in the street."

Tristan turned his notebook around in slow motion.

Kiss me in the street.

I looked up. His gaze was hot. Focused. Intense.

"We're not in the street," I told him.

It was the worst thing to say. It was the best thing to say.

He turned the notebook around, his hand moving fast and furious over the page.

Kiss me anyway.

I let out a shaky breath. "I thought a gentleman always asks."

He flipped the notebook around and added one curvy line.

Kiss me anyway?

I laughed aloud, but the sound was cut off as his hands cupped the sides of my face. As he pulled me to him. As his lips covered mine.

The chorus blasted into my ears, drowning me in his voice, his scent, his mouth. The song lifted to a crescendo as the melody raced toward the bridge.

Suddenly, Tristan was everywhere.

He was turned up so loud.

He was everything I heard. Everything I tasted. Everything I felt.

That kiss might have lasted a few seconds or it might have lasted days. I'll never be able to tell you which one, because I lost myself in it. I lost my own rhythm in his drumbeat. I lost my own words in the soulful lyrics he was belting into my ear. I was a wandering melody with no direction. No goal. No reason. Ready to be pulled into his.

If given the chance, I don't think I would have ever stopped kissing Tristan. But eventually he pulled away, leaving both of us breathless and besieged.

That's when I first heard the silence and realized there was no longer any sound coming through the headphones. The song had ended and I had no idea how long ago that was. I had been listening to empty static but it still felt like music.

He pulled the headphones off and a rush of cool air brushed against my ears.

"I never said yes," I whispered to him as he rested his forehead against mine.

He smiled into me. "I took a leap of faith."

THE FIFTH MONDAY

Here I Go Again

7:04 a.m.

Bloop-dee-dee-bloop-bloop-bing!

No. It's too early. I need to sleep in. I've had almost a week of Mondays. I deserve a weekend already. I deserve some rest.

Besides, who's texting me this early? Owen? He needs to chill.

Groggy and blurry-eyed, I grab for my phone, knocking over a cup of water on my nightstand, and blink against the light of the screen. I bolt upright when I see Tristan's name on the screen.

Tristan's texting me?

About what?

Our romantic evening last night? How hot I looked on stage next to him? How happy he is that we're together?

Obviously, those are the only three options.

Obviously . . .

Tristan: I can't stop thinking about last night.

No. It's not possible. It can't be. It's not . . .

Bloop-dee-dee-bloop-bloop-bing!

Tristan: Let's talk today.

NOOOOOOOOOOOOOOOOOOOOOOOOOOOOO OOOOOOOOOOOO!!!!!!!

I quickly tap over to the calendar app and my bedroom shrinks down to the size of a tuna can.

Monday, September 26.

Monday.

Monday.

MONDAY!

How in the name of everything that is holy can it still be *Monday*?

I fixed the problem. I righted the wrong. I did exactly what I said I would do when I made that moronic, ill-fated wish to the universe and asked for another chance. It can't still be Monday.

I shake my phone, willing it to change.

Wake up, phone! Get with the program! It's Tuesday, you piece of crap!

The calendar doesn't change.

"What the hell do you know!?" I scream, and violently chuck the phone across the room. It crashes against my mirror, shattering both. Glass and broken phone parts rain down to the carpet.

A moment later Hadley bursts through the door, eyeing the mess and gasping. "What happened?"

"Get out!" I yell at her. "Just get OUT!"

Her injured expression sends a shot of guilt into my chest

as she quietly ducks out, looking like a dismissed Disney character.

Whatever. I don't care. Let her be hurt. Let my mirror shatter. It'll all be reset tomorrow, because obviously nothing I do matters anymore.

Nothing.

I could set fire to the house, run naked through the school hallways, assassinate the mayor, and tomorrow no one will even remember. I'll just wake up right here in this bed, with those stupid text messages.

Over and over again.

I'm trapped in a nightmare. I'm going to live the rest of my life in this awful, awful day.

Why couldn't it have been a Saturday? Or a Sunday?

Why couldn't it have been my birthday or Christmas or the day Tristan and I had our first kiss? I would have been perfectly fine reliving *that* day over and over again. But this one?

The one where Tristan hates me?

Where he's on the precipice of ending everything we had?

Not to mention the election speech and the rain and the school pictures and the softball tryouts and the ticket and . . .

Gah!

I can't do it. I can't relive it all over again. I can't keep trying to make things right with Tristan only to have my efforts erased the next morning. It's like running on a treadmill. You run and run and run, but in the end you've gone nowhere. What's the flipping point?

I lie in bed, resolved not to move. I won't go to school. No one can make me. It's not like I'll get an absentee mark on my permanent record. I *have* no permanent record anymore!

I don't know how long I lie there, because my phone with

my only clock on it is smashed in the corner, but eventually my dad knocks on the door and enters.

"Owen is on the landline for you. He said he's been calling your phone but it goes straight to voice mail. Are you sick?"

"No. Go away."

My father doesn't move. I guess that line only works on little sisters. "I'm not going to school," I vow.

"If you're not sick, then you're going to school. Plus, you have softball tryouts today."

I groan and roll over, facing the wall. "What's the point? I'll just try out tomorrow."

"The email your coach sent said it was a one-day tryout. No makeups. Today is your only chance, Ellie."

I press my face into the pillow and let out a scream.

When I look up again, my father is sitting on the edge of my bed. "Is this about Tristan? Your sister told me that you two had a fight last night."

Dang it, Hadley!

I can feel the tears welling up but I refuse to cry in front of my dad. Especially about a boy.

"No," I mumble, but it sounds about as convincing as a confession of love on a reality show.

My father lets out a sigh. "Well, I'm sorry if you're having . . . boy trouble, but that's no reason to miss school. Junior year is incredibly important when it comes to colleges, and you can't let a little crush ruin your chances at a good future."

I growl and push the covers off me. "It's not a little crush, Dad. May I remind you, you married your high school sweetheart?"

He surrenders his hands into the air. "Right, right. Of course. Sorry."

I drag myself to the bathroom and run the hot water in the sink.

"Does that mean you're going to school?" he calls after me.

"Yeah, sure. Whatever," I call back, and then I slam the door.

I stare at my reflection in the mirror. It's the same old me. On the same old Monday. With the same old stupid life.

I tug at my cheeks and run my fingers through my hair.

And the same old hair.

I open the drawer under my sink and rummage around until I find a pair of scissors. I gather all my hair into one fist, suck in a deep lungful of air, and start cutting. The scissors aren't sharp enough to get through the entire thing in one snip, so I have to work at it, sawing through the wad of hair like a lumberjack.

Finally, it all falls in a clump into the sink as the remainder of my now-jagged, shorn locks tumble around my shoulders. It looks absolutely horrible. Choppy and uneven. Some shorter strands curl around my ears while the longer ones drag across my shoulder. It looks like I visited a barbershop run by toddlers.

Well, at least it'll grow back by tomorrow morning.

I pull on a pair of ripped jeans and zip up a ratty once-black-now-gray hoodie that hasn't been washed in decades, pulling the hood up over my avant-garde haircut. I glance at my reflection in my busted bedroom mirror. The warped, splintered image is all too fitting.

As I pack up my schoolbag, my gaze falls to the reading chair by the window. That's where I put the stuffed poodle Owen won for me at the carnival last night. The chair is now empty. The whole night has been erased, including our fight. Part of me feels relief, part of me wants to cry.

8:20 a.m.

When I get downstairs, Hadley is already gone and my parents are in the midst of their heated argument, obviously the culmination of my mother's cabinet door slamming earlier.

I catch a glimpse of the clock on the microwave. School starts in ten minutes. Owen is going to kill me.

"If you would just tell me what's wrong, I can fix it!" my dad is saying to my mom, trying to put his arm around her.

She pulls away. "If you paid any attention to anything, I wouldn't have to tell you!"

She opens her briefcase and starts loading it up with files. "Just forget it. I'm fine." She slams her briefcase closed.

"Obviously you're not fine," he tries. "And I'm sorry if I've been preoccupied lately with—"

"With Scrabble!" my mom shouts. "Preoccupied with playing board games with strangers on the other side of the world."

I roll my eyes. I really don't have the patience for this.

"You forgot your anniversary!" I yell, causing both my parents to stop and stare at me openmouthed. "That's why she's pissed!" I push my bag farther up my shoulder and storm through the garage door. "Sheesh! Grow up, you two!"

Good Golly, Miss Molly

It's raining. Again. Of course. It's always raining. My life is one big rain cloud that I can't ever escape. I consider running back inside the house to grab my umbrella but then I think, *Screw it. What does it even matter?*

I slam the car door closed, rev the engine, and back out of the garage, tires screeching and squealing on the slick pavement.

When I pull into Owen's driveway a few minutes later, he comes running out from the cover of his front porch where he's been waiting for me.

"Yeah, yeah, it's really chucking it down out there," I grumble as soon as he opens the car door. "Get in."

Owen scowls and drops into the front seat. "Well, someone woke up on the wrong side of the universe today."

I slam the shifter into reverse. "You can say that again."

As I speed down his street, Owen starts searching for something in my car. Finally, when he can't find it, he asks,

"Where's your phone? Someone needs her 'Psych Me Up Buttercup' playlist stat."

"I threw it against the mirror this morning and it broke."

Owen sits in stunned silence for a moment. "What happened to you?" His voice takes on a cautious tone, as if I'm a serial killer and he's just now noticing after seven years of friendship. "Did you and the rock star break up or something?"

"Nope. Not yet."

I turn left onto the main road without even pausing to check for oncoming traffic. Owen braces against the window as a car swerves around us, laying on the horn.

"Are you crazy?"

I ignore him and step on the accelerator until I've caught up to the car that honked at us. I pull up beside him, matching his speed, and press down on my horn until the driver looks over at me. Then I flip him the middle finger.

Owen grabs my hand and yanks it back down. "Do you *want* to lose your license? Or get shot?"

"Relax. Nothing's going to happen. I'm invincible."

"Invincible?" he echoes dubiously.

"Yup. I'm done playing by the rules. I'm done being the goody-goody sugar-and-spice girl that everyone can rely on. Do you know why I've always played by the rules?"

"No," Owen says uneasily. "But I have a feeling you're going to tell me."

"Because I've always been terrified of consequences. If I fail a test, I won't get into a good college. If I ditch class, I'll get detention. If I say the wrong thing, or act the wrong way, or fail to be the cool, no-drama, easy-breezy, cucumber girl that Tristan wants, he'll break up with me. But you know what? I was wrong. All this time. I've been worried about consequences my whole freaking life, when in reality there *are* no consequences. None. Nothing I do matters. So why should I bother following the rules?"

Owen looks terrified. I eye the fateful red light up ahead at the intersection of Providence Boulevard and Avenue de Liberation. It's just starting to turn yellow and I'm still a good two hundred yards away.

"Uh, Ellie. That's a yellow light. *Aaaand* now it's a red light."

I floor the accelerator.

Owen grips the door handle. "Ellie!"

As we race through the intersection, I let go of the steering wheel and yank up on the bottom of my hoodie, giving the cameras a nice clear shot of my bra. "Eat your heart out!" I shout.

Flash! Flash! Flash!

I feel like a Victoria's Secret runway model.

With *slightly* less cleavage.

When I lower my sweatshirt and return my hands to the wheel, I notice Owen is staring openmouthed at me.

But not at my face.

At my . . .

"What are you looking at?" I ask. My tone is not accusatory. It's amused.

He quickly averts his eyes, turning the color of a fire truck. "Uh . . . nothing."

I let out a cackle. "You act like you've never seen boobs before."

His face turns an even deeper shade of red. "I've . . . um . . . just never seen . . . you know, *your* boobs before."

"Wait," I say, suddenly overwhelmed with curiosity, "whose boobs *have* you seen?"

No response.

"Interesting," I muse.

"What's interesting?"

"Nothing." I shake my head, a playful smile dancing on my lips. "Now, where's my bloody fortune cookie?"

8:35 a.m.

"So, are you going to tell me why you're acting like a suicidal maniac?" Owen asks as he crumples up his fortune and tosses it into my backseat.

Once again, his said the same thing, while mine changed to:

You make your own happiness.

Not helpful.

I tried to make my own happiness. I've tried for more than four days now and nada. So needless to say, mine got crumpled up and tossed into the backseat as well.

"Do you want the long version or the short version?" I ask, replying to Owen's question.

He glances out the window. "Well, seeing that we're about twenty seconds from the school and first period started five minutes ago, the short version."

"This is the fifth time I've lived this exact same day."

Owen's face scrunches up. "Okay, maybe I need the long version."

I turn in to the parking lot and find a spot in the back.

When I park the car, Owen makes no move to get out. He crosses his arms expectantly over his chest. "I'm waiting."

"You're already late."

"Precisely. I'm *already* late. So spill."

I let out a sigh and push back the hood of my sweatshirt.

Owen's eyes widen when he sees what I've done to my hair. "Holy crap! Ells, what did you do?"

I don't answer the question. It will all become clear soon enough. "Maybe this time I should start with the proof. It might speed things along."

"What proof?"

"Did you by chance have a dream about skinny-dipping with Principal Yates last night?"

8:55 a.m.

By the time I get to my first-period class twenty minutes later, I'm soaking wet and the class has already returned from school pictures.

"Do you have a pass?" Mr. Briggs asks as I waltz through the door and drop into my chair.

"Nope."

"Then I hope you have a very good excuse."

I shake my head. "Nope. Don't have one of those either."

He flashes me an aggravated look. "Well, then I have no choice but to write you up."

I nod. "I would expect nothing less."

"Ellie?" he asks, like he doesn't even recognize me.

I reach into my bag and pop a piece of gum into my mouth. Chewing gum isn't allowed in class. "Yeah?"

"What's gotten into you?"

I shrug. "What's gotten into *you*?"

Mr. Briggs's face turns a faint shade of purple. "You better watch it. Any more lip from you and I'll send you to see Principal Yates, and *that* will go on your permanent record."

I pop my gum. "I wouldn't bet on that."

The entire class snickers. Mr. Briggs stomps back to his desk, pulling a thick pad of pink slips from the top drawer and scribbling furiously. He rips off the top sheet. "Ellison Sparks. Out of my class. Now."

I release a heavy sigh, scoop up my bag, and walk to the front of the room to accept my fate.

"Well, it's been fun, boys and girls," I say to everyone. "Stay in school. Don't do drugs."

Then, with a salute, I disappear out the door.

There's a Bad Moon on the Rise

I make the long walk down to the principal's office. Normally, I would be freaking out right about now. In my sixteen years of life, I've never actually been sent to the principal's office. My only real exchanges with Principal Yates have been when she hands me another award for making the dean's list or having perfect attendance. (Well, if you don't count the run-ins I had with her this week, which I obviously don't.)

Past Ellie would be mortified right now. For her, this would be the equivalent of a walk of shame. But not me. Not anymore. That old Ellie is gone. She's been gobbled up by the universe and spit out like undigested food.

Now I couldn't care less what the principal thinks of me.

When I open the door to the main office, I'm surprised to see a familiar face waiting in one of the chairs outside of Principal Yates's door. His body is hunched over, his hands clasped between his knees.

"Owen?" I say in disbelief.

He picks up his head, a faint smile fighting its way to his lips. "Hey."

"What are you doing here?"

"I thought about what you said. About how there are no consequences. How nothing we do or say matters. And I figured, why not? So I gave the teacher a little taste of O-Town Filly."

O-Town Filly is the rapper name Owen gave himself in middle school when we were bored one night and stumbled upon an online Rapper Name generator.

Mine was Luscious E-Freeze.

Now he uses that name when he wants to think of himself as hard-core.

I shoot him a dubious look. "You told off Mrs. Leach?"

"Yes." His lips say the words, but his eyes give him away.

"Let the record show that the witness is lying."

He bows his head again, his voice losing all the bravado it had only a second ago. "Okay, okay. She sent me here for being more than thirty minutes late to class and I didn't have a pass."

I bite my lip. "I'm sorry, O."

He shrugs. "It won't matter tomorrow, right?"

"Nope. Not in the slightest."

He rubs anxiously at his chin. I can tell he's still trying to process what I told him in the car. Make sense of it. Basically the same thing I've been doing for the past five days. "So. Let me get this straight. You and"—he won't say his name; he never says his name—"*blondie* had a fight yesterday."

"Sunday. Which was four days ago for me."

"Right. And today he's going to break up with you. But yesterday—or yesterday for you—you were able to stop him from breaking up with you because you dressed up like a stripper?"

Okay, when he puts it that way, it does sound kind of ridiculous. "In a nutshell, yes."

"But today you woke up and it was still the same day."

I nod. "And I have no idea why."

"But," Owen argues, biting his lip, "wouldn't he have just broken up with you anyway?"

"What? Why?"

"Because that wasn't *you*. You were playing a part. You said so yourself. You would never have been able to keep that act up forever and eventually he would have ended it anyway."

"You don't know that," I say quickly.

He shrugs. "No, but . . ."

"But what?"

"Never mind."

"No. Finish your statement, counselor."

I sense another fight coming on and I really really don't want to argue with Owen again.

"What happened *after* he didn't break up with you?"

I have a feeling that's not what he started to say only a minute ago but I don't object. "I left the carnival, Tristan went to hang out with the band, and then . . ."

Tell him, I urge myself. *Tell him the truth. We hung out. We had a blast. He hustled a carnival employee at the ring toss game. And then we got into the worst fight of our friendship.*

"And then?" he prompts.

"And then . . . nothing," I finish.

Why did I say that? Why can't I just tell him? He deserves to know the truth.

He gets very quiet, staring at his hands. Then finally he says, "Ellie. Can I ask you something?"

I have no idea where this is going, but for some reason I feel a lump form in my stomach.

"Sure" is what I say, but it's a big fat lie. I'm most certainly *not* sure about anything anymore. If anything, I'm one hundred percent unsure about everything.

He runs a hand through his hair. It's not a casual gesture. It's a conflicted one. He looks like he wants to tug the strands out by the roots. "Do you think you could ever—"

The door to Principal Yates's office swings open and her large frame fills up the entire doorway. She looks at each of us in turn, seemingly deciding which one she wants to deal with first.

She sighs. "Mr. Reitzman."

It was a wise choice. Save the most difficult for last.

He stands and follows Principal Yates, but before he disappears into the temple of doom, he catches my eye. I notice something in his gaze. An intensity I've never seen before. It stirs up emotions deep in my chest. Emotions I don't even recognize.

I don't like it.

I don't approve of whatever invisible electricity is surging between us right now.

"Behave in there," I tease with a suggestive raise of my eyebrows. "The pool is only a few steps down the hall, you know."

We both stifle a laugh as Owen continues into the office and Principal Yates shuts the door behind them.

Just like that, Owen is Owen again. The boy who convinced me to climb a telephone pole at summer camp seven years ago.

And I'm . . .

Well, the jury is still out on that one.

Hold On! I'm Comin'

9:32 a.m.

Principal Yates gave me detention. She looked all torn up about it, too. Like it pained her to do it. Owen, I discovered from a text message later, skated by with a warning, but since I was late *and* talked smack to Mr. Briggs, I'm apparently the bigger threat to school security.

When Principal Yates asked me what I had learned from this morning's events, I told her I'd meditate on the question and get back to her.

She gave me detention for tomorrow, too.

To this, I snorted. "Wouldn't that be nice? If there actually *was* a tomorrow?"

Then she tacked on detention for Wednesday.

Wow, I really am John Bender from *The Breakfast Club.*

Ellison Sparks: Wanted Criminal. I kind of like the sound of that.

I don't meet Tristan at his locker before third period because there's really no point. I could argue and plead and change my look and follow all the commandments in the world and it wouldn't matter. He's either going to break up with me or he's not and tomorrow it won't make one bit of difference.

I ignore him all through Spanish class. When that stupid, suicidal bird flies into the window and everyone makes a big stink about it, I yell, "Oh shut up, he'll be alive again in the morning."

Throughout the whole period, I sense Tristan trying to get my attention. But I'm too busy sleeping on my desk to be bothered with relationship drama.

Can't he see I'm tired?

I've had a very long week.

When the bell rings, I grab my stuff and disappear into the hallway. He catches up with me a few seconds later and grabs my arm, pulling me into an alcove between lockers.

"What's up with you?" he asks. "Are you still mad about last night?"

"Nope. Not mad."

I try to walk away, but he blocks me. "Then what's gotten into you? And what did you do to your hair?"

"I don't know what you mean."

He sighs, shifting his weight. "You *are* mad. Look, I want to talk about what happened. About the fight."

"Tristan. I'm not mad. I just don't give a crap. Okay?"

I push past him and walk away. This time, he's too stunned to try to stop me.

11:20 a.m.

In third period, I fail my American history quiz, but that's probably because instead of circling one of the multiple choice answers, I write in my own.

Britain met its manpower needs during the Revolution by:
A) Raising the recruiting bonus
B) Lowering physical requirements
C) Hiring foreign troops
D) All of the above
E) Selling Erotic Harry Potter Fan Fiction Online

12:40 p.m.

During lunch, I make a bunch of new friends outside in the parking lot. They sit in their cars and smoke cigarettes and talk about TV shows I've never even heard of, but definitely need to record on my DVR. Who knew this was where the cool kids were hanging out the whole time?

When we sneak back into the cafeteria before lunch is over, I notice the cheerleader bake sale in the corner and the long line of people waiting to hand over their money.

Daphne Gray is at the microphone, announcing that this is the last chance to buy baked goods to help support the team.

I excuse myself from my new acquaintances, strut over, and grab the microphone from her hand.

"Um, excuse me," she protests. "What are you doing?"

I ignore her. "I would like to make a public safety announcement. It really pains me to be the one to tell you this, but unfortunately Daphne Gray had explosive diarrhea yesterday when she was making some of these yummy treats, and she did *not* wash her hands before handling the ingredients. I just thought you should all know. The banana bread is delicious though. *Bon appétit!*"

I step off the stage and do nothing to hide my smirk as I watch the long line of people scatter. Daphne calls my name, but I don't respond. I have nothing to say to her so I keeping walking.

I'm almost to the hallway when I hear Daphne's voice come back over the loudspeaker. "You little skank!"

I stop, still facing the door.

"Everyone knows Tristan Wheeler only started dating you because of how desperate you were to get into his bed."

The cafeteria suddenly gets very quiet. Or maybe that's just the ringing in my ears drowning everyone out.

I slowly turn around and stalk purposefully back to the table. I just remembered I *do* have something to say to Daphne Gray.

She sees me coming and crosses her arms over her chest, like she's challenging me to come closer. I climb the three steps up the tiny stage, cock my fist back, and shove it into her face.

We Gotta Get Out of This Place

1:08 p.m.

I've never been in a fight before. It's kind of anticlimactic. I was expecting epic throwdowns and slow-motion spin kicks, but it's actually just a lot of hair pulling and screaming and hands in faces.

"That night was supposed to be about *us*!" Daphne growls as she rolls me over and straddles me. "I threw that party for Tristan and me! Not so you could swoop in and steal him!"

Well, that makes a lot of sense. At least now I know why Daphne Gray hates me so much.

I push her off me and jump to my feet. "Then why was he sitting outside by the pool bored out of his freaking mind?"

She roars and charges me, shoving me into the circle of students that have surrounded us. They're all yelling and egging us on. I can't exactly make out what they're saying, but I think most of them are rooting for Daphne.

Surprise, surprise.

A dozen hands push me back into the ring just as Principal Yates breaks the whole thing up.

"Thank God you're here!" Daphne cries. "Ellison Sparks attacked me out of nowhere!"

I roll my eyes. How original.

"Sparks!" Principal Yates bellows. "Back into my office."

"I have a speech to give in like two minutes. I have students to inspire," I protest, slightly breathless from our skirmish.

Principal Yates drags me by the elbow into the hallway. "Not anymore you don't."

1:30 p.m.

Rhiannon Marshall is going to be livid. I've been in the principal's office for the past fifteen minutes. She's probably tearing her hair out wondering where I am. The mental image does kind of make me smile.

Principal Yates has been yammering on, but I haven't been paying a lot of attention. I'm too busy contemplating what I should do with my hair next. I was thinking maybe a really crazy spiral perm. Or maybe I'll dye it purple. I've always wanted purple hair.

"I have no choice but to suspend you from school for a week," I hear the principal say.

I lazily turn my attention back to her. "Only a week? Why not a month? Why not forever?"

She sighs like she's completely given up. "What has gotten into you? Last week you were one of my most promising students, and today it's like you're an entirely different person."

"A lot can happen in a week," I mumble.

1:50 p.m.

I'm supposed to wait for my parents to come pick me up. Apparently suspended students are not allowed to drive themselves home. But as you can probably guess, I'm not really inclined to do what I'm supposed to.

Instead, I wait for Owen outside his seventh-period class. When he rounds the corner and sees me, his eyes go all wide. Before he has a chance to say anything, I grab him by the elbow and pull him into a nearby janitor's closet.

It only takes me a few seconds to realize it's the same closet Tristan and I made out in yesterday. Not that it matters.

"What's going on?" he asks, glancing uneasily around the small, cramped space. "Why do you smell like cigarette smoke?"

"Never mind that."

"And why is Daphne Gray spreading some ludicrous rumor that you started a fight with her?"

"Oh, that's not a rumor. That's true."

He drops his bag to the floor with a thud. "Ells, what's going on with you?"

I groan. "We've been through this. I told you what's going on with me."

"Yeah, but you? Fighting?"

"Look, it doesn't matter. I need to get out of here and you need to come with me."

He presses his lips together, looking very torn. "I don't know, Ells."

"C'mon! My parents are going to be here any second!"

"Your parents? Why?"

"Principal Yates suspended me."

I think Owen's head might actually explode. "What? For how long?"

"Does it matter? Let's go!"

He hesitates. "Ditching school? I don't know. I'm already on Yates's watch list today. I can't get into any more trouble."

I let out a frustrated growl. "Owen. Have you not listened to a single word I've said? There is no trouble. There are no consequences!"

He shifts his weight, clearly conflicted.

I rest my hands on his shoulders, forcing him to look at me, but instead he looks at my hands. "O, what would you do if there was no tomorrow? If you could do anything and it wouldn't matter?"

"I don't know, Ellie. What if you're wrong?"

"Objection. I'm never wrong."

"Objection. I can think of plenty of times you were wrong."

"Like when?"

"I have two words for you: spray tan."

"Withdrawn. But listen, Owen, I'm not wrong this time. You've gotta trust me on this. How long have we played by their rules? Done everything we're supposed to do? Don't you think it's time for O-Town Filly and Luscious E-Freeze to have a little fun?"

I can almost hear the wheels clicking into place inside his mind. I can almost see his inner rebel pushing its way to the surface.

A cunning smile finally breaks through his hesitation. "What did you have in mind?"

Money (That's What I Want)

2:05 p.m.

"I'd like to make a withdrawal please," I say sweetly to the bank teller. I can tell my ratty, stained hoodie is making her nervous. Not to mention the bruise that's forming under my left eye from Daphne's mean right hook.

I slide my debit card across the counter along with my driver's license. She double-checks the picture against my face several times, looking extremely skeptical. "I got a haircut," I tell her, primping my choppy, uneven locks. "Do you like it?"

"How much do you want to withdraw?" she asks, ignoring my question.

I'll take that as a no.

"All of it," I tell her.

She frowns. "All of it?"

"Yup. Every last cent."

"Are you closing the account?"

"No. I just want all my money."

She doesn't seem to follow. "Did you experience any dissatisfaction with our bank?"

"Nope. Just want the money."

She gives me another dubious look before punching a few buttons on her keyboard. "How would you like it? Hundreds? Twenties?"

"I'll take singles," I say. I glance at Owen. "Then we can roll in it like gangstas!"

He gives his head a sad shake in reply.

The teller does little to hide her annoyance as she begins counting out three thousand two hundred and forty-nine dollars of my hard-earned money in one-dollar bills. I shoot Owen a toothy grin and stuff the cash into my bag. "Let's go."

Our first stop is the supermarket to stock up on sustenance. We push the cart down the aisle and dump every single junky, chemical-filled, sugar-bloated food we can find—all the things my parents never allow me to eat—right into the cart.

As we wait at the checkout line, I grab every cheesy gossip magazine on the rack and toss them onto the conveyor belt. The majority of them have the same story on the cover—a famous heiress is marrying some middle-class former intern of her father's company. Apparently they met when her dad forced her to work a bunch of low-wage jobs in order to earn her trust fund and the intern was assigned to be her chaperone. The tabloids are calling it the role-reversal Cinderella story of the decade.

Owen grabs boxes of candy and gum from the impulse shelf and overturns the contents onto the conveyor. "See?" I ask. "Isn't this fun?"

"That depends. We aren't going to get tattoos next, are we?"

My eyes light up. "Ooh!"

"No," Owen say sternly.

"It'll be gone by morning!"

"So why suffer through the pain?"

"Good point."

We skip the tattoos and instead spend the rest of the afternoon driving around town, eating junk food until we nearly throw up. I bought purple dye at the supermarket, and like the fugitives that we are, Owen helps me dye my hair in a gas station bathroom. But we don't really follow the directions too closely and my hair ends up looking more green than purple.

We spend the rest of the evening pigging out on appetizers and desserts at the fanciest restaurant in town. At first they didn't want to seat us, but I slipped the hostess a wad of singles and suddenly it wasn't a problem.

"Can we be serious for a minute?" Owen asks from across the white linen tablecloth.

I bring the empty sundae bowl to my lips and tip back my head, slurping down the last melty gooey drops of ice cream. "There's nothing more serious than this sundae," I say, setting the bowl back down. Several people are staring at us, but ask me if I care.

Owen laughs and reaches out with his napkin to wipe chocolate syrup from my face.

"I mean it."

"So do I! It was amazing."

Owen gives me a harsh look, and I plant my hands in my lap and give him my most somber-looking face. "Yes, Owen?" I ask in a deep, serious voice.

"What is this about?"

"What is what about?"

He gestures around the restaurant. "This? This day. The

junk food and the hair and the driving like a maniac and the—"

"I told you," I interrupt. "There are no consequences! So I can do whatever I want!" I yell this last part, attracting even more attention.

Owen cringes. I have a feeling he's not fully getting the whole "no consequences" thing because he still seems way too concerned about what people think of us.

"You can keep saying that all you want," Owen says, keeping his voice frustratingly low. "But I know you, Ellie, and none of this stuff is you."

"That's the whole point!" I don't know why, but there's a sudden sharpness to my tone. Why is he trying to ruin all the fun with his stupid serious questions?

"*What's* the whole point?"

"Being someone else!" I shout. "Not having to be yourself anymore."

"What's wrong with yourself?"

I throw my hands in the air. "Everything! I'm too dramatic. I'm too clingy. I'm too jealous. I'm not a Creature of Mystery. I'm not a cool cucumber. I'm a skank who Tristan only asked out because I'm desperate to get into his bed!"

That, apparently, was a bit too far. A man in a crisp dark suit approaches our table. He doesn't look pleased by my commentary.

"Excuse me, miss. I'm afraid we're going to have to ask you to leave the restaurant. You're disrupting the dining experience of our other guests."

"And!" I shout to Owen. "I'm disruptive!"

"Please, miss. If you don't remove yourself from this table, we're going to have to remove you ourselves."

This makes me laugh. Like really, really laugh. The idea of me being physically manhandled by restaurant security is too much.

"Oh yeah?" I snap to the man in the suit. "I'm sure you've got, like, five burly men with earpieces in the back just waiting for something to do."

The man in the suit—who I assume must be the manager—motions to someone behind me. Before I can crack another joke, I'm actually being lifted out of my seat by at least three pairs of hands. They jostle me through the restaurant and stand me up on the curb outside. Owen walks out a moment later carrying both of our bags. He doesn't look happy.

"Well, that was fun." The sarcasm is practically dripping down his chin.

I sigh. "Just shut up, okay? I don't want to fight again."

Confusion flashes over Owen's face. "Again?"

Uh-oh. I've said too much. I was really hoping to keep our fight last night to myself.

I start walking toward the parking lot. "What should we do next? Rob a convenience store?"

But Owen is suddenly in front of me. "Why did you say 'again'?"

"Forget it." I try to sidestep him, but he blocks my path.

"No, I won't forget it."

The electric rush of this day seeps out of me, deflating me like a balloon. "Fine." I huff out an exaggerated sigh. "We had a fight. A big one. Okay?"

"When?"

"Yesterday. And the day before. But yesterday was the big one."

The conflicted expression on Owen's face pains me. "What was it about?"

"The Ferris wheel? Tristan? I really don't know. One minute we were fine, joking around, and the next you were accusing me of being on Mute."

"On Mute?" he repeats.

"Yeah. You said when I'm around Tristan I play dead."

Owen averts his eyes, almost embarrassed. "I said that?"

"Yup."

"What about the day before that? What was that fight about?"

I sigh. "Book club, I guess."

He scoffs incredulously. "Book club?"

"Yeah, you accused me of having read the book or something."

"And?" he prompts. "Did you read the book?"

I press my lips together and look toward the fairgrounds. From here, I can just see the top of the Ferris wheel, all lit up and spinning. Tristan's band won't be playing tonight. I didn't go get him the gig and I never had the conversation with Owen about it for Daphne to overhear. The stage will be dark tonight.

"Ells?"

"Yeah, I read the book, okay? I read all the books."

Owen rubs at his eyebrow. "You read all the books for book club but didn't want to join?" He laughs at this last part, and I admit it's kind of amusing. As far as dirty little secrets go, mine ranks somewhere near the severity of a hidden stamp collection. "Why would you do that?"

I scuff the ground with the toe of my shoe. "I don't know. I wanted to read them. They sounded good."

"But you didn't want to join because it would get in the way of your time with him."

Owen is not asking this as a question. He's stating it as a fact. Because he knows me so well. Too well sometimes, it seems.

"What does it matter now?!" I yell. "He's going to break up with me and I'm going to wake up tomorrow and you're not going to remember any of this and I'll have to start all over again."

My voice breaks and I can feel the tears welling up again.

I'm so tired of crying.

I'm so tired of losing.

I'm just so tired.

Suddenly Owen's arms are around me. His shoulder is cradling my forehead. His chin is resting atop my crazy, greenish-purple hair.

His shirt absorbs my tears. His strong arms absorb my shudders.

The Owen that I've known for nearly half my life—my best friend—absorbs a little piece of my heartbreak.

"Maybe this is it?" he whispers into my ear as he gently strokes my back. "Maybe you'll wake up tomorrow and it'll be Tuesday."

"It won't," I say miserably. "I'm stuck in this day forever."

I can feel his chest rising and falling in short breaths. I can feel his heart pounding under my cheek.

"Maybe," he begins again, "we should go to the last night of the carnival. You know, just in case you're wrong."

I sniffle and lift my head. Our eyes lock together in a way they've never done before. It's the kind of look that changes things. Things you never thought you wanted to change.

Owen reaches down and brushes the wetness from my

cheeks. His face is only inches from mine. I can feel his breath on my lips.

"If I'm wrong," I say softly, "I'm going to have a *lot* of explaining to do tomorrow."

Then we both break into uncontrollable laughter.

It's Been a Hard Day's Night

8:05 p.m.

"We have a winner!"

Owen leaps into the air and pumps his fist. "Oh yeah! Who's the man? That's right, it's ME!"

I laugh and once again stare incredulously at the five rings resting on the five bottle necks. A group of spectators have gathered once again, and it suddenly dawns on me that *this* was the crowd I had to push my way through that first night, when Tristan broke up with me and I ran away in tears. Owen seemed to appear out of nowhere to ask me what was wrong. But it wasn't out of nowhere. He was playing this game.

"Someone's been practicing," the employee comments.

Owen stops dancing and shoves his hands in his pockets. "Nah, I think it was just beginner's luck." He turns to me and points at the prizes. "Which one do you want?"

"I think you know which one I want."

We share a knowing smile before he turns back to the booth. "We'll take the poodle."

The employee hands me the stuffed dog and we push our way through the onlookers. I lead Owen to the horse race game and take a seat at number four this time. Owen tries his luck at number five. "Let's see if your skills transfer," I challenge.

We feed our dollars into the machine and the buzzer rings. As soon as the little red ball is released, I grab it and send it rolling upward with a subtle flick of my wrist. It sinks right into hole number three. My horse moves three paces forward.

"Aha!" I cry out.

Owen looks up at the horses. "Did you win already?"

"No. I just finally managed to get the stupid ball into the stupid hole. It's all in the wrist."

I sink three more balls into holes two and three over the course of the race, but I still don't win. At least I'm not in last place this time when the buzzer rings. I consider that an improvement.

"I don't like this game," Owen complains, getting up to leave. I glance at the scoreboard. Horse number five is still at the starting line.

I laugh. "I guess your skills *don't* transfer."

"Let's go do something else."

As we make our way through the aisle of carnival games, I catch sight of a slender raven-haired girl standing alone near a concession stand. I immediately recognize her as the new girl who just moved from L.A.

"Sophia!" I call out and she turns around, but there's absolutely no recognition on her face.

"It's me. Ellie. We met at lunch, remember?"

It's clear she doesn't remember, and then it dawns on me. That wasn't today. That was *yesterday*, when Tristan and I were practically entangled in the cafeteria. I stopped her from getting tripped by Cole Simpson and she came and sat with us.

"Sorry," she says, "are you in one of my classes?"

I'm about to mumble "Never mind" and get out of there, when a guy in dark jeans and a black sweater appears holding a cotton candy and a soft pretzel. It's the same guy I saw her holding hands with during Tristan's show a few nights ago. He gives Owen and me a once-over as he hands Sophia the cotton candy.

"Thanks," she says, and when she looks at him, I see the same doting expression I saw the other night. Not last night—last night she was alone—but *two* nights ago.

Then a startling realization hits me.

This is the guy she spilled food all over in the cafeteria. She only met him because Cole Simpson tripped her with his bag. Yesterday, I stopped that from happening and she came to the carnival alone. Today, I wasn't around to prevent it, and they're here together.

Is it possible that something good actually came out of Cole Simpson being a total jerk?

"Well, it was nice to meet you . . ." Sophia says, fishing for my name.

"Ellie," I say, then point at Owen, "and this is Owen."

"I'm Sophia, and this is Nate. Maybe we'll see you around school?"

I nod. "Yeah. See ya."

I watch them walk away, shoulders brushing. Nate reaches over and tries to steal a piece of Sophia's cotton candy. She giggles and pulls it away, but he snags it anyway. She does the same thing with his pretzel.

"Friends of yours?" Owen asks.

I shake my head. "Just someone who I thought needed help, but it turned out she didn't."

A few more seconds pass and Owen asks, "So, are we going to stalk them, too?"

I laugh and punch him on the arm. "Shut up."

"I'm just asking so I can be prepared. I should warn you, though, I left all my spy gear in my other pants."

I start walking. "You're obnoxious."

"I'll tell you right now, though," Owen says, trying and failing to sound serious. "There's no way that Nate guy can rock the ring toss as well as me and Dr. Johnson."

"Halloway," I correct him. "And about that, are you going to tell me how you did it or what?"

Owen shrugs. "I told you. Beginner's luck."

"No way. I don't believe you. You have to have been practicing. Do you have, like, a ring toss game set up in your basement or something?"

He guffaws. "Um, that would be weird."

I grab on to his arm and give it a petulant tug. "Then tell me!"

"Nope."

"Owen!"

He playfully yanks his arm from my grasp, trying to get away, but our hands catch, and for a moment we're just standing there, both staring down at our tangled fingers, wondering what to do next. Wondering who will let go first.

"There you are," a voice says, breaking into the bubble that seemed to have formed around Owen and me. My head whips up in surprise and I see Tristan standing in front of us. His eyes are locked on our intertwined fingers.

I pull my hand free and let it fall to my side.

Tristan clears his throat. "I've been looking everywhere for you. Where have you been?"

I take a step sideways, away from Owen. "Here. At the carnival."

"I figured," he says. His voice is so monotone. Like a blank white wall with no pictures. "You weren't answering your phone or any of my texts so I thought I'd try to find you here."

"My phone is busted." I keep my voice equally flat.

Tristan's gaze darts between me and Owen. "Can we, um, talk?"

I turn to Owen. "I'll just . . . give me a minute?"

"Sure. Whatever." I don't miss the irritable edge to his words as he walks away.

Tristan nods his head toward a nearby bench—the same bench where he first broke up with me, where this crazy Alice in Wonderland of a week started. "Do you wanna sit down?"

"No, I'll stand."

Tristan shifts his weight nervously from foot to foot. "Okay. Um. I'm not sure where I should start. I just came by to talk to you about something, and I didn't want to do it over the phone."

"Yeah, yeah, you're breaking up with me," I say impatiently. "What's your lame excuse this time?"

I am *so* not in the mood to stand here and listen to this same babbling speech all over again. I figure I better just move things right along.

Tristan flinches, looking completely taken aback. "Uh . . ." he stammers.

"I'm too clingy? We're not a match? Something is broken. What?"

"Something *is* broken," Tristan says, sounding relieved that I plucked the words right out of his head. "I'm just not sure what it is."

"Have you ever stopped to think that maybe *you're* the one who's broken?"

For a moment, Tristan is completely speechless. Then he appears to gather his thoughts. "I just don't want any drama in my life."

"Oh, right!" I say, like I'm having some big epiphany. "The *drama*!" My voice is loud enough to attract the attention of passersby. I can tell the attention—and my volume—is making Tristan uncomfortable. So I keep going. "You and your drama queens! You don't want *any* drama. You just wanna sail through life on the smoothest, glassiest sea. And as soon as you get one inkling of an incoming wave, you jump ship. *Sayonara,* baby. Isn't that right, Tristan?" I practically spit his name.

He opens his mouth to say something, but only a stutter of air comes out.

But I'm just getting warmed up. "Well, I'm sorry. Sometimes life is dramatic. Sometimes relationships are dramatic. You go out with all these girls and then you end up dumping them for the exact. Same. Reason. Every time. They're too crazy. They're insane enough to actually *want* your undivided attention. What a novel concept! Here's a hint for you. Girls don't like it when you Snapchat with other girls! Girls don't like it when you flirt with other girls right in front of them. This is not rocket science. *We* are not rocket science! Did it ever occur to you that maybe you bring out the crazy in these girls? Did it ever occur to you that maybe they're dramatic *because* of you? No. Of course not. You're too busy picking them apart, finding reasons not to be with them anymore, and then trying to pass those reasons off as 'feelings' so you can claim to just be 'staying true to what you feel.' I'd be willing to bet that if you actually dated the kind of girl you think you want to date, you'd get bored with her in a matter of minutes and dump her anyway. So how is this, Tristan?" I raise my voice another few decibels, shouting for the whole carnival to hear. "Is this dramatic enough for you?"

Tristan eyes the growing circle of nosy eavesdroppers around us. "Uh," he falters, "I'm sorry, Ellie. I really am."

"Yes, I know," I tell him, "and this is how much I care."

I turn, grab the first guy I see—I think he's actually a freshman at my school—and plant a big, wet, sloppy kiss on his lips. By the time he unfreezes from the shock and starts to kiss me back, I'm already pushing him away and disappearing into the crowd.

What a Wonderful World

8:33 p.m.

There's a funny thing that happens when you have all the time in the world. Theoretically, you would think there'd be no rush. You can slow down. You can take a thousand steps to reach a destination that's only ten steps away. But it's actually the opposite. When time is on your side, you suddenly have this burning desire to make the most of it.

When I find Owen loitering next to a popcorn cart, I grab his hand and don't let go.

I walk fast, dragging him behind me, not looking back until we've reached the very front of the line. I pull every last dollar bill I have out of my bag and thrust it at the short female carnival employee. "We want to get on this thing *now*."

She doesn't even bat an eye. She pockets the wad of cash, yanks on a lever, and an empty car slows in front of us. "It's all yours," she says, gesturing to the two side-by-side seats.

My stomach is on spin cycle. I'm squeezing Owen's hand so tightly, I'm sure his fingers are white.

"Ells, you don't have to do this," he says quietly.

"No," I tell him. "I do. It's exactly what I have to do, and you're the exact person I have to do it with."

I draw in a long inhale—a breath I'll probably hold until my feet are back on solid ground—and plop myself down on the seat. Owen sits next to me, watching my reaction carefully as the carnival employee lowers the safety bar and locks it into place.

That's it? That's all that stands between me and certain death?

A flimsy metal bar.

Relax, I command myself. *It'll all be over soon.*

"What was it you said to me when I wouldn't climb the telephone pole?"

Owen is rigid beside me. Nervous about how nervous I am. "I told you that falling was the best part."

I watch the employee yank on her death lever and we jerk backward. I scream and squeeze Owen's hand tighter. He squeezes back.

"Something tells me that same piece of advice doesn't apply here," I squeak.

Owen laughs. "No, it doesn't."

The Ferris wheel continues to move. We're sailing backward and then up. The platform is no longer beneath us. Now there's only air. I watch the ground get farther and farther away beneath my dangling feet.

"I can't!" I shut my eyes. "Oh my God, Owen. This was a bad idea. I can't do this."

How did I ever think this was romantic? This is about the least romantic thing I've ever done. I feel like I'm going to throw up. I feel like I'm actually going to heave not only the food in my stomach, but my entire stomach as well. Spleen, liver, kidneys, everything!

How are we still going? How are we still rising? Does this thing ever stop?

Just as the thought enters my mind, I feel a shudder and the world jerks to a halt.

"Oh God. This is it, isn't it? It's broken. There's a screw loose. We're going to die up here!"

"Ellie," Owen whispers next to me, his hand still firmly clasped in mine. "We're not going to die. Open your eyes."

I shake my head obstinately. "No. I'd rather die with my eyes closed."

He chuckles. "No, you wouldn't. You're not that kind of girl."

"I think I've somehow managed to fool you into thinking I'm someone I'm not."

There's silence next to me, and for a minute I consider opening my eyes just to check that Owen is still there. That he hasn't slipped out from under this bar and plummeted to the ground. He could easily slide right out from under this thing. He's skinny, you know. Well, at least he used to be. Before he totally bulked up over the summer without telling me.

Then I realize I'm still holding his hand. He's still there.

"I know exactly who you are," Owen says, but I can tell he's not looking at me when he says it. His words get swept up by the wind.

I open my eyes and my heart hitches.

It's breathtaking up here. So beautiful. And quiet. And terrifying.

We're so high. It's like the world is nothing but a scale model. One of those 3-D re-creations you see in museums. The lights of our little town are twinkling far below. I can even see Providence Boulevard, the main road that leads to the fairgrounds. I follow it with my eyes—one, two, three, four stoplights—then I turn left, and another left.

"Look!" I release Owen's hand and point. "I can see my house." I backtrack three streets. "And there's yours!"

Owen chuckles at my enthusiasm. "Pretty cool, huh?"

"It's like we're gods or something. Even the air is different up here."

"Gods," he repeats, trying the word on for size. "I like it. I'll be the god of wit and frivolity."

I snort. "That's not a real god."

"Yeah, because realism is what we're going for here."

"Fine. Then I'm the god of classic rock."

"I thought that was Jim Morrison."

"You're right. I really can't take that from him."

"Besides, you're clearly the god of Mondays."

I groan. "Don't remind me."

"How many has this been again?"

"Five."

"And you *still* haven't managed to watch the season finale of *Assumed Guilty* yet?"

"I've been busy."

"That's a load of cobblers."

I snort. "A what?"

"It means a lot of rubbish."

"Right."

"I'm telling you," Owen says righteously, "you have to watch that episode. You're missing out."

I peer over the side of our car at the carnival below. "Actually, I don't think I am."

I can see the ring toss game and the bumper cars and even

the concession stand where Annabelle and Dr. Jason Halloway shared their milk shake. It's all there. Everything on my little fantasy date checklist. I suddenly feel silly for thinking I could re-create a night I witnessed between two strangers six years ago. Who has a fantasy date checklist?

Is there anything *less* romantic than a checklist?

It's like I became so obsessed with doing things right, I forgot to enjoy them.

Feeling bold, I lean forward in my seat, trying to view the rest of the carnival, but the bucket starts to tip. I let out a yelp and grab Owen's hand again, bolting upright.

He laughs. "Don't worry. It's supposed to tip."

All of my former confidence has vanished. "I don't like the tipping."

"But the tipping is so fun."

I shake my head. "I swear, if you rock this thing on purpose, I will kill you in your sleep and make it look like a mafia hit."

I smile as soon as I realize I've stolen his own words and used them against him.

A far-off look crosses his face. It's almost as though he can remember the words. The entire conversation. Maybe all the conversations. Like some distant reverberation through space. A ghostly echo through time.

But of course that's impossible. He can't remember those other conversations. Those alternate versions of us. They live somewhere else. In another universe.

And we live here.

In this one.

He squeezes my hand. "Don't worry. I won't let you fall."

My gaze drifts to him. "I thought falling was the best part."

His laughter has faded but the amusement still lingers in his eyes. He lets go of my hand only long enough to lace his fingers through mine. It's the subtlest shift—a simple rearrangement of extremities—and yet it makes all the difference in the world.

"It can be," he murmurs softly.

My throat is dry. My stomach is still churning, but now I don't know if it's because I'm an acrophobic who's suspended two hundred feet in the air, or if it's something else.

What am I really afraid of?

What is truly paralyzing me right now?

Is it the height? The thought of plunging to my death?

Or is it the fact that Owen is right here? Right now. Moving closer to me. Leaning into me. His lips parted, his eyes soft yet focused.

Or maybe it's the realization that he's been here the whole time.

I can feel myself being drawn into him. It's an unfamiliar sensation. The desire to be closer to Owen. The sudden desperate need to know what his lips taste like. For just a fleeting second, the rest of the carnival disappears. The lights flicker out. The noise mutes. We are no longer dangling from the top of a Ferris wheel. We're dangling from the top of the world.

And the fall would definitely kill us both.

I close my eyes. The nearness of him is tangible. I feel it in my toes. His hand is cold as it rests upon my cheek, yet the warmth spreads through my entire body.

"Ellie," he breathes, knocking the wind out of me.

His hand guides me closer to him, steering my mouth to his. Our lips barely brush. I feel it everywhere.

The Ferris wheel jolts violently, pulling us apart as I let out another startled shriek. Our eyes meet for one long, tense moment before Owen looks away, taking his hand and his warmth and his air with him.

Then suddenly we're moving again. Descending from the skies. Coming back down to earth.

I Second That Emotion

8:48 p.m.

The first thing I see when our car reaches the platform at the bottom is my mother. She's standing next to my father and neither one of them looks very happy.

The operator stops the ride and raises our safety bar. I step off and walk hesitantly over to my parents. I'm barely within earshot when my mother yells, "What on earth were you thinking!?"

Talk about a return to reality.

Yikes.

I'm not the kind of kid who gets in trouble very often, but I know better than to respond. Anything I say will only make matters worse.

"You got suspended from school for *fighting*?"

I almost laugh when my mother says it. It does sound too incredible to be true. Of all the things anyone would expect me to get suspended for, starting a fight with another student is definitely near the bottom of the list. Staging a sit-in to demand better-quality textbooks? Maybe. Arguing with a teacher over an unfair grade? Probably. But physical violence? No way.

"Do you have anything to say?" my mother asks.

I turn to my dad, who gives me a subtle warning shake of the head. The message is understood. *Stay silent if I want to keep my fingers and toes.*

"No," I mumble.

"Well, I hope you know you're grounded," my mom goes on. "Starting first thing tomorrow."

Owen and I share a conspiratorial look.

My mother grabs me by the elbow and steers me toward the parking lot like a toddler.

I don't even have a chance to say goodbye to Owen.

9:45 p.m.

Hugging my newly won poodle to my chest, I sit on my bed and stare at the window. For the past thirty minutes, I've done nothing but wait.

Will Owen even show up?

Or does he only climb through the window after he's seen me cry?

I can't make sense of what happened between us tonight. I'm not sure I even want to try. But I know that I want to see him again. I *have* to see him again.

My phone is still lying in a broken heap at the foot of my mirror, so I keep getting up and checking my laptop screen for the time. At what point does the whole thing reset? Midnight? 7:04 in the morning, when the first text message from Tristan comes through?

What if I don't go to sleep?

Will everything just fade away? Will my vision cloud over? Will it be like fainting?

Tap tap tap.

I jump up and run to the window, yanking it open. Owen falls clumsily inside, like a baby giraffe trying to stand for the first time. I laugh and help him to his feet. Then we just stare at each other, neither one of us sure what comes next, or even what to say.

I break the ice first. "I didn't know if you'd come."

"I didn't know if you'd want me to."

"I do. I mean, I did." I huff, feeling flustered. "I'm glad you're here."

He nods, and then it's that stupid silence again. The kind that never used to exist between us. The kind that makes me feel like I'm stumbling around in the dark looking for a light switch that has always been right there.

"So, are you busted big-time?" he asks, and I'm grateful for the lightheartedness of his tone.

I plop down on the bed and pull the poodle back onto my lap. "Yeah. Good thing they won't remember it tomorrow, huh?"

He sits down next to me, but keeps his gaze glued to the floor. "Yeah. Good thing." But there's an uncertainty in his words. A hesitation.

"I'm really glad I didn't get the tattoo. I might not be alive right now."

He laughs, but doesn't respond. We just sit there, awkwardly facing the window, saying nothing. I'm itching to check the clock on my laptop again, convinced that an eternity has passed.

"Why does this feel weird?" Owen finally asks.

I breathe out a sigh. "I don't know."

"Was it weird the other nights when I climbed through your window?"

"No. It was . . . you know, like it always is."

"What did we talk about?"

I smile at the memory. "One night we talked about Hippo."

"He needs a new name," Owen declares, grabbing the stuffed animal from behind him. "Calling something by its literal genus is not a real name."

I smile. "That's what you said before, too."

"Well, what can I say? Alternate me is a smart guy."

"And the other night, we talked about what was happening to me."

"That's only two nights," he points out. "I thought you said this is your fifth day."

"It is."

"So what happened the other nights?"

I pull my legs up and hug them to my chest. "The third night I didn't see you at the carnival so you never came, and last night, we got into that fight."

"Right," Owen says, sounding distant. "The fight. You've been doing a lot of fighting lately."

I laugh. It lightens the mood somewhat. "Tell me about it."

"We could watch *Assumed Guilty*," he suggests, nodding at my TV.

"Nah, I'll watch it tomorrow. I'm tired."

He nods and stands up, heading for the window. "Okay, I'll let you get some sleep."

I reach for his hand. "O?"

He turns and peers down at me. There's so much going on in his eyes. "Yeah?"

"Will you stay?"

His body goes rigid. "You mean, sleep here?"

"Like when we were kids."

He shifts uncomfortably, and I'm afraid he's going to say no. But he doesn't. He says, "Sure."

The first summer I went to Camp Awahili, I came back with a best friend. A boy named Owen Reitzman. I never thought I could be friends with a boy. When I was nine, boys were stupid. They were immature and dirty and made fart noises. But Owen was different. He wasn't like the other boys I knew.

He started spending the night in my room when we were ten. He had come over to watch a movie. I wanted to watch *Sleepless in Seattle* for the one-thousandth time. He insisted we watch *The Ring.* Neither of us had seen it before so neither of us knew what a huge mistake it would turn out to be.

I was too afraid to go to sleep that night. Too afraid to even shut off the light. I was convinced some creepy girl was going to come crawling out of my TV screen. I made Owen stay over, and I also made him put my TV in the hallway.

We slept on opposite ends of the bed. His feet next to my head and my feet next to his head. I was so grateful to have him there, I didn't even complain that his socks smelled. We spent a lot of nights like this—mostly in the summers—lying foot to head, making shadow puppets on the wall or practicing our psychic abilities (one of us would think of a number, or an animal, or a country, and the other would try to guess it telepathically).

As soon as we entered middle school, the sleepovers just stopped. We didn't talk about it. We didn't debate the pros and cons. It just wasn't something we did anymore. Like an unspoken rule that had been decided.

When Owen gets into bed with me tonight, he doesn't move the pillow to the other end, like he used to do. He climbs under the covers with his jeans and T-shirt still on and curls onto his side, facing me.

We lie there. Head to head. Feet to feet.

As I start to drift to sleep, his eyes—open, green, beautiful—are the last things I see. His soft, even breath the last thing I hear.

Until . . .

"Ellie?"

"Yeah?" I murmur, half awake.

"I won't remember any of this tomorrow, will I?"

My throat stings as I feel the tears form behind my closed eyelids. "No."

Tomorrow I'll wake up, he'll be gone, and I'll be alone again.

I assume he's fallen asleep, because for a long time there's nothing but silence. I feel myself drifting off. I feel the darkness taking me under. I steel myself for what I know will happen next.

The morning light will stream through my window. My phone—back together in one piece—will ding with Tristan's first text message. I'll knock over my water reaching for it. I'll pick up Owen from school and everything—*everything*—will start all over again.

I wait for it.

I wait for it.

I wait for it.

And just as sleep pulls me under and the last glimmers of consciousness flicker out, I hear Owen say, "Then I won't remember telling you that I've been in love with you since middle school."

The Way We Were (Part 5)

Four months ago . . .

You have no idea how fast news can spread in high school until you become that news. The Monday after Tristan kissed me in his bedroom and took me out for pizza, I became a different person. I became a known entity. My name didn't matter. All that mattered was my new status: "Tristan Wheeler's Girlfriend."

For the first half of the day, I thought I had put my clothes on backward, stepped in dog poop, broken out in hives, been the victim of a social media hack. Hundreds of explanations for the sudden attention flooded through my mind. None of them were the right one. Because never, in a million years, would I have ever guessed that dating Tristan Wheeler would attract this much attention. People whispered about me in the hallways, girls sized me up in the bathroom, I got at least twenty new followers on Instagram in a matter of hours.

I felt like the mistress in a political scandal.

I was grateful when school let out for summer break a

month later. The sudden interest was unnerving me. I had started taking longer routes to class to avoid inquisitive eyes. I had stopped using the bathroom at school, convinced that girls were judging the sound of my pee.

The entire time, I don't think Tristan ever knew.

This was his life. The attention was part of his existence. It never occurred to him that it wasn't part of mine. And I never mentioned it. I dealt with it myself, in private. I didn't want to be the girl who complained about her boyfriend's popularity and its adverse effect on her.

The first time I witnessed Tristan's influence over people—namely girls—was the first Whack-a-Mole gig I ever attended. It was on the last night of school, at a small club two towns over that allowed minors inside before eleven p.m.

The place was packed. I didn't know how my entire school could fit into this cramped space, but somehow they managed.

"You know you're my good luck charm," Tristan said to me backstage, a few minutes before they went on. He was tuning his guitar and I was sitting on a black drum case, fiddling with the metal snap, flicking it open and closed and open and closed.

"You probably say that to all the girls you take backstage."

He stopped tuning and looked at me, his blue eyes serious. "I've never taken anyone backstage."

My fingers froze against the snap.

"It's true," Jackson, the drummer, vouched. "You're the first." He patted my side, urging me off the case so he could pull something out of it.

I hopped down. "Really?"

Tristan flashed me his killer dimple. "Really."

"Why is that?"

He shrugged. "I didn't want to be distracted right before a show. I wanted time to focus."

I walked up to him, tilting my chin up to look into his eyes. "Am I not a distraction?" I asked coyly.

He bent down to graze his lips against mine. "You are the very best kind of distraction."

"Maybe you should kick me out then," I murmured into his mouth.

His hands fell from the strings and wrapped around my waist, pulling me into him. The guitar banged against my hip but I didn't complain. "Never," he said, and then he kissed me hard. I tasted the adrenaline on him. I tasted the excitement of the upcoming gig. He put it all into me, and the kiss left me feeling dizzy and breathless.

"Okay, lovebirds," Lance, the bass player, said. "We have a set to play."

Tristan released me and then instantly yanked me back. "This summer is going to be amazing."

I felt my throat go dry. I still hadn't told him that I was signed up to work at Camp Awahili again this year, and that I would be gone for three months—basically the entire summer. I was supposed to leave the very next week.

"About that—" I began, but I immediately knew it was the wrong time. I couldn't lay this on him right before he went on stage. I'd never been a groupie before but some knowledge is just instinctual.

He nuzzled my nose. "What?"

"Nothing," I said, and pushed him away. "Now, go . . . you know . . . rock the house."

He raised his eyebrows. "Rock the house?"

"Yeah. Knock 'em dead. Punch 'em in the gut. Whatever it is you do up there."

Tristan shook his head. "Oh, I have much to teach you."

I flashed him a winning smile. "I'll be in the back, trying not to plug my ears from all the noise."

"Hey!" Lance and Jackson said at the same time.

Tristan held up a hand. "She's joking. It's an inside joke." Then he gave me a playful warning look.

I started to leave but Tristan grabbed my hand. "Wait. You can't stand in the back. You have to be in the front."

Butterflies took flight in my stomach. No one had said anything about standing in the front. He just asked me to come to the gig. He didn't say I had to be in the front row.

"I don't know," I faltered. The idea of being up there, with all those people behind me, was terrifying. I got claustrophobic just thinking about it. "I'll have a better view from the back."

"But then how will I know that you're there?"

I laughed. "I'm not going anywhere."

"I want to see you. I want to look in your eyes when I sing 'Mind of the Girl.'"

His words were like a vise squeezing around my chest. I wanted so badly to say yes to him. To give him everything he wanted. Everything he asked for. I'd already given him my heart. What else did I have to lose?

"I'll try to find a space up front," I promised him.

His smile brightened the whole room and I thought, *Why do they even need stage lights with a smile like that?*

An emcee introduced them and they charged the stage like bulls. I scurried through the door that led back into the front of the club and watched them take their positions. I eyed the space in front of the stage. It was packed wall-to-wall with people—mostly girls. I would need a helicopter to even get there, and the thought of elbowing my way through was enough to make my legs give out.

Making sure Tristan's gaze was trained on the crowd, I sidled my way around the edge of the room until I reached the bar. I ordered a cranberry and soda water and clutched the tumbler like a life preserver.

I was so nervous. Nervous for Tristan. Nervous for the guys. Nervous that I would hate the show, hate the way they sounded, and I'd have to spend the rest of our relationship lying to him.

Then Jackson kicked off on the drums and suddenly the energy of the club changed. It was like someone had run a live wire through the whole room and it could blow us all to smithereens any minute. That was the anticipation. That was the thrill. That was the edge I lived on for the entire forty-five-minute set.

Tristan was magic up there. He was so confident and charming, his voice throaty and masculine, his lyrics deep and poetic. His presence captured everyone in the room. Including me. All the way in the back.

I don't even remember the music. It was irrelevant. Tristan was the show, and I was a convert.

As soon as the set was over and he emerged from backstage, he was surrounded. He could barely move. Everyone wanted a piece of him. Everyone wanted whatever they had just felt from that stage, but he came straight for me. He pushed and swam and waded through the bodies like they were nothing but tall weeds.

When he reached me, he cupped both of his hands around my cheeks, stared deeply into my eyes for five long seconds before guiding my mouth to his.

He kissed me.

In front of everyone. In *spite* of everyone.

I'd never felt more significant in my life.

"I thought you were going to be up front," he said, pouting.

I laughed. "There was no room. I would have had to drive a tractor in there to hack through all of your adoring fans."

"You're the only adoring fan I care about."

My knees gave out. It was a good thing Tristan's hands were still holding me up.

"I'll stand in front next time."

"You promise?"

"I promise."

First thing the next morning, I called the director of Camp Awahili and told him I wouldn't be coming this summer.

THE SIXTH MONDAY

I Look Inside Myself and See My Heart Is Black

7:04 a.m.

Bloop-dee-dee-bloop-bloop-bing!

I must be dead.

There is no other explanation. I've died and am now living in some kind of purgatory.

Please, just let me out.

Shut it down. Stop the ride. I want off. I can't do this anymore. I take back everything I said about wanting another chance. I take back everything I said about everything. Just don't make me do this again.

What if I don't open my eyes? What if I refuse to wake up? As long as my eyes stay closed, anything is possible, right? Owen is still lying next to me. The text message that I just received is a wrong number. The sun is shining outside my window.

Today is Tuesday.

The universe is not a cruel, devious prankster who thinks it's funny to trap poor, innocent teenagers in the same horrific day over and over and over.

Bloop-dee-dee-bloop-bloop-bing!

Don't do it, I scold myself. *Whatever you do. Don't open your eyes. Let's just go on pretending.*

I open my eyes. The space next to me is empty. I search for a stray strand of Owen's hair, a crease in the pillow, a lingering scent. Something to prove he was there. To prove that last night happened.

But there's nothing.

Nothing.

Nothing.

My life is one big meaningless cycle of nothingness.

See, some nagging voice in the back of my head says. *This is why you don't open your eyes.*

I shut off my ringer, roll over, and try to go back to sleep.

Maybe I can sleep through the rest of the day.

Maybe I can sleep through the rest of my life, which coincidentally is the same thing. My life *is* this day. There's no escape.

I'm trapped here forever.

What did I ever do to deserve this? Was it the candy bar I stole from the supermarket when I was six? The four dollars and eighty-five cents in fines that I've owed to the library since last year? That time I lied to my teacher about our dog being sick so I could get an extra day to finish my paper?

We didn't even have a dog. And now I'm paying for it.

My dad knocks on the door and sticks his head in. "Ells? Owen is on the landline for you."

Owen.

My mind instantly flashes back to the Ferris wheel. To his lips brushing ever-so-slightly against mine. And then, to that thing he said just before I fell asleep. Was that real? Did that really happen, or was I dreaming?

I push the memory from my mind. I can't deal with that right now.

"He said he's been calling your phone but it goes straight to voice mail," my dad goes on. "Are you sick?"

"No," I correct. "I'm dead."

My dad huffs out a laugh. "You look pretty alive to me."

"It's an illusion." I pull the pillow over my head. "I can't go to school. Call Owen and tell him he needs to find another ride."

"What about softball tryouts?" my dad asks, disappointed.

I pound the pillow with my fist. "I'm not going to those either."

"But it's your chance at varsity."

I tear the pillow from my face. "You know what, Dad? Maybe I don't care about making varsity. Maybe I don't want to play softball. Maybe I don't want to do anything. Maybe all I want to do for the rest of my life is lie here."

Comprehension flashes across his face. He sits down on the edge of my bed. "Ah. Is this about a boy? Is this about Tristan?"

Pillow. Face.

My father lets out a sigh. "Well, I'm sorry if you're having . . . boy trouble, but that's no reason to miss school. Junior year is incredibly important when it comes to colleges, and you can't let a little crush ruin your chances at a good future."

"I'm not going to school," I mumble into the fabric. "Ever again."

"Well," my dad says, "if you're not sick—"

"I *am* sick. I'm very, very sick." It's not a lie. Clearly something is horribly wrong with me. It's just not something that's diagnosable on WebMD.

My dad stands up. "Okay. I'll bring you some toast and soup, and I'll call your coach and talk to him about rescheduling."

7:59 a.m.

My parents argue downstairs. An untouched bowl of soup and plate of toast are sitting on my nightstand. I try to fall back asleep but it's pointless. The universe isn't even merciful enough to give me that.

For the rest of the day, I lie in my bed with "Paint It Black" by the Rolling Stones playing on Repeat, and watch the minutes tick by on my phone.

8:02 a.m.—Owen gets in the car and says, "It's really chucking it down out there."

8:11 a.m.—I run the red light at Providence Boulevard and Avenue de Liberation and get a ticket.

8:42 a.m.—I take a horrible school picture.

9:58 a.m.—A kamikaze bird dive-bombs Señora Mendoza's classroom window.

11:20 a.m.—History quiz on the American Revolution.

1:22 p.m.—I give the world's blandest election speech.

2:10 p.m.—Mr. Goodman gives me another brochure. Pow! Pow!

3:25 p.m.—Coach tries to fool me with a curveball.

Round and round it goes.

I get three text messages from Tristan and five from Owen. I don't read or respond to any of them. What's the point? It won't make one bit of difference tomorrow.

4:34 p.m.

I hear the front door slam and my sister trudges up the stairs. She'll be soaking wet but I still have no idea why. I count her footsteps down the hall and then she disappears into her bedroom.

I turn on my TV and flip through the recordings on my DVR. The season premiere of *Assumed Guilty* is at the top of the list. It's the episode Owen has been bugging me to watch for the past five days. I press Play.

Owen was right. The episode is pretty amazing. It's about a woman named Simone Hudson whose identity gets stolen by this other woman who looks uncannily like her. The real Simone Hudson ends up suing the fake Simone Hudson for stealing her identity, but then in a fourth-commercial-break twist, the fake Simone Hudson *countersues* the real Simone Hudson, claiming *she* was actually the victim of the identity theft, not the other way around. The fake Simone Hudson's attorney does such a convincing job at arguing her side that by the end of the episode, you actually have no idea *who* the real Simone Hudson is.

The episode is so intense that by the time it's over, I feel breathless and light-headed. How scary would it be if someone stole your identity and then turned around and claimed that *you* actually stole theirs? Both Simone Hudsons had birth certificates and social security cards and passports with their names on them. Obviously one of those sets of documents was fake, but which one? And does it even matter? How do you *really* know that you're you? Is it because your name is on a piece of paper?

I reach for my bag and pull out my wallet. I stare at my driver's license for a good five minutes, studying the girl in the picture and the text printed next to it.

Ellison Beatrice Sparks.

546 Briar Tree Lane.

5′4″.

109 lbs.

Birthday: July 15.

The picture certainly looks like me, and that's definitely my name and my birthday and my address. But what if it's *not* me? What if the real me is out there somewhere living some other life? At some other school?

I bet that Ellison Sparks has it all figured out. I bet her boyfriend never broke up with her in the first place. I bet *she* never almost kissed her best friend on top of a Ferris wheel. She's probably not even afraid of heights.

I bet, for her, it's Tuesday.

I watch the episode again. When it's finished, I watch it again. I search for clues, something to help me figure out my own twisted existence, but I only end up more confused.

Eventually I lose track of how many times I've seen the episode. All I know is, it's dark outside my window now. My mom comes knocking at my door to tell me that Tristan is here and wants to talk to me.

"I don't want to see him," I tell her. "He's just here to break up with me."

An hour later, my phone vibrates nine times in a row. I glance at the messages.

Tristan: I'm sorry to have to do this by text.

Tristan: But you won't answer your phone or talk to me.

Tristan: I don't think I can do this anymore.

Tristan: Us, I mean.

Tristan: Something is broken and I don't know how to fix it.

Tristan: I don't know if it can be fixed.

Tristan: I'm sorry. It breaks my heart to do this.

Tristan: I wish I didn't feel this way. But I do.

Tristan: And I have to stay true to what I feel.

I shut off the phone and toss it onto the floor.

I'm about to press Play on the remote to watch the episode of *Assumed Guilty* yet again when someone knocks on my door. It's my sister.

"I was about to put on a movie. Do you want to watch it with me?"

I smile and push myself off the bed. "Sure. But not *The Breakfast Club,* okay? I've seen that too many times."

She looks at me in surprise. "How did you know I was going to watch that?"

I shrug. "Just a hunch."

My sister runs back to her room to get the movie ready and I walk over to my window and stare out at the lonely tree in our front yard. The one Owen climbs on so many other versions of this Monday. I don't know what will happen tonight. I've already messed with every single moment of the day.

But I crack the window open anyway.

Because despite being dead and stuck in purgatory, it turns out I still have some hope left.

Break On Through

9:45 p.m.

Hadley chose *Some Kind of Wonderful,* another teen movie made in the eighties about a guy who empties his entire college savings account to take the popular girl out on a date, but then discovers that he's actually in love with his best friend.

As the credits roll, I turn to my sister. "Hads, what happened today? Why did you walk home from school soaking wet?"

Flustered, she searches for the remote in her tangle of blankets and presses Stop. "How did you know about that? Did they put it on the Internet?" She grabs her phone off her night-stand and swipes it on. "Is there a video?"

"What?" I ask, confused. "Did *who* put it on the Internet? Hadley, what happened?"

But once again, she completely shuts down. "I'm tired. I need to go to sleep."

I know this is my cue to leave but I don't budge. "Hadley, you know you can talk to me about this, right?"

"No!" she screams and I flinch. "I can't!"

"Why not?"

"Because you wouldn't understand. You have everything figured out."

This makes me laugh, and I immediately realize what a mistake that is because Hadley clearly thinks I'm laughing at her. "I have *nothing* figured out!" I tell her.

She crosses her arms, evidently not believing me.

"Do you know why I stayed home from school today?" I ask. "Why I *really* stayed home from school?"

"You were sick."

"No. I was scared."

This was obviously not even in the same galaxy as what she thought I was going to say. "Of what?"

"Of my life. Of facing it. Of being me. The same old stupid me, day after day."

"But your life is perfect," she argues.

"It's not."

"You get perfect grades and all the teachers like you and you're going to be on the varsity softball team. *And* you have the cutest boyfriend in school!"

I sigh. "Actually, I have none of those things. And Tristan broke up with me today."

Her jaw drops. "Because of one fight?"

"No, because . . ." I trail off. Because why? Six breakups and I still don't seem to have a straight answer to that question. "I guess things were just broken between us."

"But you can fix it!"

I look at her sweet, innocent face and feel a pang in my chest. She's so desperate for me to tell her that she's right. That I can fix it. That my seemingly perfect life will go on exactly the way she wants it to.

"I don't know," I admit. "Maybe some things aren't fixable."

"Maybe *everything* is fixable."

I reach out and ruffle her hair. "When did you get to be the wise one?"

She laughs. "I've always been the wise one. You're just noticing it for the first time."

I nod. "You're probably right." I stand up and start for the door.

"Ells?" my sister calls out.

"Yeah?"

"They told me Avery Frahm wanted to kiss me. He's the cutest boy in our class. I never should have believed them. They told me to wait for him on the soccer field. Then they turned the sprinklers on."

I open my mouth to demand *who*. Who would do this to my sister? But before I can get the word out, I realize I already know.

The giggling girls. They came running out of that side door when I was looking for Hadley. Now I know what they were giggling about.

I run back to my sister and pull her into a hug. I can tell by the stiffness of her body that she's trying not to cry. She's trying to stay strong. Stronger than I would have been if I were in her shoes.

"Don't worry," I tell her. "Tomorrow we'll make it right."

10:02 p.m.

When I get back to my room, Owen is sitting on my bed flipping through my copy of *The Book Thief*, which he must have found on my bookshelf.

Seeing him in my room brings an onslaught of unwelcome memories. I try to force them from my mind, but they attack from all sides. I can suddenly see Owen in every single version of this day. Bending down to examine my lips in the girls' bathroom, wishing me good night in Cherokee as he climbs out my window, telling me he likes my outfit as we stand outside the school in the pouring rain, jumping up and down like a lunatic after winning the ring toss game, squeezing my hand on the Ferris wheel.

And last night, telling me that he's in love with me.

This one hits the hardest. In the most vulnerable spot.

I'm suddenly overwhelmed with relief that he doesn't remember. That I don't have to talk about it. Because what would I say? What *could* I say?

He's my best friend. My *only* friend.

Yet somehow it feels like it didn't even happen. Or rather, it happened between two other people. A different him and a different me.

"This is read," he accuses, holding up the book and pointing at a dog-eared page.

I let out a soft chuckle. "I know. I read all the book club books."

I watch his reaction. The shock in his eyes. The revelation of hearing this confession for the first time.

Then I burst into tears.

Owen closes the book with a *smack*. "What's the matter?"

I sit down next to him on the bed and hold my head in my hands, sobbing quietly. I can feel Owen's franticness. He's trying to figure out what to say, what to do, how to fix it. How to be Owen.

Maybe some things aren't fixable.

Maybe everything is fixable.

"I have to tell you something," I murmur between shudders.

Owen grabs Hippo and pushes him into my lap. "We're listening."

"It's something you're probably not going to believe."

Owen takes a deep breath, like he's steeling himself for bad news. "Try me."

God Only Knows What I'd Be Without You

I've confessed my secret to Owen so many times, you would think it would get easier. It doesn't. I start from the beginning—the first Monday—and I don't stop talking until I get to this very second. I tell him about Tristan's text messages, my parents' fight, my ticket, the fortune cookies, Owen's dream, Daphne Gray's attempt to poison me, the election speeches, my history quiz, the carnival, *The Girl Commandments*, my extreme make-over, yesterday's rebellion, and even Hadley's unexplained walk home.

The only parts I leave out are the Ferris wheel and his confession to me last night. Because I just can't deal with it right now.

When I finish, Owen grabs Hippo from me and squeezes him tightly to his chest. "I think I need this more than you."

I laugh, but it quickly dissolves into more tears. "I don't know what to do. I just want my life back. I want to wake up tomorrow and not know what's going to happen. I thought I had it all figured out. I thought if I could just keep him from breaking up with me, the day would be fixed, but it wasn't. And now I'm afraid I might be stuck here forever."

I collapse onto my back, letting the tears roll down the sides of my face.

"Ellie," Owen says after a long moment, twisting his body to look at me. "You can't keep changing yourself to please one guy. If he doesn't love you for who you are, then he's not worth it."

I sniffle. "You sound like one of those inspirational GIFs."

"I happen to *like* those inspirational GIFs."

I grin through my tears. "You would."

He ponders for a moment and then asks, "What exactly did you say that first night?"

"Huh?"

"That first Monday when you wished you could have another chance. What were your exact words?"

I think back, trying to remember. It feels like forever ago. "I didn't *say* anything. It was just a thought in my mind."

"Okay, what did you *think*?"

I sigh. "I dunno. It was something like 'Please give me another chance. I swear I'll get it right.'"

Owen silently turns away from me. I can hear him breathing. In. Out. In. Out. Like he's trying to remind the air where to go. And then, "You never mentioned him."

I sit up, wiping my eyes. "What?"

"You never specifically mentioned *him*. You said 'I swear I'll get it right.'"

"I think the 'him' was implied," I say defensively.

"What if it wasn't?" Owen challenges. "What if this day was never about getting him back?"

His question renders me speechless. I never even considered the possibility that this wasn't about Tristan.

Owen's next words are barely a whisper. "What if it was about getting *yourself* back?"

"Now you really sound like an inspirational GIF."

He laughs and stands up. At first, I think he's going to leave and I feel a flutter of panic, but instead he reaches into the pocket of his jeans and produces two fortune cookies.

"Choose your tasty fortune!" His voice is artificially cheerful.

I shake my head. "My fortune is bleak. I don't need a cookie to tell me that."

He nudges his hand toward me. "C'mon."

I oscillate between the two, finally deciding on the one on the left. I toss it next to me on the bed and collapse onto my back again. Owen sits down and cracks his open.

"If your desires are not extravagant, they will be granted," I recite in a bored voice.

He laughs. "My desires are *always* extravagant, but that's not what it says."

"What?!" I bolt upright and grab the tiny strip of paper from his hand.

Tomorrow will bring unexpected things.

It changed. Owen's fortune *changed.*

But how? Why?

I rummage through my tangled sheets until I find my cookie, scrambling to get it open and read the message inside.

All we ever really get is today.

"Owen!" I exclaim, bounding to my feet.

He's startled by my outburst. "What?"

"I think you might be right."

"Of course I'm right. I'm always right."

"You're not always right."

"Uh, objection. Yes, I am."

"Objection. I can think of plenty of times you were wrong."

"Like when?"

"I have two words for you: sheep's milk."

"Withdrawn," he mumbles. "But, hey, speaking of me being right, did you ever watch the season premiere of *Assumed Guilty*?"

"No," I lie. "Do you want to watch it with me now?"

Owen glances at the time on his phone. "It's too late, isn't it?"

Maybe some things aren't fixable.

Maybe everything is fixable.

Or maybe it's just about knowing which things actually *need* fixing.

I shake my head and flash him a smile. "I don't think it's too late."

The Way We Were (Part 6)

Sunday night . . .

It wasn't the movie I wanted to watch, but once Tristan pressed Play and snuggled up next to me, it didn't matter anymore. All I cared about was having him next to me. It was our first night alone together in a long time. Whack-a-Mole had had a busy summer. They were booking gigs like crazy, but now that school was back in session things had started to slow down. I knew Tristan was anxious about that, but I was secretly grateful. It had been an exhausting few months, spending my nights in clubs, and my days in Jackson's garage listening to the guys practice and strategizing on marketing ideas.

Then school started a month ago. My schedule was crazy and my homework load was crazier, which made it hard to get together. At school, we were back under the social microscope. I knew everyone was just counting the days, waiting until that inevitable moment when Tristan would dump me like he dumped every other girl, and just knowing that made me all the more determined to prevent it from happening.

But now, we were finally alone. Tristan's mom was on a date and we had his house to ourselves. I suggested a movie because it seemed so low-key, especially after our whirlwind summer of crowded rooms and loud music.

Although the real reason I suggested the movie was that we'd just spent twenty minutes in his bedroom in almost total silence. I couldn't decide if something was on Tristan's mind or if we had simply run out of things to say to each other.

Tristan chose some action flick that he had missed in the theaters. I would have preferred something a little more romantic, but it didn't matter. As long as we were together.

We were only twelve minutes into the movie when the alerts started going off on his phone. There hadn't even been a single explosion in the film yet, but his phone was already blowing up.

I recognized the sound of the alert. It was from Snapchat. Someone (or multiple some*ones*) was messaging him. I knew Tristan relied heavily on Snapchat to promote his music. That and Instagram were how he kept in touch with his growing fan base, but it irritated me that he kept looking at the screen. He didn't actually respond to any of the messages (he'd just casually glance at them and then set his phone aside), but the fact that he kept looking—like he was checking to see if something more interesting was going on in the world—made my temper start to flare.

I had switched my phone off the moment I arrived at Tristan's house.

I didn't *want* to be distracted by anything.

But Tristan was almost welcoming the distractions.

By the seventeenth ding, I finally sat up and asked, "Who's

messaging you so incessantly?" I tried to keep my voice light. Friendly. A casual observation of his phone activity.

He waved away my concern with his hand. "Just some girls from last week's show."

Girls.

The word felt like a slap across the face. It's amazing how five little letters can pack so much punch. He said it like it was the most innocent word in the English language. As harmless and unremarkable as "bread," or "spoon," or "chair."

But to me, the word implied so much more.

All I saw through my red-tinted vision were flirty promises, too-short skirts, high-pitched giggles, and manicured fingernails.

I told myself to keep calm. Chill out. Stay cool.

You are the anti–drama queen.

"What did they say?" I asked.

He shrugged. "Not much. Just wanting to know when our next show is."

"Seventeen times?" The question rushed out of my mouth before I had a chance to stop it.

Tristan pushed Pause on the remote and turned to look at me. "Excuse me?"

I tried to backpedal. "I just meant it's weird for you to get seventeen messages all asking the same thing."

"Were you counting them?" It wasn't a question. It was an accusation.

"It's a little distracting," I admitted. "You know, while we're trying to watch the movie." I rubbed his shoulder in an attempt to disarm him. "I was kinda hoping we could have some alone time."

"We *are* alone."

I bit my lip. This was going downhill fast. I had to fix it. "I know. I mean, without our phones." I pulled mine from my bag. "See? Mine's off."

"Fine," Tristan said. "I'll put it on Silent."

Disappointment flooded me but I refused to let it show. I grinned. "Thank you. That wasn't so hard, now, was it?"

It was meant to be a joke, but Tristan barely even smiled. The tension between us was suffocating. What had happened to the playful, affectionate guy who used to run to me the moment he got off the stage?

As I cuddled up against him, I vowed to keep my jealousy in check for the rest of the night.

You're being ridiculous, I told myself. *Tristan is a musician. He has to stay connected to his fans. It's part of the job.*

My little pep talk seemed to work because my frustration eventually dissipated and I found myself pulled into the plot of the movie, which admittedly wasn't half bad. It was a spy thriller about a CIA agent who is wrongfully accused of treason and has to go on the run to prove his innocence.

When the hero narrowly managed to escape an intense, high-octane chase through the streets of Rome, I glanced up at Tristan to share in a moment of relief, only to find that he wasn't even watching the movie.

He was focused back on his phone.

And this time, I got a glimpse at the screen.

It wasn't a message. It was a photo. Of a girl. She was posing provocatively, the phone held high above her to capture the perfect angle down the front of her shirt.

Enraged, I launched from the couch and stomped toward the front door. I yanked it open and charged onto the lawn.

Tristan was behind me in an instant. "Ellie? Where are you going?"

"Home!" I shouted.

"Why?" I was devastated to hear annoyance rather than concern in his tone.

"Why are random girls sending you selfies?"

He sighed. "Because that's what they do. I don't ask them to send those. They just do it. I can't control what people send me. I'm a musician. It comes with the territory."

"Why don't you just shut off your phone?"

"I can't. What if someone calls about a gig?"

"Someone incapable of leaving a voice mail?" I roared back.

"Ellie," Tristan said, his voice aggravatingly condescending. "You're overreacting. It was just a picture. I didn't even respond."

"That's your big comeback? That you didn't respond?"

"I didn't realize I needed a 'big comeback.'"

"Of course you do!"

"Ellie," and there was that tone again. "I didn't do anything wrong."

I wanted to scream. I wanted to hit him over the head until he got it. My mind was telling me to just go. Get in my car and drive away before I could do any more damage, but my irrational side wanted more. She wanted to make an impression. Leave her mark. Prove just how livid she was.

She wanted to *throw* something.

I peered around my feet, my gaze landing on the only thing within reach. An adorable garden gnome stood unassumingly among the flowers that lined the walkway. He was the least likely of weapons, with his long white beard, red pointy hat, and permanently cheerful expression, but he was all I had.

I scooped him up and hurled him at Tristan's head.

He ducked but it didn't matter. The gnome was about a foot off target. My irrational side had terrible aim. The gnome hit the pavement of the walkway and smashed to pieces.

"What the . . . ?" Tristan yelled. The condescension was long gone, leaving nothing behind but disbelief.

Well, at least I had made an impression.

I turned around and ran to my car. I collapsed into the front seat, my hands shaking, my thoughts vibrating like they'd been injected with caffeine.

What did you do? I asked myself over and over again. *What did you do?*

When I got home, I sat in my car in the garage and switched on my phone. I prayed for correspondence. Text, voice, Instagram comment, I didn't care. As long as it was from him. As long as there was some indication that everything was okay. That I hadn't ruined the best thing to ever happen to me.

The phone connected to the network and I held my breath.

Bloop-dee-dee-bloop-bloop-bing!

I exhaled.

Bloop-dee-dee-bloop-bloop-bing!

Bloop-dee-dee-bloop-bloop-bing!

Bloop-dee-dee-bloop-bloop-bing!

The phone wouldn't stop beeping. The texts were coming in faster than I could read them. Grinning, I swiped open the message app.

Until I saw who they were from.

Owen: Assumed Guilty is starting in seven minutes. Where are you?

Owen: Two minutes and counting! Are we doing this or not?

Owen: Ellie! It's the season premiere! This is not the time to go MIA on me!

Owen: Okay, I just watched the first five minutes. This episode is killer. Why aren't you texting me back???

I let out a whimper and tossed my phone aside. There were about twenty more messages from Owen, but I couldn't bring myself to read them.

The ceiling of the car felt like it was crushing down on me.

I had completely forgotten about our Sunday ritual.

In one night, I had managed to disappoint the two most important people in my life. What was happening to me? Who was this person I had become? She was a stranger. A jealous, short-tempered, unreliable, gnome-throwing stranger.

My fingers itched to text Owen back, my heart panged to call Tristan and apologize, but I couldn't bring myself to do either of those things.

I was afraid this new, scary version of myself would only make things worse.

So I did the only other thing I could think of. I dropped my head in my hands and cried.

THE SEVENTH MONDAY

Take a Sad Song and Make It Better

6:30 a.m.

I put the finishing touches on my omelet, garnish the plates with parsley, and top off the tray with a single red rose in a vase. I've been up since 5:30. I was too excited to sleep. Too eager to start my day.

I can hear footsteps upstairs. My dad must be awake. I send him a quick text message, telling him to meet me downstairs.

He arrives a moment later, still in his pajamas, hair rumpled.

His sleepy eyes widen when he sees what I've done. "What is this for?"

I beam. "Your anniversary." I hand him the tray containing two omelets, fresh-baked muffins, and orange juice. "Tell Mom that you did it."

I watch his reaction go from disbelief to recognition to gratitude. "Oh my God. I would have totally forgotten."

"I know."

"You saved me big-time, Ells."

I laugh. "I know." I kick my foot in his direction. "Now, go."

Careful not to spill the tray, he leans forward and gives me a kiss on the cheek. "I owe you one. Good luck at softball tryouts today."

"Actually, Dad."

He stops halfway out the kitchen. "Hmm?"

"I don't think I'm going to try out this year."

He sets the tray down on the counter. "What? Why?"

I shrug. "Softball has never really been my thing. I think it's always been *your* thing. I started playing because it seemed to make you happy."

He presses his lips together contemplatively. "Are you sure you're not just scared you won't make varsity?"

"I know I could make varsity." My dad laughs. "I'm just not sure I want to."

I watch disappointment weigh on my father's features as he picks the tray back up.

"I'm sorry if I let you down," I offer.

He gives me a sad smile. "Ells Bells, I want you to do what makes you happy."

I smile at the childhood nickname. "I want that, too."

7:04 a.m.

Bloop-dee-dee-bloop-bloop-bing!

The first text message comes through right as I'm getting out of the shower.

Tristan: I can't stop thinking about last night.

I pick up my phone and watch the screen, counting the seconds—thirty-two—until the next one arrives.

Tristan: Let's talk today.

Then I carefully type out my response.

Me: Me neither. Meet me in front of my locker before Spanish so we can talk.

I set the phone down on the counter and start getting ready. The dress I pull out of my closet is a short-sleeved navy wrap dress with white polka dots. I've only worn it once—two summers ago at a camp dance—but as soon as I put it on, I wonder why I don't wear it more often.

I scrunch my wet hair, opting to let it air-dry, apply a subtle layer of makeup, and complete the whole look with a navy blue headband that I borrow from Hadley.

"You look pretty," she says, standing in the doorway as I put the finishing touches on my look.

"Thanks." I catch a glimpse of her reflection in the mirror and notice the slight downward curve of her mouth as she watches me.

"Today is going to be a good day," I tell her.

She nods but I can tell she doesn't believe me.

"We're going to make it right today."

Her eyebrows knit together in confusion.

"Hey," I say, changing the subject. "Since I'm borrowing

something of yours, why don't you pick out something from my closet?"

Her entire face lights up like a Christmas tree. "Really?"

I walk past her toward the hallway. "Yup. Anything you want." I pause, reconsidering. "Just stay away from the fishnets."

It's Gonna Work Out Fine

7:54 a.m.

The rain streams down my windshield as I drive to Owen's singing along to "Son of a Preacher Man" by Dusty Springfield.

I pull into Owen's driveway and he casually saunters to the car, getting drenched in the process. "Wow. It's really chucking it down out there," he says, dropping into the passenger seat.

"Isn't it, mate?"

He gives me a funny look.

"What?" I ask.

"Mate?"

"You're not the only one who can steal words from the Brits."

"Okay." He dives for the radio and turns up the volume. "Ooh! Good song. 'Top of the World' playlist?"

I beam. "Uh-huh."

"What's the occasion?"

"No occasion. I just know you like this one."

He gives me another strange look. "Someone's in a good mood today."

"That I am, old chap. That I am."

I put the car into Reverse and back out of the driveway. Owen is unusually quiet as we drive. I can feel his eyes on me, watching me suspiciously.

"Are you kissing up to me?" he finally asks. "Is this your lame way of trying to make up for last night?"

I come to a complete stop at the corner and turn toward him. "Owen." My tone is so serious he looks worried.

"Do not tell me you're dying. I'm not emotionally equipped to deal with that."

I shake my head. "I'm not dying."

"Then what?"

I place my hand over his. "I just wanted to say how sorry I am. For blowing you off last night."

He glances down at our hands. "It's okay," he says stiffly.

"No, it's not. And I'm sorry I blew you off this summer, too. It won't happen again, I promise."

"Did you join a twelve-step program or something?"

I laugh. "Or something." I return my hand to the steering wheel and step on the gas. "How good was that episode though?"

Owen goes into full-on rehash mode. "Right? I mean that whole closing argument that Olivia gave at the end?"

"Chills!"

"Total chills!"

"The best kind of chills!"

"I can't *believe* they didn't tell us who won though."

"I don't think that was the point of the episode," I argue.

"I know, I know. It was all about the viewer forming an opinion about who is the real Simone Hudson, but still!"

"Obviously it was the woman who sued first."

Owen makes a funny noise with his throat that sounds like a bullfrog being suffocated. "Objection! Obviously it was the woman who countersued."

"That woman was just trying to cover herself. It was a total ploy."

"Are you kidding?" he screeches. "The writers just wanted you to *think* that. And you fell for it."

A huge grin spreads across my face.

"What?" Owen demands.

"Nothing. I've just missed this."

"Missed what?"

"Us. Being us."

He's profoundly confused. "Were we not us yesterday?"

I bite my lip, fighting the urge to tell him the truth. I've done it countless times now. I know I can make him believe. I can make him an accomplice in this craziness once again.

But I hold it in.

All of it.

This isn't his burden to bear. Not today. Today, it's mine and mine alone. I can't keep dragging him into something that I clearly have to figure out on my own.

"Hey," I say, nodding toward his bag on the floor. "Have you forgotten something?"

He gives me a blank look before the realization hits. "Oh! Right!" He unzips the front pocket and pulls out the two crescent-shaped cookies. "Choose your tasty fortune!"

"You pick first this time," I tell him.

He frowns. "But you always pick first. My fortune is always the result of your choices. That's like the whole basis of our friendship."

I know he's kidding, but there's something in his joke that

rings so true, it unnerves me a bit. "I guess it's time to do things differently."

Owen shrugs, selects a cookie, and hands me the other one. I hold it in my lap while he breaks his open. I keep my eyes on the road, waiting for him to read the mysterious message inside.

"Huh," he says after a moment.

I glance over at him. "What?"

"It's empty."

Empty?

I pull to a stop at the next red light and instantly dive for my own cookie, scrambling to get it open and completely disregarding the crumbs that fall everywhere in the process.

Owen leans in to read over my shoulder.

But there's nothing to read.

Mine is empty, too.

"That's *so* weird!" he exclaims.

"Yeah," I murmur softly.

"Green light." Owen points at the stoplight and I look up. It's only now that I notice where we are. At the intersection of Providence Boulevard and Avenue de Liberation. The very spot where I'm supposed to get the ticket.

Goose bumps prickle my skin.

"What do you think this means?" Owen asks. "I once heard that it's bad luck to have empty fortunes. Do you think it means something horrible is going to happen?"

"No," I say, stepping on the gas. "I think it means exactly the opposite."

Walkin' Back to Happiness

8:42 a.m.

"Say 'Two more years!' " the photographer trills.

"Two more years!" I trill back. She snaps the photo and I climb off the stool to check the viewfinder. I'm surprised by what I find. The girl on the little screen is so calm and relaxed. Her shoulders aren't hunched, her posture isn't ramrod straight, her smile doesn't look forced.

She looks . . .

"You look happy," the photographer's assistant comments.

Yes. That's it. I look *happy*.

Why has she never made that comment before? Had I really looked that miserable in the countless other photos I've taken this week?

9:50 a.m.

The bell rings, ending first period, and I file into the hallway with my classmates. I'm supposed to meet Tristan at my locker right now, and I can't help feeling nervous at the thought of seeing him.

I know he won't remember anything from the past six days. I know, for him, this day has been completely reset. But *I* remember. I know all the things he's said, all the reasons he's given me for wanting to break up, all the reactions I've had as a result.

Reminiscing about it all at once—like a mental collage—is twisting my stomach into knots.

He's already at my locker when I arrive. He doesn't see me yet so I have a few seconds to observe him. He leans against the locker banks, his guitar strapped to his back, peering down at his phone.

He sees me approach and stands up a bit straighter, pocketing his phone.

I smile and dial in the combination at my locker.

"Hi," I say.

"Hi," he responds rigidly. He clears his throat. "So, that thing last night. I thought we should talk about it."

I grab a pen from the holder, stick it into my bag, and close the door. "Yes," I say, and turn to face him. I draw in a courageous breath. It's taken me a week to get here. Now it's finally time to say all the things I haven't been able to say in the last six days.

"I've been wanting to talk to you about that, too. Look, I'm tired of acting like I don't care. I'm tired of hiding my feelings from you. The reason I behaved the way I did last night is because I trapped those feelings and thoughts inside for so long that they just exploded. From the day we met, I've been pretending to be someone else. I've been pretending to be the girl I *thought* you wanted. But I'm not her. I get jealous when you flirt with other girls. I get angry when you Snapchat with them when you're supposed to be watching a movie with me. That's who I am. I'm sorry I misled you for so long. It wasn't fair to you or to me."

Tristan stares at me for a long moment. I can tell this isn't what he expected me to say, and to be honest, one week ago this isn't what I'd expect me to say either.

He blinks rapidly, trying to gather his thoughts.

"We should get to class," I say, walking past him, but he stops me, gently reaching out for my hand.

"I'm sorry, too," he says.

Now it's my turn to be stunned. "What?"

"For last night. I should have put my phone away. I shouldn't have made you feel ignored. That was really insensitive of me. I know I'd hate it if you were texting other guys when you were with me."

I'm so speechless, I can't move. Tristan is apologizing to me?

"Do you forgive me?" He bends down and gently touches his lips to mine. His kiss is so disarming, his apology is so heartfelt, all I can do is nod.

The bell rings, snapping me out of my reverie. I glance at my phone.

Crap!

If I run, I might just make it. I take off at a sprint down the hallway.

"Ellie?" Tristan calls after me.

"We're late!" I yell over my shoulder. "He's not dying today! No one is dying today!"

I hear footsteps behind me. "What are you talking about? Who's dying?"

Why didn't I suggest we meet at Tristan's locker? It's right next to our Spanish classroom, while mine is on the other side of the school.

The hallways are emptying as I race up the stairs, past the library, and into the foreign language corridor.

"Why are we running?" Tristan pants from somewhere behind me.

By the time I burst through the doors of the classroom a few minutes later, Señora Mendoza is already halfway through her future conjugation of the verb *ver.*

"Nosotros veremos," she declares to the class. She pauses when she sees me. "Señorita Sparks. It's nice of you to join us today."

I ignore her and fly across the classroom, weaving around chairs and knocking textbooks off desks in the process.

"Señorita Sparks," she repeats, this time with a tinge of exasperation. "Will you please take your seat?"

I reach the window, flip the lock, and thrust it open just in time. The massive black bird comes soaring into the classroom, right over my head. Some of the girls scream.

"*¡Dios mío!*" Señora exclaims, clutching her chest. The bird makes a full lap around the room, forcing the teacher to duck to avoid getting dive-bombed. Then, just as suddenly as it entered, it flies back out the window. I slam it closed, flip the lock back into place, and saunter to my desk.

Every pair of eyes in the classroom is trained on me. Tristan is still standing in the doorway, staring at me in astonishment.

I slip into my chair and ask, "What?"

"Señorita Sparks," Señora says reprovingly.

"Oh, sorry, I mean, *¿Qué?*"

Black Magic Woman

11:25 a.m.

My history test is a breeze. If I don't know those questions backward and forward by now, then there's absolutely no hope for me. Daphne Gray, once again, is extremely annoyed that she has to write "100%" at the top of my paper. And she's even more annoyed when she notices Tristan waiting for me outside our classroom when fifth period ends.

She gives me a dirty scowl and stomps off down the hallway.

"Hey," Tristan says, his fingers lacing through mine. "Are you coming to the band room for lunch?"

"No," I say apologetically. "I'm going to the book club meeting."

His face scrunches in confusion. "We have a book club?"

I playfully bump his hip with mine. "Yes, we have a book club."

"When did you join it?"

"Today."

He still seems baffled by this turn of events. "But have you even read the book?"

I nod. "Actually, I have, but you can walk me to the cafeteria. I'm going to grab something to take to the library."

Not only does Tristan walk with me, he even waits in line with me and pays for my turkey sandwich.

"So, you're sure you don't want to come?" Tristan says, putting his wallet back into his jeans.

I smile and stand on my tiptoes to kiss his cheek. "I'm sure. Thanks for the sandwich." I start to walk away but then turn back. "Oh, one more thing. You may want to visit the carnival manager down at the fairgrounds. I heard a rumor that he's looking for a band to play tonight."

I wave goodbye and disappear into the hallway just as I hear a loud clatter behind me. That would be Sophia's tray tumbling to the floor and her chocolate pudding finding its way down the front of her future boyfriend's shirt.

I check my phone.

12:49 p.m. Right on time.

You gotta hand it to Cole Simpson. He may be a giant knobhead, but he sure is punctual.

12:51 p.m.

"What did I miss?" I say, as I approach the group of tables pushed together in the center of the library.

Owen stops midsentence and gawks at me. "What are you doing here?"

"Isn't this book club?" I ask, sliding into the chair next to him.

"Yeah, but aren't you—"

"I'm joining," I say, looking around at the seven other members. "If that's okay with all of you?"

Everyone nods back in response. I turn to Owen. "Is that okay with you, Owen?"

"Of course," he blubbers. "We were just talking about the reasons the film wasn't as good as the book, but since you haven't read it, I guess you can observe—"

"I personally think the movie didn't work because we lost the powerful impact of Death as a narrator," I launch in, instantly igniting an impassioned debate among the other book club members.

I glance at Owen and give him a wink. For some reason, he can't seem to close his mouth.

"Don't you have a speech to practice?" he whispers to me a few minutes later.

I grin. "I thought I'd stir up some trouble here first."

"I thought you spent your lunches in the band room now."

"Trust me, this is much more exciting."

"More exciting than hanging out with rock stars?"

"Oh, *infinitely* more exciting."

Owen barks out a laugh. The rest of the book club stops their discussion and stares at us like we're from another planet. I duck my head into Owen's arm and stifle a fit of giggles.

For the first time in a long time, I know I'm exactly where I'm supposed to be.

Break On Through (to the Other Side)

1:33 p.m.

"Running for vice president of the junior class, here's Ellison Sparks, Sparks, Sparks." Principal Yates's voice reverberates through the gym and Rhiannon gives me a little shove.

"Where are your notes?" she hisses.

I pull the note cards from the pocket of my dress and tap them against my hand. Then I step up to the microphone and clear my throat.

"Hello, everyone. I'm Ellison Sparks," I begin, looking down at the index cards. The truth is, I've given this speech three times already, I don't really need the notes. I pretty much have the whole tedious thing memorized.

I find Owen in the bleachers. He's back in the front row. He gives me an encouraging nod, and I let my gaze drift to the rest of the faces staring back at me. The hundreds and hundreds of people who didn't even know my name until I started dating the lead singer of a local rock band.

I glance back at Rhiannon. She gives me another one of her perfected dirty politician looks.

Why am I even standing up here? Why did I ever say yes to her?

Was it so I could write down another impressive statistic on my college applications? Was it because I'm just incapable of saying no to pushy tyrants like Rhiannon Marshall?

Or is there possibly another reason?

"Don't just stand there," I hear Rhiannon growl through her teeth. "Talk."

I clear my throat again and peer back down at my notes. Then, before I can second-guess myself, I return the cards to my pocket.

"Hi. I'm Ellison Sparks," I begin again. "Although most of you probably know me as Tristan Wheeler's Girlfriend."

A few sniggers from the crowd. I find Tristan sitting four rows from the back and flash him a smile. He gives me that delicious dimpled grin in response.

"I admit, as far as titles go, it's not a bad one to have. Especially if you've seen him without his shirt on."

The sniggers instantly turn into catcalls. Principal Yates shoots me a look, while from somewhere behind me Rhiannon hisses, "What are you doing?"

I ignore them both.

"And although that is an accurate title—I am, indeed, Tristan Wheeler's Girlfriend"—I look to Owen but he's suddenly more interested in something next to his feet than my speech—"it's also not my *only* title."

The room falls silent. I take that as a cue to keep going.

"I figure if I'm going to ask you to vote for me, if I'm going to ultimately represent you for the rest of the year, then you should probably know more about me than just who I make out with in the hallways."

Another round of whoops breaks the silence.

"The truth is, we are never just one thing. We all have many titles and many labels, but far too often, we get trapped inside a single definition. The Teacher's Pet, the Rule Follower, the Cheerleader, the Athlete, the Princess, the Basket Case, the Criminal . . . the Rock Star's Girlfriend. Whether we wrote that definition or whether it was given to us, it somehow becomes our only identity. We get so lost in it that we forget about all the other pieces that make up who we are. I know I've been guilty of falling into this very trap. But in addition to carrying the title of the Girl Who Dates Tristan Wheeler, I also proudly claim the title of the Girl Who Knows the Lyrics to Every Rolling Stones Song."

This elicits more cheers.

"The Girl Obsessed with Legal Dramas," I go on. "The Girl Who Makes Playlists to Match All of Her Moods. The Girl Who Starts Fights in Book Club. The Girl Whose Lips Look Like a Photo from a News Story About Plastic Surgery Gone Wrong Whenever She Eats Almonds."

The audience hoots with laughter. It gives me the fuel I need to keep going.

"The Girl Who Still Sleeps with a Stuffed Hippo. The Girl Who Sings in the Shower. The Girl Who Watches Too Many Documentaries That Make Her Paranoid About Stuff That Will Never Happen . . . Probably."

Even Principal Yates snickers at this one.

I take a deep breath. "The Girl Who Would Repeat the Same Day Over and Over Again Until She Got It Right. Because I've recently discovered that I'm also the Girl Who Never Stops Trying to Fix Things.

"And that's what I intend to do for you as your representative. I intend to fix things. I won't stop until I get it right, because that's just the kind of girl that I am. I see problems and I simply have to find solutions. For instance, there is a serious shortage of palatable food options in our cafeteria."

Judging from the reaction in the bleachers, my peers agree with this assessment.

"So how do I intend to fix this? I'm going to work with the administration to get local restaurants to sell items from their menus at our school."

The students erupt in cheers. Well, everyone except Rhiannon, who I can feel seething behind me.

"Also, I've seen how many of you come out to Whack-a-Mole's shows. Some of you are willing to drive over a hundred miles to see them play. And yet, we've never had a rock concert here at our school. That's why, if I win, I'll be starting a semiannual Battle of the Bands night."

They seem to like this idea even more.

"So among the countless titles I already have, I'm standing here now, asking you to help me add yet another to my list. With your vote today, I would be honored to also be the Girl Who Won the Junior Class Vice Presidential Election. Thank you."

The students erupt in applause. Some of them even stand up, although admittedly I think that's only Owen and a few book club members. I find Tristan once again. He's not clapping or stomping his feet like so many others. He looks utterly stunned, like he has no idea where I just came from.

I step away from the mic and join the other candidates.

Rhiannon looks like she can't decide whether to applaud me or stab me. I give her a hearty pat on the back that makes her stumble forward. "They're all yours."

1:55 p.m.

The bell rings, signaling the end of homeroom, and I deliver my ballot to the teacher's desk. Owen is waiting for me in the hallway.

"So, when did you become Tony Robbins?" he asks, falling into step beside me.

I shrug in response. "I had some time to practice."

"Seriously, that was some speech."

"Thanks. Did you vote for Rhiannon and me?"

"No," he replies in all seriousness.

"No?"

"I wrote your name in for president."

I stop walking. "You did what?"

"You don't deserve to work under that fascist dictator."

"Owen," I whine. "That's a waste of a vote. That's one less ballot we'll have."

"I'm sorry, but I have to vote my conscience. And I can't conscientiously vote for Rhiannon Marshall to be in charge of my after-school activities."

I laugh and keep walking. "You're such a dork."

"Takes one to know one," he counters. "Wait, why are we walking toward the guidance counselor's office?"

I pause and point up at the ceiling. Right then, the school secretary's voice comes over the intercom system. "Ellison

Sparks, please report to the counseling office. Ellison Sparks to the counseling office, please."

"That's why," I say.

Owen stares at me in bemusement. "How did you do that?"

I raise my eyebrows at him. "Remember when we were kids and we used to practice our psychic abilities?"

"Yeah."

I pull open the counseling office door. "I guess mine have finally kicked in."

2:02 p.m.

"Hello! You must be Ellison!" Mr. Goodman says, offering me the chair across from him. "Great to see ya. Really swell. I'm Mr. Goodman. But you can call me Mr. *Great*man, if you want." Har. Har. Swat. Swat. "Just joshin' ya! So how ya doing? Ya holding up okay?"

"I'm great, Mr. *Great*man. Just swell!"

He brightens at my enthusiasm.

"Good to hear it! Good. To. Hear. Now, let's get down to business. Junior year. It's a toughie, am I right? Or am I *riiight*?"

Wink. Wink.

"It sure is! Wow. This day alone has been a trial, let me tell ya."

"And don't forget about those colleges. It's time to start thinking about your future." He forms his hands into pistols and shoots them at me. "Pow! Pow!"

I do my best imitation of someone being shot in the heart. It cracks him up. His laugh could easily be confused with a donkey's bray. I wake up from the dead and laugh along with him.

"Okay, time to get serious," he says, wiping the amusement from his face by pantomiming a windshield wiper. "Us trusty guidance counselors have been assigned to meet with every student in the junior class to talk about the next two years. Have you given any thought to where you want to apply?"

"Not yet," I say with a sigh, "but I was hoping you could help me figure it out."

Something Tells Me I'm into Something Good

3:20 p.m.

I close my locker and check the clock on my phone. Two minutes and counting.

I'm not sure why I'm so nervous. Maybe it's because today is the day I actually care about what happens.

I tap my fingers anxiously against the screen of my phone, willing the time to move faster.

"Hey!"

I pop my head up to see Tristan walking toward me with his usual sexy swagger. "That was some speech you gave today. You were amazing up there."

I grin. "Thanks."

"I also wanted to say thank you for the tip about the carnival. I was able to get us the gig for tonight! By the way, how did you know that—"

I shush him when I hear the ding of the announcement system. I bite my lip and knead my hands together as the school secretary starts to speak.

"Attention, students. I have a couple of announcements before I reveal the results from today's election."

This is it. Judgment day.

"First off, the cheerleaders would like to thank you for supporting their bake sale today. They raised over one thousand dollars! Also, a reminder that the auditions for the fall musical will start tomorrow afternoon. The deadline for signing up to audition is four o'clock today. This fall, the drama department will be bringing us the hit musical *Rent*!"

My heart pounds in my chest.

"And finally, here are the results from today's election."

Tristan grabs my hand. I listen intently as the results of the freshman and sophomore classes are read first.

"For the junior class, we had a bit of an unusual situation."

Unusual?

That can't be good. Unusual is never good.

"There was an abnormally high number of students who utilized the write-in feature of the ballot this year. After tallying up the votes, including the write-in additions, we can now confirm that your new junior class president is . . ."

Tristan squeezes my hand. I squeeze back.

". . . Ellison Sparks!"

I drop Tristan's hand.

What?

Tristan lets out a whoop and picks me up, swinging me around. When he sets me back on my feet he's beaming, but I'm scowling in confusion.

"You won!" he exclaims.

"B-b-but how?" I stammer. "I didn't even run for president."

"Enough people wrote your name in. Everyone wants you to be their president."

"They do?"

"The people have spoken," Tristan says in a deep movie-trailer voice. He gazes at me with something in his eyes that I'm not sure I've ever seen before. I don't even recognize it at first, but after a moment I'm pretty convinced that it's pride.

"President Sparks," he says ceremoniously. "I like the way that sounds."

He leans toward me, his dimple practically glowing. I feel myself being pulled into his gravity, his energy, his atmosphere.

Our lips touch just as I hear someone screech my name. It's not a pleasant sound. It ranks somewhere up there next to nails on a chalkboard and metal grinding against metal.

Tristan and I both look up at once. Rhiannon Marshall is barreling down the hallway like a fireball in one of those highly unrealistic explosion scenes. This is the part where Tristan and I are supposed to start running so we can dive in slow motion under a car and avoid being blasted to bits.

But neither one of us moves.

"How dare you!" Rhiannon shrieks when she reaches me. "How dare you swoop in and steal *my* presidency."

Tristan steps in front of me, opening his mouth to speak, but I gently push him aside. "I didn't steal anything, Rhiannon," I say calmly. "The students voted for me."

"You sabotaged me. You rigged this election."

Her accusation stuns me. "And exactly how did I do that?"

Her face turns every shade of red as she angrily fumbles for a comeback. "I may not have an answer to that right now, but trust me, there will be a full investigation. I will get to the bottom of this."

I nod. "You do that. Let me know what you find out." I close my locker door with a decisive slam and walk away.

Tristan jogs to catch up with me. "Don't worry about Rhiannon. She's all talk."

"I'm not worried."

"Where are you going?" Tristan asks. "Isn't the locker room the other way?"

"To the auditorium," I tell him. "The auditions for the school play are tomorrow. I've decided to sign up."

Tristan sputters to a halt. "The play? But you hate singing in front of people."

"Actually," I say, stopping in front of the signup sheet and scribbling my name under the role of Maureen, "it turns out, I kind of like it."

An alarm goes off on my phone. I check the screen and turn to Tristan. "I gotta run."

He looks flustered. "What? Where are you going? Should I come with you?"

I shake my head. "That's okay. I got this."

He wraps his arm around my waist and pulls me toward him. "Should I come over later, then?" He's using that seductive voice. The one that not only usually melts me, but melts all my resolve as well.

"You should get ready for your gig," I point out, untangling myself from him. "I'll see you at the carnival tonight, okay?"

Before he can respond, I'm already halfway down the hallway.

Wooly Bully

3:55 p.m.

By the time I pull into the parking lot of the middle school next door and hop out of my car, the buses have left and the parent pickup line has mostly emptied. I park the car and run to the side door of the building, the one I saw the girls exit from.

I carefully ease it open to find that it leads to the school's security office, which is currently empty. Everyone must be at some kind of staff meeting. I hear whispers coming from the other end of the office and I quickly duck behind a file cabinet. A moment later, the girls are there. One of them—a tall brunette who is undoubtedly their leader—sits down at the desk and switches on the computer. I peer around the side of the cabinet to get a view of the monitor. She clicks the mouse a few times and suddenly a video feed of the soccer field is on the screen.

Security cameras.

The school must have them installed throughout the building.

There's movement on the feed and the girls start to giggle. The leader shushes them and points to the screen. Quietly, I take my phone out of my pocket, pull up the video camera, and press Record.

"She's walking onto the field now," the leader says. "I told her that Avery would meet her out there in a few minutes. She thinks he wants to make out with her. Can you believe she actually thought someone like Avery Frahm would want to kiss her? She's so freaking gullible."

My blood boils as the girls burst into laughter.

This is what my sister has been dealing with? These horrible girls making her life miserable? No wonder she buries herself in those movies and books. She hasn't only been turning to them for wisdom, she's been turning to them for a distraction.

"Like he would ever want to touch those hideous frog lips of hers," one of the other girls chimes in, leading to another round of laughter at my sister's expense.

"Look," the leader says, "she's in the middle of the field. Activating the sprinkler system in five, four, three, two—"

"This is all very entertaining," I say, stepping out from behind the file cabinet.

The girls jump. Two of them actually let out a shriek.

The tall brunette takes charge, standing up from her throne to face me. "Who are you?" she asks rudely.

"An interested party."

She rolls her eyes. "Well, why don't you make yourself useful and go away. We're busy."

"Yes." I nod. "I can see that. You're clearly very, *very* busy, and I'm sure your principal would be extremely interested to know just how busy you are."

Pink Miniskirt groans, like I'm wasting her time. "Do whatever you want." She resumes her place behind the computer.

It takes all of my strength not to reach out and smack her across the head, but I force myself to stay calm and keep my cool.

"Oh, I will," I say, taking a step toward her. I queue up the video. "And what I really want to do is push Send on the email I've drafted with this video attached." I push Play and the girls' voices are echoed back at them through my phone's tiny speakers.

"She's walking onto the field now. I told her that Avery would meet her out there in a few minutes. She thinks he wants to make out with her. Can you believe she actually thought someone like Avery Frahm would want to kiss her? She's so freaking gullible . . ."

I turn the phone around and hover my finger over the screen.

The leader stands up again. "What do you want?"

"I want you to apologize to Hadley Sparks. Right now."

She shakes her head like this is all so juvenile. "That's it?"

I shrug. "Yup. That's it."

She huffs. "Fine. Let's go." With a cock of her bony hip, she leaves the office, the other girls following closely behind her.

"And if you ever mess with her again," I call after them, "this video will also find its way to the police."

I send a quick text to my sister and then hurry over to the computer monitor. Through the feed, I can see Hadley checking her phone. She looks confused by my text, but thankfully starts walking toward the parking lot.

A moment later, the girls exit through the doors of the gym. They strut out to the soccer field, like they own the whole darn thing. They reach the center of the field and search for Hadley, confused by her unexpected absence.

That's when I activate the sprinklers. It was nice of them to set up the controls for me.

There's no audio, but I can assume from their horrified faces and open mouths that screams are accompanying their mad dash for cover. But it's so hard to run in those spiky-heeled shoes. Especially on grass. Especially on grass that's now wet. The leader of the pack takes a nasty tumble as the other girls scurry past her.

I switch off the computer monitor, pocket my phone, and disappear out the door I came in from.

Hadley is waiting by the flagpole where I told her to meet me.

"What are you doing here?" she asks.

"I was just running a little errand." I grin, and put my arm around my sister's shoulders. "Wanna go knock off a candy store with me?"

Wouldn't It Be Nice

8:16 p.m.

"Okay, we have one more song for you tonight," Tristan breathes into the microphone as he brushes away a damp clump of hair from his forehead. "This one is dedicated to the girl who got us this gig, and the *new* junior class president of our high school: the beautiful Ellie Sparks."

A tingle of excitement travels through my body as Whack-a-Mole launches into the final song of their set—"Mind of the Girl." It's the song Tristan and I first kissed to. The song that turned Tristan's music from noise to art. The song that turned me into a fan.

Watching him on that stage, hearing him say my name to a carnival full of people, listening to him sing the lyrics that I truly believe were written for me, it's an amazing feeling. It wraps around me and squeezes me like a hug. It lulls me into a sense of security.

Yet, as I listen to Tristan sing, I can't help but think about all the other times I stood in the middle of this carnival.

The first Monday, when I never saw the heartbreak coming.

The second Monday, when I couldn't believe it was happening again.

The third Monday, when I still couldn't fix it.

The fourth Monday, when I thought I had.

The fifth Monday, when I refused to care anymore.

But what about tonight? What will happen in less than thirty minutes? Will he do it all over again?

Will he break my heart a seventh time? Does it even matter anymore?

What do you want, Ellison? I ask myself. But it's suddenly the most complicated question in the world. One that I'm not even sure I trust myself to answer.

The music intensifies, leading into the chorus.

On stage, Tristan is singing about my impenetrable mind, my bewildering thoughts, my inscrutable emotions. It's no wonder they've been such a mystery to him. I can't even figure them out myself.

Frustrated and with tears stinging my eyes, I turn away from the stage and wander through the carnival. After many aimless steps, I somehow find myself back at that stupid horse race game. I pick the very last seat—the unlucky number thirteen—and sit down. I feed my dollar into the slot and wait for the game to begin.

Someone drops onto the next stool and I turn to see that it's Owen. He looks at me. I look at him. Neither of us speaks. And yet it's like we're both saying everything.

No. Not saying it.

Screaming it.

For years we've communicated in silent words. Thoughts that we never had to say aloud, but this is a new conversation.

This is a subject we've never broached before.

And I can't be certain that I even understand it.

The buzzer rings, snapping us both out of the moment. I reach for the little red ball and with a practiced flip of my wrist, fling it up the ramp. It drops directly into the number three hole and rolls back down. I repeat the action, same position, same flick, same result.

Again and again, I sink the ball into that coveted high-point slot.

I must fall into some kind of trance, because suddenly Owen is shaking me, pointing at the horses. "You won!"

I blink and look up. There's number thirteen, all the way at the finish line, a scattering of losing horses frozen in its wake.

"I won?"

"You won," he confirms.

The carnival employee comes over and hands me a giant stuffed turtle. "Here you go, little lady. Nicely done."

Before I can think, I turn and thrust the turtle into Owen's arms. It's so unexpected, he nearly drops it.

"For you," I mumble. "I want you to have it."

He frowns. "Me?"

I reach out and pet the turtle's soft head. "Slow and steady wins the race, right?"

Owen laughs. "Not in your case." He gestures to my winning steed. "That was pretty impressive. Have you been practicing?"

I shrug. "Beginner's luck, I guess."

"There you are," someone says, and I tear my gaze from Owen to see Tristan walking over, the post-gig glow still radiating off his skin. "Where did you run off to?"

I scuff my feet against the dirt. "Sorry. We were—I was just playing some carnival games."

"Cool," Tristan says. "So, do you want to check out this carnival? Maybe ride the Ferris wheel?"

I glance at Owen, immediately falling into his vibrant, pleading eyes. Another barrage of silent words comes charging in my direction, but I understand them perfectly.

Say no.

Stay here with me.

Choose me.

It's only taken me a week to hear them, but that doesn't mean I know what to do with them.

That doesn't mean I'm brave enough to face them.

I flash Owen a friendly smile. "I'll text you later, okay?"

It seems to take forever for my response to reach him. Like bullets traveling in slow motion. When they hit, he hides the wounds well. But I've known him too long. I see through his façade, and the pain on his face ricochets back to me, making me feel like *I'm* the one who's been shot.

"Sure," he mumbles. "Later."

Then he walks away, and I watch him drop the stuffed turtle into the nearest trash can.

When You Change with Every New Day

8:50 p.m.

We lift into the air, the ground beneath us growing farther away with every passing second. I yelp and grab Tristan's arm.

He chuckles. "Are you afraid of heights or something?"

"Maybe," I squeak.

He puts his arm around my shoulders and pulls me to him. "Don't worry, I won't let you fall."

Falling is the best part.

I snuggle up to him, trying to absorb his warmth, the surety of his embrace. But none of it seems to penetrate the surface. When we reach the top, the Ferris wheel stops and our little car begins to sway from the momentum.

I try not to look down, but for some reason my eyes are drawn to the ground.

Drawn to the people I left behind.

They're so small from up here. Indistinguishable. I can't make out any of their faces. And that makes me want to cry.

"Looking for something?" Tristan asks, peering over me.

I shake my head and focus my attention back on him. On this. This was my fantasy from the very beginning. A romantic night at the carnival with the boy I love, ending in a moonlight kiss on the top of the Ferris wheel.

I glance up.

There's the moon.

I glance to my left.

There's the boy.

It's everything I wanted.

So why does it feel so anticlimactic?

"Ellie," Tristan says, pulling my attention back. His voice is suddenly serious. "I wanted to talk to you about something."

My stomach drops. Here it is. The reality of this moment. The reality of every single Monday I've lived through.

Tristan isn't here to share some romantic moonlit kiss with me. Tristan is here for the same reason he's always here: To end it. To crush my fantasy. To break my heart.

"Yeah?" I ask, my throat suddenly bone dry. I close my eyes and wait for the words I've heard countless times. The same vague speech that leaves me feeling frustrated and so terribly empty.

Tristan takes a deep breath. "I woke up this morning feeling like something was wrong. I couldn't put my finger on it. Everything just felt . . . off. I didn't know if it was our fight last night, or something else, but I quickly realized that this feeling wasn't new. It's been building and building for the past five months."

Wait, what?

This isn't the speech. This sounds nothing like the speech. I almost want to interrupt him and feed him the right lines, put this night back on track, but I stay silent.

"I came to school thinking I was going to end it," he goes on. "You and me. I couldn't see any reason for us to be together anymore. I didn't really know why. It was just a feeling. It was like we were broken somehow and I didn't know how to fix us. But then something happened today. You were . . . I don't know how to explain it . . . you were so different. You were . . . *radiant.* Everything about you. And I realized, maybe the problem was, I just couldn't see you before. I couldn't see how much you shine. All on your own. But now I do. I see it. I see *you.*"

I wait for him to say more. There *has* to be more.

"Hold on," I say, confused. "You mean you're *not* breaking up with me?"

He laughs. "No. The opposite. I wanted to tell you how happy I am that we're together."

A thrill ripples through me.

I can't believe it. I did it. I actually did it. I stopped Tristan from breaking up with me. I didn't need any tricks or how-to books or fishnet stockings. I just needed to be me.

I suddenly feel like Dorothy in *The Wizard of Oz,* who had the ruby slippers on her feet the whole time. She was just too focused on other things to notice.

I turn to Tristan. He's wearing that irresistible smile that's pulled me in so many times.

He rests his palm on my cheek. He guides my mouth to his. He kisses me. The way only Tristan can kiss me.

Six days ago, this was all I wanted.

Six days ago, this was my fantasy.

But a lot can happen in six days.

For the past five months, Tristan has been the music I couldn't live without. He's been the song stuck in my head, playing over and over again. I've spent this entire week trying to keep the music going. Trying to keep him in my life.

But now, when I kiss him, I no longer feel the lips of the boy who wrote a song for me. Who shouted the lyrics from a stage for the world to hear. I only feel the lips of the boy who told me goodbye *six* times. Who broke my heart night after night. Who wanted the music to stop.

It wasn't until I showed him who I really was that he decided to stick around.

I couldn't see how much you shine. All on your own. But now I do. I see it. I see you.

But there's someone down there who's seen me all along. Who didn't need me to prove anything to him.

I was so blinded by the spotlight shining on Tristan, I couldn't see what was right in front of me. Tristan's music was turned up so loud, it drowned out everything else. It was the only thing I could hear. The only thing I wanted to hear.

But it was never my kind of music.

It was a temporary soundtrack. A placeholder until I could find the real song.

I gently push against Tristan's chest, tearing my lips away from him. Tears are streaming down my face.

"What's wrong?" The concern in his voice is raw and real.

"I can't do this anymore," I blurt out.

"What? The Ferris wheel?"

"No. I mean, us."

"What?"

The ride shudders back into motion and we start our descent toward the ground.

"It took me an entire week to show you the real me," I tell

him, "because I was afraid. I didn't think I *could* be myself around you. I didn't think you'd like who that was."

"And you were wrong," Tristan argues. "I do."

"I know." I let out a tiny sob. "But it's too late."

"Too late?" he asks. "I don't understand."

"You and me. We don't work."

Comprehension floods his features. "Wait. Are you breaking up with me?"

Our bucket reaches the ground and the ride stops to let us off. I turn to take in Tristan's baffled, distraught face. "I'm sorry," I say with genuine sympathy, "but I have to stay true to how I feel."

I lift the bar and hop off. It feels good to be on solid ground again.

I start running. I don't stop until I get to my car. I start the engine and turn on the radio. The "Top of the World" playlist is still streaming from my phone.

It's Owen's favorite.

I turn up the volume. "Ruby Tuesday" by the Rolling Stones blasts through the speakers. It gives me the courage I need.

The Stones always do.

"She would never say where she came from," I sing along as I put the car in Drive and pull out of the parking lot. *"Yesterday don't matter if it's gone."*

As I drive away, I catch a glimpse of the fairgrounds disappearing in my rearview mirror.

I think I'm done with carnival rides for a while. I need something a little more stable.

Build Me Up Buttercup

9:15 p.m.

Seven minutes later, I pull into the Reitzmans' driveway and throw the car in Park. I run up the walkway and bang on the door. Owen's mother answers a moment later.

"Where's Owen?"

"He went to the carnival," his mother says, confused. "I thought he was with you."

"He was. I mean, he is. I mean, I hope he will be."

Owen's mom gives me an odd look.

"I mean, I'll go find him," I say, backing away. She watches me curiously from the doorway as I stumble to my car.

I get in and close the door.

Where could he be?

Did he really stay at the carnival?

I pull out my phone and send him a text message.

Me: Where are you?

There's no answer. Well, I guess I'll wait here. I mean, he has to come home eventually, right?

I turn on the engine and listen to three more songs from my playlist. But with each song, I'm feeling less and less like I'm on top of the world and more and more like I've made a huge mistake.

I can't stop thinking about Owen's injured face when I ditched him at the carnival. When I told him I'd text him later and then ran off with Tristan.

The memory of it now is like a punch in the chest.

What if that was my last chance?

What if the universe only gave me one more day to get it right and I failed?

What if I wake up tomorrow and it's Tuesday and Owen wants nothing to do with me anymore?

What if—

My phone beeps. I fumble to pick it up and swipe it on, my fingers trembling.

Owen: I'm in your room. Where are you?

I don't even take the time to tap out a response. I throw the phone onto the passenger seat and peel out of the driveway. I get to my house in a record fifty-three seconds. I park at the curb, scramble out of the car and up the tree in our front yard.

Of course, I could use the door.

It's my own stupid house.

But I don't want to risk bumping into anyone. I don't want to talk to anyone.

The tree is a lot harder to climb than I've ever given Owen

credit for. It takes core muscles that I just don't have and balance that I never thought I needed. I look across to the window. It's already open. Apparently this is how Owen got inside as well. Holding on to the trunk for as long as possible, I shimmy along the branch that connects with the house, trying not to look down for fear of losing my nerve. That's when I realize the branch I'm standing on is a lot lower than the windowsill. I peer beneath my feet, my vision blurring when I see how far above the ground I am.

Why didn't my parents build a one-story house?

I suck in a breath, rest my hands on the windowsill, and jump, using all my strength to hoist myself up and scramble inside. I tumble onto the floor of my bedroom with an *oomph.*

Owen jumps up from my bed and runs over to me, helping me up. "Are you okay? What on earth are you doing? Why didn't you use the door?"

"All we ever really get is today," I say breathlessly.

His forehead furrows. "What?"

"That was my fortune. It said, 'All we ever really get is today.'"

"Your fortune cookie was empty. So was mine."

I shake my head, still trying to catch my breath. "No, it wasn't. I mean, yes, today it was, but yesterday, it wasn't. And the day before that it wasn't. But none of those other days matter, because all we ever really get is today."

"Objection," Owen says playfully. "Witness is acting irrational."

"Objection," I counter. "Irrelevant."

"Objection. Absolutely relevant."

"Permission to approach the bench?" I ask.

Owen scowls. "Huh?"

But I'm already moving. The gap between us is already closing. My arms are already wrapping around his neck, pulling him down to me. My lips already know exactly where to go.

It doesn't take long before he's kissing me back. Before his hands are on my waist, lifting me off the ground.

We topple backward, landing on the bed. It's clumsy and uncoordinated and us.

Owen pulls back and looks at me.

"Do you know how long I've wanted to do this?" he whispers, stroking my face.

I smile. "No."

"A bloody long time."

He dives for my lips again, kissing me hard.

And it's good.

And it's like falling.

And I hear music. The kind you can dance to. The kind that drowns out the rest of the world. Because when you find what you're looking for—when you finally get it right—everything else is just noise.

Epilogue

7:04 a.m.

Bloop-dee-dee-bloop-bloop-bing!

Bleary and disoriented, I pull my heavy eyes open and stare at my phone. It's sitting on my nightstand, the screen lit up from an incoming text.

My hands are shaking with anticipation as I reach for it and swipe it on.

When I see the message waiting for me, a heavy weight drops into the pit of my stomach, making me want to throw up.

I can't stop thinking about last night.

No. It can't be. This isn't happening. It's a dream. It's just a bad dream.

I slap my cheeks, trying to wake myself up.

Please, I beg silently, then I say it aloud, "Please!"

I shut my eyes tight, then open them again. The screen

slowly comes back into focus. That's when I first notice the sender's name.

Owen.

I bolt upright.

Owen?

I blink three times and look at it again, certain I must have misread it.

But the name doesn't change.

Owen is the one texting me? Not Tristan?

I glance around my room, searching for evidence, but everything looks the same. I paw at the screen of my phone, scrambling to get to my calendar. I need to see the date. I need to be one hundred percent sure. But before I can open it, another text arrives.

Bloop-dee-dee-bloop-bloop-bing!

With my heart in my throat, I click the message. It's from Owen. And it says:

Happy Tuesday.

Acknowledgments

Bloop-dee-dee-bloop-bloop-bing!

Jessica Brody: A million billion gazillion thanks to Janine O'Malley, Brendan Deneen, and Mitchell Kreigman for letting me tell Ellie's story to the world.

Bloop-dee-dee-bloop-bloop-bing!

Jessica Brody: Crazy-huge and blindingly shiny thanks to Jim McCarthy, a superhero in disguise as an agent. (Don't worry, your secret's safe with me.)

Bloop-dee-dee-bloop-bloop-bing!

Jessica Brody: Thank you to the stellar hardworking people at MacKids who keep believing in me book after book and who keep making it all look so easy (even though I know it's not)—Mary Van Akin, Angie Chen, Joy Peskin, Allison Verost, Molly Brouillette, Angus Killick, Simon Boughton, Jon Yaged, Lauren Burniac, Lucy

Del Priore, Liz Fithian, Katie Halata, Holly Hunnicutt, Kathryn Little, Stephanie McKinley, Mark Von Bargen, and Caitlin Sweeny.

Bloop-dee-dee-bloop-bloop-bing!

Jessica Brody: Elizabeth Clark, you continue to blow my mind with your staggeringly brilliant cover designs. You really outdid yourself this time! Thank you!

Bloop-dee-dee-bloop-bloop-bing!

Jessica Brody: Thank you to Terra Brody, who makes everything more stylish . . . even my characters. And to my insanely supportive parents, Michael and Laura Brody.

Bloop-dee-dee-bloop-bloop-bing!

Jessica Brody: Squishy hugs to my pups, Honey, Gracie, Bula, and Baby! If you don't understand why they deserve their own thanks, follow me on Instagram. You'll get it.

Bloop-dee-dee-bloop-bloop-bing!

Jessica Brody: As always, thanks to Charlie. If I had a week of Mondays, I'd spend them all with you.

Bloop-dee-dee-bloop-bloop-bing!

Jessica Brody: The biggest, bubbliest, giddiest thank-you goes to my readers. There will never be a day of the week when I'm not grateful for you. There will never be a book where I don't tell you that.